BETRAYED

LEGACY OF MAGIC, BOOK 2

LINDSAY BUROKER

1

MY ARTISTIC ABILITY TO CARVE BEAUTIFUL SHAPES OUT OF WOOD DID not extend to pruning rhododendrons, hydrangeas, and red twig dogwoods into pleasing shapes. And the quest to remove the invasive Himalayan blackberry brambles? I would rather have tangled with orcs and werewolves. I usually bled less after those encounters.

"Are there supposed to be more branches and leaves in your hair than in the waste bin?" Zadie, my friend and real-estate agent, asked from behind me.

"Yeah, I'm saving them to make a twig crown later." I dashed sweat from my eyes and kept working. With the photographer already snapping photos of the house, I wanted to finish as quickly as possible.

"That's more elf than dwarf couture, isn't it?"

"I have elf friends now. It could be for them."

Technically, the haughty assassin Varlesh Sarrlevi was the only full-blooded elf I knew, and I had zero interest in giving *him* gifts, though the thought of him wearing a twig crown as he sprang into battle against fearsome enemies amused me.

I hacked at the base of a two-inch-thick blackberry vine trying to choke a lilac bush and used all of my half-dwarven strength to tug at it. It was barely sufficient, and only years of martial-arts training kept me from tumbling backward on my ass as the roots finally pulled free.

"Goats might have been a better choice," I muttered.

"I can have the photographer skip pictures of that side of the yard if you want, but I'm sure prospective home buyers will appreciate grounds free of invasive weeds."

"I've heard that's a selling point."

The rumble of machinery drowned out our conversation as my six-foot-ten half-troll business partner, Abbas, strode from the backyard to the front, pushing a lawn mower. Our intern and my roommate, the three-and-a-half-foot-tall green-skinned goblin, Tinja, was riding it.

"Faster, faster," she urged, waving a spade in the air.

"Tinja is a college student, isn't she?" Zadie watched with bemusement as the odd duo passed us.

"She's halfway through earning her architecture degree, yes."

"Sometimes, she seems younger than that."

"Goblins of all ages cackle with glee when they ride machinery. It's in the blood."

Dwarf mongrel, a familiar voice spoke telepathically into my mind. *You requested two of your Earth weeks. I have given you three. Are you not yet done with your project?*

"Speak of the devil." *You may recall that my name is Matti. And I'm almost done. Hold your horses.*

My people domesticate and ride evinya—*giant birds*—*not equines.*

Hold some of them then. Maybe they like your rough, impatient touch.

Unbidden, the memory of him massaging my scalp as he tried to convince me to assist him with his quest came to mind. His touch hadn't been impatient *or* rough. No, it had evoked pleasure, passion, and intense yearning. Unfortunately, my body refused to forget that.

This work you do is not as important as finding your mother and reuniting her with her father, the dwarven king.

I scowled, not reiterating that my mother was dead, that I had, at four years old, seen her shot twice in the chest before a burning building collapsed on her. Sarrlevi had heard the story. He simply refused to believe I could be right.

"Superior bastard," I said, though I couldn't deny that recent events had gotten my hopes up. Maybe I *was* wrong, and the mother I'd missed and longed for almost my entire life was still alive out there.

I brushed thorns and smashed blackberries off my gloved hands as I frowned toward the backyard. Though I couldn't sense Sarrlevi—he often camouflaged himself from other magical beings—I could tell his voice had originated from that direction.

"Problem? Besides the obvious?" Zadie waved as the photographer, who'd been distracted making adjustments to a drone gathering aerial images, squawked and backed away from the lawn mower.

The woman hadn't been in danger of being run over, but hulking Abbas did have a tendency to startle people who didn't know he was a borderline pacifist and wielded nothing deadlier than carpentry tools. Though, as the woman's gape settled on Tinja, it was possible she was more alarmed by the green-skinned mower rider. After all, according to the media and government, goblins and other magical beings did not exist. *Usually,* Tinja camouflaged herself from mundane humans, but she must have been having too much fun with the ride to remember to do so.

"The elf has arrived, and I haven't made his twig crown yet." I waved toward the front door. "Feel free to take the photographer inside. Everything is finished and freshly cleaned in there."

"And free of short greenies?"

"That's my only goblin assistant."

"Good." Zadie adjusted her *Star Trek* messenger bag and hurried to the side of the alarmed photographer.

Bracing myself for more irritation than the thorny brambles had given me, I marched into the backyard. The backyard that was *beautiful* now, especially compared to its original moss-blanketed, overgrown state.

Screw Sarrlevi. My work *was* important. Once the house sold, a family would love living here.

As I'd suspected, he was among the towering firs, pines, and cedars that we'd left natural on the back half of the large lot, but his *Lord of the Rings* attire camouflaged him as much as his magic, and it took me a moment to pick out his green cloak, beige tunic, brown trousers, and short blond hair.

His arrogant angular face didn't fit in with the serene surroundings nearly as well, so it shouldn't have taken me that long to locate it. His achingly *handsome* arrogant face, with a knowing smirk on his lips as I approached. As if he knew I'd been thinking about the appeal of his touch scant seconds earlier.

Hopefully not. He'd said my half-dwarven mind was hard to read, probably because it had the density of the rock my mother's people mined. And all I did was scowl at him when my heart sped up, beating rapidly as nervous adrenaline surged through my veins.

"I hope you brought me more exotic cheese from other worlds." I stopped several feet away from him.

It wasn't that he would spring forward and inflict his touch on me—as he'd made clear, he had no interest in mixed-blood, or *mongrel*, dwarves—but it seemed safer farther back. My hormones would be less affected by his stupid allure.

"Does your work not earn you sufficient funds to buy food?" Sarrlevi asked.

"My funds are fine, but you know our deal."

Admittedly, we hadn't started the search for my mother yet, and I'd been too busy to do more than make a couple of phone calls, so our agreement that he begin an elven cheese-of-the-month club for me hadn't officially started. Sadly. I'd finished off the brick of *orax* cheese two weeks earlier, and Tinja, who seemed to eat her body weight daily in snack food, had devoured the wheel of pink *dokdok* cheese.

"Indeed." Sarrlevi reached past the hilts of not one but two longswords sheathed on his back to slide his magical bag off his shoulders. It contained everything from a cot to a blanket to the heads of his slain enemies to who knew what else but was no larger than a runner's hydro pack.

As he unfastened the lid, my mouth watered. I rolled my eyes at the response. Did normal, full-blooded human women have so little control over their bodies?

"I have a brick of the *orax*, which I know you enjoy, and a new one for you to try. *Vejek*. An ogre delicacy sourced from the *vejerikai*, one of only two types of birds—large and aggressive birds —in their world to form a milk-like substance. They regurgitate it to nurse their young. As you can imagine, it's not easy to acquire. Only great hunters are brave enough and strong enough to climb the towering cliffs to their aeries, subdue the birds long enough to force out milk, and escape with their prize and their lives. Not all make it. Many are attacked by the flock and fall from the clifftops to their deaths."

"Is that your way of telling me that this cheese is even more expensive than the others?" I debated whether milk regurgitated from a beak was grosser than milk squeezed out of a nipple. As an open-minded eater, I resolved to try it and let my taste buds decide if it was acceptable.

"It is exceedingly rare and highly prized."

"So that's a yes."

"Yes." Sarrlevi handed me the familiar ocean-blue brick and a smaller wax-wrapped circle. His eyelids drooped halfway, his eyes intent as he regarded me through his lashes. "I trust this offering will place you in the mood to put aside your mundane work for a time and assist me."

"Yeah, yeah, your bribe is sufficient." I made myself thank him as I accepted the cheese, though we both knew it wasn't out of kindness or an interest in doing nice things for me that he'd brought them. "I called Artie's Axes yesterday to confirm that the dwarf lady you terrorized has returned to work."

I'd been tempted to introduce myself and question her over the phone but had only inquired about the hours her business was open. Dwarves weren't known for being garrulous, and I'd been sure she would hang up if I started asking about the secrets of her past. Hopefully, if I came to her in person, with the photos I had of my mother, she would believe I was who I said I was and want to speak with me.

"I did not terrorize her," Sarrlevi stated stiffly. "As I told you, she attacked me first."

"Because you're an assassin who once accepted the gig to kill her friend—my mother." I squinted at him, still not positive that I could trust him. Forty years had passed since then, and he'd claimed he'd recently accepted a new assignment from the dwarven king, one to *find* my mother, but who knew what went on behind his enigmatic blue eyes?

"That is likely the reason, yes."

"It's either that or she found your face so smug that she couldn't resist throwing an axe at it." I smirked at him, not shy about letting him know how I felt. Mostly because I hated that I was attracted to him and he knew it. Any chance I could find to take his ego down a notch, I would.

"Dwarves are quick to belligerence," was all he said, unfazed by my insult.

"I'll go see her this evening and find out what I can. Do you want to meet up tomorrow morning?"

"I will go with you to interrogate her."

"I'm not going to *interrogate* her. Didn't you already do that and find it didn't work? I'm going to introduce myself and have a chat with her. Dwarf to dwarf. Or half-dwarf. Having you there would be problematic."

If his second visit went like the first, Artie would throw axes at us both, then run away and disappear for days.

"To ensure there isn't trouble, I will wait outside while you *chat* with her."

"Are you expecting trouble?"

He gazed at me without answering. What did *that* mean?

My phone rang, and I held up a finger, though I almost didn't answer it. Colonel Willard hadn't been in touch since I'd reluctantly agreed that I would take on work for her, most likely thumping magical bad guys when her Number One civilian contractor, Val Thorvald, was out of town.

"Hello?" I answered as Sarrlevi watched.

Some people backed off when others took phone calls, but maybe he was interested. He'd been the one to suggest that if I worked for Willard and did a good job, she might be able to get me into the military prison where my father had been incarcerated for the last thirty years. The Army had always rejected my requests to see him, saying that those in maximum security weren't allowed visitors.

"I need you in my office, Puletasi," Willard said.

"Uhm." Did that mean she had a mission? I was sure she wasn't inviting me for a coffee chat. "Today or tomorrow? I was about to head over to Port Townsend to—"

"*Now.*" With her curt message delivered, Willard hung up.

I stared at the phone and wracked my brain, trying to think of something I'd done that could have pissed her off. But it had been weeks since I'd employed my form of vigilante justice, as she called it, to thump a miscreant.

"I need to make a stop before heading to Artie's," I told Sarrlevi, though I was positive his pointed elven ears had heard Willard. "It's on the way and hopefully won't take long."

"I will accompany you." No doubt he wanted to *ensure* there weren't any further delays.

"Oh, good. My life is empty and joyless when you're not in it."

"Most people are not irreverent to assassins."

"Yeah, but you need me to complete your mission. You're not going to kill me."

"One day, my mission will be complete," he said, though he sounded more amused than irked. I doubted he was fantasizing about my strangulation or throat-cutting.

"At which point, you'll have developed too much affection for my snarky mongrel antics to contemplate my death."

"An interesting hypothesis."

"I thought so."

2

I WOULD HAVE PREFERRED TO TAKE MY MOTORCYCLE TO PORT Townsend, since ferry passage cost less for it than for a vehicle, but there was no way I would invite Sarrlevi to sit behind me in the saddle. As a mage as well as an assassin, he could create portals to whisk himself from world to world, but when I'd asked if he wanted to meet me at Willard's office, he'd given me a blank look.

Someday, I would request details on how portal travel worked. All I knew was that few magical beings had the power to create the temporary passageways, which meant Sarrlevi was a badass in more ways than with his swords.

We rolled off the 520 bridge and into Seattle in my dented beater of a truck with garbage cans full of blackberry brambles in the back. Sarrlevi shifted uncomfortably on the bench seat, rolled down the window, wrinkled his nose at the scent of exhaust, and frowned out the dinged windshield whenever brake lights came on ahead of us. Either he'd never been in a car before or my truck wasn't up to his standards. Maybe both. There was, as numerous passengers had pointed out, a spring attempting to thrust through the worn upholstery on that side. The seat on my side, thanks to being copiously patched with duct tape, was well armored against such affronts.

"Have you accepted missions from the human military officer while I've been gone?" Sarrlevi shifted again, either rubbing his shoulder blades on the seat back or worrying that its cooties were getting all over his cloak. His weapons and pack rested between his knees.

"Nope. I'm saving myself for you."

One of his eyebrows rose as he looked over at me, and, non-native to Earth or not, I had a feeling he knew that term was usually used in regard to sex.

"The cheese bribes must be working," he said.

"They do get me excited." For some reason, my cheeks warmed. I needed to watch what I said around him. "I'm hoping this won't take long and that Willard isn't going to send me off on a mission. I do want to get to the bottom of my mother's past. I just had to get the project finished first. My business had to take out a big hard-money loan to afford that place, and the longer we hold it before we sell it, the more we have to— What are you doing?" I frowned over at him.

He'd removed a kerchief from a pocket, one I'd seen before and that gave off a faint magical signature, and was wiping the dash.

"Your conveyance is begrimed."

"It's just some dust. This is my work truck. I haul sawdust, cement mix, and landscaping pavers in it. My *conveyance* can handle some grime."

Sarrlevi leaned farther forward to wipe the windshield, the kerchief remaining white, no hint of dirt on it. "Should you be attacked while in it, would it not be useful to better see your enemies coming?"

"Nah, I like their arrival to be a delightful surprise." While we waited at a light, I watched him finish cleaning his side of the cab, including the gear shift, and then eye my side. "You're not climbing in my lap to wipe down the dash over here."

"No," he agreed, though he continued to eye the film of dust.

His magical kerchief did a good job, but I'd seen him use it to clean blood off his swords after beheading werewolves. I hoped it resided in a jar of bleach and disinfectant when it wasn't in use.

"I didn't know you were a neat-freak," I said.

Maybe that was why he carried a cot and rug with him everywhere he went. So he wouldn't *begrime* himself by sleeping on the forest floor.

"Most people also don't call assassins *freaks*," he said coolly.

"It's not an insult when it's hyphenated with neat."

We turned onto the street that held Willard's offices, an IRS building, according to the sign out front.

"Ask anyone," I added when his sidelong look suggested he didn't believe me.

His gaze shifted toward the three-story brick building, a tidy grass lawn surrounding it. "Thorvald and her *dragon* are inside."

His tone was even cooler for the word *dragon*, and his hands twitched toward his swords. He didn't, however, draw them, maybe because he would have had to put away the kerchief first. He glanced at it and seemed reluctant to do so.

Maybe he intended to pounce on my side of the truck as soon as I got out. The passenger side *was* vastly improved. I hadn't known the dash could get that clean.

"Maybe this *is* a coffee date." I sensed Thorvald and her mate now that Sarrlevi had pointed them out.

The magical aura of the dragon—Lord Zavryd'nokquetal, I'd learned—wasn't as noticeable when he shape-shifted into human form, but one could still tell he had tremendous power. An elf's power was far less significant next to that of a dragon, and I wondered if Sarrlevi's arrogance would ratchet down a few notches in the presence of one.

After parking, I stepped out, shutting the door behind me. Sarrlevi *did* lean over to wipe off the steering wheel, dash, and windshield. That made me wish Thorvald and Willard were out there to witness it. An assassin who moonlighted as a maid had to be rare.

Surreptitiously, I slipped out my phone and took a photo before he finished. He noticed and gave me a flat look before putting away the kerchief, grabbing his gear, and joining me at the curb.

"How much do I owe you for the detail?" I asked.

He frowned at a smudge of dust on his cloak and brushed it off. "You will complete this errand so we may return to my mission."

"A fair trade. Do you do tires, by chance?"

"What?"

"Apply a little Back-to-Black?" I made a scrubbing motion and pointed at the tires, but my attempt at humor received another blank look. "Never mind."

Maybe I should have worried more about what he might do to me once he was done using me for his mission. It was possible my mongrel snark wasn't earning his affection, after all.

When we entered the building, the door to Willard's outer office was closed—probably to protect innocent passersby from whatever projects her goblin assistant was building this week. I lifted my fist to knock, but magic whispered past my shoulder, courtesy of Sarrlevi, and the door opened.

The goblin Gondo, Willard's informant/secretary, poked his head up from behind his desk. There weren't any aerial fans whirring around the office today, but a machine hummed hungrily in a corner, and colored shreds of paper were piled about him and dangled from his pointed ears. He reminded me of a stuffed bunny poking up from the green plastic grass in an Easter basket.

Gondo hopped up on the seat and extended an arm toward the closed inner-office door, my senses telling me Thorvald and Lord Zavryd were inside.

"You are anticipated," he said grandly.

When Sarrlevi walked in after me, Gondo fell off the chair with a thump, ribbons of paper wafting up from behind the desk.

I hurried forward, peered over the top, and wondered if the pile of shredded paper had softened his landing. "Are you all right?"

"Am *I* not anticipated?" Sarrlevi asked dryly.

"Are assassins ever anticipated?" I asked.

"I believe it depends on how much cheese they bring."

Gondo jumped up, his head appearing above the desk again. "Cheese?"

"Get in here, Puletasi," came Willard's voice through the door.

"Is there any chance she's crabby for reasons that don't involve me?" I whispered, wondering if Gondo would dish on his boss.

"Oh, yes," he said. "Many reasons. Not five minutes ago, Lord Zavryd'nokquetal incinerated a plant she recently added to her office."

"Do dragons find plants offensive?" I headed for the door, not wanting Willard to think I was delaying.

"There was mold in the potting soil," Gondo said. "Don't tell her enemies, because the Ruin Bringer might not want her secrets to get out, but she is allergic to mold."

I imagined orcs and ogres pelting Thorvald with moldy bread and was smirking as I stepped into the office. The stern-faced Colonel Willard, the beautiful half-elf Thorvald, and the haughtily handsome Lord Zavryd all frowned at me, and I wiped the smirk away. Their gazes immediately shifted from me to Sarrlevi. Their frowns deepened.

"There's a stray elf following you around, Matti," Thorvald said.

Remembering we'd invited each other to use first names, I resolved to start calling her Val, though my inclination was to keep her and Willard at arm's distance. It didn't help that she, with her elegant features, six feet of height, and long blonde braid, managed to look stunning even in ripped jeans, a duster, and combat boots, whereas I always felt like a schlub. Even when I remembered to tweeze my eyebrows before leaving the house in the morning.

"That happens when you feed strays," I told her.

Though I didn't look over my shoulder, I could *feel* Sarrlevi's eyes narrowing as he considered the back of my head. *I am the one who has fed you,* he said telepathically, foisting an image of cheese into my mind.

Since I'd sampled both types he'd brought before getting in the truck, I couldn't deny that. Nor could I deny that the bird cheese had been even more amazing than the blue brick, with the runny insides of a ripe camembert and a pungent umami flavor like nothing I'd had before. Before eating the rest, I wanted to find a crusty baguette to go with it, or maybe some dried fruit to alternate with.

I know, I replied silently, wrenching my mind from cheese fantasies. *It's a joke. Here on Earth, it's accepted that if you show kindness and put out food for stray dogs and cats, they'll soon move in with you.*

On Nirathra, if you do that, the yeshando *will destroy your house and devour you whole.*

Is that... another name for the elven home world?

No. It's the world where the house you've visited is.

Ah, right. One of many houses you own, as I recall.

Yes.

"If you object to my presence," Zavryd told Willard, his arm around Val's shoulders, "then, surely, you must wish the elf assassin to leave your office immediately."

When I glanced back, I found Sarrlevi glaring at Zavryd, not the back of my head, as I'd believed. And the dragon was glaring back.

Val patted her mate on the chest before stepping out of his reach and placing herself between him and Sarrlevi, as if to play peacekeeper. Or maybe to act as an obstacle to prevent them from springing for each other's throats. I remembered that Sarrlevi had once been hired to kill Val.

"I object to your presence because you incinerated my fern," Willard grumbled, then pointed at Sarrlevi. "We'll be speaking of top-secret government matters, and you're not cleared to be here."

Sarrlevi shifted his gaze from Zavryd to Willard, though he carefully angled himself in the corner of the room so that nobody, not even the paper-shredding Gondo, was at his back. "The dwarf mongrel has agreed to assist me in completing my mission. I have already patiently waited for her to finish her mundane work. You will not give her an assignment before she helps me complete mine."

"The *dwarf mongrel*?" Willard mouthed and looked at Val. "So much for your belief that he's into her."

I barely stifled a groan. They had to bring up *that* discussion in front of Sarrlevi?

Val shrugged. "Zav called me a mongrel for *months*."

"All the while secretly coveting you?" Willard's eyes glinted with amusement.

I'd liked it better when she'd been crabby.

"I believe the onset of the coveting was gradual." Val smiled at Zavryd.

"You are a mongrel," he stated. "It is the appropriate term for a mixed-blood individual."

"And doesn't imply scorn and dismissal from the often-arrogant full-blooded user of the term?" Val arched her eyebrows.

"It may imply those things," Zavryd surprisingly admitted. "It took me some time to realize your value."

"I noticed."

I looked back at Sarrlevi, but his face was still cool and hard to read. I didn't know if it was because his terminology was being dissected or he was irked to be in the same room as Zavryd.

"Mr. Sarrlevi," Willard said, "as much as I appreciate individuals from other worlds coming into *my* office and giving me orders, in this instance, I can accede to your demand. I wish to show Puletasi something, get her opinion, ask a few questions, and then she can go back to *assisting* you." She lowered her voice to mutter, "Lucky girl," under her breath.

"Very well." Sarrlevi inclined his head ever so slightly.

"But I need you to wait outside the building," Willard added. "And Thorvald, ask your mate to wait out there as well. This is a matter of Army secrecy, if not national security."

"You don't think he can help with the problem?" Judging from Val's head tilt, she also hadn't been filled in on what was up.

"It's possible, but I don't want more people knowing about this than necessary."

"You know he can read minds, right?" Val glanced at Zavryd, but he was examining his footwear.

Once again, he wore yellow Crocs with even more meat-shaped charms than before filling the holes. Another time, I would ask the story behind those shoes. I couldn't imagine he'd picked them out himself.

"I'm willing to take the risk that he's sublimely uninterested in government problems," Willard said.

"That's possibly true." Val touched Zavryd's arm and asked him to wait outside.

No assignments other than mine, Sarrlevi said into my mind before also leaving the office.

Have I mentioned how endearing it is when you give me orders like I'm your lackey? If I hadn't already agreed to head to Port Townsend and work with him, I might have asked Willard if she needed any file cabinets organized or any other task that would force him to wait for another day or two. But I was a half-dwarf —*not* a mongrel, damn it—of my word.

You have not. Do I need to come up with further bribes to make you eager to work for me?

I didn't know if he telepathically placed the memory of him massaging my scalp into my thoughts, or if my own treacherous mind dug it up, but I couldn't keep from scowling. *No, dude. I said I'd help, and I will. I'll be out there as soon as I can.*

Good, he said, approval lacing the telepathic word, as if he wanted me to know he liked it when I was obedient.

"Such a bastard," I grumbled.

After the males were gone, Willard said, "This way, you two," and led us out.

Val cast a worried frown toward the window in the outer office, one that looked toward the lawn in front of the building. My senses told me Sarrlevi and Zavryd were both out there, not that far away from each other.

"Do you think it's all right that we sent them away together?" I doubted the glares they'd been trading had been feigned or for dramatic effect.

"I hope so," Val said, "but they don't like each other. Hopefully, this won't take long."

"Do *you* like Sarrlevi?" I asked curiously as we followed Willard down a hallway with recently buffed floors toward stairs leading to a basement level.

"I don't hate him, now that he's no longer trying to kill me, but I don't think anyone *likes* assassins." Val must not have realized how many people in the magical community still referred to her, the Ruin Bringer, as an assassin. "They're not the cuddliest types, you have to admit."

"True," I murmured, though I remembered the hints I'd gathered that Sarrlevi was ostracized by his people. A strange twinge of sadness came over me at the thought that he might not have any friends. If he didn't, it was his own fault for choosing that profession, but I was sometimes mildly curious about what had driven him to it. He clearly had his own agenda and admitted he was using me, but he didn't seem like a bloodthirsty psychopath.

"You left the artifact vault open?" Val asked as we descended the stairs into a windowless hallway, and a solid metal door, the only one, stood open at the end.

Willard gave her a dark look. "I *found* it open this morning."

Val grimaced. "Not dark elves again, I hope."

"It's possible, since we know they're capable of getting past our security and gaining access—unfortunately—but considering someone *else's* artifact went missing recently, I'm considering other suspects."

Was she referring to the magical dwarf power reactor that had been under the park?

Not clarifying, Willard stepped through the doorway and into a dim but spacious cement-walled room with rows and rows of deep metal shelves. *Empty* metal shelves.

"Oh, shit," Val breathed.

"That's an understatement," Willard said.

3

SINCE I'D NEVER BEEN TO THE BASEMENT VAULT BEFORE, I WASN'T AS stunned by its emptiness as Val, but I could imagine the shelves usually overflowing with magical weapons and doodads, things the Army had found or taken custody of over the years.

"There aren't any bullet casings on the floor, are there?" I asked, thinking of the tunnel under the house.

"No," Willard said, "but there also wasn't a fearsome metal furnace guardian protecting this place."

Val must have given her a thorough report of what had happened during our battle.

"Maybe you should get one." Val rotated in a slow circle, taking in the empty shelves.

"Why?" Willard asked. "It didn't help Puletasi's dwarves keep their stash."

"At least it killed a few of the thieves."

"I need you to hunt around—get Zavryd to help if he's willing, ideally without filling him in on *all* the details—and find out who took everything. If it's on Earth, I need you to find it all. Hell, if it's *not* on Earth, I need you to find it. I've cataloged everything and sent reports up my chain of command. If I have to tell them that I *lost* all this stuff..." The usually stern and stoic colonel shook her head, her dark eyes daunted as she stared bleakly at the shelves. "Let's just say that if you've ever fantasized about a new boss in charge of this office, it could happen."

"No, thanks. I've had that experience before." Val's grimace suggested her previous employers hadn't been appealing. She touched the cat-shaped figurine on her neck to summon her tiger. "I'm partial to being bossed around by you. I'll see what I can find."

Willard nodded, then looked at me as Sindari formed in silver mist beside Val.

I waited, having no idea what she would ask. She'd already told Sarrlevi she wasn't sending me on a mission.

"You have any ideas, Puletasi?" Willard asked as Val conferred with Sindari and asked him to sniff around for clues.

I couldn't sense any magic in the room other than Val's aura and those of her weapons and trinkets, nor did I have a tiger's keen nose, so I could only shrug. "You think this is related to the people who took the reactor?"

"It's crossed my mind. Especially since these thieves didn't leave any clues—nobody wandered past cameras, the way the dark elves who stole from the vault did—that would suggest they weren't familiar with human technology. The cameras went down for two hours last night, starting at one a.m. My captain thinks we were hacked from the outside, then the thieves used magic to get through the wards protecting the door. I have—*had*—both mundane and magical security measures." Willard shook her head. "When the cameras came back online, the vault was empty."

"That's not much time to move all the stuff that was in here." Val waved at the shelves.

"Unless they had magical help," Willard said.

"The guys who were dead under Matti's house were human."

"Humans can't have magical help?" Willard waved at Val's charms and tiger.

"Well, charms and artifacts aren't easy to come by."

"That programmer you dated had piles of them."

"I was his *bodyguard*, not his date, and he was wealthy and could afford to throw large sums of money around."

Willard waved dismissively. "Puletasi, you can go, but when you're out hunting for signs of your mother, keep your ears open. If you hear anything about this or that reactor, I want to know."

I didn't point out that I suspected the military was behind the missing dwarf artifact, even if *she* hadn't been filled in, and I still didn't trust her fully or want to help her that much. She was aware of how I felt and squinted at me, as if she knew exactly what I was thinking. Unless she had a charm that let her read minds, and I didn't sense anything like that on her, she shouldn't be able to, but I was probably an open book.

"I'll keep my ears open," I said.

"Shit." Val spun toward the doorway. "Zav and Sarrlevi are fighting. Your elf wasn't hired to assassinate him, was he?"

"He's not *my* elf," I said as alarm flashed through me. Sarrlevi was a magnificent fighter, but he couldn't match a dragon.

I was closer to the door than Val, but she had longer legs, and she beat me to the stairs. Together, we raced up to the hall above and out the front door, the clangs of swords ringing out ahead of us.

Where had the dragon gotten a *sword*?

But sword-fighting was exactly what was taking place. Val and I rushed outside but halted at the display on the grassy lawn.

Zavryd had produced a glowing yellow sword from somewhere, as well as what looked like a dwarven shield, and was engaged with Sarrlevi and his twin longswords. They battled with tremendous speed, thrusting and parrying so quickly that the clangs of their weapons turned into one continuous ringing of metal that assaulted our ears.

Our eyes, on the other hand, were mesmerized. Val and I ended up shoulder to shoulder in front of the door, watching their display.

Though Zavryd was in human form, he had as much speed and agility as his elven foe. Or perhaps *almost* as much. I sensed magic aiding his movements, his power allowing him to block and parry more quickly than his limbs might otherwise have managed. Sarrlevi had magic of his own, but he didn't seem to use more than what was infused in his blades. His prowess was purely physical, his feet moving so rapidly that few foes could have matched him. Only magic, I believed, allowed Zavryd to keep pace.

Even though I was worried, afraid they would kill each other, and puzzled as to why they were fighting, the battle was a thing of beauty to watch.

Until they started slinging insults.

"Bloodthirsty, orc-kissing murderer who dares raise a blade to a dragon," Zavryd bellowed, magic amplifying his voice so the Mariners fans probably heard him all the way over at the stadium, "you'll know the wrath of the entire Stormforge Clan if you touch me again."

"Swaddled dragonling who's afraid of leaving the nest," Sarrlevi replied as he *dared* swing a blade toward Zavryd's chest. "Go complain to your relatives that an elf threatened you. Perhaps you can hide behind your mother's tail."

"You *dare* accuse me of being puerile and cowardly." Zavryd parried, then rushed him, swinging for his head.

Sarrlevi ducked, sprang to the side, and slashed at Zavryd from behind. Though the dragon spun in time to face him, one of those lightning-fast blades darted under his defenses. It sliced through the black elven robe, and I thought Sarrlevi could have drawn blood if he'd wanted, but Zavryd jerked his body to the side and armored himself with magic, so perhaps not.

"'Ware, dragonling. My blades can cut through magical defenses."

"The blades you've stolen from those you've slain? Why you were not on the list of criminals the queen wished me to capture for punishment and rehabilitation is a mystery, but I shall bring you in as a bonus." Zavryd charged him.

Once again, Sarrlevi was fast enough to evade blade and shield, diving and rolling in several fast somersaults before springing up to face his opponent.

"Look out," Val warned, gripping my arm and pulling me back into the doorway as Zavryd hurled a great wave of magical power.

It targeted Sarrlevi, but that didn't keep it from ripping up grass and bushes and knocking a mirror off a car parked in the street. I expected Sarrlevi to go flying, but the power didn't so much as ruffle his hair. He smiled tightly and sprang for Zavryd, blades slashing toward his head and chest.

"I'm a prominent dues-paying member of the Assassins' Guild, you overgrown reptile. *Not* a criminal."

"You tried to slay my mate!" Zavryd's next attack was one of fire, a great inferno that roared across the lawn, incinerating grass before it engulfed his foe in a great swirling ball of flame.

"Sarrlevi!" I cried, running several steps, though I didn't know what I could do. I had no way to fight fire, and I hadn't even brought my hammer in from the truck.

"I was legitimately hired to assassinate her," came Sarrlevi's voice from within the inferno, shockingly calm behind the crackling of flames. "That is not a crime; it is a business transaction."

Zavryd stopped outside the ball of flame still burning atop

Sarrlevi. "Only a fool with a death wish accepts a *business transaction* that involves slaying the mate of a dragon."

After a pause, Sarrlevi surprised me by saying, "It was probably unwise."

"How do we stop this?" I asked Val, worried that whatever protection Sarrlevi was employing against the flames would wear off, or that Zavryd would find a way around his defenses.

"Zav," Val called. "We've been given a mission, and we'd better leave now so we can stop for takeout on the way to clue-hunt for Willard."

His gaze shifted from the fireball, the flames now dwindling, and locked on to Val. His jaw was bloody from a cut, and he looked perturbed from the fight. I expected him to state that dragons didn't accept *missions* from human colonels.

Instead, he asked, "Takeout *food*? Such as chicken slabs from one of the meat-delivery buildings?"

"Chicken strips, yes." Val lifted her phone. "I'm putting in an order now. Make sure to save some of your fire so you can incinerate the breading."

I looked curiously at her.

"He's on a full carnivore diet," she explained. "No fries, no breading, no dipping sauces."

"He sounds finicky."

"It's a dragon thing."

As the last of the flames died, leaving not only burned grass but a smoking crater in the lawn where the dirt itself had melted, Sarrlevi walked toward me, though his gaze remained over his shoulder and locked on Zavryd. Neither his blond hair nor clothing was singed. His swords glowed icy silver, and I remembered the command word Val had taught me to waken the power of cold within my hammer. Maybe his elven blades could do something similar and extend their protection around him.

"Why were you fighting a *dragon*?" I whispered to him as Val joined Zavryd near the crater.

Since Sarrlevi was breathing heavily and bleeding, I didn't mention that he could have been doing something more constructive and less deadly, like applying his magical kerchief to the exterior of my truck.

He lifted his chin, still holding Zavryd's gaze—or would that be considered a glare? "We were merely sparring."

Zavryd, who'd traded his goofy Crocs for black slippers, touched the cut on his jaw dripping blood onto his robe. A few slashes in that garment suggested there might be more than one injury. Was striking a dragon even *permitted*? Would there be repercussions from other dragons? The Stormforge Clan?

"Yes." Zavryd also lifted his chin. "A dragon enjoys a spirited match, though I was of course limited by agreeing to remain in this lowly form. Had I been in my natural state, your blades never would have sliced through my scales."

"Feel free to shape shift, and we can go another round," Sarrlevi said.

"I do not fear you, *or* your mongrel companion."

Uh, why was he bringing me into this? I looked at Val, but she was rubbing her head in puzzlement.

"How did this, er, sparring match start?" She didn't sound like she believed that was all it had been.

"I haven't the faintest idea what brought on the attack," Zavryd said. "We were discussing mongrels and how they might in time overcome their mixed-blood handicaps. I said that you, my mate, might instruct his mongrel female to better be able to acquit herself in battle and among the magical beings of the Cosmic Realms."

His mongrel female? If the dragon was talking about me, I was insulted.

"He said the dwarf mongrel did not *need* the Ruin Bringer's instruction. Believing he'd slighted you, I may have challenged him." Zavryd lowered his voice to speak privately to Val, though my hearing was good enough to catch the rest. "Unwisely, I agreed to do battle in this diminished form. I also did not immediately think to switch my footwear for something surer for such activities." He touched the gouge on his jaw, though it had already stopped bleeding. Dragon magic meant it would probably heal and disappear completely within the hour.

"Just to be clear," Val said, "he wasn't trying to kill you because someone hired him to assassinate a dragon lord but... because you insulted his, ah, lady friend?"

I raised a finger. "We're not friends, and I'm not *his*."

Sarrlevi merely raised an eyebrow.

"That is correct," Zavryd said, ignoring us and responding to Val. "I do not believe he was trying to kill me. Had *that* been the case, I would have smote him with my great power."

"Naturally," Val said.

"As I recall, you *did* try to smite me," Sarrlevi said, "when I pricked your chin—and your ego. *Twice* you enveloped me with fire, but my armor protects me against such magic."

Ah, so the blades hadn't been responsible. Though they were still glowing and emanated strong power of their own.

"There are other ways to smite an assassin. Had I continued through my repertoire, I would have found a way." A hint of smugness crossed Zavryd's face as he glanced at Val. "As I recall, assassin, you are susceptible to some elven magic, such as entangling roots."

Sarrlevi clenched his jaw for a moment before responding. "That was once true, as I did not wear enchanted items to protect against the magic favored by my own kind, but I have since remedied that mistake. Should your mate wish to challenge me to another duel..."

"She does not," Val said, even as Zavryd's violet eyes lit, as if he wanted to see Val pummel Sarrlevi.

Judging from what Val had admitted about their previous encounters, she wasn't sure she would come out on top again and wasn't eager to challenge Sarrlevi.

"Why is there a *crater* in the lawn of my supposedly inconspicuous office building?" Willard demanded from the front door. "You all have missions, do you not? Get out of here, and don't light anything else on fire." She made a shooing motion toward Zavryd and Sarrlevi.

More than ready to depart, I pointed for Sarrlevi to head to my truck, but he didn't take his eyes from Zavryd, who was shifting into his huge dragon form. Soon, inky black scales covered powerful muscles, and he flexed and spread his great wings. His eyes glowed as he looked back at us, and I had the distinct feeling he was showing off his magnificence.

"Never have I seen two males so full of themselves," Willard grumbled. "You know what they say, Thorvald."

"What?"

"One day a rooster, the next a feather duster."

"A dragon's scales would make a lousy dusting tool," Val said.

"Those horns ought to be good for something. Are they ivory?"

You fantasize about detaching my horns and carving them? Zavryd boomed telepathically. *As if I am one of your walruses?*

"Move faster," I whispered to Sarrlevi, daring to give him a shove toward the truck, "in case he really gets cranky."

Sarrlevi snorted and didn't object, finally taking his gaze from his supposed sparring opponent.

Though I was hurrying to get in and drive off, I didn't miss that the outside of my truck was now as dirt-free as the dash. Even the tires were free of grime. Damn, that looked good. If Sarrlevi had been a normal guy, instead of a haughty elf overly certain of his sex appeal, I would have hugged him and kissed him on the cheek.

I refrained, merely turning the key in the ignition to take us out of there. I had to drive up on the curb on the opposite side of the street to keep from running over the long scaled tail extending out onto the pavement. Though Zavryd was busy glowering at Willard and educating her on proper respect for dragons, I had no doubt he would notice me running over one of his appendages. In the last month, my already odd life had taken a turn for the weird.

4

As we drove off the ferry and headed through Kingston on the way to Port Townsend, I glanced over at Sarrlevi. For most of the ride, he'd been silent, other than shifting now and then on what he clearly considered a deplorably uncomfortable seat. I was tempted to ask for his version of how and why the *sparring match* with Zavryd had started. But if it had truly been about me, I wasn't sure I wanted details.

It had *sounded* like he might have been defending me, or at least saying I was a capable warrior without need of Val's instruction, but since he wasn't exactly effervescent in his praise for me, that was hard to believe. The one time he'd somewhat grudgingly said I was doing good work was when I'd been carving the posts on the stairs in the project house.

"How come your armor didn't have protection against elven magic before?" was what I ended up asking.

It seemed safer. If I'd misunderstood Zavryd's comments, and Sarrlevi *hadn't* been defending me... Well, I would prefer not to know it. Maybe it was dumb, but I wanted Sarrlevi to be nobler than he probably was. Which was a strange thing, since I knew—

he'd fully admitted—he'd once taken an assignment to kill my mother.

"My people rarely attack me, nor am I often hired to assassinate elves," he said, gazing out the window instead of looking at me.

"Because elves don't piss off powerful people?"

"Because elves often *are* powerful people."

"Wouldn't that make others more eager to get rid of them through, uh, alternate means?" I waved toward him.

He didn't answer.

"Or is it that you have a rule against, uhm, preying on your own kind?"

"I do not."

Given his terse answers, I assumed that was all he would say, especially since he wasn't looking at me but rather continuing to gaze out the window as we drove out of the city and into the countryside, the grass turning yellow as summer progressed. Then, in a quiet voice, he added, "The first person I ever killed was my father."

I digested that for a moment, debating if I wanted to ask for details. Curiosity prompted me to continue. "On purpose?"

"On purpose."

"You weren't hired to assassinate him, were you?"

"No." Sarrlevi finally turned his face toward me, but only to give me a cool what-kind-of-a-monster-do-you-think-I-am look. At least, that was how I interpreted it. In truth, it held little expression. "I did train hard for many years so that I could survive a battle against him. He was a capable weapons master and a powerful mage, and I knew he wouldn't hesitate to kill me if I failed."

"No love lost between you, huh?" I was late noticing a curve in the road and hurried to adjust the wheel. Distracted by Sarrlevi's story, I was glad we'd driven into a rural area and there wasn't much traffic.

"No." Not alarmed by the swerve—the broken coil in the seat seemed to bother him more than my driving—he returned his gaze to the countryside.

Long seconds passed before I realized he didn't intend to continue.

"Why did you want to kill him? You can't tell me only *part* of the story."

"It was long ago. It doesn't matter, and you..." He flicked his fingers in a dismissive gesture.

I scowled. "What? You remembered I'm a mongrel and therefore not worth sharing with?"

"When we reach the dwarf's domicile, I will camouflage myself and wait outside while you question her. If you are effective and learn where your mother is, I will not show myself."

"You're a pain in the ass, Sarrlevi." I lowered my voice to mutter, "I should have been rooting for the dragon to win."

"Perhaps so," he said softly.

Boy, he was in a mood this evening. Maybe his insult-throwing with Zavryd had reminded him of his failure to slay Val. Though from what Val had said about that mission, it had sounded like Zavryd had worked to get the contract canceled, not that Sarrlevi had given up. Something told me that he wouldn't stop going after a target, even if he lost a battle along the way. He was probably like a Terminator. Relentless, inexorable.

So... had he truly given up on his mission to kill my mother?

I looked uneasily at him, but his gaze remained on the countryside.

As we continued the drive in silence, I wondered if he hadn't previously acquired defenses against elven magic because he didn't *want* to fight his own people. Despite what he said. Maybe he had some mental hang-ups about it. Or about a lot of things.

"Maybe I should get the number for Val's therapist," I said, still muttering.

As if his pointed ears couldn't pick up everything. He squinted over at me.

"Welcome to Port Townsend." I waved to the sign, deciding to drop everything else and focus on the mission. "Are you camouflaged yet? She's a full-blooded dwarf and will be able to sense you from a distance."

"I am aware," he said, without answering the question.

Hoping that meant yes, I bypassed Artie's house and headed to the axe-throwing establishment, figuring she might be there—and that she might be less disgruntled if I showed up at her business instead of her unlisted private address.

After parking in the lot, I touched the Polaroids and ring in my pocket, reassuring myself that I had them. I'd stopped toting around the clunky iron chest they'd been hidden in and left it in my house. The last I'd seen, Tinja was using it to store the tabs from aluminum cans. Apparently, those had uses in *dozens* of goblin projects.

"She is inside." Sarrlevi nodded.

I also sensed Artie's aura, as well as that of the half-dwarf teen who'd been taking money and handing out axes when Val and I had come.

"Good. Stay here, and keep my truck from being stolen." It was a joke—there was nothing seedy about the neighborhood a handful of blocks from the waterfront—but his expression suggested he didn't get it.

"Is that a likely occurrence?"

"It is looking pretty rockin' now that you cleaned it." I managed a smile for him. "Thanks for that."

He frowned at my smile, as if I'd pulled a knife on him, then grunted and looked out the windshield.

What a tool.

When I opened the building's front door, I looked back to make sure Sarrlevi was staying put. But he'd disappeared from the truck.

I hoped he was still sitting in there, and his camouflage hid him from me, not that he was skulking around and peering through the windows like a stalker. He'd *said* he would wait outside while I spoke with her. Hopefully, that hadn't meant outside her office window.

"I should get a tiger for a partner instead." I stepped inside to eighties Metallica playing on the speakers for a few people in the axe-throwing lanes as well as the teenager up front.

Nerves started squirming in my belly as I walked in. I wasn't sure why, other than that I hoped Artie would talk to me and be a decent person, not someone dismissive who shooed me away. A pang of wistfulness accompanied the nervousness, a longing to speak with someone who'd known my mother and who might tell me about her world and what it meant to be a dwarf.

My grandparents were good people and had done their best to raise me and my half-sister—admittedly, prim and proper *Penina* hadn't been that trying for them—but they had only met my mother a few times before she'd passed, and they hadn't even known she hadn't been human. She'd simply been that quirky short and stout woman their son had been shacked up with.

"You're back," the teen said gruffly, eyeing me without warmth before looking past my shoulder. He held a stack of paper targets and a stapler and had been on the way to affix them to the plywood boards in the lanes. "Is the hot half-elf with you?"

"No, and she's married to a dragon, so you might want to keep any horny thoughts you've had to yourself."

"Thoughts can't get you in trouble." He smirked.

"They can around mind readers. Is it okay if I see your boss?" I pointed to the closed office door down the short hallway behind the bar, though I would go whether he said *yes* or not.

"Only if it's about business. She's not the social type." He shifted his gaze, no doubt disappointed by the lack of a hot half-elf behind me, toward the hammer slung over my shoulder. "And she doesn't like *solicitors*." Even though he said the last word slowly, he still managed to mangle the pronunciation.

I spun and hurled my hammer down the closest lane. Since it wasn't an axe and had no blade, it shouldn't have lodged in the plywood board, but it did, the head precisely in the center of the target.

The kid's jaw drooped.

"It's about business." I walked down the cage and pulled it out. It would have been even more impressive if I'd used the power word that made lightning shoot out of the head, but I hadn't wanted to accidentally zap someone.

"Yeah," the kid said when he recovered from his surprise. "She'll probably want to see you." He gave me a thumbs-up.

If one couldn't travel with a blonde beauty to distract teenage boys, then hurling hammers into walls was the next best thing.

I used it to knock on the door.

"Who are you?" came a gravelly voice from inside. Not exactly an invitation...

"Matti Puletasi." I hesitated, then added softly, "Daughter of Rodarska Ironhelm."

For some reason, it struck me as a little dangerous to shout that where others might hear, as if someone might still be hunting my mother—and her offspring. Not necessarily Sarrlevi. I thought instead of the soldiers who had taken Mom down thirty years earlier. And how it might have been soldiers who had killed the renter at the project house before stealing the reactor. Thus far, those people hadn't shown their faces to me, but that didn't mean they weren't watching me. After all, *Willard* had a file on me that went back years and that didn't, as far as I knew, have anything to do with my mother.

After a long silent pause, footsteps approached the door.

I pulled out the Polaroids, intending to show the ones of my mother to Artie as quickly as possible to keep her from putting a fist through my nose, or anything else a dwarf might do to a suspected imposter.

But when the door opened, the four-and-a-half-foot tall brown-haired dwarf woman peering up at me, she merely nodded. "I thought it was something like that. Your aura is familiar."

Encouraged, I offered the stack of photos anyway. Just in case she realized my *aura* was familiar because it had been in her house a few weeks back, not because she could sense something of my mother in it. Could she? I didn't know.

For me, I could tell if magical beings were familiar, each person's aura being unique, akin to a fingerprint, but I wasn't sensitive enough to determine someone's heritage through it. Sarrlevi had needed that magical blood analyzer to know I was my mother's daughter. Of course, he hadn't likely known her well. Maybe that made a difference.

"I remember him taking these," Artie said as she flipped through the Polaroids.

"Who?"

"Norgoth. He went back to our world long ago. Most of them did."

"But not the dwarf who was guarding the house in Bellevue. You know he passed, right?" I eyed her warily, hoping I wasn't the deliverer of the news.

"I just learned of it and that—" Artie looked at me and cut herself off.

"The magical reactor you guys made was taken?" I asked.

She frowned at me, and I braced myself to tell the story—and explain that I'd had nothing to do with the theft—but she said, "You have the aura of a dragon about you."

"I was in a room with one today."

"And... someone else." Her frown deepened as she squinted at me.

Hell, she couldn't sense that I'd been in the truck with Sarrlevi, could she? I had no doubt that Sindari would have been able to smell his scent since we'd been close, but could someone *sense* that in my aura?

"*He* is here." Artie's blue eyes flared with anger—and maybe fear. She spun, looking around the office before peering into the hallway again. She cursed and yelled in Dwarven, words that I wasn't familiar with, but I caught Sarrlevi's name.

"He won't hurt you." I lifted my hands to pat the air.

Artie reached for the door, and I lunged, putting my foot inside, in case she meant to slam it shut. I couldn't leave yet; I hadn't learned anything.

"He's trying to rectify a mistake from his past," I told her. All right, Sarrlevi hadn't *said* that, but I wanted to believe it, to believe his claim that the king had hired him. "He doesn't want to hurt my mother anymore, just find her."

"Your mother isn't alive," Artie said.

"I know. But— Oh." It wasn't as if I hadn't expected her to say that—it was what I'd always believed—but hearing the words spoken with such certainty quashed a hope that had bloomed within me. That my memories would be proven wrong, or at least incomplete, and that my mother would somehow—some way—be alive.

"Let the past be the past," Artie said. "Because of *him*, Hennehok and I are refugees on this world, doomed never to see our families back home again, forever watching over our backs..." She glared at the door.

"Why? What happened?"

Artie shook her head.

"Please tell me. My father has been in jail for almost my whole life, and I don't even know why exactly. He shot people when he was defending my mother, but *why* did they have to defend themselves?"

"Safer for you not to know and get involved. They're still out there."

"Who is?"

If she had been referring to Sarrlevi, or *only* Sarrlevi, she wouldn't have used *they*.

Jaw set, Artie shook her head again.

I groped for something to say that would sway her. "Where did you go when Sarrlevi visited you before? Your worker said you went to warn someone."

"He did not *visit*. He attacked me."

"He said you attacked him first." Sarrlevi wasn't who I wanted to talk about, but I didn't know how to get the answers I longed for from her.

Artie frowned at me, her aura growing stronger, as if she were summoning magic and planned to push me away for my own good. Maybe I should have been worried about my safety, but I remained rooted to the floor. I wanted to know about my mother and what had happened.

"He's coming. Come inside." Abruptly, Artie grabbed my arm.

Since I'd expected her to shove me away instead of pull me in, she caught me off guard and succeeded at tugging me into her office.

"Sarrlevi? He won't hurt us."

She gave me a scathing look. "If he has been around you, it is for his own vile and nefarious reasons. That one is trouble. All of the Cosmic Realms know that."

Artie grabbed the door to slam it shut.

There was nothing blocking it, so it should have closed, but it halted inches before reaching the jamb. I sensed Sarrlevi in the hallway on the other side, close enough that his camouflage had stopped hiding him. Or he'd deliberately let it stop hiding him.

But what was he *doing*? Besides ruining my chance to make friends with a real dwarf and learn more about my mother's death?

Sarrlevi's aura grew stronger, as if he was about to summon a huge blast of magic to blow the door—or maybe the entire building—down. But Artie's aura did the same, and she clenched her jaw and growled like a pit bull.

Not wanting to be caught in the middle, I slipped out of her grip and stepped to the side. Though Artie didn't move, I sensed her unleashing her power. It didn't knock the door down but went through it like an apparition. On the other side, Sarrlevi unleashed *his* power.

What are you doing? I almost shouted it aloud but hoped that he was monitoring my mind and would hear the words.

Helping you.

Magic pounded at the door like a murderer with a vendetta.

How are you helping me?

Artie ran behind her desk, yanked open a cupboard against the wall, and pulled out an axe much larger than anything people threw at targets out front. The two-handed weapon was as big as my hammer and emanated similar magic.

"Stand with me," she ordered. "His magic is strong."

"Uhm. All right."

I still had no idea what Sarrlevi was doing and couldn't imagine I would be forced to fight him. Unless he'd been lying to me and had come along to interrogate the poor dwarf again. Even then, would he attack *me*? He'd said he was helping, but as magic railed at the door like a hurricane gale, I couldn't see how.

Though Artie's power reinforced it, the door quaked on its hinges. More power flared outside, twin points of magic that mingled with Sarrlevi's aura. He'd drawn his swords.

"What the hell, man?" I yelled through the door.

It quaked and shuddered again.

Artie said something in Dwarven. Several magical tools on

shelves and windowsills around the office, items I'd barely noticed on my first visit, started glowing, humming, or both. Their power flowed into the walls of the room. Reinforcing them as Artie was reinforcing the door?

"Here." She pointed for me to join her at her side.

She crouched with her axe raised, its power mingling with and adding to hers. I lifted my hammer and stood beside her to face the door, but if Sarrlevi charged in, I didn't know what I would do.

5

As I crouched side by side with Artie, our weapons pointed at the door, Sarrlevi seething with magic on the other side, her power curled around me. It wasn't alarming but reassuring, as if it welcomed me as an ally.

To my surprise, my hammer warmed in my grip and glowed silver-blue. I'd seen it do that before, but when tendrils of power floated out of it to join with golden tendrils that flowed from Artie's axe, that was something new to me.

The tendrils twined together and sailed into the door, reinforcing it and the wall around it. In the hallway, Sarrlevi stepped back. Or was he *pushed* back? All my senses told me was that he was moving farther away, the magic he'd been throwing at the door waning.

"He had better not hurt Ethan," Artie growled and leaned forward.

Thinking of chasing Sarrlevi all the way out of her building?

Artie glanced at the door—at splintered wood from where a throwing axe had stuck in it the last time I'd been there—and must have decided Sarrlevi was too dangerous for that. If she left her office, she wouldn't have the added assistance of whatever the magical doodads around the room were doing. They hummed with power and had helped keep Sarrlevi from getting in.

Even if I hadn't meant to, thanks to my hammer's assistance, I had also helped keep him from getting in. Would he hold a grudge about that?

I sensed him leave the building before his aura faded from my awareness, his camouflage back in place. Slowly, I lowered my hammer. It and Artie's axe stopped glowing, though she remained in a wary crouch, squinting toward the front of the building, as if she could see through the walls and could continue to track Sarrlevi.

I doubted she could. The powerful *brysarrusi* in the park hadn't been able to sense him from ten feet away. When he wanted to hide, he was good at it.

You are welcome, Sarrlevi spoke into my mind.

For what? You terrorizing this dwarf woman? Again?

I did nothing of the sort, merely gave her a chance to test her building's security. And for you two to stand together against a common enemy. It should increase her feelings of empathy toward you and make her more likely to open up. I was listening. She was not going to give you the information we seek, and I knew you would not threaten her to gain it.

No, I would not. Even if such a thing had crossed my mind, I had a feeling Artie had the power to kick my ass, with her magic if not with her axe.

So I assumed.

So you manipulated her.

I did.

The way you manipulate me.

Sarrlevi paused before answering. *I did not bring her cheese or rub her head.*

I doubt that would have worked on her.

Likely not. One must use different tactics on different people.

Right. Cheese for mongrels addicted to it. *You're still an ass, you know.*

A fact that will likely not change. Acquire what information you can. I will be waiting in your conveyance for you.

What a treat for me.

Artie finally lowered her axe. "I don't know if he's gone, but I don't sense him anymore."

"Me either." I almost added that he'd told me he would wait in the truck, but Artie would be even less likely to speak with me if she believed we were working together. Still, going along with Sarrlevi's manipulation, whether I'd had advance warning about it or not, made me feel squicky, so I thought about telling her everything anyway.

"He's following you around?" Artie asked. "Hoping you'll lead him to your mother?"

"Yeah." That much was true. Admitting it wasn't holding anything back.

Her voice lowered to a growl. "Has he hurt you?"

"No."

She squinted at me. Trying to read my mind? I didn't feel the crawling sensation under my skull that I got when Sarrlevi tried to read my thoughts, so probably not. Maybe she was just trying to guess based on my face. Since my expression was sour, who knew what conclusions she came to?

"It would not be a failure on your part if he had," Artie said, her tone growing gentler. "He is a powerful mage as well as a weapons master. Even a well-trained full-blooded dwarf—" she touched her chest, "—would struggle to stop him. I sense that you have some of your mother's power, but her talents were for crafting and enchanting. She could defend herself, but she was a kind person and a gentle soul, not one to train obsessively for battle or long to slay enemies."

My throat tightened with emotion at the confirmation of what I'd always believed. That my mother had been a good person. It angered me anew that Sarrlevi had once accepted the mission to assassinate her, even if he'd since given it up. Had he even met her? Did he *research* his targets before he took on assignments? Or did he not care one whit if he killed a good person?

No. He didn't. He'd admitted as much. I ground my teeth.

"It is why I left with her." Artie smiled faintly for the first time. "And why the others did as well. She needed more militant souls to protect her so she could do that which she excelled at and loved, creating magical tools for the good of our people."

"Why does—did—her sister want her dead? Sarrlevi said she was the one to hire him."

Artie's smile vanished. I shouldn't have mentioned him again.

"Princess Barothla is *not* a kind person. She's ambitious and was always envious of her older sister. Not only did she want to be the heir to their father's throne and the ruler over the largest kingdom of our people, but she wanted his affection. Especially after their mother passed, she was needy and coveted it. I cannot know for certain, but I believe she plotted a long time before hiring the assassin." Artie scowled in the direction of the parking lot again.

"You said my mother was a crafter. Was she the one to make that power source? Or did you all bring it along, and she was able to activate it?"

"For your own safety, I will not speak of such things. You wouldn't be able to defend yourself from Sarrlevi if he mind scoured you, and we do not give even elves we are allied with information about what we can craft. Long ago, I swore to keep your family's secrets. Not that I know the details of them, but I know enough."

"He said my mind is hard to read because I have a natural dwarven defense to such magic."

"I'm sure you have *some* innate mental defenses, such as would stop a lesser mage, but if he wanted your thoughts, he would have them. It's possible he's read your mind and simply didn't admit to how much information he gained. He also may not have wanted to harm you if he believes he can use you to get what he wants. A true mind scouring is quite painful."

Sarrlevi hadn't hurt me, but I shivered a little as I remembered the night in the pantry when he'd rested his hand on my head. How many of my thoughts *had* he extracted then?

"Are you *sure* he hasn't hurt you?" Artie asked softly, watching my face.

"He hasn't."

"I'm surprised. Do not let yourself trust him."

"Oh, I won't."

"Did he say what he wants? Is it... the artifact? Or does he not realize your mother is dead, and he still seeks to slay her?"

"Are you sure she *is* dead?" I peered into Artie's eyes, wondering if she might be lying about that as another way to protect me.

"I believe she is. Don't you? I'd heard the military men shot her and burned her building to the ground around her."

Another verification that it *had* been the military who'd been responsible. Not that I'd doubted it.

Artie shook her head sadly, continuing before I responded. "I regret that we weren't there to protect her, but we foolishly went along with her plan, her wishes."

"What wishes?"

"For those of us who came to this world with her to disperse so she could integrate into human society and attempt to disappear among them. I did not think it would work, as a dwarf is most distinctly a dwarf, but she was in love and—my apologies—not making the best decisions. Hennehok and I were unwise to do as she asked, but she was our princess, and your father's heir, and we'd long ago sworn oaths to protect and obey her." Artie's mouth twisted. "Whether we wished to do the latter or not."

Even if this confirmation that someone else believed she was dead was depressing, it heartened me to know that my mother had genuinely loved my father. I'd believed that had been the case, since I had memories of them hugging and holding hands and leaning on each other, but everything I knew was filtered through thirty-year-old memories and the eyes of a four-year-old.

"How did she meet my father?"

"She told us he helped her escape from the soldiers when they imprisoned her on their base. At the time, she'd disappeared on us for six months. We'd looked everywhere, and several of us had gone to other realms searching for her. We feared Sarrlevi had finally thought to look on Earth and had found her, but it was the soldiers. They had her."

"Why? Was that after you guys built those tunnels and stashed the reactor?"

Artie winced. "Please do not speak of that. It is worrisome that you know as much as you do when you cannot guard your thoughts from enemies."

"Don't take this the wrong way, but a lot of people know about that place now. The reactor is gone. Someone got to it before us— before the orcs that were forcing us to help them get it."

Artie swore softly and turned away, her back to me as she started pacing. "I told him we should have taken it home long ago. It was madness to leave it on this world, even with the furnace guardian protecting it."

"Why did you?"

"Hennehok made the decision."

"He was your engineer, right?" I thought of the painting in Artie's house, the portrait of her and my mother standing with the armored dwarf from the group, the one Sarrlevi remembered from the king's court.

Artie looked toward the ceiling, as if it, or maybe the heavens, might advise her on whether to answer my questions. Though I reminded myself that dwarven gods lived underground, supposedly working and crafting at the Eternal Forges.

"Yes," she finally said, as if she'd decided she could admit that much without breaking decades-old oaths. "He never believed your mother was dead and wanted to keep the artifact here on Earth for her, so that when she returned, we could still do what we'd planned. Start a colony here, create a safe haven for any other dwarves who had to flee the Cosmic Realms because they'd gone afoul of the dragon rulers or—" her tone turned bitter, "—cruel and ambitious siblings."

"Why did he believe she's still alive?" Once more, a hint of hope stirred in my chest. "Is there any chance—"

"No," Artie said sharply, turning to frown at me. "Do not allow yourself to obsess for years over finding her when there is no evidence to suggest she is alive. Accept that she's gone. Please. It's what we should have done. We should have gone home years ago, as the others did. Instead of sitting here on this backward, magic-depleted world, waiting for her return."

"Why did you wait? If you're certain she's gone..."

"Because I'm a fool. And Hennehok has been a friend for a long time. If he hadn't loved *her*..." Artie waved a dismissive hand.

The engineer had loved my mother? But she'd loved my father? And had Artie loved the engineer?

I rubbed the back of my neck, feeling knots tightening between my shoulder blades. It seemed that the more stones I overturned, the more complicated the past became. And there was still no evidence that my mother was alive, not unless the engineer had some. Was that who Artie had gone to see—to warn—after Sarrlevi had shown up at her place the first time?

"Does Hennehok live in the Seattle area?"

Artie gazed at me, her eyelids drooping. Maybe she *could* read some of my thoughts. "Yes."

"Will you tell me where? I'd like to learn more about my mother and why he thinks she's still alive."

"She's not alive."

"I just want to learn as much as I can. Can you understand that? My whole life, I've wondered about her. My father is in a maximum-security military prison, and I haven't been able to ask him anything. Honestly, I don't even know for sure if he's alive, or if they... did away with him." I didn't have to feign the emotion that made my voice tight.

"As long as that assassin is trailing you around, I dare not tell you anything."

"If Mom is dead, what does it matter? All he'll find, if anything, are her remains." I attempted to swallow the tightness. I barely knew Artie. Even if she'd been friends with my mother, I didn't want to fall apart in front of her.

"More than that may have drawn him here. Someone might have paid him to recover that which we hid."

"He wasn't that interested in it."

She gave me a pitying look, probably because I sounded like I believed the things Sarrlevi had told me.

I didn't trust him and took everything he said with a grain of salt, but his *actions* hadn't suggested he'd cared about the reactor. He'd fought the *brysarrusi* to buy time for Val and me to get Tinja and deal with the orcs without the creature piling on. He might have saved our lives. Mine, at least. I didn't have a tiger bodyguard.

Even if he hadn't helped me for altruistic reasons... he'd still helped.

"I never saw her body," Artie admitted so quietly I almost missed the words.

It took a few seconds for her meaning to sink in.

"So, you're not as positive as you sounded that she's dead."

"She *is* dead. I'm certain of it. But... if she weren't, and she'd hidden herself from all of us for some reason, maybe because she worried her sister—her sister's *minions* were still after her... and you led him to her..." Artie spread her hands.

"Sarrlevi says he's not working for the princess anymore, that the dwarven king has hired him to *find* my mother, or her remains to bring home."

"King Korvik Ironhelm would *never* hire an assassin, nor ask an outsider for help."

"He may have believed Sarrlevi would best know where she was, since, uh, he was after her once."

Artie folded her arms over her chest. "Have you *met* your grandfather?"

It was strange to hear the words *your grandfather* and not have them refer to my Samoan family. A weird pang of longing came over me, a desire to meet my mother's father and have him be a decent guy. Have him accept me and give me a hug. They were silly things to crave at my age, but I couldn't help but wish for them.

"No," I said. "I didn't know anything about him or even who he was until a few weeks ago."

"He's an honorable leader of the dwarven people, not someone who would have anything to do with an assassin. Girl, Sarrlevi has been *lying* to you. Manipulating you for his own gain."

"I know that. But he's not *successfully* manipulating me. I'm aware of what he's doing, and I'm..." I was what? Not helping him? But I was, wasn't I? Because he'd helped me in fights and gotten me out of a pickle with the police. And because I'd promised I would help him. Whether he was manipulating me or not, I was bound by my own word.

Artie's pitying look was all too knowing. "You need to get away from him. I'm tempted to offer to house you here and give you a job, but I doubt I could keep him from reaching you if he was determined." Her eyes narrowed, contemplation replacing the pity. "You should learn to use your power so you can better protect *yourself*. And you should meet your grandfather, both because he'll want to know that you exist and so you can ask him if he hired that assassin. I'm *positive* he did not, but maybe you need to hear that from him."

She made that claim with more confidence than she'd said she was positive my mother was dead. What should I take away from that?

"If I had the power to conjure portals," Artie continued, "I would send you to Dun Kroth now."

I couldn't keep the wistful expression off my face. I would love the opportunity to meet my dwarven grandfather, ask him about my mother, and find out if he'd hired Sarrlevi. Especially if he was a good guy. And Artie made it sound like he was. Though that didn't mean he would approve of *me*. Did he know anything about what his daughter had been doing once she'd left the dwarven home world?

"Hennehok can create portals," Artie said slowly. "I could send you to him."

I raised my eyebrows hopefully. Earlier, she hadn't been willing to tell me where he lived. If her change in attitude truly was a result of Sarrlevi's plan, I... Well, I wouldn't thank him, since it had been a dick thing to do, but...

Hell, I didn't know. Why was he so difficult?

After she finished whatever internal debate she was having, Artie nodded. "Yes. You should meet your grandfather. But—" she pointed her finger at my nose, "—you won't ask Hennehok about the artifact nor try to extract clues about your mother's location, *should* she live, and I'm sure she doesn't." She frowned, not appearing *sure* at all. "I'll let him know that you're coming and remind him of his oaths. If you visit Dun Kroth and your grandfather wants to tell you more, then that's his choice and his right."

"I understand." This was what I'd hoped for when I came. "Thank you."

Artie huffed and walked around to her desk. "I don't want you leading that assassin to Hennehok. Or having anything else to do with him." She opened a drawer.

Curious about what she was retrieving, I didn't object, though my promise to Sarrlevi lingered in my mind. But if he'd been lying to me about being hired by the king, did I owe him anything? My loyalty ought to be to my mother, whether she was alive or not, and her kin.

"Here." Artie extracted a beautiful stone hammer on a keychain, a hint of magic emanating from it, as with the other knickknacks she had around the room. "You're familiar with camouflage charms?"

"Yes. My goblin friend has one, but it looks like a wad of gum with staples sticking out of it."

Artie grunted. "Sounds like the goblin aesthetic, yes. Your mother made this one for me. She had a similar one that she wore."

"Oh?" The polite and proper part of me felt I should reject the offering, not accept an item that had been a gift to Artie, but... "I would be touched to have something she made," I admitted.

After the fire, there'd been nothing left of our apartment building. Years later, when I'd been old enough to wonder and ask my grandparents to take us to see it, we'd found the burned remains long gone, replaced with an eight-story condo complex with a gym and a grocery store on the bottom floor.

"Your mother made your hammer, you know," Artie said dryly and walked toward me with the charm.

I blinked. "She *did*? I thought—I think someone implied—it was an ancient weapon made by some long-dead master smith."

"Some recently dead one." Artie's tone went swiftly from dry to grim.

"Yeah." I touched the double heads and engraved runes with new reverence.

Artie waved for me to hold out a hand, then pressed the charm into it. "Rub it and imagine disappearing. Within seconds, even an elf tracker—or elf *assassin*—will struggle to find you." She gave me a pointed look as she tilted her head toward the parking lot.

Oh. She wanted me to ditch Sarrlevi.

"Don't let him manipulate you further, girl," Artie said earnestly, holding my gaze. "And please don't lead him to Hennehok. I won't forgive myself if *he* ends up with an assassin's hand around his throat—or worse."

I wanted to tell her that Sarrlevi wouldn't do that, but hadn't he already?

"Where can I find him?" I asked instead.

"He lives in a cabin on the outskirts of Woodinville. I don't remember the address, but he's been working at Wolf Winery of late, so you can probably find him there."

I blinked. Hadn't the werewolves in Bellevue mentioned that place? They'd had something snide to say about the pack that ran it. "Would that be *Were*wolf Winery?"

"That's not on the sign out front, but essentially."

"All right," I said, though it was hard to imagine a dwarf engineer working with werewolves. Maybe Hennehok was a big wine fan and they gave him free samples. "Thank you, Artie."

"Artnoroka." She nodded. "Rub that, so the assassin can't track you there."

I hesitated, not sure how she expected me to elude Sarrlevi when he not only knew where I worked and lived but was currently waiting in my truck.

"You can go out the back door and get a taxi," Artie said, guessing my thoughts. "Come back for your car later. I won't have it towed."

"Thank you," I said, not commenting on the rest.

She squeezed my shoulder. "Glad to have met you, girl."

"I'm glad to have met you too."

Because she was watching expectantly, I rubbed the charm, and its camouflaging magic enveloped me. A whisper of her magic opened the office door for me. As I walked out, I debated if I should heed her warning and ditch Sarrlevi. At the least, I would accept a portal ride from Hennehok and go check on Sarrlevi's story with the king.

6

As I left Artie's office, more customers were coming in the front door, paying the teenager for trios of axes to take to the cages. Sarrlevi must not have bothered anyone on his way out, for all appeared normal. With my new camouflage charm activated, the kid didn't notice me.

I looked toward the front door, then headed for the back, my thoughts a jumble regarding Sarrlevi. Getting a ride all the way to the Kingston ferry terminal wouldn't be cheap, but I could do it, and then get another ride home—or to Woodinville—from Edmonds.

When nobody was looking, I opened the back door and slipped out.

But it wouldn't take Sarrlevi long to realize I'd abandoned him. He, too, had the power to create portals. He could beat me to the other side of Puget Sound, and he would eventually show up at my house or the project house. As far as I'd seen, he hadn't been to my home in Lynnwood yet, but I had a feeling he knew where I lived. He was, after all, a professional stalker.

And if I disappeared on him, would he blame Artie? Would he

go in and attack her more earnestly? If he'd spoken the truth earlier and had been trying to make her feel protective and want to help me, he might not have thrown everything he had at her. Maybe he could have come into that office any time he wished. If I didn't return, maybe he would, and he would interrogate her to find out where I'd gone.

Sighing, I headed for the corner to walk around the building. I couldn't risk him turning his ire on Artie. Besides, I was still struggling with the fact that I'd given him my word about helping. Until I knew he was lying about being hired by the king, maybe I ought to give him the benefit of the doubt.

"Something I'd feel better about if he weren't an assassin," I muttered.

No wonder I had knots of tension in my neck and shoulders.

When I stepped around the front of the building and into the parking lot, I almost snorted before remembering the charms didn't camouflage *sound.* I caught myself and didn't utter anything further as I headed for my truck where Sarrlevi sat on the passenger side with the window down and his boots up on the dash.

Since he'd cleaned that dash recently, and would doubtless wipe off any dirt he left, I didn't object, but I walked up and said, "You're not getting muddy prints up there, are you?"

The only indication that I'd surprised him by being camouflaged was a slight flutter of his eyelashes as he looked toward me. "You've acquired a new charm."

"Yeah. A gift from Artie. She wanted me to go out the back and ditch you." I fished my keys out of my pocket and walked around to the driver's side.

Sarrlevi lowered his boots and watched me as I got in, glancing once toward the front door, which he'd been observing closely enough to know I hadn't come out that way. "Why did you not heed her advice?"

"What can I say?" I turned the key in the ignition. "I'm drawn to your magnetic personality."

He kept watching me, presumably because he was trying to figure me out, not because my profile was alluringly beautiful and he couldn't look away.

"Besides, I told you I'd help you find my mother. I'm not a liar." I looked over at him, holding his gaze. "I just hope *you're* being straight with me, because Artie is *positive* you're bullshitting me about having been hired by the king."

His gaze didn't flicker away, nor did his face give any indication that he was being dishonest. "She has reason not to like me."

"You think?" I envisioned his hand around her throat and him trying to batter down her door, though he probably referred to his original mission to take out my mother. "We're going to Wolf Winery in Woodinville. Hennehok may be working there. This time, you *will* stay in the car, got it?"

I squinted, expecting him to object to me giving him orders.

Sarrlevi smiled faintly, maybe a little mockingly. "Of course."

He'd said that last time, so I only shook my head, afraid he would end up making trouble again. Would he try to keep Hennehok from making a portal to send me to Dun Kroth? Or would he make one of his own and follow me through?

"I won't interfere with your questioning next time," Sarrlevi said more seriously. "I only intruded this time because she wasn't going to tell you anything."

I almost snapped that he didn't know that, but he'd admitted he'd been spying on our conversation. And he was right. His manipulation of Artie had worked. That didn't mean I liked it or wanted him to do it again.

"You shouldn't feel compelled to intrude this time. Artie is going to send word ahead so Hennehok will be expecting me." I decided not to mention the portal. Sarrlevi would assume I was following leads, gathering more information about my mother.

"Good."

I grabbed the gear shift to take us out of the parking lot. He startled me by reaching for my hand. I almost yanked it back but glowered defiantly at him instead. "What?"

His faint smile returned, less mocking and more genuine this time. Maybe even... gentle? "I'm pleased you did not *ditch* me."

"Dude, you were in my truck."

His smile turned smug, as if he knew there had been more reasons than that, and nerves fluttered in my belly. He was handsome even when he was being fierce and cold, but the smile and glint of humor in his eyes made him breathtaking. Damn it, I didn't *want* my breath taken.

His thumb brushed the back of my hand, sending a zing of pleasure up my arm and through my entire body. Every part of me tightened with a longing for him to touch *more* than my hand.

I scowled ferociously at him, shifted gears, jerked my hand away, and planted it on the steering wheel. He wasn't going to touch anything else of mine, and I wasn't going to feel disappointed about that. I had a mission to complete, and he was still a bastard.

With his smile lingering, Sarrlevi dropped his arm and gazed out the window.

7

ON THE DRIVE BACK, WITH LITTLE INTEREST IN CHATTING WITH
Sarrlevi and darkness shrouding the truck, I tried a few different
types of music for him. I started with things I associated with
elves, albeit the fantasy Dungeons & Dragons kind of elves, such
as *The Lord of the Rings* soundtrack, Enya, and anything else serene
and inspired by nature. These songs earned bored looks of disin-
terest from him.

"It is not necessary to fill your conveyance with noise to entertain me," he said as we drove off the ferry, me fiddling with the
music library on my phone. "I am comfortable with silence."

"The guilt from all the people you've killed doesn't haunt you
in quiet moments, huh?"

I expected him to scoff and say such things didn't bother him
in the least.

But after giving me a flat look, he said, "Such emotions mani-
fest themselves in my sleep. I can control my mind when I'm
awake."

"So killing people *does* bother you? On some level?"

"I have occasionally regretted completing an assignment. It is rare. Most people I'm hired to kill are deplorable, and the Cosmic Realms are better for their passing."

"My mom wasn't."

"Perhaps not."

"Did you ever talk to her?" It was strange to think that Sarrlevi might be a resource, someone with insight into my mother that I craved. I wished I'd had a chance to speak with Artie about things unrelated to the mission. What had my mother's favorite food been? Her favorite hobby? Her proudest achievement?

"No. As I later learned, someone eavesdropped on my conversation with her sister and warned her even as I accepted the mission. She'd left Dun Kroth before I started looking for her. I spent about four months searching various worlds and seeking her out, amid completing a few other assignments, and finally got busy with other work—it was a period of political instability and assassin-hiring on another world. Afterward, I didn't return to hunting her."

We'd stopped at a light, and I watched his profile, trying to tell if he spoke the truth. Or had he continued to, at least casually, hunt for her all these years?

"Is that typical? That you aren't able to complete an assignment?"

"No, but it happens from time to time, especially if a target is capable of creating portals, flees to another world, and goes completely underground. It's ideal when you're able to find them before they know anyone is after them."

"Does it gall you when they're able to elude you?"

"It depends on the target and how eagerly I look forward to finding and challenging them." Sarrlevi looked over at me. "I wasn't that pleased to accept a mission given by a conniving princess to hunt down a *crafter*."

"Yeah, *warriors* give so much more to the world than those who make things to help their people." I scowled at him.

His return look was cool, a reminder that *he* was a warrior and had spent his whole life training with his swords.

I wouldn't retract the words. His belittling of my mother and her chosen profession was galling.

The light turned, and I had to focus on the road again, but my curiosity lingered, not squelched by his glare. "If you weren't into it, why did you take such an unappealing mission?"

"Reputation means a lot in my business. When world leaders and their scions, or others who've gained a lot of power and influence in the Realms, hire you, it's a good idea to perform adequately."

I remembered Val's story of how Sarrlevi had been manipulated into *performing adequately* for the fae queen.

"I prefer to hunt down warriors and mages, conquerors and despots. Those who'll put up a strong fight when I find them. Those who know what it is to face death and are prepared to meet theirs at the end of a blade."

"Like Val?"

Sarrlevi slanted me a sidelong look. "The Ruin Bringer had earned a reputation as a cold-hearted assassin of magical beings on this world. I looked forward to facing her."

"When you get to know her, she's not that bad," I said, though I didn't know if he would agree, especially after Val's dragon mate had tried to incinerate him. "I gather she only assassinates criminals."

He grunted. It could have conveyed agreement, or it could have meant he was not interested in discussing the matter further.

Reminded of the music that had been playing at Artie's, I tried Metallica. Sarrlevi had too dark a soul for Enya.

"Here you go. 'Disposable Heroes.'"

His eyebrows quirked. Maybe it was my imagination, but he seemed to listen with more interest. He didn't start head banging with glee, but he may have tapped his fingers. I snorted. I should have known to try songs about war and death and killing.

By the time we reached Wolf Winery in Woodinville, Sarrlevi was nodding his head to "Sanitarium."

"My grandparents hated that I listened to this stuff as a kid," I said, turning into a parking lot, the trees that lined the Sammamish River visible at the back of the property. The sign was a lit wolf's head with bottles of wine crossed like swords under it, and I sensed magical beings—werewolves—inside. "My sister listened to appropriate teenage-girl music about boys and love."

"You were not interested in those things?"

"I mostly wanted to bash the boys at school in the head with my hammer." I remembered I was talking to someone almost three hundred years old. Even if his school years had been anything like mine, he might not recall them. I shrugged and parked. "I was angry a lot. Losing your parents horribly at a young age leaves a mark on you."

I wondered if he'd ever had to spend time with the offspring of someone he'd killed.

"If you care for them, yes," Sarrlevi said. "I do not sense a dwarf inside."

He was gazing intently at the stone castle-inspired building we'd driven up to, lights and signs inviting visitors to pass over the drawbridge, under the portcullis, and into the tasting room.

"Maybe he's camouflaging himself. Artie said she was going to contact him and let him know I was coming. She may have mentioned I have a stalker." Especially if she'd seen or sensed me driving off with Sarrlevi, instead of ditching him as she'd suggested.

"You have an *ally* who will assist you in getting what we both want."

The stubborn part of me wanted to argue with him and say he was totally a stalker, but he'd upgraded me from his assistant to his ally. Whether he'd meant anything by the word choice or not, it was an improvement.

"That should prove handy. Wait in the truck, please."

His eyebrows arched. Not an outright refusal, but I interpreted it as one and sighed.

"At least don't attack anyone or threaten them," I amended.

Giggles came from the well-lit manicured lawn near the drawbridge. Three young girls were posing with... That wasn't a dog. It was a pretty gray wolf with blue eyes—a *werewolf*. One girl was hugging it.

"I take that back," I said. "You may attack and threaten any werewolves thinking of eating children."

Fortunately, that wolf did not seem to have such activities in mind. It—she, I decided—patiently let the girls pat her while an older sibling took photos.

"If the owners made a habit of doing that," Sarrlevi said, "it's unlikely they would retain their clientele."

"True, but I don't know if that's an owner. It could be..."

"A mascot?"

"Maybe. I'll go see if Hennehok is around." I waved, grabbed my hammer, and didn't bother to ask him to stay in the truck again. If I hadn't been playing the music on my phone, I would have left him some more metal to tap his fingers to, but the old truck only had an AM/FM radio that hadn't been state-of-the-art even when the vehicle rolled off the assembly line.

A hammer was perhaps an odd thing to take into a winery, but I wouldn't walk unarmed into a werewolf den. If they were acquaintances of the shifters I'd battled in Bellevue, they might be predisposed to dislike me. Besides, with the medieval theme of the building, the hammer wouldn't be that out of place.

"It would be odder to walk across a drawbridge *without* one," I assured myself.

Welcome, a young female voice spoke into my mind. *The tasting room is open for ten more minutes. Please go in if you wish to sample our current vintages.*

It took me a moment to realize the sleek wolf with children hanging off her was the owner of the voice. *Do you always greet your guests telepathically?* I sensed a few more magical beings inside the winery—the castle—and thought they were other shifters rather than guests, but maybe this was like the Coffee Dragon and catered to special patrons.

Only the ones with magical blood who look like they enjoy drinking. She chuckled into my mind and swished her tail, not commenting on my hammer.

I don't necessarily enjoy drinking. I might *need* a *drink.* I glanced back at the parking lot.

For the moment, Sarrlevi remained in the truck. How long would that last?

Are elves trying?

That one is very trying. I headed for the front door, not wanting the establishment to close for the night before I could ask about Hennehok.

From what I see, he looks very handsome. Her tone took on the dreamy wistfulness of a teenage girl enraptured by a crush. Maybe the werewolf *was* a teenage girl.

Oh, he is. I kept myself from adding *and he knows it*, not wanting to disparage Sarrlevi behind his back—to his face was acceptable —and switched topics. *My name is Matti, and I'm looking for a friend of a friend, a dwarf named Hennehok. He works here, right?*

I'm Belle. He's upgraded a lot of our fermentation and filtration equipment, yes. I haven't seen him for a few days, but you could check with my mom. Annette. The werewolf inserted an image of a sexy black-haired woman with her midriff on display as she poured glasses of wine behind a bar.

That's your mom?

She didn't look any older than I.

Yup. Belle opened her jaws to give me a lupine version of a smile.

Until a boy in the parking lot shouted, "Check out that dope wolf. I want to get a picture."

"That's a husky, son," a weary-sounding mother said.

"No way. It's *Wolf* Winery, isn't it? It's got to be a wolf. And he's *huge*. Like two hundred pounds, I bet."

Belle lifted her snout. *Mundane humans are so oblivious. It should be clear that I'm not male. Nor am I more than one-twenty. As if.*

Will you let him take your picture? I pushed the door open.

Of course. It's good for business. And my tip jar.

I glanced back in time to see Belle point her snout at a basket on the lawn next to her. The mom whose kids had been hugging her dropped a couple of dollars in as the teenage boy ambled up.

Inside, I found Annette, a sultry black-haired beauty, regaling a number of men, most of the geeky tech-job-looking sort. They perched on their stools and gazed raptly at her as she spoke of tannins, the growing season, and the tasting notes of chocolate and blackberry in the current offering. A couple of the men seemed to be attached to wives, though they might have forgotten that, for the women were down at the far end of the bar, in front of a graying but striking older lady who might have been Belle's grandmother. She was also a werewolf, and a few more female shifters worked in the kitchen, washing dishes and bringing out small plates to accompany the wines. If there were any male were-wolves in the building, I couldn't sense them. Maybe they hunted while the women ran the business.

Between pours, Annette peered at me and waved me over, though she soon looked past my shoulder toward the wall. Or maybe she was using her senses to check out the elf in the parking lot? I couldn't believe the teenage boy who thought her daughter was a husky interested her that much.

"Ten dollars for six one-ounce pours," Annette said, tugging her gaze back to me, "but the tasting is free if you end up buying a bottle or six. Dwarves are known to be hearty drinkers."

The nearest tech guy peered at me through his glasses, then whispered to Annette, "I think you're supposed to call them little people. Or people of short stature."

"She's not *that* short," his drinking buddy said, elbowing the speaker.

I sighed and straightened to my full five-foot-one height as I took out a ten-dollar bill, willing to pay for information and not that interested in wine. I had nothing against an earthy red, but as long as Sarrlevi was around, I wanted to keep my wits about me. Besides, I was his driver.

"I'm looking for another dwarf," I told Annette quietly, "a *full-blooded* dwarf. A friend sent me to see him. Hennehok. I believe he works here?"

"He does some work for us, yes. You look like someone with a sweet tooth."

I squinted at her. What did *that* mean? My curves might be on the voluptuous side, but I wasn't overweight. And muscles of steel lay underneath everything soft. I reined in my temper and nobly resisted the urge to hurl my hammer the way I had at the axe-throwing place.

Ignoring my glower, Annette said, "We don't usually start with a dessert wine, but I have a hunch you'll enjoy our moscato." She poured wine that looked like liquid nectar from a bottle. On the label, a wolf was biting a bunch of grapes, the imagery outlined in white on black. Her pour was a lot more generous than the ounce she'd promised. Maybe she found drunk tasters were more likely to purchase bottles afterward. "Hennehok has improved a lot of our equipment."

"He's not here or coming in soon, is he?"

"He comes by monthly to check on everything and usually a few times a week to sample the wines. You know, to make sure the equipment is producing satisfactory beverages." Annette smirked. "He hasn't been by for a while though."

I should have gotten a phone number from Artie, but who knew if dwarf engineers even had phones? "Do you know where he lives?"

She hesitated, then shook her head. "No."

"You're sure he didn't leave his address?" I couldn't help but think that hesitation might have indicated a lie. "Or maybe a phone number?"

Annette shrugged. "A lot of people in the community maintain low profiles or don't have permanent addresses. One of our dish-washers shacks up with a different member of the pack every week, so we never know where she's living."

Maybe promiscuity was a werewolf thing. I hadn't encountered a lot of the females before, but all those shifters in the park had to have come from somewhere.

"I'll be back with our late-harvest Riesling and port when you're ready. I *know* you've got a sweet tooth." Annette winked and waved at a fancy silver bucket on the counter where I could dump the contents of the glass if it wasn't to my taste.

It made me think of Zadie and her wine hobby. She regularly met with others to compete in blind tastings. I would be far more interested in a blind cheese-tasting contest.

After nodding at Annette and sipping the sweet wine to be polite, I took the glass and wandered around the wood-paneled room and under antler chandeliers dangling from wood beams high above. The walls were made from the same castle-inspired stone as outside and lined with bookcases featuring tomes about the industry, bottle openers with wolves on them, and other non-alcoholic items one could purchase.

A hallway leading into the back half of the castle drew my eye. Doorways led to the kitchen, what looked like a classroom, and a couple of offices. Maybe one held a filing cabinet full of employee

—or equipment contractor—addresses. But could I sneak back unnoticed to snoop? Even as I considered it, someone spoke from behind me.

"Cheese, cracker, or apples, ma'am?" a twenty-something werewolf with a tray asked.

She was as beautiful as Annette and looked to be a relative but had most of her flesh covered. Not that I would have noticed if she were naked and belly dancing. Pieces of Gruyere, Blue Stilton, Gorgonzola, and goat cheese drew my entire focus to the tray.

"I recommend the Gorgonzola with the moscato," she said.

"Thank you. Ah, is there a restroom back there?" After plucking up some of the cubes she'd indicated—and some of the others, since it would be rude to leave without trying *all* the cheeses—I pointed down the hallway.

"Over there." She pointed toward the front of the tasting room.

"Right. Thanks." I didn't want to go in *that* direction. I popped the Gorgonzola in my mouth and decided it was better than the wine. "I was supposed to meet Hennehok," I said before she could walk away. "But the lady at the bar said he hasn't been by?"

"Oh, for a date?" She grinned at me. "I bet you'd be *just* his type. He likes them curvy and tall." Her grin turned into a wink.

Yes, by pure dwarf standards, I was tall. I wasn't *that* short for a normal human. That guy at the bar was an idiot.

"Yeah," I said. "He said to meet him here, but you're about to close, aren't you? Do you know where he lives? I might have misunderstood, and he wanted me to come there." I touched my lips, attempting to look a little dim.

"I bet he does." She winked again. "I don't know his address though. He's got a cabin up on one of the wooded acreages here." She waved vaguely inland from the Sammamish River Valley where the wineries had their tasting rooms.

"That's most properties in Woodinville, isn't it?" I plucked a few more cubes of cheese off the tray, using my napkin so I could hold more. I barely kept myself from making it a few *dozen* more.

"Well, yeah." She shrugged. "My aunt might know more." She waved toward the bar, where the midriff momma was waving a bottle of port at me.

"Thanks." I rubbed my face as the girl walked away, afraid Sarrlevi was watching from somewhere nearby and would, as soon as he realized I wasn't getting what I needed, spring through a door and threaten to attack people.

As I looked longingly toward the offices, fantasies of rummaging in file cabinets returning to mind, a door at the end of the hallway opened with a bang.

A hulking male orc in bronze armor decorated with finger-bones stood there, his muscled arms bare, his hands gripping a sword as long as I was tall. More than seven feet tall himself, the orc had to bend his neck to peer inside. Though he looked more like a warrior than a shaman, he had a prominent aura and was bigger and had more of a dangerous edge than other orcs I'd faced.

Mongrel dwarf, he growled into my mind as he turned his tusks and squat snout of a nose toward me. *You will come outside, or I will destroy this building and rape these females.*

I gaped at the startling—and alarming—threat.

What the hell do you want? I replied silently and glanced around the tasting room. Had anyone else sensed the orc's approach?

Yes, the mother and her niece were conferring head to head, the tray set aside. They announced closing time and shooed the clients toward the front door. Fortunately, I didn't sense any orcs outside on that side of the building.

You, he said, *and your hammer.*

He ran his dark tongue over his blue-tinted lips and slid it up one tusk. I wasn't sure if it was a sexual gesture or not, since he was looking at my weapon.

Come to me, and maybe I won't kill you after I take it from you.

You're not taking it anywhere, Tusks. Though walking outside to face him seemed stupid, I couldn't risk him coming in, hurting people, and demolishing the winery. If he was here because of me, I *especially* couldn't let that happen.

8

SARRLEVI. AS I STEPPED OUT THE BACK DOOR OF THE WINERY INTO misty night air to face the single orc standing on a cement walkway that split a lawn, I attempted to project my thoughts toward my truck out front. Since nobody had instructed me on the art of telepathy, I doubted it would be effective, but maybe I would get lucky and he would be monitoring me. *There's a big orc back here who said elf ears are effeminate. You might want to come help me deal with him.*

I *thought* I could handle this guy, but it wouldn't hurt to have backup around. Just in case. The orc's strong aura and huge sword, which he held above his shoulder like a ninja poised to strike, were a touch daunting.

"Who wants my hammer?" I stopped well away from him and took it from my shoulder while wishing there was better light, but the back half of the building faced the river instead of the street and parking lot. Other than a few dim pathway lamps, little brightened the area. The *orc* could probably see in the dark. "Or are you looking to add it to your personal collection?" Under my breath, I whispered, "*Eravekt.*"

The silver-blue illumination that spread from the hammer heads would help me see that sword but might not keep me from tripping over something in the grass. If I hadn't heard the laughter of kids in the parking area and cars starting up, I would have suggested we take the battle to the pavement out front.

The orc answered out loud in his own guttural language, a tongue that made German seem lyrical by comparison. He'd either recently arrived on Earth and hadn't picked up English, or he didn't care if I understood him.

Belatedly thinking of the camouflaging charm that Artie had given me, I considered trying to disappear on the orc. But he was close enough to rush forward and spring at me before I fully faded from view. Besides, his promise to hurt the people in the winery stuck in my mind. Orcs weren't known to make hollow threats, and the brute seemed like the type to take out his frustrations over losing his prey on innocent bystanders.

Without warning, he rushed me, making up my mind about what I would do. I had no choice but to fight him.

He swung his sword toward me as if I were a log to chop up for the fire. Given his size, and the size of that weapon, he was faster than I expected, but I sprang to the side in time to avoid the blow. He halted it before the sword struck the walkway—it probably would have gouged out chunks of cement—and spun toward me.

I dodged another attack, wanting to get a feel for his speed and tactics before committing. He feinted toward my head, then swept the huge blade toward my feet. Keeping my hammer up, I leaped out of reach again. Snarling, he rushed at me, this time launching a chain of attacks. They were faster than before, and I had a feeling he'd been testing me—my speed.

I dodged and darted out of his reach, making sure I didn't let him back me toward a wall. When I got a feel for his rhythm, I ducked and lunged in behind a horizontal swing attempting to take my head off. As he completed the maneuver, I swept my hammer toward his ribs. He couldn't bring his sword back around quickly enough to counter, but he jerked his elbow down so that the head struck his meaty arm instead of the gap in his armor I'd been aiming for.

Though my blow was solid, he didn't so much as flinch, merely whirling to face me again. I skittered back and would have avoided his next swing, as I had the others, but magical power burst from him and wrapped around me. Right away, as it tightened around my body, I knew it was meant to hold me in place while he bashed me.

My hammer flared brighter, and his magic only partially held me, but as he slashed toward my head, I feared any hold would slow me down too much.

Roaring, I cried, "*Hyrek!*" and willed my body to shake off the bonds as I whipped my hammer up. It obeyed in time, and my weapon caught his over my head, the haft holding against his heavy blade, though his power almost drilled me into the ground.

Lightning sprang from my hammer, arcing along his sword and up his arms to his armor. I willed it to do damage, but as electricity crackled all around him, the orc smiled and laughed, thumping one of several charms embedded in his chest armor. Star-shaped, it glowed and flashed yellow, wrapping a barrier around him and protecting him from my hammer's magic.

Before the lightning died out, he swung at me again. I growled in frustration, still slowed by the magic he'd enrobed me in. I could move fast enough to parry, but it felt like I was waist-deep in water, unable to spring about as rapidly as usual.

My hammer parried his sword, another blow so powerful that deflecting it made my joints hurt. He let go of his weapon with one hand and tried to snatch mine. I jerked the head up and clipped him in the chin.

When he staggered back, snarling and cursing, it must have made his concentration lapse, for his power released me. But he recovered quickly and threw another magical attack. A great wall of power struck me like a battering ram, hurling me ten feet.

Though startled and discombobulated, I twisted in the air and managed to land on my feet in a deep crouch.

He sprinted toward me with his sword raised, but he slowed down when I lifted my hammer, ready to parry.

Release that weapon, mongrel female. And I will let you live.

You'll have to kill me before I let it go, you bastard son of a drunk walrus. Maybe I shouldn't have said that...

He leaped for me again, anger—or maybe blood lust—filling his eyes, and swung for my head. Distracted by his fury, he hadn't employed his magic again to slow me down. I ducked his swing easily, using my hammer to deflect his strike high, then switched my grip with practiced speed and slammed a head into his chest plate, aiming for the star-shaped charm he'd touched before.

A normal weapon wouldn't have destroyed a magical aid, but my hammer crunched it. Sparks flew from it, one singeing his eye. His head jerked back, giving me the opportunity to swing again.

"*Hyrek!*" I yelled and hammered at another charm embedded in his armor.

As the blow destroyed it, lightning streaked out and arced all around him. This time, the orc had no defense against it. He threw his head back and roared in pain. Lightning flowed past his lips and flashed brilliantly, highlighting the roof of his mouth and his yellow teeth.

Doubting that would kill him, or even incapacitate him for long, I struck again, smashing a vulnerable kneecap instead of his armored chest. He screamed in pure raw pain. *That* might take him out of the fight.

He started to crumple, and, reminded that he also had magic he could bring to bear, I hit his chest plate once more, unleashing all my strength. As big and heavy as the orc was, he flew backward, his feet leaving the ground. He landed hard on the cement walkway and hit his head. His sword slipped from his limp fingers and thudded onto the ground.

Two sets of growls came from high grass near the river. My first thought was that a couple of the werewolves might have shifted into their lupine forms and come out to defend their property, but two more orcs crouched there. Two more *large* orcs with huge swords and strong auras.

I swallowed uneasily, certain they hadn't been there before. Unless they'd been camouflaged. As with the orc on the ground, my senses detected powerful auras that suggested they had access to magic as well as their towering brawn. As one, the pair strode forward.

Once more, I crouched with my hammer raised, but I debated sprinting around the building toward the front. I'd almost been overpowered by one. Two, especially two who'd trained to fight together, would be too much.

But a familiar aura came out of the shadows behind me. Sarrlevi.

When he spoke, it was in the orc tongue. Usually, his voice was as smooth and elegant as he, but even an elf couldn't manage to sound appealing when speaking Orcish.

My two new opponents halted and glanced at each other.

Sarrlevi stepped up beside me and rested a hand on my shoulder as he faced them.

This female is spoken for, he told them, switching to telepathy, so I could understand—or because Orcish tied his tongue in knots. *If you want her, you must fight me first.*

We are not afraid of you, assassin, one replied, also using telepathy.

I raised my eyebrows, surprised they recognized Sarrlevi. But if he'd been working in the Cosmic Realms for hundreds of years, maybe he was well-known. There probably weren't that many elf assassins. It was hard to imagine most of his tree-hugging kind gravitating toward such a violent profession.

Then you will challenge me to a duel for her? Sarrlevi asked.

"Uh." I raised a finger. *I'm not a prize in a duel.* "Besides, they want my hammer, not *me*."

The speaker pointed at my hammer but then lowered his finger toward my chest. He leered, thrust his hips forward, and he and his buddy laughed.

Hell, maybe they did want more than my hammer.

With his hand still on my shoulder, Sarrlevi drew one of his swords and stepped closer to me, holding the weapon in front of us. *If you disrespect this female, I will slice off your cock and shove it down your brother's throat.*

The speaker prowled forward. *She is that good? We came only for the hammer, but if she is worth dueling over...* He leered again, sliding his tongue along one tusk, as the other had done.

Sarrlevi growled, his grip tightening on my shoulder.

"Knock off the possessive male posturing," I muttered. "You take the one on the right, and I'll take the one on the left?"

Let him have the tusk licker. My body ached from being battered by magic in the first fight, and the other orc was hanging back. He didn't appear as eager to jump into battle with Sarrlevi, even if there were two of them.

She is worth it. Sarrlevi kept his gaze on them instead of responding to me. *You will have to duel me if you want her. Or leave now. You'll not steal from my female.*

"*Sarrlevi*," I whispered.

"It's what they can understand with their limited minds," he murmured back. "They regularly waylay females of their species, and other species, and drag them back to their caves and hovels to claim them."

"Another reason I'll happily help you take these two out."

The one I'd defeated groaned. While Sarrlevi and the

mouthier orc exchanged more threats in the foreign tongue, I stepped forward, picked up my guy's fallen sword, and jogged it across the lawn to chuck it in the river. It landed with a heavy splash, as if I'd thrown in a dumbbell. The thing had been heavy enough to qualify as one.

Duel accepted! the mouthy orc announced.

A snarl and the jangle of armor sounded as the speaker charged Sarrlevi.

I turned back, glancing at the other orc, in case he also attacked. He rested the point of his sword in the grass and leaned casually on it to watch.

Sarrlevi and his opponent came together in a flurry of blows, the light elven blades moving thrice as quickly as the heavy orc sword. By the time I circled the battle, wanting to return to the walkway to make sure the one I'd downed didn't rise and interfere, Sarrlevi's opponent bled from a dozen cuts.

The orc blasted him with power, but Sarrlevi's armor, or his own magical defenses, blocked it. He didn't slow down in the least. As weapons strikes rang out, competing with the traffic noise from the street out front, I noticed light coming from the open back door of the winery. Annette and her niece stood watching the battle. Ready to get furry and help if need be?

The niece pointed at the orc on the walkway and gave me a thumbs-up, making me wonder how long they'd been observing. During the fight, I'd been too busy defending myself to scan the area for the auras of magical beings.

Annette's gaze was glued to the fight, a slight smile curving her lips in appreciation of the battle. I couldn't blame her. The orc was strong and fast for his size, but Sarrlevi was grace and agility personified when he fought, and it was always a pleasure to watch him. Though I should have been keeping an eye on the other two orcs, I couldn't help but grow a little mesmerized as he evaded the powerful swings from his foe, dodging or ducking, then springing under the big weapon to slice or stab. Sometimes, his blades clanged off the orc's armor, but just as often he found vulnerable seams or struck at one of the brute's bare arms.

He was so much faster than the orc that I started to wonder if he was drawing out the battle, making it last longer than it needed to. It was possible he was being wary because the orc kept throwing in magical attacks, but it crossed my mind that he might know the sexy werewolf lady was watching and want to impress her.

I was sure he didn't care about impressing *me,* but I couldn't help but wonder how his agility might come into play in the bedroom. Annoyed with the thought as soon as it appeared, I quashed it. But I didn't look away from the battle or stop admiring him.

With a snarl almost redolent of a wolf's, Sarrlevi sliced off his opponent's hand. The orc's sword flew free, almost slamming into the other orc's legs, and, though Sarrlevi's foe yelled in pain, he wasn't done fighting. With his remaining hand, he yanked something out of a pocket and hurled it.

Instead of ducking or springing away, Sarrlevi lunged in and swung his sword. With a soft *tink,* his blade struck the thrown item and knocked it away. It sailed toward the river and exploded, highlighting the water and incinerating some of the tall grass. Startled ducks that had been sleeping farther up along the bank quacked uproariously and took to the air.

Sarrlevi leaped, swinging down with one longsword as the other slashed horizontally toward the orc's neck. His foe tried to scurry back while jerking his arms up to defend himself, but the blades moved too swiftly. As one cut deep into the orc's shoulder, the other sliced through his thickly muscled neck as if it were butter. The tusked head soared free and splatted into the grass.

Before the orc's body hit the ground, Annette had her fingers in her mouth, whistling her appreciation.

Not sure what the other orcs would do, I kept my hammer pointed toward them, but that didn't keep me from rolling my eyes. Maybe it was petty, but I couldn't help but think that nobody had whistled for *my* victory.

The sole orc still standing strode toward the walkway, and I braced myself. Sarrlevi moved to stand beside me again, his hand on my shoulder, his sword now bloody as he held it between us and our remaining enemy.

But the orc only helped up the one I'd knocked down. After hoisting him to his feet, he led his limping comrade away from us.

Magic swelled near the river, and the silvery disc of a portal formed. That surprised me. I hadn't realized they were that powerful.

Before departing, the orcs picked up the sword and a necklace from their beheaded comrade. In front of the portal, they paused, and the one I'd fought looked back at me. His eyes were glassy, and one of his tusks had broken when he'd fallen, but that didn't keep him from delivering a parting threat.

The elf won't always be at your side. I will get your hammer yet.

Great. Already, as they disappeared through the portal, I regretted not finishing him off. But I wasn't a heartless killer, damn it. Not by choice anyway. I was a civilized businesswoman.

"You smell like cheese." Sarrlevi, still close, looked at me with amusement.

"Fighting with that idiot probably smashed all the cubes in my pocket." Not that a little smashing would keep me from eating the rest of them. The winery gave out good cheese.

"He may return."

"So I gathered. You can let go of my shoulder. They're gone, and I assume you don't want to drag me off to a cave."

That knowing smirk of his crept onto his face, the one that I always read as an indication that he knew I would *like* him to take me off for a wild night. I squinted at him, wondering if he'd caught me ogling him during the fight.

Sarrlevi released his grip, and his face grew more sober. "Do you understand Orcish?"

"My night school didn't offer it, no."

"You have a new problem."

"That they're after my hammer? I know."

"That *many* people may be after your hammer, not only Way Rover orc mercenaries. Someone is offering a reward for it."

I groaned. "Someone on Earth? Or elsewhere?" I waved toward the stars visible between the clouds to indicate the Cosmic Realms as a whole.

"He wouldn't tell me who put it out or where it originated, but those mercenaries are not from this world, so it was likely someone out there."

"Who *out there* even knows I exist? Or that I have this hammer?"

"It is possible the word got out among the orcs and werewolves who survived battling with you a few weeks ago." Sarrlevi hesitated. "It is also possible Slehvyra said something. She saw you with it, did she not?"

"Yes, but why would an elf care about a dwarven hammer?" She *had* implied the dwarves would hunt me down if they found out about it, but would she have bothered running off to another world to tell them?

"She probably doesn't. I only mention it as a possibility. I can attempt to learn more the next time I leave this world."

"Thanks. I would appreciate it."

The idea of having to look over my shoulder for the rest of my life made me groan again.

Sarrlevi turned to face the back of the winery. The niece had gone back inside, maybe to gather her relatives to help toss the heavy orc corpse in the river, but Annette was walking toward us.

No, toward *Sarrlevi*. She didn't so much as glance at me as she sashayed toward him, her chest thrust out, her lean abdomen still on display.

"What magnificent fighting, noble elf," she said.

Sarrlevi bowed politely toward her. I couldn't tell if he used the gesture to covertly ogle her. Probably not. He didn't strike me as the type to be subtle about his interest. If he found her appealing —and she was gorgeous, so how not?—he had probably taken in all of her attributes when he'd first arrived. While I'd been panting and grunting and trying to survive being pummeled by an orc.

"I've never been with a full-blooded elf before." Annette smiled, touching a finger to her pouty lips as she looked him over. "I've heard your people are *very* agile." Her eyes crinkled at the corners. "Have you ever been with a woman who howls?"

How was this fair? Sarrlevi got hit on by the sexy werewolf lady, and I got hit on by the tusked, blue-skinned orc.

"I've been with many women who ended up howling," Sarrlevi said dryly.

That comment deserved eye rolling. And more. Would they notice if I made gagging sounds?

As Annette sashayed closer to Sarrlevi, I waved a hand. "I'll be in the truck when you're done here."

Without waiting for a reply, I strode around the building toward the parking lot. I told myself I had bigger problems to worry about than Sarrlevi flirting with a werewolf, but that didn't keep me from wincing as she laughed, either at her own wit or something he'd said. For some reason, I thought of his guest room in his house and all those sheer nightgowns he kept in a dresser there. Would he invite her back for a night of wild sex on another world?

It didn't matter, and I didn't care. I had a dwarf to find.

9

I SAT IN THE CAB OF THE TRUCK, LOOKING AT A MAP ON MY PHONE, and debating where to go next to search for Hennehok. People's vague descriptions of a cabin in the woods hadn't been helpful. Woodinville was full of such properties.

I pulled up the number for Artie's Axes so I could call, though she had said she didn't know her friend's address. Maybe she could at least direct me to the right street.

Before I could make the call, I sensed Sarrlevi approaching. He opened the door and slid inside. I eyed him warily, half-expecting his clothing to be askew from a quickie, but I doubted enough time had passed for that.

"Do you have a piece of paper?" he asked.

I found a pen in the glove box and turned over an expired insurance card so he could use the back. He wrote down an address, then handed it to me.

"She told you where Hennehok lives?" I guessed.

"I asked her where he lives, and she wouldn't tell me, but a payment paper with his address on it appeared in her thoughts while she was fondling my chest."

"That's not what *I* would be thinking about while I was fondling your—a guy's chest."

"No?" His knowing smile curved his lips.

Damn that slip.

"I used a small amount of magic to coerce her into thinking about such things," he said. "Werewolves do not have the natural mental defenses of dwarves."

"They're well-endowed in other areas."

"Indeed."

He wasn't gazing back at the castle with longing, but I couldn't imagine that he hadn't admired Annette's *endowments*.

"I can go see Hennehok by myself, if you'd like to stay here and make her howl." That would actually be perfect. Artie had instructed me to visit Hennehok, at least in part so he would make a portal and take me to see the king, where I could, among other things, check on Sarrlevi's story. It would be easier to do all that if Sarrlevi wasn't at my side. "I didn't hear any ululations coming from the back, so I assume you didn't show off your elven agility to her."

"Had I done that, it would have taken far more than five minutes." His smile lingered as he watched me.

"Seven or eight, huh? Good to know you've got stamina."

He snorted but fortunately didn't brag about how many hours he could go and how great it was for the ladies. If he had, I really would have gagged.

I plugged the address into the phone's GPS, and a route through windy streets came up. The place was only a ten-minute drive away.

"Thanks for getting this," I made myself say, not sure why it was so difficult for me to express gratitude to him. Probably because he was so smug about everything. It didn't make me want to admit he was useful. I also didn't want him to think I needed his help. One way or another, I would have found Hennehok. Sarrlevi and his fondle-able chest had simply made it easier. "And for coming back there to help with the orcs," I added.

"I must ensure you live."

"So you can follow me to my mom, right." I pulled out of the parking lot and headed for the first turn. That he hadn't come because he'd been worried about me shouldn't have bothered me. It wasn't as if I had any delusions about him. "You're not going to become my permanent bodyguard now that there are bounty hunters after me, are you? *Hammer* hunters." I didn't know if it could be called a bounty if all the issuer wanted was my hammer. Either way, it would be hard to sneak off to the dwarven king's court with Sarrlevi looming nearby. Though I supposed it didn't matter if he came along. If his story was true, he had no reason *not* to come along.

But what if it wasn't?

"I will have to consider that," he said. "You defended yourself adequately against the orc mercenary."

"Yes, people I work with often praise me for my adequateness."

Sarrlevi gave me one of his bland looks, and I wasn't sure if he caught the sarcasm or not. He probably did and didn't think it was worth responding to. "The Way Rover orc mercenaries are outcasts who band together, fight hard to hone their skills, and pay shamans to teach them magic. They're more difficult opponents than most of the orc refugees hiding out on this world."

"So you're saying I might have been *more* than adequate?" I resisted the urge to look at him. The roads had grown narrow, curvy, and hemmed in by trees. There wasn't a streetlamp in sight. Houses lurked behind the foliage, with interior and exterior lights on, but they did nothing to illuminate our route.

"For a mongrel trained to fight on this backward world, you do well."

I shot him the dark look that backhanded compliment deserved. "Remind me not to fish for praise from you."

"Assassins aren't known for rhapsodizing effusively about others."

"No wonder you live alone."

His eyes narrowed. Maybe I shouldn't have been sniping at him, but he and everything about his manner brought it out in me.

I fished in my pocket, moderately pleased to find the cheese cubes still nestled in the napkin. I'd stuffed it in there before the fight. It would have been a shame if they had fallen out. I pulled out a couple of only slightly smashed cubes.

"Cheese?" I offered Sarrlevi.

In the dark, I couldn't tell if pocket lint stuck to the cubes. Maybe I should have stopped at a grocery store or drive-thru for less-mangled snacks.

He took a piece of cheese and sniffed it. I popped one in my mouth. After the long day and battle, I was hungry enough to risk lint.

"I *choose* to live alone," Sarrlevi said after he ate the cube. "I could have company if I wished."

"Yes, I remember the nightie collection."

My phone rang, interrupting the GPS voice giving directions. My sister's number popped up, and I grimaced, memories of the previous Sunday brunch coming to mind.

After three weeks of successfully dodging her invitations, I'd caved and accepted one, going to spend a couple of hours with her, her husband, and their children in their posh suburban house that literally had a white picket fence out front. The accountant she'd wanted to fix me up with had been there—even better, he was friends with the husband and hadn't *known* it would be a fix-up. She'd waylaid both of us and then had the audacity to be appalled when I'd shown up in ripped jeans and a baggy sweat-shirt. It hadn't been my fault I'd been painting the project house that morning...

I answered, more because I didn't want the ringing to keep interrupting the map's directions than out of a desire to talk, especially with Sarrlevi in the seat next to me. Further, with this new information about people looking for my hammer, I had to worry once more about my family. What if some thuggish orc mercenary showed up at my sister's house to take her kids hostage? Penina might grate on my nerves at times, but her kids were cuties, and her husband was a decent guy. I didn't want any of them to be hurt.

"Hey, Matti," she said before I spoke. "Tyler told Bob that you're pretty and he wouldn't mind seeing you again. Just the two of you. That's what he said! He didn't even mind that horrible baggy hoodie you were wearing, though I think he got more interested when you took it off and had just the tank on to play badminton with Josh and Jessie. Way to work it, girl. I didn't know you had it in you to jiggle appealingly for a guy."

Aware of Sarrlevi looking over, I couldn't keep my cheeks from flushing with heat. I hadn't been jiggling to *appeal* to anyone. That just happened when you swung vigorously for badminton birdies. And I didn't play any sports without vigor.

"Do you want me to set up a date? He wanted to know if you like poker. I guess he hosts a game. But you should go out *alone* with him somewhere, not to his house to hang out with a bunch of beer-swilling guys. Do you want to call him and see what movies he's into? Or can I give him your number?"

"Uh." Having no idea what to say, I looked at the next turn on the map while I groped for an answer. Letting my sister set up a date sounded horrible. Setting one up myself wasn't a priority at the moment either. Even if the tall, gangly, but boyishly cute Tyler was more appealing than a tusked orc, I couldn't imagine sharing popcorn with a guy at the movies while bounty hunters snuck down the aisle toward us. "Sure."

That would end the call with my sister more quickly. Besides, talking to Tyler wouldn't hurt, and I could put off dates until the hammer thing had been resolved. *If* it could be resolved. How did one get a reward for one's weapon removed? Knock the person who'd put it out on their ass, presumably, but if it was that elf ex-princess and she lived on another world, how would I reach her?

Maybe Hennehok could take me to her house on the way to see the dwarven king.

"Fabulous, Matti. This is so great. He does the books at a tech startup. He's got *stock options.* If you married someone with prospects like that, it would be so much better than those blue-collar knuckle draggers you usually go for. Maybe you could get a house in my neighborhood!"

"Or maybe, by continuing to work hard at my own business, I could afford a house there on my own." Not that I had any interest in her white-picket neighborhood dotted with signs threatening heinous fines from the HOA if people parked in the street or didn't scoop their dogs' poop.

"Of course, sweetie, but it wouldn't hurt to be supported by someone well-off. I'll give him your number. He'll call you. It'll be perfect."

"Almost there," I said apologetically to Sarrlevi as I hung up and took another turn. In the quiet car, there was little doubt that he'd heard every word of the conversation. Nobody, even smug and snooty elves, should have to listen to my sister's matchmaking attempts.

"What are stock options?" Sarrlevi asked dryly, as if he was already sure they were ridiculous.

"Something self-employed businesswomen don't get."

That prompted the bland sidelong look again. I was beginning to interpret that as: *Your response is inadequate; do you wish to correct this deficiency?*

"I'm not sure exactly beyond that if the company you work for does really well in the stock market, you do really well."

"Financially."

"Yes."

"When you are self-employed, you must excel and be rewarded entirely on your own merits." His tone had gotten snooty.

It took me a moment to realize he was referring to himself and his work, rather than my comment about being self-employed. Technically, since Abbas was my partner, I had a small business, but it amounted to the same. What we earned was in direct correlation to the time and effort we put into our work. I refused, however, to see myself as similar to an assassin.

"You've arrived at your destination," my phone announced.

If not for its certainty, I would have kept driving. Trees and shrubs rose densely to either side of the narrow road, and if not for the presence of a dented mailbox, I might have missed the narrow gravel driveway heading back into the gloom.

A dog barked in the distance, hopefully not from the dwarf's house. I didn't want to have to defend myself a second time that night.

After turning, I drove down the pothole-filled driveway, branches scraping at the side of the truck. "You'd think an engineer would keep his place up better," I murmured.

"Dwarves are not known for a fondness for landscaping. Foliage is rare underground on their home world."

"Rare but not nonexistent?"

"There are mushrooms almost as large as trees in some of their caverns, and a photoluminescent algae spreads like carpets around their underground lakes."

"But they don't prune it, huh?"

We went back farther than I expected—how *large* was this property?—before my headlights reflected off glass. One of the windows of what was a *very* rustic log cabin. I was almost surprised it had glass and the windows weren't simply shuttered against the night.

"Speaking of carpets of growth," I muttered, eyeing the roof. If any of the shingles were visible under the moss blanketing it, I couldn't see them.

"I do not sense anyone inside," Sarrlevi said.

I almost snarked that the lack of lights or a car parked out front told me to expect that, but I was too busy being disappointed that Hennehok wasn't home. There wasn't a garage or carport where a vehicle could have been hidden. Did Hennehok even drive? After thirty-odd years on Earth, he should have learned, especially if he lived way out here.

"Maybe if we wait, he'll come back." I hoped Sarrlevi hadn't gotten the address wrong.

After I parked, he opened the door. "We will search inside for clues."

"That's illegal on Earth," I said, but I got out too. I might only peer through the windows and search *outside* for clues, but I would like to find confirmation that this was indeed Hennehok's home.

"Is it likely your authorities monitor this remote locale?" Sarrlevi headed for the front door.

"No, but that doesn't make committing crimes any less illegal."

From the cracked-cement front stoop, he looked over his shoulder at me. I'd left the headlights on, so I had no trouble seeing his smirk. "Were you not employed by the military colonel because you are a vigilante who rarely obeys laws?"

"I obey *most* laws *most* of the time." I crossed my arms over my chest and lifted my chin. "Only when someone is committing a crime do I jump in to put a stop to it, whether it's legal to pummel people with a hammer or not."

The lingering smirk suggested he either didn't believe me or didn't see the distinction. I half expected him to kick the door in, but he merely rested his hand on it and tilted his head thoughtfully. Only then did I sense a hint of magic about the knob and lock. There was more magic inside.

My nerves jangled. This was the place. It had to be.

10

"THERE IS MAGIC ENCHANTING THE DOOR, BUT I DON'T BELIEVE IT'S A booby trap." Sarrlevi's gaze drifted to a copper head mounted on the log wall nearby. It looked like a stone golem with a serpent's forked tongue sticking out. Something out of dwarven mythology?

"What does it do then?" I stood on a flagstone walkway a few feet behind him, thick tufts of grass growing up between the cracks.

Sarrlevi tapped the tongue. A faint glow emanated from the head, a clank came from behind the door, and it swung open with a *bong*. Had Hennehok been home and sleeping, that would have woken him.

Inside, lights came on, and a music box started playing a tune I'd never heard. I wanted to call it a work dirge. Whirring and what sounded like wheels rolling on a wood floor also came from the interior.

Sarrlevi snorted and stepped aside, extending his hand toward the interior. Inviting me to go first.

"You're *sure* it's not booby-trapped?" I peered inside without stepping over the threshold.

Even though Sarrlevi hadn't forced open the door, nobody had invited us in.

A metal dog on wheels whirred toward us, barked cheerfully, then spun three circles and rolled toward a workbench covered in tools and half-finished projects. The entire room was full of such, with nothing so typical as a sofa or a chair. There were chests and crates, but they were too covered in books, sketches, and tools to sit on. Chalkboards containing diagrams and equations filled the walls, and in more than one spot, someone—Hennehok, presumably—had gone off the board and written in chalk on the logs.

The back corner contained a small kitchen, but the sink was full of unidentifiable gizmos, and stacks of Lunchables on the counter suggested the dwarf didn't cook often. Or ever. I didn't even *see* a stove.

"You're supposed to refrigerate those." I waved at the boxed meals.

"Dwarves have hearty constitutions."

"Meaning it doesn't matter if mold is growing on their crackers?"

"I saw you savor the moldy cheese you plucked out of your pocket."

"That cheese is *supposed* to be moldy. It's what makes it flavorful."

"Maybe your dwarf engineer likes flavorful crackers." Sarrlevi's smirk had returned, as if he found the whole house amusing.

Not certain if it was because he felt superior about it, since his sprawling home wasn't stuffed with projects and clutter, I had the urge to defend the place. Better to have passions that filled one's life than an empty existence where one had nothing better to do with one's free time than invite over bitchy elves to sleep with.

Deciding I was overreacting, I tamped down my indignation. Sarrlevi hadn't *said* anything. Besides, his office held books and game boards. He clearly had *some* hobbies, if more cerebral ones.

And he hadn't had sex with the elf ex-princess. Thankfully, since I'd been in the next room. Just because he had ladies' night-gowns in his guest room didn't mean he hosted orgies every weekend. He was three hundred years old. Maybe he'd acquired all those garments when previous guests had left them over the years. Or—I snorted at the thought—maybe his magical laundry device had stolen them and not returned them before the recipients left.

Sarrlevi headed for the single bedroom. It, a loft full of more crates and projects, and a tiny bathroom were all that remained to explore in the cabin.

The strongest magic came from the bedroom, and I followed Sarrlevi curiously, looking hopefully around for clues about where the dwarf had gone. A few bottles from Wolf Winery rested on a shelf, dust on them. Numerous things had dust on them, and I worried Hennehok had been gone longer than we'd thought. What if he'd taken off weeks earlier, after Artie's first warning that Sarrlevi was on Earth?

She had, however, expected Hennehok to be here. Maybe he just didn't bother dusting when he was home. I didn't see magical gizmos floating around and cleaning things.

"One wonders where he sleeps," Sarrlevi mused, waving toward a bed covered in books and scrolls. "Do you think he nestles in there with them?"

"Maybe. It would be like sleeping with cats, except books are less likely to hog the covers."

His eyebrows lifted, and he looked me over. Searching for feline fur on my clothing?

"My grandparents have always had cats," I said. "I'm not home enough for pets of my own."

"Ah." His eyes glinted with amusement. What, was he imagining me in baggy pajamas, eating ice cream in bed, and surrounded by Himalayan cats?

Nothing like that had happened since high school... Not with cats, anyway.

I looked around, the magic I'd sensed calling to me. It came from a suit of armor in the corner, the plate armor Hennehok had worn in the photo he was in with my mother. It was the first proof that we were indeed at the right house, though there were probably few cabins in Woodinville filled with dwarven projects.

"Where would he have gone without his armor?" I wondered.

"Perhaps he has more than one set. His weapons are gone." Sarrlevi pointed to hooks on one of the logs.

Had this been a normal person's house, I would have assumed skis or a bike usually hung there, but a sword did seem more likely.

Sarrlevi headed to a desk as covered in clutter as everything else and opened the second drawer down, as if he expected to find something in particular in there. I did sense more magical items in that corner of the room, but I couldn't tell one signature from another and had no idea what he would pull out.

As soon as he opened the drawer, a golden glow seeped out. He withdrew a colorful ceramic platter and leaned it against a stack of books so the surface faced us. A few dwarven runes were painted around the wide rim, but I didn't know what any of them meant.

"That's an odd place to keep a plate. Any cracker crumbs on there?"

Sarrlevi slanted me a pitying look. "It's a communications device."

As if I was pathetic for not knowing that. "It looks like a nacho tray, dude."

The pitying look continued.

"Look, there's a cup in the middle, like where you'd put your salsa." I wasn't the crazy one here... Really.

He touched a finger to the center of that *cup*, and the color faded from the platter. It turned into a screen of sorts, a face forming on its surface. Artie's face.

I blinked. "Is she... calling him?"

Sarrlevi gripped his chin. "I believe I commanded it to play previous messages."

"So it holds nachos and salsa, *and* it's an answering machine? Handy." My humor vanished when Artie started speaking. Hell, was she going to talk about me and my need for a portal to see the king? To verify Sarrlevi's story?

Whatever she said, the words ringing out in the room were in Dwarven. Sarrlevi watched, his chin still gripped in his hand. Could he understand? I caught a few words and also my mom's name and *hevki*. Daughter. It *was* about me. Uh oh, and there was Sarrlevi's name. She had to have been explaining why I needed a ride to see the king.

At the end of the message, Artie touched her brow, then her chest, and bowed before disappearing.

Sarrlevi squinted over at me, and my heart double-timed, pounding in my chest. I felt like a naughty kid caught in the act and about to be punished. Or worse. How pissed would Sarrlevi be if he found out I planned to check up on him?

"Did you understand her words?" he asked, his face hard to read. His earlier humor was gone.

"No, did you?"

"She said your mother's name, that her daughter would visit, and something about a portal." Sarrlevi raised his eyebrows, as if he expected me to explain further.

"Huh," I said.

"You wished to see this dwarf to find out if he has clues about where your mother might be, correct?"

"Yeah, *if* she's alive. Artie was almost positive she isn't."

"*Almost.*"

With Sarrlevi's gaze locked on my face, I struggled to maintain my equanimity. Maybe if I told him *most* of the truth, he wouldn't be suspicious. It didn't sound like he'd understood much more of the Dwarven message than I had.

"Artie said the engineer stuck around because he never fully believed my mother had died. If there are clues that could lead to her, he would be the one to ask. She also said he knows how to make portals and might be willing to take me to see the king. I thought if I talked to him, maybe I could learn more about Mom, and that would help in our quest." I smiled at him, hoping that including him would remind him that we were both on the same side in this. At least, I hoped we were. His expression wasn't changing, wasn't giving anything away, as I spoke. "King Ironhelm didn't tell *you* anything about my mother that might help, did he?"

"No."

"Well, I'm nicer and cuddlier than you, so maybe he'll confide in me." I widened my smile, inviting him to laugh, snort, or at least change expression.

For a long moment, he didn't react at all, and I had a feeling he sensed I wasn't being entirely forthright with him.

But he finally leaned back, crossing his arms over his chest. "You consider yourself *cuddly*?"

"I'm a lot cuddlier than you. You're all lean and angular with no body fat. Who'd want to snuggle up to that?" I hoped he didn't give me the knowing smirk that suggested *I* would. I wouldn't. I could see having sex with him, because my dumb body couldn't help but find the thought intriguing, but he definitely was not the type for postcoital snuggling. He probably pulled out, slapped a girl on the butt, and strode off to clean himself with his magical kerchief before putting all his weapons back on.

"You'd prefer a cat, perhaps."

"Or even a book." I waved to the bed. "Yes."

"You are an odd mongrel."

"Well, you're an odd elf."

He smiled faintly. "I *am* atypical."

Hoping he wouldn't press me further on the message, I walked back out to the living room, where the robot dog was circling, occasionally issuing tinny barks. I was tempted to root through some of the projects, hoping to find clues, but what I *really* wanted was to speak with my dwarven grandfather. Maybe if Sarrlevi didn't believe my desire to do so had anything to do with him, *he* would make a portal and take me to the king's court. But had I succeeded in assuaging his suspicions?

The sound of Artie's voice came from the bedroom. At first, I thought she might be calling again, and Sarrlevi had answered, but I recognized the same message. That sent a little chill through me. Why was he repeating it? So he could memorize it and get it translated later?

That was the only reason that made sense, and nerves fluttered in my belly. If I was going to ask him for a favor, I had better do it *before* he found someone to translate the message.

"Hey, Sarrlevi?" I asked as I ambled back to the doorway, trying to make my words come out as casual. "*You* can create portals. Since the engineer isn't here, is there any chance you could take me to the dwarven home world so I could speak with the king?"

His back was to me as he considered the communications device. The message had finished, but Artie's face remained on it. A face of earnest warning. She must have been telling Hennehok that an assassin was manipulating me and might still be hunting for my mother...

"Why did you not ask me before?" Sarrlevi asked without turning around.

"Because I'm still indebted to you for the *last* favor I asked you for." I'd promised to help him find my mother, or her remains, when he'd created a portal to get me out of the park when the police had been surrounding me.

"And you hate asking for help."

"From you, yes."

Sarrlevi turned to regard me. "From anyone, I suspect."

That wasn't untrue, but I particularly didn't want *him* thinking I needed help. "Will you take me or not? I don't have much I can offer a wealthy assassin with multiple homes on multiple worlds. I'm still working on the *last* thing I promised to help you with." I flung a hand around the cabin to indicate the quest for my mother. The robot dog, or maybe it was a *clockwork* dog, wound down in a corner, its metal tail drooping.

Sarrlevi gazed at me, and I sensed that he wanted to say *no*. It couldn't be because creating a portal was too taxing for him. I'd seen him do it with a wave of his hand, even when he was injured.

Was it because he didn't want me to have that meeting with my grandfather? I didn't ask the question but raised my eyebrows.

"One cannot make a portal directly into the king's court," Sarrlevi said. "As with the elven court, and the important cities for many magical civilizations, there are protections in place to prevent that."

"How about a half mile outside that protection? I don't mind walking. My legs are sturdy. They work well."

His gaze lowered to regard them, and I blushed for some reason. It wasn't as if he was checking out my ass, but who knew what went through his head?

"The protection extends some ways," he said. "And due to my career and reputation, I am not beloved by the king's guards or dwarves in general."

"Dwarves aren't drawn to you? Shocking." I clamped my mouth shut, wishing I could retract my sarcasm. I was asking him for a *favor*. Being polite would be wise. I refused to suck up, but there had to be a middle ground I could walk.

"Few are." Sarrlevi lifted his chin. "I prefer it that way."

I thought of his house overlooking the wild ravine with no

other signs of civilization—of people—in sight and decided that probably was his preference. It seemed lonely.

"How did you get in to see him and be assigned the gig to find my mother in the first place?" I was tempted to also ask how he'd originally gotten in to see Princess Barothla when she'd given him the assignment to *kill* my mother, but I didn't want any details related to that. Maybe she'd gone to him. I doubted assassins were like appliance installers and made house calls.

"An acquaintance arranged it."

"Any chance your acquaintance would like to arrange for an earnest young half-dwarf to be united with her grandfather?"

"It's doubtful."

"I dislike him already."

"Her," he said.

I grimaced. "It's not the elf ex-princess, is it?"

Why would *she* have an in at the dwarven court? Or did all the royals—and dragon-foisted-from-power ex-royals—chat with each other? That was possibly true. On Earth, the leaders of countries always seemed to be visiting each other to discuss trade and alliances and such.

"I will see if I can arrange a meeting for you," Sarrlevi said without answering my question. "I will also attempt to find out who put the reward out for your hammer. It may take some time. You will remain here until the dwarf returns?"

Remain here? What did he think? That I would sleep on the floor with the clockwork dog and eat moldy Lunchables? "I'll go back to my house tonight and check on this place again soon."

He gazed thoughtfully at me. Did he object?

"Perhaps, since you are being hunted, you should stay in close proximity to a strong ally. I believe Thorvald's house has extra rooms."

I propped my fists on my hips. "I'm not going to ask the *Ruin*

Bringer to be my bodyguard. Or show up on her doorstep with a suitcase. I barely know her."

"It is her mate that I thought would be a suitable bounty-hunter deterrent."

"The dragon who tried to kick your ass earlier today?"

"He may have *tried*. He was not successful. Regardless, his presence should keep you safe until I return."

"Look, I'll be fine. After the trouble that the whole reactor artifact brought, Tinja and I put some alarms and booby traps up around our house. If anyone comes to kill me, I'll know about it."

"Goblin booby traps." Sarrlevi didn't sneer, but his tone conveyed his disdain.

"Goblin and half-dwarven booby traps. They're excellent." Never mind that I'd done little more than provide materials of a higher quality than the recycled junkyard stuff Tinja usually favored. It wasn't as if I knew how to enchant anything.

"You could also wait in one of my homes. They are well protected. By *elven* booby traps."

"Which are far superior to what a goblin can make, I'm sure."

"They are powerful and not comprised of stolen gewgaws."

I lifted my hands. "I appreciate the offer, but I've got to be here in case an offer comes in on the house I've got listed for sale now, and I have to spend time researching our next property. We only get paid for projects we complete, and I can't abandon Abbas for days."

"You can do such things from Thorvald's house." His mulish expression suggested he was thinking of forcibly taking me there.

I folded my arms over my chest, tempted to tell him that he could *try*, but a thought sprang into my head, and I lowered my arms. "All right. I'll call her and ask her for help."

Sarrlevi squinted at me, and I tried to keep my mind blank in case he attempted to read my thoughts. If he did, I didn't feel it. Maybe he was starting to trust me. That probably *wasn't* the case

—he might simply think it wasn't worth arguing about—but the thought that he could read my mind almost made me squirm. Because I wasn't planning to do as he'd asked.

"Good. You must survive until I complete this quest."

"At which point, you don't care if I trip and fall off a cliff and die."

His faint smile returned, and he rested a hand on my shoulder for a moment before walking out the front door. I had no idea if that had signified agreement or if he'd been implying he might care a tiny bit.

"No way," I muttered, reminding myself of what he was. *Not* someone who cared for the well-being of dwarves. And certainly not mongrel half-dwarves.

Silver light beyond the window indicated a portal forming. His presence faded from my awareness, and, as the portal also disappeared, I called Val.

"Yeah?" she answered amid a surprising amount of hissing, bubbling, gurgling, and clanking. It sounded like she was in a mad scientist's laboratory with ten experiments threatening to boil over.

"It's Matti."

"Hey, girl. Got any leads on Willard's missing artifacts?"

I grimaced with guilt since I hadn't thought once about Willard's problem.

"Sorry, no. I have a question." I wasn't thrilled about asking her for favors, but I took a deep breath and made myself do so. "I'm being hunted by crazies trying to get my hammer, and I need to talk to the dwarven king about my mother and, uhm, some other stuff." I was fairly certain Sarrlevi had left through the portal and wasn't crouched outside the window, using his magic to camouflage himself and eavesdrop, but he *was* an assassin who stalked people for a living, so I couldn't be positive. "Is there any chance you and, uhm, your mate, would be able to give me a ride to the dwarven home world?"

"Zav hasn't offered to take anyone else from Earth to other worlds, but I'm expecting him back in the morning." A small explosion sounded somewhere near Val. Where *was* she? As far as I knew, she didn't have any goblin roommates, so engineering projects shouldn't spontaneously combust often. "I can ask him. And I definitely commiserate with you on people hunting you for your weapon. That's always a pain in the ass. Do you know who's paying the crazies?"

"Sarrlevi said he would try to find out. There's apparently a reward out for it."

"I'll text Willard. Maybe she's heard something."

"Does she mind you texting this late at night?"

"She does, but I do it anyway if it's important."

"Oh." I wasn't sure whether to thank her for pestering her boss on my behalf or not. I was more interested in arranging the meeting with the king. "Do you think your mate would be more inclined to help me if he knew Sarrlevi had refused to take me to the dwarven world?" Maybe it wasn't fair to say that, since he had said he would try to arrange something, but after seeing Zavryd and Sarrlevi trying to prong each other with swords, I thought the dragon might be willing to assist me if it would irk Sarrlevi.

Val snorted. "He might. Even better would be if you brought some meat."

"Like the meat cubes he mentioned?"

"*Any* kind of meat. He likes barbecue."

"Who doesn't?"

"Come on over tomorrow morning. I'll text you the address."

A stern male voice in the background said, *Not like that!* and another explosion sounded.

"Is it safe?" I asked.

"Rarely. Will you be all right tonight? You can crash here if you want." A different male voice said, *Should not your half-elf assistant be wearing safety goggles and a filtration mask? She yet breathes.*

She yet *breathes*? Who was there with Val? And what *were* they doing?

"I'll stay at my house, thanks." Whatever Val was dealing with sounded at least as dangerous as bounty hunters.

"Right. Honk when you get here tomorrow. I'll need to adjust the magic of the topiaries to let you in."

I blinked. Speaking of booby traps... "What happens if I walk to the door *without* adjustments?"

"The barbecue will get extra crispy."

"And the delivery dwarf too?"

"Exactly."

11

Afraid I wouldn't be able to find a barbecue place early in the morning, I picked up a couple of pounds of pulled pork, sausages, and brisket on the way home. The price of pounds of meat—no sides necessary, thank you—made my eyes bulge, and I hoped the bribe worked on Lord Zavryd.

When I walked through the door to my house, the booby traps around the yard appearing—fortunately—unmolested, Tinja was still awake, blueprints spread all over the living room and draped over the furniture and even the television. A pen and pencil perched behind her ears, and protractors and compasses clanked in her pockets as she moved around on hands and knees.

With some bemusement, I realized my house wasn't that different from Hennehok's cabin, at least not since I'd gotten my goblin roommate. Before that, it had been more sparsely furnished and relatively project-free since I used the shed and backyard for most of my hobby work.

Despite her obvious engrossment, Tinja sat up, her green nostrils twitching. "Is that barbecue?"

"Yes, but I need it to bribe a dragon tomorrow."

"So... we can eat only a small sample?"

I snorted, having intended to only have some leftovers before going to bed—dinner had long since come and gone without an offering greater than cheese cubes made to my stomach—but it *did* smell good. "I'll fix you a plate. You working on homework?"

"Not this time. I've turned everything in for the week. *This*—" Tinja spread her arms toward the drawings, most showing exteriors and floorplans for surprisingly diminutive dwellings, and were those *wheels* on one? "—is the project that's going to make me rich."

"No kidding." I fished plates out of a cupboard in the kitchen. "Did you get a gig for a wealthy client?"

"No, I'm not supposed to take on clients until I finish my architectural degree and get licensed."

"You do stuff for me all the time."

"As your intern. That's perfectly acceptable. I have checked your laws. Do you know that your people have more laws than any other civilized race in the Cosmic Realms and wild worlds?"

"Is that true?" I spooned pulled pork, slices of sausage, and chopped brisket on the plates.

"Well, I'm not that sure, but you have more laws than goblins. This I know."

"Do goblins have *any* laws?" I was positive they didn't have any about acquiring goods from other people.

"Not many. Our main tenet is that you should strive to do work that improves the lives of all goblinkind while not impeding the freedoms of others."

"Wise."

"As goblins obviously are."

"Obviously." After tucking the rest of the meat in the fridge, I returned to the living room, handed one of the plates to Tinja and debated where to sit. The dining-room table and its chairs were also covered in projects, so my options were returning to the truck, using my bed, or eating while standing.

"Except for stuck-in-their-ways *rural* goblins who insult you instead of supporting your hopes and dreams of integrating into human society."

"Do you want to integrate?" I asked. "I thought you only wanted to be able to live and work here without being bothered."

"While having the freedom to make lots of money improving the abodes of your people. You know my dream of buying land—unlike my bumpkin cousins, I would not simply *squat* in the woods and presume that gave me the right to the property—to create a fabulous sanctuary in the city for goblins like me who enjoy the amenities of this world." She popped a sausage slice in her mouth and savored it. "Yes, mm, *amenities*."

"It is hard to get good barbecue in the woods."

"The last time I saw my rural cousins, they were roasting road-kill on a spit. It wasn't even *seasoned*."

"Barbaric."

"Exactly what I said. Next time I visit, I intend to take them exotic spices."

"Exotic? Like saffron? Turmeric? Grains of Paradise?" I only knew the names from cooking shows and had no idea what those spices tasted like.

"Like *salt*."

"Even better. How is that going to make you rich?" I waved at the papers.

"I've learned that some architects sell many copies of some of their basic plans on the internet. Since everything is digital, it is very inexpensive for them, aside from the initial work."

"And finding people to buy the work, I imagine."

"That will be a simple matter of learning internet marketing."

"Something easy, no doubt."

"For a bright and determined goblin, certainly." Tinja waved an airy hand. "I have also learned that in these times of economic disparity in your world, those without great means enjoy building their own tiny homes. They are much more affordable than large homes on foundations."

"Ah, the little houses on wheels. I've seen them."

"Yes. As a goblin, I am naturally an expert at all things tiny."

"I have no doubt."

"Maybe I'll make that part of my marketing pitch. Tiny person, tiny home expert? What do you think?"

"Just that you better remember in your designs that most humans can't walk under counters." My phone rang as I was noshing on pulled pork. Zadie.

She didn't usually call this late, and worry thudded into the pit of my stomach. What if one of the would-be hammer hunters had shown up at her apartment? She was still recovering from the *last* orcs who'd visited—and the ear that Sarrlevi had chopped off one and left on her living-room floor.

"Everything okay?" I answered.

"Uh, yes." Zadie sounded surprised by the question, and that assuaged some of my worry. "But you didn't call back. Didn't you get my message earlier? Or check your email?"

"I haven't been home all day." I checked my voice mail and was surprised that a new message *had* come in. "Sorry, there must not have been good reception at the cabin in Woodinville. It was out in the sticks."

"You're not buying a *cabin,* are you? Like with logs? Those don't go for top dollar, Matti. People don't want their toilet paper holders mounted on logs."

"I was visiting a dwarf," I said dryly, "but thanks for the real-estate tip."

"That's what I'm here for. And to let you know I've got an offer on the Bridle Trails home."

"Wow, that was fast. So the listing is live on the MLS?"

"It went up today, yes. There were several showings this afternoon."

"Didn't you say the market had softened and not to expect anything right away?"

"Yeah, but who couldn't fail to be wowed by hand-carved staircase railings that look like trees with birds and squirrels perched on the branches?"

"Well, *I* would buy a house with such things."

"Your potential buyers loved it. Actually, *both* of your potential buyers. We have two offers. Have I mentioned that you're my favorite client to work with?"

"Yes, and also that you refuse to give me a discount, despite the ease with which you sell our homes."

"I can't afford to give discounts. Have you seen the HOA dues for my condo building?" Zadie's tone grew tart as she added, "Especially since we've got a special assessment coming up, due to someone knocking our rooftop door off the hinges. There's also damage to the roof itself. The manager said it looked like a hippopotamus was jogging around up there."

"Just... a dragon landing."

"The water-tank support was damaged, and someone snapped the antennas."

"Odd. Do the offers on the house need a quick response?" They usually did. I was glad she'd called again. I might need to check my inbox and sign documents before leaving Earth. Presumably, one didn't have access to Gmail from the dwarven home world.

"Within twenty-four hours, yes. The first one is from an institutional buyer who's offering full price, cash, and a two-week closing. I think he's going to rent the house, then try to partition the land and build another home on the back half of the lot."

"The half with all the trees and nature intact?"

"You sound like an elf."

"I have been hanging out with Sarrlevi."

"Didn't you say he's an *assassin*? How much does he care about nature?"

"He travels with his own moss rug to put his cot on. I think he's all right with it."

"You're my weirdest client. And you ask why I don't give you discounts. You should be paying *me*."

"Because I know someone with a moss rug, I'm weird? For all you know, they're trendy and all over Etsy."

"Trust me, they're not."

"What's the second offer?"

Zadie sighed dramatically, which I took to mean she wanted me to take the first offer. "A family offering a hundred thousand under our list price, because it's supposedly all they qualify for. You do *not* come in under list on a house that just came on the market, Matti. Their agent should have known better, but supposedly they're in love with it. They have kids and a dog and all that."

"Well, I'd want to try a counter, regardless of what their agent said, but they sound like who I'd want to live in one of my homes." Before making any decisions, I would text Willard and ask if the werewolves were bothering people in that park. I *hoped* the neighborhood was once again safe for families.

"Dogs don't appreciate nature either, Matti. They pee all over it."

"Urine doesn't prompt a forest to die, not the way bulldozers do."

"Don't get all tree-huggy on me," Zadie said. "If you take that much of a hit, you won't make a profit."

"We'd make *some* profit."

"I'd tell you to wait and see if more offers come in, full-price offers from tree-hugging families, but since you're a flipper, I'll assume you have a crappy hard-money loan and have already held the house longer than ideal due to the extenuating circumstances."

"It's not *that* crappy of a loan, but... yes to the rest." Not to mention that my life had gotten crazy and now included trips to other worlds. Though I hoped the stuff with my grandfather wouldn't take long, it was possible it would keep me away for days, and Abbas and I both had to be available to sign paperwork.

Tinja had taken a break from eating and drawing to frown over at the conversation. Her ears were as sharp as an elf's, so I had no doubt she was catching everything.

"Given all the death and fighting and everything that happened in that house," I added, "before and after we bought it, I wasn't expecting to make a profit at all."

"Neighborhoods have short memories, and none of that ever appeared in the news," Zadie said. "I'll send both offers for you to look at, but you'd better consult with Abbas before getting your mind set on anything."

"I always do." Fortunately, Abbas was a softy and usually agreed with my desire to see people who would actually *live* in our houses get them, not investors. Especially institutional investors who were driving up home prices and making it hard for families to buy.

Zadie sighed dramatically again. "Let me know in the morning."

"I will. Bye."

"You should take the offer for more money," Tinja said as I texted Abbas the details, not sure if he would still be awake. "Then you'll be able to afford to pay me more than a pittance."

"You're a college student, an intern, and you live here for free. You're supposed to make pittances. It's character-building."

"I must acquire an urban goblin sanctuary, Matti."

"Isn't the tiny-house scheme going to get you that?"

Abbas, bless him, promptly texted back that we should sell the house to the family.

"It may take some time for my tiny-home venture to gain steam. I believe marketing costs money too. Thus, the more funds you pay me for my blueprints, the more I can spend on internet advertisements."

"Do goblins know the saying *shoestring budget*? It's what most young entrepreneurs start out with."

"Goblins know how to *make* things out of shoestrings, yes. But how will that help me with marketing?"

"Never mind." I patted her on the shoulder. "After I finish this stuff with Sarrlevi and my mother, I'll double down on the next house project so we can afford to pay you a little more. You are, after all, invaluable."

"I know this. I just need *other* people to realize it. You have no idea how hard it is being green."

"I've heard that from Muppet frogs."

That earned me a puzzled look.

"Never mind," I repeated and was on my way to bed when my phone dinged with a text from Val.

Willard wants to see us in the morning. Be here by 8.

I groaned. If Willard was more worried about her missing arti-facts than my quest, she might send me off with Val. I wanted to meet my grandfather, damn it. And find out if Sarrlevi was telling the truth.

12

WITH MY RECENTLY REHEATED BARBECUE TAKEOUT IN AN INSULATED bag to keep it warm, I drove to the address in Green Lake that Val had sent, arriving at a large corner lot without a driveway or garage. The three-story Victorian house, complete with a window-filled turret above the porch, had been built before cars had been a mainstay in the city.

Despite that deficiency, I couldn't help but gape in envy out the window as I parked behind Thorvald's black Jeep. The home had been beautifully renovated, was only a couple of blocks from the lake, and I wagered that turret had a killer view of the water.

"This place has got to be worth millions," I muttered. "Who knew killing magical bad guys paid that well?"

It wasn't until I was out of the truck with my bag of barbecue meat that I noticed large dragon-shaped topiaries growing up from the corners of the property and on either side of the walkway leading to the house. My senses twanged, promising magic all over, from the turret to the basement and dotting the front and back yards. Maybe the neighbors somehow knew about it too. On the streets leading to the address, cars filled every available inch of curbside parking, but I'd had no trouble finding a spot behind Val's Jeep. The entire corner around her property was empty of other vehicles.

"So, did the house come with quirks that made it available under market value, or did she bring the quirks with her?" I texted Val instead of honking, since it was early, and grabbed my hammer.

Unfortunately, I didn't sense her dragon. I worried that meant we wouldn't be able to leave as soon as the meeting with Willard was over. I did detect a surprising number of other magical beings in the house—no, in the basement.

Come around back and down the steps to the basement, Val replied. *I'm being pressed into holding something, but Zav is on his way.*

I eyed the topiaries warily as I stepped from the sidewalk to the walkway between two of the looming creations. I couldn't tell what shrub they were made from—was it even native to Earth?—but they oozed magic. Two eyes in each foliage head glowed red, and I paused, but after the topiaries surveyed me, the eyes dimmed again, as if to say I could pass.

"I *hope* that's the message." Still wary, I inched farther up the walkway.

The topiaries remained dormant. I imagined UPS drivers chucking packages onto the porch from the safety of the sidewalk.

Nothing else glowed at me as I veered off the walkway toward the side of the house, but magic oozed from a fairy ring of mushrooms growing on one half of the lawn. Some instinct told me to be careful not to step on any of them.

A fence surrounded the backyard, and I scowled as I rose on tiptoes, fumbling at the gate to reach the latch that fastened it from the other side. People who installed such things were always at least six feet tall and didn't think about the vertically challenged.

Had I not sensed more magic near the fence and gate, I might have used my hammer to open it. But it was bad form to smash things on property belonging to a person you were asking for a favor. Or anyone's property.

It wasn't yet eight, and I hadn't seen a car that might belong to Willard, but I could envision her scowling at me while thinking, *Vigilante.*

The backyard was nicely landscaped, with a large flagstone patio, a fountain, and raised garden beds made from rocks. Bamboo and other tall-growing shrubs around the perimeter ensured privacy and also half-hid wooden structures attached to an old cedar hot tub.

Make sure to close the outer door of the light lock before opening the inner door, another text came in from Val as I descended cement steps to the basement.

What was a *light lock*?

The sturdy windowless door was brightly painted to match the trim of the house, but a dour sign read: *Beware of vampire.*

My first thought was that it was a joke, but I then recalled Val mentioning a vampire roommate. At the time, I hadn't thought much of it or believed her serious, but some of the magical beings I sensed *might* be vampires. Since I'd never encountered one before—thankfully—I wasn't familiar with their auras.

As I opened the door, I wondered if I should have borrowed the steel gorget from Hennehok's suit of armor. Hopefully, Val's roommate wasn't known for sucking the blood of visitors.

As she'd implied, I found myself in a small windowless chamber with a second door. I closed the first behind me, but not before the light let me read a second sign: *No, really. Vampire. Disturb at your own risk.*

Even though we'd been texting and I sensed Val in the basement with the other magical beings, I knocked.

"Come in," Val called through the door.

As I eased it open and stepped into the basement, infrared

light brightening the space, an urbane male voice with an Eastern European accent said, "Really, dear robber. Do I invite strangers into *your* home when they knock on the door?"

"Matti isn't a stranger." Val waved me into a chemistry laboratory lined with counters full of equipment I couldn't name. Above and below them, cupboards with glass panels revealed hundreds, if not thousands, of vials, bottles, and tins. A cabinet of curiosities to one side housed jars of organs—and was that a fetus?—in formaldehyde. I flashed back to my high-school biology class. I'd always assumed the weird stuff shelved in the back of the room had been for show, possibly to horrify meek-hearted students, but maybe scientists had an actual need for such things. "Willard just hired her," Val added. "She's going to help out with capturing bad guys."

The owner of the voice stepped into view, a pale-skinned man in a lab coat over a suit and bow tie, his black hair swept straight back from a widow's peak. He might have been handsome if that pallor hadn't made him look like he'd stepped out of a coffin.

Oh, I realized dumbly. If he was a vampire, he probably *had* stepped out of a coffin. Yes, there was one in the back corner of the basement, a bedroom area set off from the laboratory. A few more vampires sat in plush chairs around a low table while watching something on a laptop. Their complexions were similar, save for one man with almond-shaped eyes and what must have been darker skin in life—he still managed to look pale.

"Matti, that's Zoltan." Val pointed as she introduced me to the speaker. "Zoltan, Matti."

"Oh, joyous," Zoltan said. "Another overly muscled magical being with a giant weapon she'll doubtless use to threaten innocent vampires."

"I didn't even use it to threaten the gate," I said, though it had crossed my mind. "And did he call you *dear robber*, Val?"

"Yeah. It's his pet name for me. It's a long story."

"The tale of how you originally burst into my home and slew my giant guard spider is not that long," Zoltan said, "and does not the term *pet name* imply a romantic relationship? Let us call it a sobriquet, shall we? Or even better, a cognomen. I do not want to give your menacing mate a reason to come down here and breathe fire on my neck."

"He's never done that," Val said, "and your neck isn't flammable anyway."

"My *wardrobe* most certainly is." Zoltan smoothed his suit and brushed a speck off his white lab coat. "And I'm not confident that vampire magic can withstand dragon fire. I do not wish to put that to the test."

Val's phone rang, and she held a finger up to me. "It's Willard," she said before answering.

Zoltan walked closer to me, eyeing my hammer, and did his gaze linger on my neck? Maybe I *should* have borrowed that armor.

"You are a half-blooded dwarf, yes?" he asked. "The blood that flows through your veins is magical and hale."

"Good to know."

"And you have the aura of a full-blooded elf about you? A mate?"

"No."

"I've yet to have the opportunity to drink from the veins of a full-blooded elf or dwarf. Of course, I do not fantasize about such beings the way I do about dragons. You cannot imagine the temptation of having one in the house, sleeping a couple of floors above your coffin. But I dare not make an entreaty on his neck, even when he is in human form. You know what they say. The more appealing the blood, the more dangerous the person filtering it through their body."

"Yeah, I get that saying in fortune cookies all the time."

"We're in the basement, Willard," Val was saying. "I think Zoltan is making a pass at Matti's veins."

"Hm," was all Zoltan said.

"Are you a chemist?" I asked, more to distract him from my blood than because the field interested me.

"An *alchemist*. I use magic as well as scholarly knowledge to run experiments and invent new formulas. I also run a very successful YouTube channel where I instruct legions of followers in how to make mostly harmless tinctures and formulas."

I blinked. "You're on YouTube?"

"Naturally. I have a face for film, do I not?" He showed me his profile.

"And you have followers?"

"Teenage girls, mostly," Val said. "They like to learn how to make warts grow all over the ex-boyfriends who've wronged them."

"I'm happy to oblige with such instructions," Zoltan said. "Young women shouldn't be wronged."

"We pretend it's not creepy that they adore him," Val said.

"Naturally not." Zoltan extended a hand toward his seated comrades. "I am instructing my fellow vampires in how to start their own channels. The undead are most intriguing to the mortal human community, as you must know."

"The mortal teenage-girl human community." Val shook her head. "Willard is coming down. She's got a lead on the reward out for your hammer."

"Oh?" I brightened. I'd been afraid Willard wanted to send me off on a new quest that would get in the way of my trip to Dun Kroth, but if she knew who was sending goons after my hammer, I wanted to know. "An elf ex-princess, by chance?"

"Uh, I don't think so. It sounded like someone here on Earth, and since my half-sister went back to Veleshna Var, I haven't heard of any elf princesses, ex or not, spending time here."

Maybe I didn't have Sarrlevi's snooty visitor to blame, after all.

A heavy knock came from the outer door.

"Do not let your uncouth employer open both doors at once," Zoltan ordered, scurrying to join the others in the seating area and throwing a black curtain behind him.

"She won't," Val said. "She's been here before."

The inner door opened, and Willard walked in with papers in her hand. "Good morning, Thorvald. Puletasi." She raised her voice to call through the curtain. "Strange vampire roommate who doesn't pay Thorvald rent to live here."

"Dreadful human woman who doesn't respect vampires," Zoltan called back without moving the curtain, "you are not welcome in my abode."

"I wish *I* wasn't welcome in his abode," Val muttered. "But with Dimitri and Freysha both gone right now, he needs someone to hold the camera when he records his videos."

"His students can't do that?" I asked.

"Apparently, they're not yet properly trained. Besides, he was busy showing off his alchemical abilities to them last night. *All* night. You'd think they would be tired and asleep by now."

"Was that why there were explosions going on in the background when I called?"

"Last night, yes. But around here, you can never be sure about the source of explosions."

"That's the truth." Willard held out her papers—printouts of maps—and waved for Val and me to come close. "Gondo and a couple of other informants heard about a new reward out for a two-headed silver hammer full of dwarven runes." She looked pointedly at my weapon.

"Sarrlevi thought it originated on another world since Way Rover orcs attacked us," I said.

"I hate those guys," Val said.

"Information about the reward could have been shared on other worlds as well," Willard said.

"Wonderful." I felt lucky I hadn't been attacked more than once in the past twenty-four hours.

"This is the address of the issuer." Willard pulled a piece of paper out from the bottom of her stack. "Or rather the address where one is supposed to deliver the hammer once it's acquired. The reward is supposed to be waiting there."

"What's the reward?" I asked with morbid curiosity, wondering how much those orcs would have earned if they'd killed me and taken my weapon.

"One hundred thousand Earth dollars," Willard said, "according to the verbiage Gondo scrounged up and, even more interesting to me, an added incentive of a Defensive Trinket of Dark Elven Enchantment."

"Is that interesting to you because you once had one in your basement?" Val asked.

"Yeah. It's one of the pile of things you brought in after offing Weber last year."

"*I* didn't off him." Val touched her chest. "He ran in front of dragon fire."

"Which does tend to off a person."

"Yeah, but he did it to himself."

"That is the dreadful human who was responsible for experiments on vampires," Zoltan's outraged voice came from behind the curtain. "He deserved a death most vile."

I was more interested in the *Earth* dollars. Who called dollars that? Someone not from our world; that was who.

"Are Earth dollars equivalent to US dollars?" Val asked, also taking note of it.

"I assume so," Willard said. "You can ask when you and Puletasi go visit the address."

I slumped. I'd been afraid my portal trip would be delayed. But I could hardly object, not when this was about me.

"It's a logging operation in the mountains northeast of

Concrete," Willard said. "Head up there this morning, and find out if this is tied in with my missing stuff. With *all* of our missing stuff." She looked at me.

I almost pointed out that my only connection with the missing reactor under the house had been my mom's involvement more than thirty years earlier, but it didn't matter. For good or ill, I was wrapped up in this now.

Val turned toward the wall, her eyes unfocused. "Zav is on the way. Right on time. Good."

"The arrival of that beastly creature is never good," Zoltan muttered to his comrades.

One asked him if he'd ever tasted dragon blood, which led to a discussion about the culinary benefits of blood from different magical races. I did my best to tune it out while typing the address into my phone.

As it popped up on the map, I sensed Val's dragon flying in from the west. He soon landed on the roof. Given how steep and pointed it was, Victorian architecture not being known for flatness, that surprised me. Maybe he also hadn't wanted to squash the mushrooms in the fairy ring.

"How does he land up there without breaking anything?" I asked Val. "My friend mentioned some damage to the apartment-building rooftop that he landed on."

Val grimaced. "He knocked the chimney off this house the first time he landed up there. I'm fortunate that he has home-renovation skills."

"It's always handy to know someone with those." I almost pointed at my chest but decided I didn't want Val calling me if a less helpful dragon knocked her chimney off again.

"It is indeed," she said.

"I'm heading to the office," Willard said. "Let me know what you find."

"It's Saturday, you know," Val told her.

"You say that as if it means I shouldn't be going in to work."

"Well, some people take weekends off."

"Some people. Not us."

My senses told me Zavryd had jumped down from the roof and was heading toward the basement door, presumably now in human form.

I lifted the bag holding the barbecue meat. "Should I offer this to him now or wait until it's time to ask my favor?"

I smell smoked meat, Zavryd's telepathic words boomed into my mind. Into everyone's minds, judging by Willard's eye roll as she headed for the door.

"Now might be good." Val leaned over to look at the map on my phone. "Especially since that address looks to be ten miles up a forest-service road. We might want to opt to travel by dragon rather than Jeep."

I decided not to mention my fear of heights with the snarky vampire listening in. After all, I'd survived my last time riding on Zavryd's back. Assuming he enjoyed his barbecue offering, he and his full belly should fly us sedately to our destination, right?

13

Zavryd pulled his wings in, and we plummeted toward the forest below. An explosion ripped through the air we'd occupied a second earlier, the magical version of a grenade that had launched from the treetops.

He tilted wildly, and Val and I would have fallen if not for the dragon's magic holding us on his back. That didn't keep my stomach from dropping into my boots. Knuckles tight around my hammer, I didn't know whether to scream or throw up. Was it possible to do both at once?

Another grenade launched itself, seemingly of its own accord, in our direction. This time, Zavryd used his power to blow it up before it reached us, but that didn't keep him from zigzagging and flying erratically over the forest. I couldn't tell if it was because he worried about more attacks or he was simply enjoying this stimulating game of avoid-the-grenades.

"I'm glad I didn't eat any of that meat," Val called over her shoulder, the wind almost stealing her words.

Had I been taller, the wind also would have been whipping her braid into my face. Instead, it patted me on the head as we tilted left and right in the sky. My shorter hair was far more practical, and I wondered why she kept hers so long when she had to go into battle often.

"Does riding on your mate's back make you airsick?" I asked.

"Not usually, but this—"

Zavryd pulled his wings in and dropped again. We plummeted a hundred feet, another explosion pounding the air where we'd been, before he spread them to continue our flight toward the logging operation.

Val swatted him on his back. "You're doing this on purpose. I *know* you can make a barrier and keep those grenades from hitting us. *Without* detouring."

Yes, Zavryd agreed telepathically, *but this is more fun.*

His tail swished about as he flew from side to side, scaled belly skimming over the treetops.

"Do you sense anyone down there?" Val called.

I do not sense living beings, no. Now that I'm looking for them, I can pick out the magical grenade launchers mounted in the trees. I will attempt to destroy them before they can launch more grenades at us. Ahead of us, the top ten feet of a fir went up in smoke.

"Thank you."

"Why would anyone have mounted grenade launchers in trees?" I looked toward the cloudy sky above, imagining the weapons taking down aircraft, but we weren't anywhere near the SeaTac or Bellingham airports. I doubted many planes flew this way.

"To take out half-elves and -dwarves visiting on dragons?" Val asked.

"You think we, and our mode of transportation, could have been anticipated?" I could see why whatever person or group had issued the reward for my hammer might think *I* would come looking for them, but they couldn't have guessed it would be on a dragon's back.

"If we find anyone, we can ask them."

A launcher to our right that Zavryd must not have noticed blasted another grenade at us. It hurtled through the air, growing alarmingly close, before Zavryd banked sharply to the left to avoid it. When it blew up, close enough for the light to hurt my eyes, I expected the shockwave to knock us out of the sky—or Val and me off Zavryd's back—but powerful magic enveloped us, protecting us from the percussion. As Val had suggested, the power of the grenades was negligible next to a dragon's power.

"With our hands around their throats, I hope," I said, then hoped Val wouldn't accuse me of vigilante ways.

But she only grinned over her shoulder at me.

Rain started, and Zavryd flew straighter, either blowing up the grenade launchers in the trees or detonating the explosives before they reached us. My stomach thanked the clouds as he more sedately took us over the forest, following an old dirt road half hidden by trees until we reached a clear-cut area.

The naked land made me imagine the back half of the Bridle Trails lot in such a state, and I was glad Abbas had agreed to sell the house for less to someone unlikely to do that. That morning, I'd gotten up early enough to sign the paperwork and send it back to Zadie.

"Is that our destination?" Val asked dubiously, pointing to an office trailer on cinderblocks to one side of a parking area.

One of the windows was broken, graffiti covered the siding, and there were no vehicles around to suggest anyone was within ten miles.

"I can't believe someone drove all the way out here to graffiti the place," she added.

"Some people don't have a lot of demands on their time," I said.

"I can't imagine what that would be like." Val patted Zavryd and must have asked him to descend, for he arrowed toward the trailer.

Instead of landing on the open ground nearby, he alighted on the roof, its frame creaking under our combined weight.

"There's a hundred yards of flat ground all around it," Val pointed out, glancing over his side at the drop. "Why the roof?"

The ground is muddy and more puddle-filled than a bog. Zavryd kept his tail stretched out so it wouldn't droop down into a puddle that almost qualified for pond status.

"It's raining. You're going to get wet regardless." Even as she said the words, Val looked up. The raindrops weren't hitting us.

To make a magical umbrella is a simple matter. Zavryd settled on wrapping his tail around the trailer so he didn't have to keep holding it up.

"He's a good mate," Val told me, as if I had been doubting that. "He does have a few quirks. Like preferring warmth and cleanliness to the Seattle rain and mud."

"No magical kerchief like Sarrlevi has that he can use to wipe mud off his talons, huh?" I asked.

Sarrlevi! Zavryd's head swung around on his long, flexible neck, and his violet eyes peered at us. *He can do nothing that a dragon cannot do. Should I want my talons free of grime, it would be a simple matter to clean them. I merely wish to keep mud from squishing between my toes. It is an unpleasant sensation.*

"That reminds me," Val said as she slid off Zavryd's back and onto the edge of the rooftop, balancing on the scant inches of room. His large body not only took up the whole roof but extended over the sides in most places. "Would you be willing to take Matti to Dun Kroth after we're done here? She suspects Sarrlevi of shenanigans and wants to verify his story with the dwarven king."

That wasn't exactly what I'd said—I certainly hadn't used the word shenanigans—but Val must have read between the lines.

"I'd also like to meet him just because," I said, unnerved by the dragon's eyes so close, his maw parted enough for his long fangs to be visible. Even though he'd so far struck me as a touch goofy and pompous when he spoke, it was hard to feel anything but fear when I was this close, with his powerful aura radiating from him. "He may not be aware that I exist, and I'd like to let him know and also ask him about my mother." Not knowing if Val had filled in her mate, I added, "He's my grandfather."

When Val hopped to the ground, landing in a crouch and avoiding the puddles, I also slid off Zavryd's back. Though I didn't have the natural agility of a half-elf, my years of martial-arts training lent me better than average balance. At the least, I kept from slipping and pitching off the roof.

Dragons are not taxis, but you did bring me meat.

Val smirked and gave me a thumbs-up. Yes, she knew what softened her mate to a new person. Since Sarrlevi had bribed me with cheese, I couldn't judge a dragon for having a meat tooth.

"I can bring you more after the trip," I offered.

I may be able to take you, but I should speak to the dwarven king first and ensure he wishes to see you.

"Yeah," Val said, trying the doorknob, "you wouldn't want to show up unannounced and foist a daughter onto her unsuspecting father—or grandfather."

Because you are my mate, I intended to ensure the elven king wanted to see you, one way or another.

"I do remember the diplomatic skills you brought to bear. The door's locked. Give me a second." Val reached up to touch one of her charms.

Zavryd turned his gaze back to me, then startled me by shifting into human form. The rooftop grew much less crowded.

"I *would* be pleased to see shenanigans perpetrated by that elven assassin put to an end," he admitted, switching from telepathy to speaking aloud. He cocked his head as he regarded me. "But is he not forthright with you? He seems to hold you in some esteem."

"He *does*?" That put me more off balance than when his hulking body had been taking up all the space on the roof. "What makes you think that?"

Below, whatever trinket Val was using allowed her to open the door and step inside, but I wanted to hear Zavryd's response before following.

"He claimed you are as proficient a warrior as my mate and that you are not in need of instruction from her." Zavryd eyed me up and down, as if he couldn't imagine it.

I squeezed the haft of my hammer. Though his aura remained substantial, he wasn't as intimidating in his human form, and that straight and haughty nose would look better smashed in.

His eyes narrowed, reminding me that he was probably better than an elf at reading a half-dwarf's mind, and I pushed the thought from my mind. Anyone who could incinerate magical grenade launchers from afar could likely do the same to dwarves.

"He was actually defending me?" I asked. "That's what started your, ah, sparring match?"

"There was no need for *defense*. I was offering a kindness. He grew unnecessarily prickly at my unintended slight of you and goaded me into challenging him to a duel."

"Huh."

"It is no wonder he is ostracized by his people. *Most* elves are polite and suitably respectful toward dragons."

"Do you know what happened? Why he was ostracized?" It hadn't occurred to me that a dragon might be familiar with Sarrlevi, but if Sarrlevi was well-known because he'd been assassinating people all over the Realms for centuries, maybe it made sense.

"I do not. I am indifferent to elves beyond those chosen by the Dragon Council to rule over their people, such as Val's father was.

To maintain law and order, we occasionally interact with our chosen rulers."

"Sarrlevi's not from a royal family, right? He's not an estranged prince or something?"

"He was never a prince. His family is noble, and I believe his mother is a relative of the queen's. She is old and ill but protected and housed in the palace." Zavryd shrugged and shook out his black elven robes, though his magic continued to keep the rain away.

It was hard to imagine Sarrlevi with a mother.

"There's not much in here," Val called from inside the trailer. "And I don't sense any magic, certainly not one of Willard's missing trinkets." Her tone turned dry. "I also don't see a suitcase of *Earth* dollars waiting for someone who delivers your hammer. Zav, do you sense anything in the area? Maybe this isn't the only office."

"It seems more likely that your employer's goblin assistant isn't as reliable a source of information as she believes." Zavryd sniffed and levitated himself from the roof, turning in the air to float into the building without touching the ground. Instead of the yellow Crocs, he wore black slippers that matched his robe, so he didn't have to worry about mud squishing through the holes, but maybe he found it deplorable if dirt touched his feet in any manner.

I paused before jumping down, debating if Zavryd had given me any helpful information about Sarrlevi. If his mother was protected in the elven palace, a presumably well-defended palace, that might mean he couldn't visit her. He'd mentioned one could not form portals directly into the king's court, elven or dwarven, nor to their capital cities, so it might be hard to get in, even for an assassin.

But did Sarrlevi care? If he'd killed his father, his mother might have been the one who ordered him ostracized.

With Zavryd's magical protection gone, rain pattered on my head. I wiped moisture from my face and jumped down.

Inside the trailer, Val was poking at soggy papers, rain from the broken window making them clump together. The place smelled of must and mold, and I had a feeling it had been abandoned and that window broken for a long time.

"I do not sense anything magical here, no, although..." Zavryd's eyes grew unfocused as he looked at a wall—or far beyond it—using his senses. "There is a remnant of magic, a suggestion that something was here not that long ago, similar to a scent left behind that a hound might detect."

"The property might span miles," Val said. "Some of these logging operations own tens of thousands of acres. Will you fly up the mountain and poke around a bit? See if you can spot any other buildings or magic that's more than a remnant? Or any people skulking through the woods with briefcases of money?"

That last question prompted a disdainful look from Zavryd— he'd probably already made up his mind that Gondo had gotten a wrong address. I was inclined to agree, but it wouldn't hurt to look around, especially for someone who could fly across the miles quickly.

"I will search the forests and the lands shaved of trees."

Val smirked. "You cut down trees; you don't shave them."

"No? From above, the effect appears similar to what happens when one shaves a leg."

Her smirk widened. "You *do* know about leg shaving, don't you?"

I raised my eyebrows, but neither of them explained further, Zavryd simply making a *harumph* sound.

Val stepped forward and clasped his hands. "Thank you for helping out with this. I know it's not what you came back to Earth for."

"I came to spend time with my mate." He gazed into her eyes, his lids drooping halfway. "I had envisioned us eating meat in the hot box, not flying through the rain."

"Hot box?" I mouthed, then looked away and thought about going outside. The rain was unappealing, but I didn't want to intrude on their private gazing-into-each-other's-eyes moment.

"That's what he calls it," Val told me. "For a wedding gift, we received a combination hot tub, sauna, and steam room. You might have noticed its largeness in the backyard."

"Oh, is that what the privacy shrubs were trying so desperately to hide? That's quite the wedding present. I thought couples usually got toasters and crockpots."

"It was made by the goblin community." The wry look Val gave me suggested she might have preferred a toaster.

"Ah."

"Perhaps we will find enemies to battle, and the day will improve." Zavryd squeezed Val's hands, drawing her attention back to him.

"Yes, battles always perk up a rainy day."

"Indeed." He pulled her close and kissed her.

Yup, definitely time to go outside. As Val wrapped her arms around her mate, I hustled into the rain while hoping their parting kiss wouldn't take long. And that it *was* a parting kiss. Nobody would have sex in that moldy, damp trailer, surely. Wasn't Val allergic to mold?

As rain landed on my head, I tried to put my mind to work mulling over the hammer conundrum and how I could locate the issuer of the reward if we didn't find anyone here. But it was hard not to glance back and feel a little wistful about the romantic embrace in the trailer. It had been a long time since anyone had embraced *me* romantically.

Maybe I would text my sister, ask her for Tyler's number, and take the initiative and call him first. He hadn't made my heart zing, but he also hadn't been musclebound, covered in tattoos, and looked like he spent time in prison yards. That was an improvement over the guys I usually attracted. The blue-skinned tusked orc had been a new low.

Before I sent the text, Val and Zavryd finished up, and he walked out, changed back into his dragon form, and sprang into the air. He'd forgotten to levitate himself, and his tail and back talons ended up in puddles before he took off. He made a sound like a growly *gah!* and shook all three as he flew toward the mountains.

"Sorry about that." Val took a deep breath of fresh air as she walked outside. Maybe the mold-spore-laden trailer *had* bothered her. "I still get a little, uhm, smitten when he gives me his bedroom-eyes look."

She meant she got *horny*, but I didn't say so. "Understandable. He's handsome with good hygiene. Who doesn't like a man who keeps mud out from between his toes?" I eyed the road where it left the clear-cut and entered forest again, the route so overgrown that it would have been hard to drive up here even in a Jeep.

"I might agree that Willard got the wrong address," Val said, as if she knew what I'd been thinking, "but people don't put magical grenade launchers in the trees of a property that doesn't have anything valuable on it."

"True." I'd never seen magical grenade launchers on *any* property. "But maybe they were installed years ago, and there was something here *then*."

She eyed me. "Are you thinking of the empty pedestal in your basement?"

"Technically, that chamber is under the park and only *accessible* from the basement, but yes. Like that, maybe there *used* to be something here."

"But the reward put out for your hammer is recent, right?"

"I think so. Unless it took those mercs years to find me."

"Maybe someone put this address out there as a decoy." Val

looked toward the tree-covered slopes heading farther up the mountainside toward rocky peaks bare of vegetation. "Or maybe they keep an eye on the place from a distance and are prepared to come over if someone arrives with the hammer."

I waved it in the air to signal anyone looking in our direction.

"I'm sure they know you're the owner," Val said dryly, "and want to thump them, not collect the reward."

"You don't think they would believe I could be enticed by a pile of Earth dollars?"

Val rocked her hand in the air. "Given all those traps, there might not *be* any piles of dollars. Those explosives could have been meant to kill you, or whoever came, and leave the hammer intact. Whoever planted them could have hedged their bets and placed them along the road as well as in the trees. If we hadn't been traveling with Zav, one of those might have gotten us. Those were big bursts of magic he was using to destroy and defend against them."

"I suppose. Would someone have truly believed I might come by air though? Riding a dragon?"

"Well, you could have found out the road was impassable and flown here on a helicopter."

"Oh, sure. I was thinking of getting one for my business so I could avoid traffic on the way to the home-improvement store for paint." I wiped more rainwater from my face, wondering if we should have asked to go with Zavryd. I considered going back inside the trailer to wait but had a vague notion that I should be doing something more useful than standing around. But what? I tapped my hammer.

"I'm just throwing out ideas," Val said.

"I know. Thanks for helping." I crinkled my nose. "Do you smell smoke?"

"A bit, yes." Val gazed around the clearing. "Zav could be igniting things."

I hadn't heard more explosions, and the ones that had detonated before hadn't emitted much smoke. The breeze was blowing in from the other side of the trailer, and I jogged around it to take a look.

The rain made it hard to spot smoke, but the air did seem hazier in the trees off to the north.

"Your mate went east toward the mountaintops, didn't he?"

"Yeah." Val also eyed the hazy sky. "I don't sense him anymore."

As we watched, orange flames surged into view, licking at treetops to the north. There were a *lot* of flames.

"Wildfire." Val swore.

"That started in the *rain*?" Even as I spoke, I sensed a hint of magic coming from the north.

That fire wasn't natural—and it was heading toward us.

14

"GET INSIDE THE TRAILER," VAL BARKED, RUNNING FOR THE DOOR.

"The flammable trailer made out of *wood*?" I balked.

With fire crackling in the trees and heading our way, my instinct was to run in the other direction, not hunker down in a building in the path of an inferno.

"There's nothing else in this clearing to burn, and I think I can keep it from catching fire," Val called from the doorway, waving for me to join her. "I've also got a charm that protects against heat. We should only have to worry about the smoke."

"*Should.* There's magic in that fire."

"I know," she said grimly, "and it's moving fast, but running into the forest would be a death sentence. Zav should be back soon to check on us."

I didn't point out that there might be *other* booby traps in the area that would keep her dragon busy and reluctantly agreed that her plan was better than blindly running into a forest full of fuel for the fire. I, however, didn't have a charm that protected against heat. As I jumped inside, and Val shut the door behind me, I hoped she could share hers with me.

"Hunker down." Val eyed the view out the broken window, a broken window that wouldn't do anything to keep smoke out.

But the flames were what worried me. In the scant minutes since we'd first seen the smoke, the fire had grown greater, spreading into the forest far to the sides of our clear-cut area and rising high into the air above the trees. Thick gray smoke roiled upward and met the clouds, not squelched in the least by the rain.

The scent of burning firs and pines was much stronger now, the breeze blowing the smoke toward us.

Val coughed and grimaced. "I wish we had a blanket to throw over that window."

After dropping to my knees, I gripped my hammer and whispered, "*Keyk*," the command to make it cold. It had only helped protect me a little when the dwarven construct had breathed fire, but I would take any assistance I could get.

The haft grew icy cold in my hand, and the whole weapon glowed silver-blue.

Val knelt beside me and gripped my shoulder. "I've activated my fire-protection charm. Oh." She snapped her fingers and rubbed another charm dangling from the leather thong around her neck.

"You're not bringing your tiger into this, are you?"

"I *had* been thinking of asking him to sniff around for scents, but he would have snarky words for me if I—" Val paused to cough again, "—brought him into the middle of this," she finished with a rasp.

"I'm not tickled to be in the middle of it either."

"This is one of Zoltan's charms. It's supposed to protect against noxious air. I'm not sure if it'll include smoke."

"Is Zavryd returning?" I asked hopefully, afraid all the charms she had wouldn't be enough to save us from a wildfire.

"I reached out telepathically to him, but he hasn't replied yet, which is surprising. He can usually hear me from a long way off."

"Can you speak telepathically to people besides him?" I asked instead of dwelling on the possible ramifications of her not being able to reach him. Such as that something had attacked him. Or driven him from this realm.

"Yeah, but my range... isn't as great... with others." Shaking her head, Val tugged her shirt up over her mouth.

Smoke continued to blow toward us, so thick it almost kept us from seeing the flames, but their orange glow remained, visible through the haze. My senses told me the fire had us surrounded now, burning all the trees that remained in the area. The temperature had risen, and I wondered how safe we would truly be in the clear-cut.

"Maybe you can give me some tips someday. It must be a handy skill to have."

"Sure," Val rasped.

Though the smoke flowed through the broken window, it didn't bother me that much yet. Maybe dwarves had heartier lungs than elves. Someone had joked about that, hadn't they? Dwarves having evolved to live underground where odious gases weren't uncommon. Admittedly, I didn't think wildfire smoke clogged a lot of dwarven tunnels.

Something thudded onto the roof of the trailer. A hint of magic accompanied it, and the crackling of flames grew louder.

"I think it spat a piece of a burning tree on us," Val blurted, staring at the ceiling.

"It? The fire?"

"Whoever's manipulating it, I guess." Another round of coughs kept her from saying more, and she wiped her eyes.

My throat was starting to tickle now as well, and even though the temperature inside the trailer had lowered since I activated the hammer's magic, the orange of the flames outside swirled close. There *shouldn't* have been anything on the ground near us for the fire to burn, but if it was magic, maybe the rules of physics didn't apply.

The ceiling blackened from the center outward as whatever was up there burned right atop the trailer.

Val drew her sword, as if she might stop the fire with it, but it was her free hand that she thrust upward as concentration tightened her face. At first, nothing happened. Then something burst up through the carpeted floor of the trailer, startling me into rolling away from her.

But it wasn't anything burning. A thick green vine grew upward through the hole it had made in the floor, magic emanating from it. Val clenched her fist, and it grew even faster, straight up until it struck the charring ceiling and burst through it.

Thumps sounded, and I gaped as the thick vine twitched.

"What are you doing?" I finished the question with a cough. Yes, even my half-dwarven body was starting to struggle with the smoke. Tears leaked from my eyes as I watched the hole widen and the vine keep twitching. Magic smashed against magic, and I realized it was beating at whatever was burning up there.

Abruptly, something tumbled off the roof and past the window. The burning brand—no, that was more of a *log*. It struck the ground and rolled away from the trailer.

Val snarled and more vines appeared, not bursting through the floor but rising up outside the trailer. Sweat streamed from her brow, and her face twisted with effort. Her sword glowed silver-green, as if it approved of her magic. Or maybe it was assisting her in some way? Like a battery charging her?

I wished I could do something to help, but there was no enemy I could bash with my hammer, no foe I could kick in the nuts.

More vines grew up, until I couldn't see anything but green outside the window. The sounds of the crackling fire diminished, but I suspected the vines were insulating us, not that it had dwindled.

Val coughed again. I had no idea how she was concentrating and using her magic with her throat bothering her so.

"He's coming," she croaked.

I sensed Zavryd heading in our direction and sagged with relief. Hopefully, he could pluck us out of the fire and fly away. A dragon ought to be able to magically armor himself against flames, right?

A great whoosh came from outside, and the trailer shuddered.

"Is that him?" I asked. "Or the fire?"

Val could only cough for an answer. I reached over and patted her in case the cold of my hammer might somehow help. But her own blade glowed similarly, and I suspected it and her charms were already offering protection.

Outside, dragon magic mingled with—*fought against*—the magic of the fire. With the green vines still smothering the windows, and maybe the entire trailer, I couldn't see what was happening, but the power of the wildfire seemed to be diminishing.

I sure hoped so.

Coughing and wiping my eyes, I managed to say, "I'm more inclined to believe this was a trap for me now."

"And anyone traveling with you." Tears streamed down Val's cheeks.

"Sorry."

The fire magic disappeared from my awareness, and the dragon magic also faded.

A dry voice spoke into our minds. *There are elven vines blocking this door.*

Can't you get past them? Val asked, giving her voice a break and speaking telepathically.

She should have been doing that all along.

Is it not rude to destroy magic created by one's mate?

Weary magic trickled out of Val. The vines covering the

window didn't budge, but the door swung inward, revealing only a couple still rising up from the ground there, waving and wobbling like stalagmites made from Jell-O.

Zavryd, no longer worried about puddles, stood outside in his dragon form. *We have a new problem.*

"*Besides* the forest fire?" I asked, though all signs of flames were gone. Soot and ash covered everything and floated in the puddle water, but the threat had disappeared.

Yes. He looked at me as I walked outside after Val. The trailer was smothered by vines that had grown up from the ground on all sides, turning it into a strange entombed relic. *I've been called to investigate the dwarven home world,* Zavryd added.

Fresh fear lurched into my gut. "Why?"

My sister says there is a threat to the dwarven king. An elven assassin.

I halted. "Sarrlevi is *threatening* him? I thought—" I broke off, afraid I would sound foolish for admitting I'd believed Sarrlevi's story that he'd been hired by the king. I hadn't *fully* believed it, but I hadn't disbelieved it either. I'd wanted verification.

I do not know the details yet, but the queen is sending my sister and me to find out and offer protection if needed. A couple of centuries ago, the Dragon Council chose King Ironhelm and his family to rule the dwarves. He is a fair and honorable king. If that assassin *attacks him, I will slay him.* His violet eyes closed to slits as he flicked a wing and levitated Val and me onto his back. *Are these the shenanigans you spoke of?*

"I didn't think he wanted to kill the dwarven king, no. I thought he might be lying to me about... important things." Things that *weren't* important when compared to an assassination attempt on the king. I hoped whatever the dragons had heard was a misunderstanding. I didn't want to believe Sarrlevi could have helped me while plotting to kill my grandfather. Or had someone just given him that mission? Even so, if he'd taken it, I would clobber him. "Maybe he's betraying people left and right."

Betraying *me*...

Val gave me a sympathetic look.

I will take you back to our home. Zavryd sprang into the air. *The topiaries and other defenses will protect you from those seeking your hammer.*

"Will you take me with you to Dun Kroth?" I assumed he was heading that way.

If the king has been threatened, his people will not allow strangers to visit now.

"But I'm not a stranger. I'm his granddaughter."

Albeit his granddaughter that he'd never met and probably didn't know existed.

You are still strange, Zavryd said.

"Thanks so much," I muttered, though I knew what he meant.

Did you find anything in the forest? Val asked. *I wasn't able to reach you right away.*

There were some caves, yes. I flew into one that was empty but had light fixtures and electrical wiring, as well as magic insulating it from the outside world. It kept me from communicating with you while I was inside. Had my sister not arrived, I would have explored the other caves as well.

"Did you sense anyone?" I asked. "Someone had to have started that fire."

I did not. It could be that one of us triggered a trap, similar to the tree-launched explosives.

"Who burns down the trees on their own property as part of a booby trap?" Val asked.

Someone who very badly wants visitors destroyed.

As we soared farther from the forest, I couldn't help but look over my shoulder, feeling some of the answers to all that I sought

were back there, in the opposite direction from where we were
going.

15

THE RAIN STOPPED AS I SAT IN THE DARK ON THE COVERED STEPS OF Val's porch. She was inside, probably asleep. Drawing upon all that magic to create those vines had to have been exhausting.

After introducing me to her quarter-dwarven roommate—a surprisingly tall guy, given that heritage—we'd had a subdued early dinner. At least *I'd* been subdued. They'd argued about whether they needed to install sprinklers and a fireproof ceiling in the basement to protect the rest of the house from Zoltan's experiments. After our adventures in the woods, fire had to be on Val's mind.

My mind was full of musings about Sarrlevi. Why was he lying to me? And did I believe that he'd threatened the king? My grandfather. He'd once told me that assassins shouldn't be trusted, but because he'd helped me a number of times, I found myself *wanting* to trust him. Or at least give him the benefit of the doubt.

"A mistake, I'm sure," I grumbled, eyeing the neighborhood.

Night had come, and few people were out in the rain. Before departing, Zavryd had suggested I wait here until he returned, and

Val had shown me a guest room I could use, but I wasn't ready for bed. I wanted to *do* something.

A part of me wished I'd stayed in the mountains and hunted for the caves Zavryd had mentioned, but I hadn't had a way home. And if I'd remained there alone, all it would have taken was another booby trap going off to kill me.

I sensed the magic of a portal forming and rose, expecting Zavryd's arrival. Instead of manifesting in the yard or above the roof, the glowing silver disc appeared in the intersection, one edge almost licking the side mirror of Val's Jeep. That made me wonder what happened if a portal formed on top of an object.

A cloaked figure leaped out and landed in the street, and my insides tangled when his familiar face turned toward me. Damn. He had some nerve showing up here.

Unless he wasn't guilty of anything. Was that possible?

I walked down the steps but didn't go out into the rain, instead folding my arms over my chest and waiting to see what Sarrlevi said. My hammer leaned against the railing nearby, and I almost grabbed it, but I didn't. Maybe it was dumb, but I still didn't think I had anything to fear from him. Not as long as he needed my help to find my mother. And... not as long as he was standing up for my abilities to Zavryd? I didn't know.

With his pack and weapons slung on his back and his clothing clean and wrinkle-free, Sarrlevi was as tidy as always. He didn't appear to have been traveling and threatening dwarven monarchs. The rain hadn't even flattened his short hair. Maybe, like Zavryd, he could keep it from landing on him.

Sarrlevi came up to the sidewalk but stopped there and eyed the topiaries before looking to me. Their eyes flared crimson, and the magic that always enshrouded them intensified.

"I have not been able to learn who put the reward out for your hammer," Sarrlevi said, "but I did verify that it exists, with a promise of a hundred thousand Earth dollars and a magical trinket for its retrieval. I've contacted someone who's agreed to arrange a meeting between you and the king. We're to meet on Nirathra. That's the world that holds my home, the one you've visited. In the aftermath of an invasion by a dragon lich last year, the dwarves are prickly about inviting outsiders to their world and their cities and suggested a neutral location." He cocked his head. "I admit I'm surprised at the choice of *my home* as a neutral location, but since I went through an intermediary, I could not question them on the choice."

I opened my mouth, but it took me a moment to decide on a response. It was as if Sarrlevi hadn't heard anything about the threat to the dwarven king. The threat that was supposedly him.

Could Zavryd's family have been mistaken? Or was Sarrlevi tricking me? The information about the reward lined up with what Willard had learned, but maybe he was sprinkling in some truths to make his lies more plausible?

"I went with Zavryd and Val today to look for the person who issued the reward," I said.

Sarrlevi nodded, as if he'd expected nothing less. "They kept you safe?"

"I don't *need* them to keep me safe." I couldn't help but bristle at the implication that I required help. Which was stupid, because that forest fire would have taken me out if the magical grenades hadn't. I clenched my jaw, hating that my world had gotten complicated and dangerous, and missing the days when I'd been able to handle any fight. Those fights, however, had only occasionally involved magical beings and rarely full-bloods with great magic of their own.

Sarrlevi smiled slightly. "In a fair battle against one foe, you have proven yourself capable, but greedy mercenaries and thugs seeking rewards like to combine forces to outmatch their prey."

My hackles went down slightly. It might have been the closest thing to a compliment he'd given me. Being capable sounded better than being adequate, didn't it? Not that it mattered.

"Zavryd left Earth because his sister said they needed to check on King Ironhelm. Because their people, specifically their Dragon Council, chose him to be the dwarf ruler, and a certain elf assassin threatened him."

Sarrlevi's smile faded. "Elf assassin?"

"You, buddy. It's you."

"As I said, I went through an intermediary to request your meeting, and no threats were involved. All I did was pass along word of your existence and say you would like to see the king."

"How come you need an intermediary when you're supposedly on a mission for the king?" Even though I wanted to believe the dragons had been mistaken, Sarrlevi's story had never quite added up. "Can't you be straight with me? You're making me think you've been lying to me and that you *are* still after my mother."

"I am not." Sarrlevi held my gaze as he firmly said the words. "As I told you, I seek to find her and return her to your grandfather. Or at least to return her remains so that he need not continue to wonder if she lives or died." He extended a hand toward me. "Come. We should be there when he arrives."

I sensed Val in the living room before the door opened. She strode out, not in pajamas, but in her duster and boots with her big firearm in hand.

"What are you doing here, Sarrlevi?" She pointed the weapon at him.

He gazed at her, what seemed like genuine puzzlement furrowing his brow. "You've shot me with that weapon before, and it failed to penetrate my defenses."

"There's always hope I'll find a hole."

"I have not threatened the dwarves. Any of them." Sarrlevi looked at me.

"That's not what the dragons believe," Val said.

"The *dragons* are not omniscient."

"Well, someone's been telling them you're after the king," she said, the gun still pointed at his chest.

Sarrlevi's eyes closed to slits. "*Someone* may wish to damage my reputation and turn the dragons against me."

"Are you rejecting the fae queen's sex requests again?" Val asked.

"I have not seen her since delivering the brown squares she requested. The last time we spoke, she said they were a sufficient offering to calm her ire."

"You're welcome for the address to the chocolate store's factory. Why don't you run along back to your world? Matti's staying here until we figure out who's after her hammer."

Sarrlevi held my gaze, and a pang of longing went through me. Longing for him to be telling the truth. Yes, it would be practical to find out who had put out the reward, but I wanted to meet my grandfather and learn more about my mother. If Sarrlevi could arrange that, I wanted to go with him.

"You wish me to leave?" he asked softly, speaking to me and ignoring Val.

"*Yes*," Val said firmly.

I opened my mouth but hesitated.

"When we have not yet completed our quest?" he added, still holding my gaze. His words were a reminder that I'd promised to help him find her.

Damn it. If he was lying and leading me into a trap, it would be foolish to join him, but if I wouldn't assist him further, that made *me* the deadbeat who'd reneged on a promise. Besides, how else would I reach my grandfather to find out the real story? Hennehok was MIA, and it hadn't sounded like Zavryd was willing to take me to see the king at this time. If Sarrlevi *had* arranged it...

"You don't have to go with him, Matti. Don't let him threaten you or goad you into it." Val waved at her temple.

Did she think Sarrlevi was speaking telepathically to me? Coercing me?

No, he was simply standing there and waiting.

"Zav has done a lot to reinforce the magic protecting the house," Val added. "He won't be able to get to you as long as you stay here."

Sarrlevi lifted his chin, the glow from the topiaries brightening his face enough that I could see the indignation in his blue eyes. He didn't, however, voice a rebuttal to Val.

I sighed, not liking the idea of being a prisoner in her house. There was too much to do, too much I needed to learn before my life could get back to normal.

"I need to go," I told Val. "I need to meet my grandfather."

"Wait until later," she urged. "I'm sure Zav will take you. Once the *threat* to the king has been dealt with."

"If there's a threat, I want to make sure to warn him. It's possible the dragons are barking up the wrong assassin tree. And I'd hate for my grandfather to be killed before I got a chance to meet him."

Val hesitated and squinted at Sarrlevi, but she didn't stop me when I grabbed my hammer and walked toward him. Rain continued to fall, and nothing kept it from landing on my head.

Sighing, Val holstered her firearm. That didn't keep her from calling, "If you fuck with her, Sarrlevi, you know who I'll send after you."

"Your scaled mate, I am certain."

"Someone worse. The fae queen. I know what motivates her and where to find it. Fall is coming. Apple-cider caramel season."

Sarrlevi snorted before turning his back on Val. His other portal had faded, but with a burst of power, he created a new one in the intersection. In a house across the street, someone peered out the window, but only for a second before yanking the curtains closed. I had a feeling people had learned to look the other way a lot in Val's neighborhood.

A hint of pleasantly warm magic wrapped around me, stealing the chill from the air and keeping the rain from landing on my head.

I was about to thank Sarrlevi when Val jogged down the walkway after us.

"Wait. I'll go with you." *He's not telling the whole truth,* she added silently. *I'm not sure what's up, but he didn't answer you fully.*

Yeah, I know. I don't trust him. I just want answers.

Sindari and I can help you get them.

"You are not invited," Sarrlevi said.

"Why? Are you planning to seduce her and afraid I'll get in the way?"

"You just threatened to unleash an enemy at me and wonder why I do not want you along?" Sarrlevi asked.

"Please, people must threaten you hourly. You can't be that affronted."

"No," he agreed, not sounding perturbed. "The person whom I've asked to arrange the meeting might balk, however, if you arrive with us."

"Is it that bitchy elf ex-princess?" I guessed.

"A friend of hers. She made it clear that I will owe them both favors for this." He grimaced.

"Ex-princess?" Val asked. "What's her name?"

"Slehvyra-sulin."

"Never heard of her."

"She is from the family who plotted against the dragons and assassinated one of the Stormforge queen's children."

"Ugh," Val said. "Zav told me about them. Is she related to Anyasha-sulin?"

"A sister, yes."

"Double ugh. Though I don't know why they wouldn't like me.

Anyasha-sulin was the one using *me* to plot against Zav and Zondia. I didn't do anything to *her*."

"You are the daughter of King Eireth, he who replaced their family patriarch as the ruler of the elves. That is enough to ensure her hatred." Sarrlevi lifted the palm of his hand toward Val. "Remain here, Ruin Bringer. I do not intend to harm your friend." He tilted his head toward me.

One day, Sarrlevi would shock me by using my name. At least he hadn't called me *the mongrel*.

I'll be all right, I thought silently to Val, hoping she could hear me and Sarrlevi couldn't. *Thanks for offering to come though.*

Willard will be pissed if I let her newest operative die. Val held up a finger and removed her thong, the charms clinking against each other. She untied the knot, carefully unthreaded a symbol-shaped charm that might have represented a foreign word or letter, and handed it to me. *It's for translation. Rub it to activate it. You may find it handy when you're surrounded by dwarves and elves.*

Thank you. I glanced at Sarrlevi, wondering if he knew what it was or minded if I had it.

He waited patiently, with his hands clasped behind his back, and didn't seem to care. I carefully sealed the charm inside a zip pocket.

"The portal awaits," Sarrlevi told me, extending a hand toward the floating silver disc.

"Right. Let's do this." I nodded to Val, then walked toward it at Sarrlevi's side, hoping I wasn't making a mistake.

16

WE CAME OUT OF THE PORTAL IN SARRLEVI'S OFFICE IN HIS HOME, the familiar desk in front of us. I relaxed an iota, though it wasn't as if I'd expected him to take me to a cliff overlooking a lake of lava and shove me in.

A tray of salamis, cheeses, crackers, and green stalks that reminded me of asparagus rested on the table next to a bottle of wine or something similar. The stopper appeared to be made from mushroom rather than cork.

"Dwarves aren't as known to favor vegetables as elves," he told me, resting a hand on my shoulder as he nodded toward the waiting food, "but I thought you might like to—"

He broke off abruptly and spun toward the door. It was closed, but he must have sensed—

Oh, hell. I sensed her too. The elf ex-princess. And someone else. Another elf. The friend he'd spoken of?

"Are they invited to the cheese party?" I asked.

"No." Sarrlevi had been frowning, but he smoothed his face into its more usual bland expression. "I wasn't expecting them, but maybe they brought an update on the meeting. I hope that rumor of me targeting him didn't reach his ears and cause him to cancel." His voice turned cool. "I will have to find out who spread that falsehood."

When he headed out of the office, I intended to stay put, having no desire to interact with the snooty ex-princess again, but he halted so abruptly in the doorway, his entire body going rigid, that I thought she might have attacked him. Hammer in hand, I hustled up and peered around his shoulder.

The elves were not attacking him. The two females were naked and sprawled on his furniture, one on a divan and one in a chair with her leg draped alluringly over the armrest. They were *both* doing their best to be as alluring as possible, with their hair down, framing their curves, and smiles affixed on their lips.

The last time I'd come, I had noted the ex-princess's incredible beauty. She still had it, her lack of clothing making it clear she hadn't been hiding any flaws, and the other elf was almost as striking.

It took Sarrlevi a few seconds to recover from what must have been a surprise rather than a threat. Then he said something curt and dry.

The friend asked the ex-princess something. Maybe she was surprised he wasn't flinging himself across the room to ravage them. The princess lost her smile when she noticed me. She pointed, scowled, and replied to Sarrlevi.

I backed into the office. When I'd thought he was being threatened, I'd been ready to help, but whatever this was he could deal with on his own. Besides, I had no desire to look at naked females who could have made human cover models feel insecure about their bodies.

Curiosity did, however, prompt me to activate the translation charm that Val had lent me. It had sounded like these were the *intermediaries* Sarrlevi had worked through to arrange my meeting with the king. If they'd changed the deal on him, I wanted to know about it. Preferably before being forced to listen to sex play in the next room. Though Sarrlevi's tense body suggested this hadn't been part of the original deal and he wasn't interested. I hoped that was true. Even though it was none of my business, I couldn't help but feel he should go for women of substance rather than pretty girls who manipulated him. He'd already admitted he hated that.

"I said I would come to *you* on *Zerush ne Zar*, Slehvyra," Sarrlevi said, the charm not translating what must have been a place, "since you said you wanted to be *seen* with me so it would irritate your husband. You didn't mention bringing your friend along."

Slehvyra chuckled. "That's for your delight, not mine. Don't males enjoy new and exotic experiences? Varlayna has a talented tongue."

That made me roll my eyes and regret activating the charm.

"We also agreed," Sarrlevi continued, "that our meeting would take place *after* you arranged Puletasi's introduction to the king."

I should have been horrified that it sounded like he'd agreed to have sex with them as payment for my meeting, but I was so stunned that he remembered my last name that it took me a moment to process the rest. I was fairly certain I'd only given it to him when we'd first met, and I hadn't been able to get him to call me anything but *mongrel* since then.

"Who?" Slehvyra asked.

"The half-dwarf." Sarrlevi waved back toward me, though he remained focused on the elves.

Whether it was because he was admiring their naked attributes, despite his irritation, or because he didn't trust them enough to turn his back, I didn't know.

"Ah, of course." Slehvyra chuckled. "Your camp follower trailing you around, hoping you'll lose your senses and mount her."

Embarrassment scorched my cheeks, and I was glad I'd moved out of her view so she couldn't see my reaction. Unfortunately, she could probably sense it with her telepathy. Her statement wasn't the truth, but it was... closer to it than I would have liked. The thinking part of my brain might want nothing to do with Sarrlevi, but convincing the subconscious animal part of it had been difficult.

"The king's *granddaughter*," Sarrlevi stated.

"Yes, I'm certain he'll be delighted that his daughter was out on a wild world, procreating with lesser species to create her."

"King Eireth," the friend said, speaking for the first time, "seemed interested in *his* mongrel daughter. Much to his wife's consternation."

"I care nothing about who Eireth is interested in," Slehvyra said. "I'm here because of my interests. Which you *will* satisfy tonight, Varlesh, dear. If you want the meeting to occur."

"I already agreed to your terms, but we said it would be *after* the meeting," Sarrlevi said.

"After I *arranged* it, and I've done so. There is a tiny addendum, however."

Even though I'd been fighting the urge to spring out there and clobber her with my hammer, her last words made me pause. Addendum? What addendum?

I held my breath, wanting more details.

"Explain," Sarrlevi said.

"King Ironhelm is coming here, as I told you before, but he'll arrive with a platoon of his bodyguards and troops, to ensure nothing *untoward* is planned. It seems there's a rumor that an assassin is threatening him."

"Who started that rumor?" Sarrlevi's voice hadn't been warm at any point, but now it iced over.

Without answering the question, Slehvyra continued. Her voice was smug and sultry rather than icy. "In addition to bringing his troops, he'll be on the alert in case *I* come to him with a warning about your duplicity. I'm supposed to be here now, searching for threats."

"Do you find it difficult to search while naked?"

"Not in the least. If my friend and I find no duplicity and do not visit the king before the meeting, he'll assume that all is well and come as planned."

"If that's true," Sarrlevi said, "it would be a simple matter for me to keep you from reporting."

Slehvyra chuckled without fear, even though she'd lost the battle of wills—of *magical* will—the last time I'd seen them face off. "We both know that you won't harm me, Varlesh, dear. Or any elven lady."

"Don't be so eager to test that hypothesis," he said in a soft voice.

I wouldn't want to test it. He always had a powerful aura, but with that tension crackling around him, he radiated menace as well.

"Don't be so melodramatic. Come. Entertain us, and we'll have no reason to leave and give the dwarf king a warning." Slehvyra rose from the divan.

Though I couldn't see her from inside the office, I sensed her approaching him and was positive she was sashaying, thrusting her hips and breasts out with every step. Inasmuch as elves *could* thrust their breasts out. Maybe it was petty to note that there wasn't much there for a guy to cup, but I couldn't keep the thought from crossing my mind.

"We *should* check for threats though," Slehvyra said, her voice closer. "He *did* ask. It seems he doesn't trust you, my pretty assassin. Not surprising, I suppose. You tried to kill his daughter, and he knows it. He also isn't positive you weren't successful."

"Then why is he coming?"

"For *her*. If she's not who you claim, expect him to be extremely irritated. Even if she is, he may have his troops kill you."

"In my sanctuary? He can try."

I closed my eyes, certain this meant Sarrlevi had never been on a mission for the king, that Ironhelm hadn't assigned him to find my mother. Even though I'd been suspicious about that, I couldn't help but feel stung by the lies. The betrayal.

"If he didn't blame his other daughter as much as you," Slehvyra said, "he might already have tried to take you out of this universe. Tomorrow should be interesting."

"As long as he comes."

"He will. *If* he doesn't hear anything from me about duplicity on your part. I shall assess your home for threats, starting in your bedroom." Slehvyra's hands came to rest on Sarrlevi's shoulders.

Her friend chuckled—she'd moved closer too.

Sarrlevi was still standing in the doorway, and I resisted the urge to scoot into the corner so I would continue to be out of their sight—and vice versa—but stayed where I was, frowning mulishly at the desk.

"Why do I suspect you're lying to me, Slehvyra?" Sarrlevi asked, neither pushing her away nor reaching to touch her.

"Because you're a mistrustful assassin who preys on his own people at every opportunity."

"You know that's not true."

"But you *have* killed elves, including King Eireth's cousin Persylvar."

"He was a despicable bastard who brutalized females when he visited other worlds for *diplomatic* purposes." Sarrlevi sneered.

"I had heard that rumor, but I don't believe Eireth ever did, did he? Persylvar was always careful not to harass his own kind. But now Eireth has forbidden you from ever coming home. And the dwarf king wants nothing to do with you either, for obvious reasons. It wasn't easy for us to arrange this meeting." Slehvyra lifted a hand to rub the back of his head, her delicate fingers sliding through his short hair.

I looked away, wishing the portal remained open and that I could take it back to Earth. Or at least somewhere I wouldn't be forced to endure this. As much as I wanted the details and to learn everything I could, witnessing the naked elves hitting on Sarrlevi was tough to endure. Had there been a back door in the office, I would have shot out it.

"It's fortunate for you that our family isn't as out of favor with the dwarves as it is with the dragons," Slehvyra continued, her face close to his. "In fact, the dwarves, though they'll never admit it, admire us for having stood up to them. Deep down, nobody *wants* to be ruled by dragons and their sanctimonious Dragon Council, do they? Come." She rubbed one of his pointed ears. "The bedroom."

Sarrlevi sighed. Though none of the tension left his body, I realized he was going to agree. Slehvyra knew too for she smiled over her shoulder at her friend.

I cleared my throat. "Sarrlevi, can I talk to you for a moment?"

Slehvyra's smile vanished as she leaned her chest against Sarrlevi's and scowled past his shoulder at me. "Just to be clear," she whispered to him, "your camp follower isn't invited."

I almost snapped that a foursome wasn't my idea of a good time, but I didn't want to admit that I'd understood them. It might be giving up an advantage that I would need later. Their senses would have told them that I had charms, in addition to my magical weapon, but I hoped the elves couldn't tell what they did.

"I'm sure she's chagrined." Sarrlevi removed Slehvyra's hands and stepped back. "Give me a minute."

He took two more steps back and turned so he could look at me, though he didn't put his back to her. And she—rudely—didn't step away so we could speak in private.

"Look," I told him, doing my best to ignore her while hoping *she* didn't have a translation charm or understand English, "you don't have to do this—do *them*—on my behalf."

"That is the deal I was able to make," he said curtly.

"To whore yourself out as payment for a favor?"

Anger flashed in his eyes, and I regretted my bluntness.

"I'm not a *whore*. It's not my fault they won't take money or valuables and insist on *me*. Trust me, I'd prefer to pay."

"Yeah, I get what they want, but you don't have to give in for me. I'll ask Thorvald to help me. Maybe her mate—"

"—left you on Earth and did not take you with him," Sarrlevi said. "This way, you get your meeting tomorrow."

"*If* they're telling the truth." I flung a hand toward Slehvyra, who leaned against the doorframe, watching. "You just admitted you don't think she is."

"When you meet with King Ironhelm," Sarrlevi continued, ignoring my comment, "he may be willing to tell you more about your hammer and how to draw upon all of its powers. He may even invite you to stay and extend his protection over you. Until we're able to determine who issued the reward for the weapon, that could be useful."

"I can't stay on another planet. I'm in the middle of a deal on Earth. Besides, I don't want anything from him except to meet him and ask him about my mother."

"Yes." Sarrlevi's eyes narrowed, and I reminded myself that was likely why he was doing all this, not because he cared about me. He wanted to find my mother. And I still didn't know why. *Not* because the king had hired him; that was a certainty now.

"Enough, Varlesh," Slehvyra said. "We want a full night with you. After all, there are *two* of us for you to satisfy." She smirked. "We both must assure the king that there aren't threats here."

Tension continued to radiate off Sarrlevi, and I wanted him to tell them to beat it. No matter what he thought, I had a feeling they were playing him. They had skirted his question about who had started that rumor that he was after the king. He hadn't forgotten that, had he?

"Sarrlevi." I touched his arm, his muscles corded under his tunic, and groped for something else to say.

But he stepped back, bowed stiffly to me, and said, "Please enjoy the food and use the guest room." Then he walked out and joined them.

Slehvyra hooked her arm around his and said, "Send her away, Varlesh," as they headed toward the stairs. "We don't want her with her ear pressed to the wall, listening to us."

"Right," I muttered, already horrified at the idea of staying in the house while they were getting horizontal.

"I'm not sending her out into the wilderness," Sarrlevi said. "You know this world is filled with dangerous predators."

"Can't she protect herself with her ill-gotten hammer?"

"Ask her again who told the dragons you're after the king," I called, wanting to throw a wrench in their plans for the night. Not wanting to see Sarrlevi lower himself to sleeping with them. For his own sake, I told myself. Not because it would bother *me* in the least. It wouldn't.

I didn't know if Slehvyra had anything to do with that, other than a hunch that she was an evil bitch and would screw him over at the same time as she had sex with him. I peered through the doorway, curious to see if the females would react.

They'd reached the stairs, but Sarrlevi paused and looked at them.

"Who *did* tell the dragons I was after the king?" he asked coolly.

Slehvyra launched a scathing look at me before smiling and resting her hand on Sarrlevi's back, letting it slide down his spine and lower. "That was just a little insurance to ensure your cooperation. Last time, you turned me away. I didn't appreciate that. A girl has needs."

"I can't plow your garden if I'm dead."

"Satisfy us tonight, and I'll let the dragons know it was a mistake."

"Why did they listen to you, anyway?" Sarrlevi asked. "Your family plotted against them."

"*I* did not, and they trust ousted royals more than assassins who'll target anyone if the pay is high enough. Really, Varlesh. You can't blame *me* for the reputation you've cultivated."

Once more, he sighed. He looked up the stairs like a defeated man being escorted to the gallows. I knew he'd endured far worse pain than sleeping with manipulative women, but I shook my head, still not wanting him to go through with it.

Interrupt us again, Slehvyra spoke telepathically to me, *and I'll send you away myself.* She thrust an image of a magical wind sweeping me out a window and dumping me over the side into the ravine, where I plummeted hundreds of feet before landing in the snapping jaws of alligator-like creatures waiting in the river below.

Bite me, I replied.

I'm no more interested in engaging in such activities with you than Sarrlevi is. The next image she shared with me was of the three of them writhing in bed together.

Hell, I'd rather be dropped in the alligator's mouth than watch that. My grip tightened on the hammer's haft as I willed it to help me thrust the intrusion from my mind. Whether it was my willpower, or she'd grown tired of communicating with me, it worked.

Don't let them win, Sarrlevi, I thought toward him, though I didn't know if he was monitoring my mind as he walked toward his bedroom with them, one to either side of him, their hands all over him. *I understood what they were saying, and I'll tell Zavryd the truth. Don't let them blackmail you. They'll get you killed and won't even care.*

I'm confident in my ability to avoid dragons, he replied.

But why do this? When they're openly manipulating you? You said you hate that.

Yes, but if they're here tonight, they won't run off to warn King Iron-helm not to come.

Do you really care about that? About me seeing him? I asked bluntly, in part because I wouldn't waste my telepathic breath trying to help him if the answer was no and in part because... I wanted the answer to be yes. Maybe it was naive and stupid, but after what we'd been through these past weeks, I wanted to mean something to him.

If a person is fortunate enough to have family that is worth knowing and spending time with, one should be afforded the opportunity to be with them.

With that cryptic answer, he stepped into his bedroom with the elven females.

17

I MADE IT THROUGH MOST OF MY DINNER, THOUGH THE DUBIOUS—
and intensely fibrous—elven vegetables ended up in the trash bin,
before the noise from the bedroom grew too much to bear. Either
the walls and doors of elven homes weren't that insulated, or the
females were extremely enthused. I wouldn't put it past Slehvyra
to make more noise than necessary to irritate me. Though given
how many women sought out Sarrlevi, maybe he was simply that
amazing.

I snorted with skepticism, especially since he hadn't appeared
interested in having sex with them. Maybe that had been an act,
but it was hard to imagine him feigning irritation with them for
my sake.

"Should have asked him to make a portal and send me home,"
I muttered, taking a sip of the wine. It was good but not nearly
sufficient to dull my senses—my hearing.

If my grandfather came in the morning, being here and
enduring this would be worth it, but if the elves had been lying to
Sarrlevi and hadn't arranged a meeting...

"Yes, my magnificent warrior!" came a cry through the walls.

Groaning, I turned off the translation charm—I should have done that earlier—and grabbed my hammer and headed for the front door.

Sarrlevi's words about how dangerous this world was came to mind, but I would rather fight for my life than listen to more of the bedroom antics. Besides, hadn't he said his house was protected by wards and various defenses? Maybe they extended a ways around the property, and I would be safe sitting under a tree somewhere.

Outside, soft lights glowed green, highlighting the covered front porch and a walkway. It wound away between trees and alien bushes with trumpet-shaped flower heads, blue and purple berries, and something akin to fat blue pine cones. Fronds were more common than leaves, and the night air was warm and fragrant with unfamiliar scents.

Creatures squawked, hooted, and howled in the distance, their cries far less obnoxious than those of the elves.

As I headed down the lit path, I hoped for a bench or chair I could sit on until they were done, though I might have to go a ways to be out of earshot. As I recalled, Sarrlevi's windows didn't have glass. Too bad. His bedroom, at least, needed triple-pane insulation.

Rustling came from the undergrowth to the sides of the path. It sounded like nothing worse than small creatures scurrying about, but I walked with both hands on my hammer.

At an intersection, one path led farther away from the house, toward a flat, rocky plateau outlined against the stars. It looked like a landing pad for dragons. Or maybe the open area was where visitors formed portals when they arrived. The protections around Sarrlevi's home presumably kept strangers from popping up in his bedroom.

I opted for the other path, one that curved around to hug the forested ground nearer the house. Lights continued in that direction and not the other, a further reason to choose it.

As I rounded a bend, the walkway taking me down a slope and around the house in the direction of the ravine, I slowed down. Slehvyra's threat came to mind. If I ended up near the edge, her magical wind wouldn't have to work hard to knock me to my death. Would Sarrlevi, busy satisfying his guests, even notice?

If not for more lights up ahead, outlining what looked like a patio through the trees, that thought would have prompted me to turn back. But I spotted a seating area, the gray mushroom-like chairs and lounges similar to the furniture inside, and it looked like a good spot to hang out. Maybe the protective wards extended to it. And, thanks to all the trees and brush, the sounds from the house *might* not reach me.

"Rude of him not to play some loud music to drown everything out," I said, wondering if elves had the magical equivalent of stereo systems.

They probably preferred the soundtrack of nature. Though maybe not Sarrlevi. He had, after all, tapped his fingers to Metallica.

Something on the patio, half-hidden by leaves, glowed a brighter green than the lights, then turned blue. Magic came from everything in the area, including the lights, but whatever was ahead had a stronger signature.

Curious, I continued in that direction. Until a rattle of leaves came from my left, a *loud* rattle. Prompted by my instincts, I leaped forward, then dove.

Something whooshed past my head before a huge dark form landed on the path behind me. Had that been a *paw*? *Claws*?

After rolling to put distance between myself and whatever had attacked, I jumped up and spun around to face it. Just in time. It roared, the sound half lupine and half feline, and lunged at me.

The glow of the light provided enough illumination for me to make out a scaly black body, four legs, a barrel chest, and a head full of snapping teeth.

Adrenaline made me swing my hammer too quickly, and I only clipped its jaw instead of taking it in the side of the head, as I'd wished. That head was higher above the ground than mine. Fortunately, its attack faltered at the hammer's touch, giving me time to yank my weapon back and raise it defensively.

The creature prowled forward and swiped at me with one foreleg. Yes, those were indeed claws on the end. Long razor-sharp claws that gleamed under the green glow of the lights.

The deadly creature took several swipes, as if it was testing me with feints. That was exactly what it was doing. It worked its jaw from side to side as it attacked, probably stung from the partial blow I'd landed.

The probing swipes were fast, and I backed slowly, hesitant to give much ground. I wasn't that far from the ravine.

For each swipe, I raised my hammer to defend. Though tempted to counterattack, I didn't want to risk opening myself up with a big swing, not when the creature moved so swiftly, perhaps more swiftly than it had demonstrated thus far.

Then it stretched, its shoulder extending for another swipe, and I read the commitment in its body. That one wasn't a feint. With the claws flashing toward my face, I swung hard, hoping to hit it and hurt it. But its paws were too fast, and I only clipped it again. The blow kept it from reaching me but didn't noticeably hurt it. I needed to strike its head or chest, not its limbs.

Unless some lightning might help.

"*Hyrek!*" I ordered, hefting my hammer, then stalking in.

The creature swiped another paw toward me. When I smacked it out of the way, silver-blue light flared around the hammer heads, and lightning streaked toward my foe.

Startled, the creature jerked back, all four paws settling on the ground. As the lightning sizzled in the air around it, I lunged in. This time, I swept my weapon at its chest. My adrenaline made the blow hard, and it landed solidly, more lightning crackling around the creature as it lurched back.

That had to have hurt, but it roared defiantly, the sound deafening so close to my ears. Instincts came into play again, warning me that another attack was coming, that my blows might have angered it, but it had plenty of fight left. It crouched deeply, then sprang high, toward my head.

Ducking low, I scurried under its belly, raising my hammer to protect myself. While it was in the air, the creature crooked its legs to swipe at me, but I thrust my weapon upward. It struck the scaled torso, ribs cracking under the blow, and I dropped and scrambled away before its claws could catch me.

I rose as the creature landed facing the other direction. As it spun around, I darted in and swung my hammer at the side of its head, hoping to derail it before it struck again.

I connected with the power of a locomotive, and more lightning streaked forth. The blow smashed in the side of the creature's head, and it tumbled sideways off the path, only its legs remaining in view.

Expecting it to rise and attack again, I kept my hammer up, but it didn't move. My heartbeats gradually slowed as it grew apparent that the creature was either dead or unconscious.

"So much for my theory about elves protecting their patios with wards."

Maybe they enjoyed having to battle wild animals in between sipping lemonade and playing cribbage, or whatever elves did in their outdoor living spaces. Knowing Sarrlevi, he probably *did* enjoy challenges throughout the day.

"Crazy bastard."

I debated heading back to the safety of the house, especially since a fresh carcass might draw more animals to the area, but the blue glow I'd seen before pulsed warmly, as if in invitation. I decided to check it out before going back.

"How much worse could the night get?" I muttered, though it was unwise to tempt fate by asking such questions.

The pulsing light drew me closer until a pedestal with a dome atop it came into view, perched next to a raised fire pit and numerous chairs. Was the pulsing a warning? Letting me know that it would blow me up if I wandered closer? Or was this something useful? Its magic reminded me of the wards Sarrlevi had set around the project house, and its aura seemed comforting rather than menacing.

"Exactly what one would expect from a booby trap."

Nonetheless, I walked up to the pedestal. An image formed in my mind of the patio, with Sarrlevi standing in the middle and resting a hand on the dome, prompting energy to extend around it.

Instructions on how to use it?

Not sure if I should trust the thing, I might have left it alone, but a howl came from the trees not far away. I planted my hand on the top of the dome.

As I'd seen, magic swelled from it and wrapped around the patio area before fading from view. It stopped pulsing, but I could sense its magic in place. Flames also appeared in the fire pit, burning heartily despite the lack of logs inside.

"Inviting."

Maybe it was my imagination, but a sense of satisfaction seemed to emanate from the dome. Another image flashed in my mind, one of me this time. I was naked and swinging my hammer at the soap dispenser in the guest room.

"Uh." I well remembered that moment but was perplexed that some artifact on the patio did.

Had Sarrlevi recorded the event somehow? That would be disturbing. Or did the magical furniture in and around his house communicate with each other on some level? Thinking of the housewares singing in Disney's *Beauty and the Beast*, I rubbed the back of my neck, embarrassed at the notion that all of Sarrlevi's magical doodads might know that I'd demolished the soap dispenser.

Fortunately, no further images came from the dome. With what I assumed was a protective barrier in place, I relaxed a bit and let myself walk to the edge of the patio. Beyond a low stone wall, the slope turned into a cliff, dropping off into the ravine. Stars glinted overhead, constellations I'd never seen before. I stared up at them. If I'd had any doubt that Sarrlevi had taken me to another world instead of some remote place on Earth, the stars would have confirmed it.

"They and the scaly wolf-lion," I said.

As I headed for one of the lounges, figuring I could pass the evening on the patio, as long as it was protected, I noticed a hammock made from woven plant fibers strung between two trees.

"Don't elves sleep in anything that doesn't hang?" I asked before remembering Sarrlevi's travel cot.

Though I wasn't drawn to hammocks or anything that didn't offer a solid base, it looked comfortable, so I decided to try it. When I slipped in, lying cautiously back in it, the sides curled up, cocooning me in their grasp.

Alarmed, and imagining the hammock binding me like a larval butterfly, I flailed. My hammer clunked against the ground. The hammock loosened its grip, and the dome flashed again.

I made myself stop fighting, not wanting more of the furniture to believe I was attacking it. After experimenting a little, I decided the hammock hadn't been trying to trap me, just snuggle me in. Though furniture that wanted to do such things was too sentient and intrusive for my tastes, I lay back and attempted to relax and enjoy the night air. Even if predators were howling out there, it was better than being inside with the awful elves.

I vacillated on whether to include Sarrlevi under that description. He'd lied to me, and I still didn't know his real reason for looking for my mother, but I struggled to believe he wanted to kill her. Maybe because I didn't *want* that to be true. Half the time, he seemed decent to me. Hell, *more* than half the time. Yes, he teased me, but that didn't mean he was evil incarnate. Zadie and Tinja teased me too.

It was different with him because I didn't know him that well. And he was an assassin.

"An assassin who keeps helping me." I sighed.

The howling creatures settled down, and the buzz of insects and hoots of night birds returned. It was peaceful but also... lonely. I missed my home and Tinja and being able to call or text people. As the darkness deepened, I decided I missed my mother and father, too, and the relationship my family might have had if the military hadn't messed up our lives all those years ago.

When tears formed in my eyes, I decided I was glad I was alone, that the elves were all too busy with their carnal crap to witness my sadness.

18

I HADN'T PLANNED TO SLEEP IN THE HAMMOCK, BUT AFTER I GOT used to its magical fibers cocooning me, weariness convinced my body to relax enough for slumber. Maybe it wasn't wise after the battle with the predator, but I believed the dome would keep the defenses up as long as someone occupied the patio.

When I woke, it was still dark, but a hint of lightness to the sky made me think dawn approached. I was debating if it would be safe to return to the house when I sensed Sarrlevi standing a few paces away. Alone, thankfully.

Strange that being alone with him no longer bothered me. I *did* wonder how long he'd been standing there.

"You left a *yuthro* dead on my walkway," he said.

That answered my question about whether I'd killed it or knocked it out.

"I didn't know I had to dispose of the bodies after battles here. Don't you have a magical gizmo for that?"

"Not for the outdoors. But I suppose if you're going to visit frequently, I should get something." He stepped closer, and the magical flames still burning in the fire pit highlighted his face and loose pajamas with a deep V that showed part of his chest and collarbones. Fresh scratches marked his skin, and I rolled my eyes, certain elven fingernails had been responsible rather than the claws of a predator. His tone turned dry when he added, "Most of my guests don't kill the local wildlife."

The local wildlife. As if that had been a cute deer or squirrel that had ambled up, looking for treats.

"No? What do elves do when they're attacked on the way to the patio?"

"Use magic to convince the transgressor to leave."

"Well, you know the saying. When the only tool you have is a hammer..."

"You use it to brain your enemies?"

"Something like that. And I'm not planning on visiting you frequently, FYI. This has been an atypical month."

Sarrlevi stepped closer and rested a hand on my shoulder. "Are you all right?"

"Fine. It didn't even scratch me." I looked at his chest but jerked my gaze away, not wanting him to think I was checking him out. He'd been smug ever since the *first* time he'd caught me doing that.

"I know *that*," Sarrlevi said, dry again. He softened his voice to add, "I watched to make sure."

"While you were busy in bed with two women?" I thought about climbing out of the hammock but worried it wouldn't relinquish me easily, and I might dump myself at his feet.

"The wards alerted me when you left the house. I wanted to ensure nothing happened to you."

"They must have loved that," I muttered.

"I didn't tell them. Since you handled your battle without need for intervention, they did not need to know they didn't have my undivided attention."

I didn't know what to say to that, not wanting any details of how their night had gone. If I was honest with myself, I would admit I wished their night hadn't happened at all, but who Sarrlevi chose to have sex with didn't matter to me. Or at least it shouldn't.

"What I meant," Sarrlevi said, "is that I want to make sure Slehvyra didn't threaten you or hurt you. Given what she told the dragons, I'm not positive she's not behind the reward out for your hammer. It seems I vexed her the last time she visited."

I shrugged. "She was snotty again, but she didn't hurt me."

Not physically anyway. Her words had made me feel like I was back in school, the outcast that the boys all ignored while fawning over the pretty girls like her. But I wasn't going to complain about that to *him*.

I did, however, find myself asking, "Why do you put up with them? I get that they're hot, but they're jerks to you, and you're an assassin. You're *dangerous*. I've seen you fight. Don't you ever off people for being dicks? Even if it's not an assignment?" I couldn't say I wanted the answer to be *yes*, but it seemed like something an assassin would do.

Sarrlevi didn't answer at first—maybe he was digesting my Earth vernacular. "I have learned through past experience that *offing* people from powerful families or with powerful allies isn't wise, not when you yourself dare not trust many people."

"Because you're ostracized?" I asked quietly, though I didn't expect him to answer or admit that. He hadn't before.

"For many reasons. It's possible she and others like her will push me too far one day. I've accomplished most of my career goals, and I've started to care less about my fate lately. Once my mother is no more..." He shifted his hand from my shoulder to the top of my head, surprising me by brushing his fingers through my hair.

He'd done that in the project house when I'd been working on my carving. Then, it had been clear he'd been manipulating me, trying to get me to agree to help him. Now, I didn't know what his motivation was, what he wanted. If anything, the touch seemed absent, for he was gazing off into the ravine as he spoke.

I hated to admit it, especially if it *was* absent and he barely knew he was doing it, but it felt amazing. I wished he'd spent the night on the patio, hanging out with me, instead of with the frost bitches.

"My death would disturb her," Sarrlevi added. "She's been disturbed enough in her life. After she's gone, perhaps I won't care anymore. She's the only family I have left."

"Why is she disturbed? Because of your father's... demise?" I wouldn't have pried, but he *had* brought it up. And he'd shared the other day that his father had been the first person he killed.

Sarrlevi continued to gaze into the ravine and didn't answer.

"Sorry," I said. "It's none of my business. I shouldn't have asked."

"Why did you?"

"You seemed like maybe you needed to talk. And I'm a curious sort." More than that, I was trying to figure him out. "I guess I shouldn't be curious about an assassin though."

"No? Is it more appropriate to be curious about other professionals? Other plumbers?" He gave me a faint sidelong smile.

Great, he finally looked at me, and it was to tease me. "Oh, yeah. I ask them *everything*. Like is their pipe wrench, their basin wrench, or their adjustable wrench their favorite tool? A girl has to know."

"You are blunt and irreverent."

"Better than being bitchy and manipulative." I glanced at the house, half-expecting the ex-princess to realize he'd left and storm out naked, having a hissy fit because Sarrlevi was down here with me.

"Yes," he surprised me by agreeing and brushed his fingers through my hair again.

A zing of happy warmth went through me. It wasn't as if he'd said he adored my personality, but at least he'd implied I was better than they were.

So, why had he spent the night with *them*?

This time, I was the one to look toward the ravine, not seeing much as I tried to tamp down emotions I didn't want to have. I barely knew him. It didn't make sense to care, to wish the gentle touching of my head would lead to something more.

"To answer your question," Sarrlevi said, "I'd like to think my father's death was a relief to her, especially since it had been an arranged marriage, and I don't think she loved him. But I don't know. He always made it clear that he'd expected to marry a princess, not a simple noble far removed from the throne. He never stopped taking his disappointment out on her. Physically. And on my sister and me, children who would never be sufficient for his ambitions. He was brutal, bitter, and a drunk. But he also had great power, which made him exceedingly dangerous. To his family as well as his enemies. And he couldn't control his temper. He could *never* control his temper." Sarrlevi's tone had turned cold, his hand stilling. "One angry night, he killed my sister with his power, knocked her into a tree so hard that she never rose again. He almost killed my mother too. After that, I killed *him*. It wasn't in a duel, though we faced each other fairly. I was too angry to utter the official words of challenge. Because of that... it was deemed murder by our people. I was driven off Veleshna Var."

I stared up at him, more surprised that he'd answered than that he had that in his past. "That must have been awful for your mother. And for you."

"For her, yes. By that point, I'd been training for and planning to kill him, so I wasn't shocked, not like she was, though I regretted that I didn't strike sooner. Soon enough to save my sister. I hadn't thought I was yet proficient enough with blades and magic to best him, and I'd hesitated numerous times." His voice filled with self-loathing. "I was a coward, almost as afraid of him as our mother was, but after he killed Veela... I snapped."

His body had gone rigid again, the same way it had when Slehvyra had been manipulating him, and I could feel the tension in his hand.

"I doubt you've ever been a coward, and, don't take this the wrong way, but I'd prefer your fingers not be that close to my neck when you're reliving your dark past."

He removed his hand and clasped the other behind his back, though his body remained tense. "No? Do you not find me *stimulating* when I'm angry?"

His sneer and the way he said the word made me think it was a quote, or at least the translation of one. I glanced toward his house again, though it was barely visible through the leaves.

"Not really. Are they still up there?"

"Sleeping."

"Too tired to go complain to the king that you're plotting things?"

"That was the goal."

"Well, if their screaming was any indication, they used up a lot of energy last night."

"I suppose."

Since it didn't look like he would return to rubbing my head, and I refused to ask him to, I gingerly shifted my legs out of the hammock. Fortunately, its magic sensed that I wanted to rise and it loosened its hold. I managed to get out of it without falling at his feet. But maybe he wouldn't have noticed. He was back to gazing pensively at the ravine.

I wondered if his unwillingness to strike at the manipulative elves had more to do with his past than their powerful families. An aversion to treating women badly after watching his father abuse his mother? He'd mentioned that specifically as a loathsome characteristic in that diplomat he'd assassinated.

"If you ever want *me* to thump them for you, I'll be happy to." The last time I'd been at his house, he'd mused that he wouldn't mind seeing that. "You've thumped orcs and werewolves and shaggy gorilla-monsters for me, after all."

His faint smile returned, but he said, "You would also be wise not to make enemies of those from powerful families."

"I have no doubt, but we both know I'm not wise."

"No? Regular consumption of *dokdok* cheese is supposed to improve gut health, benefit the immune system, and impart serenity and wisdom."

"Really?"

"So the dwarves who make it say. I'll bring you more if you wish."

"Hell, yes." Impulsively, I hugged him.

He stiffened, and I realized, even if he *had* been fondling my head, he might not want my arms wrapped around him. Should I release him and apologize? Spring back? I would probably trip and tangle myself in the hammock...

Before I'd decided, he loosened and patted me on the back. It wasn't exactly a return hug, but he didn't push me away either. "I forgot how much cheese moves you."

"Yeah." I released him and leaned back. "Especially wisdom-inducing cheese."

His hand shifted to my shoulder, but I couldn't tell if he wanted to keep me from moving away or keep me at arm's length. The latter, no doubt, since *he* hadn't been the hugger. I told myself to step back out of his space, but it had grown brighter, the lingering fire and predawn light making the handsome angles of his face easy to see now. The *appealing* handsome angles. The captivating intensity of his blue eyes made me want to lean in for a kiss.

But I wouldn't. He hadn't been into the hug. And I... still had a lot of questions about him.

I took that step back. "The king didn't send you to look for my mother."

"No." Sarrlevi didn't sound surprised that I'd brought it up.

"You haven't spoken to him in a long time, have you? Because he knows what his youngest daughter hired you to do, and maybe he even wonders if you succeeded."

"If he believed I had, he would have tried to kill me long ago."

"Why did you tell me he hired you?"

"So you would believe I wanted to find your mother to help her."

"Why *do* you want to find her?" I watched his face, anticipating more lies, though I longed for him to tell me the truth, for it to be something he felt he could trust me with. Like that story about his family.

"I want to see my mother again before she dies," he said quietly. "She has an illness for which there is no cure."

That had to be the truth—Zavryd had mentioned it—but...

"I don't understand. I mean, I'm sure your mother would like to see you too, and I'm sorry she's dying, but how does that tie in with the dwarves?"

With *me*, I added silently but didn't say. I didn't want to sound selfish by making this about me and my mother.

"King Eireth loathes me. Not without reason. He denied my requests to come back and see my mother, and since she lives within the protection of the palace, I cannot simply show up there. I thought that by helping King Ironhelm, who is an ally of Eireth, find his lost daughter, it might make a difference. It is not exoneration I seek, as I do not regret the choice I made long ago that started me toward this career, but perhaps if I do *enough* for the royals, for those Eireth considers friends, he would permit me to visit her. I do know Ironhelm has been looking for your mother for a long time. He's asked numerous people to find her, and even offered a reward to those known to be good at locating people. If I succeeded when others failed, and if I... essentially set right what happened as a result of my taking that assignment forty years ago, perhaps it would mean something to him. To *them*."

It wasn't a quest to atone for his sins—it didn't sound like he cared about that—but if it was the truth, I couldn't blame him for taking it on. And if I ended up learning more about my mother, even if she'd passed, maybe I would even appreciate that he had.

"I hope you succeed and get to see her again," I said.

He didn't seem to hear. His face was grim as he once again gazed toward the ravine. Lost in memories of the past?

"But I'll be sad," I added, hoping to lighten his mood, "when you've achieved your goal and your cheese delivery service stops."

For a long moment, he didn't reply, his face not changing. Then it softened, and he looked at me. "But not vegetable delivery, I believe." He arched his eyebrows. "I noticed the macerated pieces spat into my trash bin."

That made me blush. I'd assumed a magical gizmo would empty the trash, that his haughty elfness wouldn't deign to glance in the bin himself. Maybe I should have hawked the discards out the window.

"They were stringy and chewy," I mumbled.

"Do you like any vegetables?"

"Of course. I'm not a health heathen."

His eyebrows arched higher.

"I like good nonchewy vegetables that don't have weird textures. Like carrots, parsnips, radishes... Oh, and my grand-mother makes the most amazing taro chips." I hesitated, not certain taro counted as a vegetable. It was probably a starch, like a potato. As Zadie had informed me on numerous occasions, pota-toes didn't count as vegetables, and French fries most *certainly* didn't count.

"Those are all root vegetables, aren't they?" His eyes glinted, and some of his usual smugness returned, as if he had already known that would be my preference. "Of course someone with dwarven blood would like vegetables that grow underground."

I wanted to object to this, if only because he sounded so certain about his hypothesis, but I paused, not certain if I had ever met a root vegetable I didn't like. Turnips were a little sketchy, but I would eat them. They were better than asparagus—and stringy elven greens *like* asparagus.

"Next time, I'll ensure I have some on hand," he said.

"Careful. Entice me like that, and I'll hug you again."

"I might allow it."

"Oh?" I decided to try. This time, he returned the embrace and rested his head atop mine. Maybe after telling me the dreadful stuff about his family, he *needed* a hug.

I leaned into it and found myself noticing the muscular arms around me, the hard swell of his chest, the strength of his shoulders. I swallowed and told myself to release him before I did something stupid. After the night he'd had, I was sure he didn't have sex or even kissing on his mind. Especially not with me.

With unexpected emotion tightening my throat, I stepped back.

"Sarrlevi?" I looked at his collarbones instead of into his eyes.

"Yes?"

"I want to trust you." It seemed a vulnerable and silly thing to admit, but hadn't he let himself be vulnerable with me? Maybe this time, he wouldn't smirk and say something smug.

"You shouldn't," was what he said, his voice serious.

"Because you're an assassin, or because you're still lying to me?"

"Because I'm an ass. You've said so yourself."

I had. Numerous times. I refused to feel bad about that, but maybe now... I believed that claim a little less.

As if he knew my thoughts, Sarrlevi brushed his fingers to my cheek, letting them linger.

A surge of power came from somewhere in front of the house, and he lowered his arm and turned in that direction.

"That's dwarven magic." He extended a hand toward the walkway. "A portal. You had better go see your visitors."

I grabbed my hammer, eagerness and uncertainty mingling in my belly. "You're not coming?"

"It might go better for you if I don't, but I won't be far." He nodded encouragingly. "If anything happens, I'll come help."

My throat grew tight again. Whether I would admit it to him or not, I decided he *wasn't* an ass.

Further, something about the way he watched me, nodding for me to head toward the portal I couldn't yet see but could sense, made me think he'd sacrificed more than his dignity and a night of restful sleep for this.

19

TREPIDATION ACCOMPANIED ME UP THE WALKWAY TOWARD THE FRONT of the house and the plateau beyond. Sarrlevi had implied King Ironhelm was a good man—a good *dwarf*—and that it was worth it for me to meet him, but how well did he know my grandfather? It sounded like it might have been forty years since he'd visited the dwarven court, and, even then, how often would an elf assassin have interacted with the king and his people?

"Just long enough to take an assignment from the treacherous Princess Barothla?" I muttered, glancing back.

But the foliage now hid the patio and Sarrlevi from view. And he'd disappeared from my senses as well. What *did* register to my senses were the auras of full-blooded dwarves. A *lot* of full-blooded dwarves. The portal also remained open. Because more would come through?

The sun rose as the plateau I'd seen the night before came into view through the trees, and the morning light glinted on shields, drawn swords and axes, and plate armor. No fewer than forty dwarven warriors stood on the flat surface overlooking the forest and Sarrlevi's house, and they all faced the walkway—faced *me*.

Had the king brought them all because he believed Sarrlevi was a threat? Or was it possible he thought *I* might be one? That this was some ruse and I would try something?

My nerves were already on edge, but now sweat broke out all over my body, my hands growing slick against the haft of my hammer. Of my *mother's* hammer. As I approached, it occurred to me that the dwarves might object to me having it. What if they didn't recognize me as her daughter? Even if I'd inherited her strength and stamina, I didn't look a lot like her. I had my father's bronze skin and dark hair and eyes. What if they didn't have the equivalent of Sarrlevi's blood-testing kit and couldn't tell by my aura that I was a relative?

Between one step and the next, magic buzzed over my skin, making my nerves tingle. I paused, then realized what had happened. I'd stepped outside of the defenses protecting the grounds.

More anxious than ever, I scanned the stoic faces that watched as I climbed the path up to the plateau. Most of those faces were grim and bearded. Their hair ranged from brown to red, with a few closer to blond, and a couple gray. They had similar broad features, bulbous noses, and stout builds, with few reaching five feet in height. If there were any females among them, I couldn't pick them out, but the plate armor would have hidden curves, and dwarven women could reputedly be bearded.

I tried to tell which one was my grandfather. One of the gray-haired ones? Given the longevity of dwarves, I didn't know if I could assume that. When I'd seen his portrait in Sarrlevi's device, his hair had been gray and red. It could have been an old picture, but I didn't see anyone who matched him.

Several of the dwarves looked from me toward the house, and I glanced back, wondering if Sarrlevi had decided to follow me out after all. But they seemed to simply be studying the architecture. Or—more likely—its defenses.

One of the armored dwarves beckoned to me with his axe, his face grave but not irritated or even suspicious. He called something in his tongue. I recognized the word *come* but nothing else and tapped Val's translation charm before continuing.

Was *he* my grandfather? Several dwarves were looking to him, as if for cues, and he had gray hair tied back from his shoulders, his beard and mustache tidily trimmed. He also bristled with weapons, carrying no fewer than six throwing axes in addition to the large two-handed blade he held. Daggers were also strapped to his armored thighs. He looked more like a general than a king, but who knew what dwarven royalty preferred?

The walkway wound up the plateau, the view of the forest and the ravine beyond growing impressive as I climbed. I glanced toward the house again, wondering where Sarrlevi had gone, and spotted the elven females out on the covered porch in front of the door.

Though they'd kept their part of the bargain and arranged for the dwarves to come, I couldn't bring myself to feel grateful toward them. Not when the price had been Sarrlevi having to lower himself to have sex with them. Distance made it impossible to tell, but I was certain *they* weren't covered in fingernail gouges.

Even with forty dwarves atop the plateau, it wasn't crowded, and the thought that this was a landing pad as well as a portal spot returned to my mind. A few dragons could have fit up there, not that I expected they visited elven assassins often. Though one must have when he'd hired Sarrlevi to kill Val.

"I am General Yagthor of Legion Oakmoor," the dwarf who'd spoken before said. "Can you understand our tongue?"

"Only a little," I admitted, sticking to English and hoping they also had translation charms. "My mother died when I was very little."

"She *is* dead then?" Yagthor scowled and looked at his men. "The assassin got her?"

Dark glowers turned again toward the house, accompanied by mutters of, "Always knew," and, "Should have killed him decades ago."

I shook my head, fear for Sarrlevi rising within me. "It was the Earth government—their military—that was responsible." I didn't mind throwing *them* under the bus. "Sarrlevi never found her."

"So he says," Yagthor said, his tone as dark as his glower. "But that he *tried* to kill Princess Rodarska is crime enough."

That drew more mutters and a lot of nods.

"Ah, did you come for him? Or me?" I wasn't sure, but I didn't think any of them were the king.

Yagthor looked me up and down. Searching for a resemblance? His gaze lingered on the hammer, and he let out a long wistful sigh. "The princess made that weapon. It is as beautiful as all her work was. She was too young to die, too kind to be targeted by an assassin."

"It wasn't the assassin who got her," I said again, worried these dwarves had decided to take revenge for the mission Sarrlevi had accepted. Maybe the king wasn't coming at all.

But if that was why they were here, why had they waited so long? The king hadn't *just* found out about his youngest daughter's treachery, had he? And that Sarrlevi had been involved?

A jolt went through me. Maybe they'd known all along, but they *hadn't* known where to find Sarrlevi. Until now. Until he'd reached out, trying to arrange a meeting for me. What if this house's location was known to few save for the elves? Maybe he usually went to his clients instead of having them come to him. It had sounded like Slehvyra had chosen this spot for the meeting. And she was in the middle of being petty and punishing Sarrlevi...

Yagthor looked toward another warrior at his side, one with fewer weapons who wore numerous trinkets around his neck and others embedded in or dangling from his armor. Maybe he was the dwarven version of a priest or shaman. Other than a few stories my mother had told me, I knew little about their religion or those who served their gods.

The priest nodded to the general. "She is a mongrel, with half-human blood, but she also carries the blood of the king."

I sighed at the irritating term, but at least the dwarf said it without a sneer or disdain, as if he were only stating the fact. "Is he... coming? I hoped to meet him."

Presumably, they knew that, but I had no idea what the elven ex-princess had told them.

"He is coming," Yagthor said, "but know that a child of mixed blood may not rule over our people. You will never have any claim on the throne of Dun Kroth."

I grimaced, hoping the elf hadn't implied that I cared about *that*. "I would just like to meet him and ask him about my mother. I know so little of her and nothing of her life before she came to Earth. I'm curious."

He glanced at the hammer again. Their interest in it made me uneasy.

A shimmer rippled through the silvery surface of the portal—it had remained open longer than I'd seen one do so before. Three more dwarves stepped out. A female wearing copious trinkets and a male armed and armored similarly to the general stood to either side of an older male dwarf with a tangled bush of gray-shot frizzy red hair that stuck out in all directions from under a helmet with horns. His beard was almost as wild. Had he not been wearing plate armor of gorgeous craftsmanship, with a gilded emblem emblazoned across the chest, I might have thought he'd wandered out from a night's sleep under a bridge. The emblem—or family crest?—featured crossed hammers under a mountain, similar to one of the runes engraved in my hammer.

His eyes—a striking green that were exactly the color of my mother's—crinkled when he saw me, and he smiled warmly. Nerves continued to assail me, but my heart lightened with hope.

It looked like King Ironhelm, my grandfather, might want to see me.

The portal extinguished behind him, and the rest of the dwarves parted to make room for him to approach me. I swallowed, surreptitiously wiped my sweaty palms, and held his gaze as he walked toward me.

"Daughter of my daughter," he said in Dwarven, the charm translating. Later, I would hug Val for thinking to lend it to me. "I am most pleased to learn of your existence and see that you are well." He looked me up and down, perhaps to confirm that I *was* well, even as he cast a quick dark glance toward the house. When his gaze returned, it went to the hammer, and a hint of sadness shadowed his eyes. But he shook his head and returned his focus to my face. "I'm glad my daughter's work was not lost and that something of her has survived."

His bodyguards watched me intently as he came closer, and I wondered if I should have set the hammer aside, but Ironhelm approached without hesitation. He gripped my shoulders and looked up—amusement, or maybe *bemusement*, entering his eyes, when he had to do so. I was only a few inches taller than him though. It wasn't as if Dad's human blood had turned me into a Women's NBA candidate.

"Me too. Uhm, I'm Matti. Mataalii Puletasi. I don't know if anyone told you."

"They did not. The elf called you *mongrel*." His mouth twisted.

The priest who'd recently used the word frowned and looked at his boots.

"She also implied you're fishing for an inheritance if not a room in the palace." His brushy eyebrows twitched, though he still sounded amused, not like he believed it.

I hoped that meant he also thought Slehvyra was a manipulative ass. "A room? No, sir. I have a house in Lynnwood. Er, on Earth. And a career. I remodel homes and build and carve things.

One day, I hope to be able to build houses from scratch." I watched him warily, wondering if a dwarf king would consider that worthwhile work.

"Engineering is an honorable profession and considered worthy for a dwarf." He smiled and nodded with approval.

Had the translation gone awry? I didn't consider myself an *engineer* and didn't even have a college degree. I didn't know if I should correct him. Though it shouldn't have mattered what a stranger thought, even one who shared my blood, I found myself longing to keep his approval.

"You may have a knack for even more," Ironhelm said. "For enchanting that which you build."

I couldn't imagine what an *enchanted* staircase or custom cabinets would do, but *Beauty and the Beast* came to mind again.

He pointed at the hammer. "You know Rodarska, your mother, made that weapon, right?"

"I... understand she made quite a few things." Remembering that Artie hadn't been willing to speak of the reactor, I didn't bring it up, and I still didn't have any idea if my mother had made that or simply turned it on.

"Yes, she was very talented." The sadness returned to his eyes.

He waved toward the edge of the plateau and gestured for his guards to stay back. They didn't look happy about the command but did so, letting him draw me away. For a private conversation?

He propped his fists on his hips and gazed toward Sarrlevi's house—or maybe beyond it to the view of the ravine.

I stopped next to him and also looked in that direction. "I don't know what the elf chick, er, ex-princess said about me—nothing nice, I'm sure—but I don't want anything from you, sir. I was hoping you might tell me about my mother. Some things have come up of late—" I kept from mentioning Sarrlevi "—and it's had me wondering about her a lot more again. I didn't actually see her die, and lately... I've wondered if there's any possibility that she didn't."

Ironhelm nodded, as if he wasn't surprised at all. "Understand-able. I have also been wondering anew about her these past three years. That is when I learned what my *other* daughter did. And that Rodarska originally fled our world because she learned that assassin was after her." He growled, losing all of his earlier humor, and pointed at the house.

"He didn't get her," I hurried to say.

"That he *tried* is crime enough. She never would have been forced to flee her home if he hadn't."

The elven females remained on the porch, and they watched us curiously. I still didn't sense Sarrlevi and was glad he hadn't come with me. My earlier thought returned, that Ironhelm might have brought all these people along, not because he worried I was a threat, but because Sarrlevi was. Maybe he even intended to *attack* Sarrlevi.

"Had I known where to find him earlier, I would have brought an army to raze his home and destroy him," he continued. "But he has numerous bolt-holes, and this place isn't known to many. It *wasn't*." He looked at me. "Why did he bring you here? And invite *me* here to meet you?"

"I believe the elf females chose this place." I debated how to explain that Slehvyra might have deliberately set Sarrlevi up to get in trouble, but he spoke again first.

"It could be a trap. Has he done anything to you?"

"No." I lifted a hand. "He's been helping me."

"*Helping* you?"

"He risked you learning where he lives to arrange this meeting for me. He wants..." I hesitated, not certain how much to say, how much to share of what Sarrlevi had revealed to me. It wasn't my story to tell, and even though I wanted to trust him and believe him, he'd once again said that I shouldn't. It was possible he was still lying to me or hadn't told me everything. "I think he regrets the choice he made to take that assignment and wants to make amends," I said, though Sarrlevi hadn't said that. I didn't know if he regretted any of the assignments he'd taken over the years. He just wanted to find a way to see the only family he had left.

Ironhelm scoffed. "Trust me, girl. That one regrets nothing. He's killed our kind numerous times over the centuries. And he's killed his own kind too. He is a heartless assassin and cares about nothing and nobody but himself."

Even though the words made sense, I couldn't match them to the person who'd let me hug him that morning. And who'd hugged me back. But maybe it hadn't meant anything, and he'd just enjoyed having someone with actual boobs squished against his chest.

I snorted in self-deprecation, doubting *that* was it. If he wanted boobs, he could find a gorgeous woman with some squish to her; of that I had no doubt.

"You do not believe me?" Ironhelm asked, misreading my snort.

"I'm not as sure as you are. He's helped me several times this past month. I know it's because he thinks I might be able to lead him to my mother—"

That was the wrong thing to say. Ironhelm's eyebrows clashed together, and a storm cloud roiled across his face.

"To finish the job. As I said." He gripped my shoulder, harder than before, his whole body tense. "You are fortunate to have survived your encounters with him so far, but don't worry. He'll soon trouble you no more."

A grim sense of foreboding trampled through me.

"What do you mean?" I whispered.

"If Rodarska is on your world, however, the assassin may be correct that you *are* the logical one to find her."

"I'm trying to do so."

"Good. Good." His gaze lowered to my hammer. "Some of my advisors—" he looked back to the general and especially the priest who'd called me a mongrel, "—don't believe you're a worthy successor for her hammer."

I lifted my chin, though I wanted to ask again what he meant about Sarrlevi, not defend myself. "They don't even know me."

"Exactly what I said. *I* believe that if you are Rodarska's daughter, you *must* be worthy." He smiled at me, though he remained tense and glanced toward the house, as if he feared Sarrlevi was nearby, spying on us.

Remembering his promise to watch out for me, I suspected he *was.*

"She was—maybe still is?—a kind soul, a strong warrior, and a great enchanter. Your human blood will mean you'll be less powerful, but greatness is not determined merely by one's magical and physical abilities." Ironhelm nodded to himself, and my relief at not having to defend myself to him was replaced by the worry that he might be giving me too much credit, simply because he'd loved his daughter. "If she lives, you will find her," he added. "Even if she's passed, if you could... bring back her remains for a proper burial..." He swallowed, moisture in his eyes.

Sarrlevi might not have spoken to Ironhelm, but he'd known exactly what the king wanted.

"That would put my soul to rest. For so many years, I've wondered and hoped and not known if I should give up or not." Ironhelm sighed. "If you can do this, that will prove to everyone that you are worthy of her hammer." He looked over at his troops again.

"I'll try, but... what if I can't?" My fears that they would take it back returned.

"You will do it," he said firmly. "They will see, and they will not try to take it from you."

Had that been on the table? I caught the priest and general

exchanging looks. *Many* of the dwarves were exchanging looks. Hell, how many of them wanted to pry the hammer from my grip? The priest might have been the only one to voice the word mongrel, but what if they all thought I was a substandard being? Not worthy to touch my mother's weapon?

"Do you know of its commands?" Ironhelm asked. "I don't know all my daughter imbued into it, but try *vishgronik* if you haven't already." He smiled faintly. "She used to cry that as she threw it, and after it landed, it returned to her grip."

"Thank you."

"You'll learn more in time, especially if she lives and you can find her. In the meantime, I'll ensure that the assassin doesn't impede you. He won't trouble you again in any way."

I opened my mouth to say he hadn't troubled me, but magic plucked at my senses as another portal formed.

Ironhelm nodded, as if he'd expected it. More dwarves coming? To tear down Sarrlevi's defenses and raze his home?

No, this portal felt different, its magic created by someone from another species than the dwarves. I shifted uneasily. It reminded me of Zavryd's aura, of *dragon* magic.

No sooner had the thought occurred than a dragon flew out. *Two* dragons. Though one was black with violet eyes, neither was Zavryd. The other had startlingly bright purple—no, lilac—scales.

"Why are they here?" I whispered, the nods of the dwarves making me even more uneasy. They'd expected this.

The dragons flew around the plateau, looking out over the forest and at Sarrlevi's house.

"To collect the assassin for something that is long overdue," Ironhelm said grimly. "Punishment and rehabilitation."

20

"Punishment and rehabilitation?" I blurted, staring at the circling dragons. "What does *that* mean?"

"For seven hundred and thirty-four days, he will be punished physically and mentally by a device that will keep him alive during the ordeal," Ironhelm said grimly. "He will endure pain equal to his crimes, enough to make him regret killing people, to feel what his victims felt as they died. Then, the dragons will erase his memories and stamp a more pliant and acceptable personality onto his mind."

I stared at him in horror. "It would be more humane to kill him."

"Normally, I agree with many of the other races that the dragon idea of punishment and rehabilitation is cruel, but in the assassin's case, I believe it is appropriate. He has killed *hundreds* of people over the years, girl. If not thousands."

"Didn't at least some of those people deserve it? Weren't they criminals themselves?" Normally, I wouldn't have defended Sarrlevi, but that dragon punishment sounded awful.

"My daughter wasn't a criminal," Ironhelm said, raising his

voice for the first time as anger flashed in his eyes. "Nor did she *deserve* it."

"No, I know. I'm sorry. I didn't mean her. But he didn't kill her, and he's not trying to now."

We shall find out, a female voice spoke into my mind. The lilac-scaled dragon. *We will scour his mind for the truth before beginning his punishment. We will find out if he slew the dwarf princess.* She rotated her head on her long neck to look at my grandfather. *We will also find out if he has plans to assassinate you, King Ironhelm.*

"He doesn't!" I called toward them, though I didn't know if they understood English. I attempted to project the thoughts mentally as well. "The elven female said that to blackmail him, to force him to dance on her strings. She said she'd tell you the truth today, but only if he *pleased* her adequately in bed."

Dozens of dwarves curled their lips. Even the *dragons* seemed to curl their lips, such that they had them. Maybe suggesting that Sarrlevi was hot to the ladies wasn't appropriate when dealing with beings from different species.

"I heard them talking to him." I raised imploring hands. Never had I thought I would so ardently try to defend Sarrlevi, but no matter what he'd done, he didn't deserve to be tortured for two years before having his brain wiped. What the hell kind of sci-fi-movie torment was *that*? They'd steal his memories, his identity, everything he was. It was worse than death. "Slehvyra was *black-mailing* him," I repeated for emphasis. "You need to scour *her* mind."

I thrust my finger toward the two elves, both of them leaning casually against pillars, no doubt using their magic to monitor our meeting. Watching it like moviegoers noshing popcorn. They didn't appear concerned in the least when I singled them out.

Mind scouring is painful, the lilac dragon said. The other, a big male with a powerful build, hadn't spoken. *It is generally reserved for enemies or those who are suspected of plotting and* becoming *enemies.*

"Sarrlevi isn't plotting against you," I said. "Or the dwarven king."

We shall see.

The two dragons banked to face Sarrlevi's home, and immense power swirled in the air around them. Though I wanted to keep shouting at them and find something I could say to change their minds about Sarrlevi, I couldn't help but quail and step back. Their power was terrifying. My whole body shuddered involuntarily.

With a great unleashing of magical energy, an attack whooshed toward the house like a hurricane gale.

"No!" I shouted, envisioning it being torn apart and hurled over the cliff. What if Sarrlevi was inside?

"Easy, daughter of my daughter." Ironhelm rested his hand on my shoulder again, his grip gentle this time. "It is not wise to interfere with the justice of dragons."

The dragons' combined power didn't blow the house to pieces, at least not yet, but it railed at the magical defenses around the domicile, and I had little doubt that it would succeed in tearing them down. Even a powerful elf was nothing compared to a dragon, much less *two* dragons.

"The justice that *you* called for?" I didn't know if Ironhelm had, but I couldn't keep the accusation out of my voice.

This wasn't right, damn it.

"Not I." He glanced at his priest and general again. "But I do not disagree with it. An assassin shouldn't be allowed in the Cosmic Realms. None who ply that cruel trade should be. This is for the best."

"No," I whispered, my senses telling me the home's defenses were weakening.

Bursts of magic to the left and right of the plateau startled me.

Many dwarves turned, combining their power to raise an invisible barrier around the area. Only my senses told me it was there, a protective dome over the plateau and everyone on it.

The dragons halted their attack, also looking toward the bursts. Magical rockets shot out of the trees toward the dragons. It seemed Sarrlevi's home could do more than defend itself.

The dragons reinforced the dwarven barrier with their own magic, and the rockets burst when they struck it, exploding with great might. Though the defenses held, the ground under our feet quaked from the shockwaves. I envisioned parts of the plateau shearing off and tumbling toward the forest floor. Or maybe the entire thing would collapse.

That elf dares *attack dragons?* the black-scaled male demanded. *And the dwarven king?*

"They must be automatic defenses." I couldn't know that for certain, but I couldn't imagine Sarrlevi being foolish enough to hide behind a tree with a remote-control device and pick a fight with this group.

The dragons roared and renewed their attack on the house as more rockets fired at the plateau.

Come to us, elf assassin, one called telepathically, magical compulsion in the words making *me* take two steps toward them before I caught myself. *Come forth and accept your punishment.*

Another shudder coursed through the plateau.

"Sire!" The general ran up to Ironhelm. "Let's get you out of here. The dragons will handle Sarrlevi, as we asked them to do."

They'd *asked* the dragons to do this?

Even though the dwarves didn't know the whole truth—I doubted even *I* knew the whole truth—I couldn't help but throw a betrayed look at Ironhelm, stung on Sarrlevi's behalf. He'd believed Ironhelm was one of the good guys.

Maybe a *good guy* was supposed to try to rid the universe of assassins, but not Sarrlevi, damn it. Even if I'd only just decided he was worth knowing and caring about, he was. And he hadn't done all the things they were accusing him of.

"Yes," Ironhelm told his general. "Come, granddaughter. We'll take you to Dun Kroth, then help you back to your home when it's safe."

When would they consider it *safe*? When Sarrlevi was dead?

"I'll be fine here." I stepped back as more rockets exploded against the barrier around us.

The ground quaked again, not only under the plateau, but under the house as well. A result of Sarrlevi's magic? Or the dragons'? I couldn't tell, but the elven females had gone from watching the meeting as entertainment to being concerned. The ex-princess flung up her arm, and a portal formed near the front door.

Apparently, the house's defenses only kept people from opening portals to come in, not from forming them to leave. Either that, or the dragons had damaged those defenses enough that they no longer worked. With nobody trying to stop them, the two elves sprang through their portal and disappeared.

Envisioning the cliff crumbling and the house sloughing into the ravine, I ran toward the lilac dragon. I had no delusions of waving my hammer or otherwise threatening her, but I had to convince them to leave Sarrlevi alone. They were only here because Sarrlevi had been helping me. And because of the stupid story the elf females had made up, the females who were no longer on this world and available to be questioned.

But the dragons could question *me*. I'd heard the elves talking, the ex-princess's confession.

"Wait." I lifted an arm toward the lilac dragon while keeping my hammer down at my side. "You can scour *my* thoughts."

"No." Ironhelm had run after me, and he gripped my arm and pointed toward a new portal that had formed, the work of one of the dwarves. "You don't know what you ask. Mind scouring is painful as well as invasive. *Very* painful."

"I want them to see that Sarrlevi was never after you," I told him as I looked up at the dragons.

The black-scaled one hadn't ceased his attacks, and trees with rockets mounted in them blew up or caught fire before they could launch. The lilac dragon, however, looked down at us.

"Read my thoughts," I called to her. "You can't trust those two elves. They *tricked* you." I flung my arm toward where the females had been, distressed that the dragons hadn't kept them from leaving. "And it's not the first time, is it? Didn't they or their family plot against you once? Why trust them in this matter?"

Their kind have *plotted against the Stormforges before.* The lilac dragon looked toward her colleague.

But another quake shook the plateau, rocks tumbling down its sides. Several huge boulders buried a section of the walkway that wound up the side. For a second, I thought I sensed Sarrlevi's familiar aura down there, but it vanished before I could focus on it. Had it been my imagination?

"Sire!" Several of the dwarves ran forward and grabbed the king. Half of their group had already left, following the general's orders, but the rest refused to go without Ironhelm. "It's not safe to stay when dragons are throwing such powerful magic around."

"My granddaughter." Ironhelm sank into a low crouch, resisting his soldiers' attempts to tug him away, and I sensed him using magic to further anchor himself. Once more, he pointed toward the portal. "Come with me."

"I can't." I met his eyes. "Sarrlevi has been helping me, and I can't leave him here to be accused and threatened and worse." Punished and *mind-wiped*—rehabilitation, my ass. "I'll let them mind scour me, and they'll see the truth. Then Sarrlevi will help me find my mother. I know he will."

Ironhelm shook his head and gathered more magic. My feet lightened as his power wrapped around me. Was he going to forcefully levitate me through the portal?

No, I couldn't abandon Sarrlevi to the dragons. What if they caught him, and I never saw him again?

"Read my mind!" I shouted at the lilac dragon in frustration.

Ironhelm winced and glanced at her. No doubt, everyone in the Realms knew it was idiotic to yell at a dragon, but, right then, I didn't care.

Rock snapped, and the wooden walls of the house tore free from the ground. The roof collapsed, even as the office blew skyward, the ground beneath it heaving upward, as if it were a volcano.

The lilac dragon had stopped assailing the compound, but the black was gleefully tearing it to pieces now that they'd destroyed its defenses. A few lingering rockets fired, but the dragons had found and destroyed most of those as well.

My feet completely lifted off the ground, and Ironhelm jogged with his men toward the portal, his magic tugging me along like a kite on a string.

"Lilac dragon!" I yelled, for she was still watching me. Contemplatively? I couldn't tell, but I kept trying. "Read my mind. See the truth. *Know* who wants to betray you."

The dragon sprang toward the retreating dwarves. One raised his axe and leaped defensively in front of Ironhelm, but most scattered, afraid she would land on them with her deadly talons.

But she landed next to *me*, and her magic overrode Ironhelm's and squashed me to the ground. She lifted one of those taloned feet and pinned me.

Fear froze me, and I forgot to breathe.

I am Zondia'qareshi of the Stormforge Clan, she announced.

Had I pissed her off by not calling her by name? By not *knowing* it?

I still had my hammer and almost swung at her, but she wasn't looking at me. She pinned Ironhelm and the dwarves with her gaze. *I will see into the mongrel's mind and learn the truth.*

"That is my granddaughter, not some nameless mongrel." Ironhelm drew a two-headed axe that had been strapped to his back and stepped forward, as if he was also thinking of bashing her leg.

"No." I flung my palm toward him, horrified at the idea that I might start a war between dwarves and dragons who had, ten minutes earlier, been amicable with each other. "I volunteered for this," I added.

She will not be irrevocably harmed, the dragon said. *You know what is involved in a mind scouring, King Ironhelm.*

"Yes, pain."

I will harm her as little as I can. I seek only the truth. If elves sought to trick dragons again, employing us in their games, we will not be pleased.

"I will wait here." Ironhelm pointed at the ground a few feet from me.

The lilac dragon's slitted reptilian eyes regarded him coolly. *A mind scouring requires concentration. I will not have you threatening to attack me while I engage in it. Leave us, dwarf king.* Magical compulsion filled the command, and if I hadn't been pinned, I might have sprung through the portal to obey it myself. *She is of your blood and sturdy. She will survive the scouring and be returned to you.*

"Of course she is sturdy and will survive, but I will remain with her." Ironhelm looked at me and opened his mouth, his brow furrowed, and I sensed he didn't *want* me to stay, but I appreciated that he was trying to watch out for me.

Before he could say more, however, the black dragon roared and turned his power on Ironhelm and the remaining dwarves. As one, they levitated into the air, and he thrust them through the portal.

As soon as they disappeared through it, it vanished, leaving me alone on the crumbling plateau with two pissed dragons.

21

As I lay pinned under Zondia'qareshi's taloned foot, I trembled involuntarily, my body certain I'd made the wrong choice and was about to die. Though afraid, I made myself look up at her, meeting her eyes when she gazed down at me.

This will not take long, she informed me.

"Go ahead." I braced myself, wanting to get it over with.

She looked over at the black-scaled dragon. He'd finished demolishing Sarrlevi's house, leaving little more than rubble, and I worried that Sarrlevi was buried underneath it or had been blown over the edge by their power.

Learn what you can. The black dragon sat on his haunches. *It is unlikely she has the strong mental defenses of a full-blooded dwarf.*

No, and I wouldn't fight them regardless. I shivered again, the rock cold under my back, and the dragon's talons even colder. I looked up at the sky, preparing myself. In case it helped her find what she wanted right away, I thought of the previous night, the ex-princess admitting she'd told the dragons Sarrlevi was a threat only to manipulate him, to force him to have sex with them.

As the lilac dragon looked at me, great talons of power raked through my mind. When Sarrlevi had tried to read my thoughts before, I'd felt his power sifting through the sands of my mind, manifesting as an itch under my skull. That had been a pleasant experience compared to this. The pain came like a mallet to the side of my head.

I stiffened, my back involuntarily arching, and clenched my jaw. I tried to keep from crying out, not wanting to show weakness in front of the mighty dragons, but I only ended up biting my tongue as daggers seemed to stab my brain. The taste of my own blood tainted my mouth.

Despite my desire to cooperate and not fight them, my body wanted to free itself. I twisted, kneeing the scaled foot that had me pinned, but those talons were like jail bars on all sides, keeping me from escaping. The dragon tore through my thoughts, ripping out not only the night's memories but my every encounter with Sarrlevi. Maybe everything *ever*. I couldn't keep my cry of pain from escaping, from echoing across the forest.

"Stop!" an angry male voice came from the edge of the plateau.

The pain vanished, but tremors gripped my body, leaving me panting as tears streaked down my cheeks.

"Let her go, and leave my home," Sarrlevi said, power in his words.

But when I twisted my head to find him, it wasn't his *power* that I noticed. He stood straight and proud, his swords glowing and pointing at the dragons, but the side of his face was abraded, his clothing torn, and his jaw smeared with dirt mingled with blood.

That rockfall. I'd thought I'd sensed him down there. The boulders must have caught him—*buried* him—when he'd been trying to sneak close.

The black-scaled male snarled and blasted Sarrlevi with magic.

Grimacing, he wrapped his power around himself, creating a defensive barrier, but it wouldn't be enough against them.

"Stop," I barked.

Surprisingly, the black dragon did. He looked not at me, but at Zondia'qareshi. He had no eyebrows to raise, nor did he say anything I could hear, but I had a feeling he was asking her a question.

She lifted her foot, and I grabbed my hammer and rolled free. I had no idea if she'd gotten what she needed, but I was terrified Sarrlevi wouldn't survive a dragon attack, Sarrlevi who'd just crawled out from under tons of rocks. Even if he'd been in perfect shape, he couldn't win in a battle against two dragons. He wouldn't be suicidal enough to leap into one, would he?

"It's fine," I told him, raising a hand and trying not to let it shake, but my muscles were weak and wobbly from the mind scour. "I volunteered for that."

"I know," Sarrlevi said, not daring to take his eyes from the dragons, the dragons who'd razed his house and wanted to do the same to him. "But if they want to know the truth, they can scour *my* mind."

"They want to take you off to their world for punishment and rehabilitation," I whispered, glancing at them and wondering how Sarrlevi could get away.

Why had he revealed himself? Even if he'd been caught in the rocks, they hadn't seemed to sense him, to know he was close.

"So I heard."

You will voluntarily submit to a mind scouring, assassin? Zondia'qareshi asked.

We're not here to scour his mind, the other dragon said. *We're here to take him for his punishment.*

"Yes, I volunteer," Sarrlevi said, though his mouth twisted with distaste.

A breeze came up, rustling his cloak, and he grimaced again.

With pain? It looked like pure determination that had allowed him to climb up here and that a stiffer wind might have knocked him over. But he clenched his jaw and didn't wobble. He did blink a few times and widen his eyes, as if he were struggling to remain conscious.

Could he *survive* the mind scouring if he'd already endured grievous injuries?

Worried, I asked the dragons, "Didn't you get enough from me? You can do more if you need to."

"No." Sarrlevi frowned at me, then repeated, "No," in a softer tone. "You will endure no more pain on my behalf."

The dragons were no longer looking at him or me but at each other. Conferring in a private telepathic conversation, I assumed.

A portal formed behind them.

We will discuss what we have learned with the queen, Zondi-a'qareshi said, *and inform you later of our verdict.*

I tensed, expecting them to levitate Sarrlevi into the portal with them, to drag him before their queen.

They turned and sprang into the air, then flew one after the other through the portal. Alone.

After it disappeared, Sarrlevi lowered his swords, resting the tips on the ground. For support. He looked like he could collapse at any second, but he blinked again, then nodded at me, and, clenching his jaw once more, he used his power to form another portal.

"That will take you back to your world." He nodded toward it. "Go, and stay with Thorvald again. Within the protection of a house that hasn't been destroyed." His mouth twisted with bitterness as he glanced toward the ruins of his.

"I'm sorry." I couldn't help but feel this was all my fault. I'd asked him to take me to see the dwarven king. If I hadn't, none of this would have happened.

"Do not concern yourself with it." Sarrlevi forced a smile,

though his pain made it more of a grimace. "There is a reason I have multiple houses."

"I thought it was because you were rich and pretentious and needed six vacation homes."

"It is because assassins must always be prepared for retribution."

"Would you have become an assassin if your people hadn't kicked you out after you killed your father? After his actions practically *forced* you to?" *If he hadn't ruined your life*, I added silently.

"Go back to your world," Sarrlevi said gently. Or... *wearily?*

Another breeze swept through, and this time, I saw him wobble. "You need help."

"I will survive."

"What if the dragons come back? Or some other enemy? Or what if it rains? You don't even have a *house*."

Nor did he look like he had the strength to make another portal to visit one of his other homes. I was surprised he'd made the one floating in the air behind me.

"Rain will not kill me." Sarrlevi didn't acknowledge that the other things could.

I strode toward him. If he passed out up here and the dragons, finding my information hadn't been sufficient, returned, they could easily kill him. Or whisk him off for that awful two years of punishment.

He eyed me warily as I clasped his hand.

"What are you doing?" he asked.

"Taking you to my house."

"Why?"

"Because I can't stand being so close to your masculine allure any longer without dragging you back to my cave like a randy orc." His hand still in mine, I tilted my head toward the portal, suggesting he walk with me. If he didn't, I *would* drag him away, or throw him over my shoulder and carry him to the portal. Thanks to my half-dwarven strength, I knew I could manage it, and I hoped my determined expression conveyed that.

Sarrlevi didn't reject the offer outright, but he didn't react to my joke, instead looking wistfully back toward the wreckage of his home.

No matter what he said about having multiple places to live, it was hard to believe the houses didn't mean anything to him.

"Besides," I added, "there isn't anything left for you here, is there? No reason to stay?"

"No," he said softly and headed toward the portal, his gait lopsided and stiff. "My masculine allure prefers I walk."

"That's probably good. I'm not known for having a gentle touch."

"You *do* sound like an orc." A fleeting smile ghosted across his lips.

"Don't let that get you too excited. You're in a weakened state and couldn't *handle* an orc right now."

"Unfortunately, true."

22

ONLY AS I WAS STEPPING THROUGH THE PORTAL DID IT OCCUR TO ME to question where it would lead. Earth, I was sure, but would I end up back on Zadie's rooftop? Or in the park by the project house? How many places in the Seattle area could Sarrlevi be familiar with?

The magic of the portal wrapped around us, dropping me into that strange dreamlike state as we whisked between realms.

To my surprise, when we landed on solid ground again, I found myself staring at my front door. The truck and Harley were parked where I'd left them, and afternoon rain fell, pattering on our heads. Surprisingly, Zadie's electric car was there too. I sensed Tinja inside and wondered if there would be any furniture not covered in tiny-house blueprints.

"I need to rest," Sarrlevi admitted, a slump to his spine.

"Because you were so busy sexing up lady elves last night that you didn't get any sleep?" I asked but immediately regretted my snark. In addition to his visible gashes, he might have internal injuries. A lot of them.

Feeling like a heel, I lifted my hammer in an attempt at an

apologetic gesture. It was hard to convey apologies with a weapon, but my other hand still clasped his.

"Because I used a lot of energy reinforcing the defenses in what turned out to be a vain attempt to keep dragons from destroying my domicile." Sarrlevi cast a sour look toward the gray clouds pelting our heads with rain, probably too weary to use his magic to keep it off us.

"Oh. Sorry." I'd thought the barrier protecting his house had held up impressively long. And maybe those rockets hadn't been as automated as I'd believed. "Come on inside."

"It didn't help that I also didn't get any sleep last night," he admitted. "And that the top of the plateau fell on me."

"What would you have done if it hadn't?" I tucked my hammer under my armpit so I could open the front door, having a vague notion that Sarrlevi might flee if I let go of his hand. He *had* other homes he could go to, after all, and maybe he would prefer that, but I worried about what the dragons would decide after their chat with the queen. If they'd known where one of his homes was, they might know where they *all* were. I deemed it unlikely they knew or cared where I lived.

"I hadn't decided yet between trying to kill them or attempting to proclaim my innocence in the particular matter that aggrieved them by offering to let them read my mind."

"Why didn't you just leave? Make a portal and go somewhere else?"

Sarrlevi wore his magical backpack as well as his sword harness. He must have been thinking of leaving.

He gave me a long look. "I didn't want them to keep mind scouring you."

I swallowed. He hadn't left because he hadn't wanted me to be hurt?

He managed a hint of dryness as he added, "I didn't know

you'd planned to volunteer to let them mind scour you in the first place."

"I figured they would be more likely to believe what they read in my head than in yours. It's not like I'm a wizard master who can trick a telepath."

"No," he agreed. "But it is an unpleasant experience."

"Tell me about it."

The door was open by then, and Tinja and Zadie peered at us from the couch, the only piece of furniture semiclear of papers. Some of the sprawl had been condensed into stacks. A third unexpected person leaned against the wall by the fireplace with her phone to her ear.

My sister. Her raven hair fell just below her jawline, the cut perfectly straight, each strand in alignment. Her pleated navy slacks, ironed blouse, and tasteful silver jewelry represented the *business-casual* attire she always believed I should wear. I had no idea if she'd come here from the office—or what she was doing here at all.

She always sneered at my modest neighborhood full of small 1950s houses with single-car garages or carports and a noticeable lack of a homeowners' association enforcing lawn maintenance and front-yard clutter rules. Mrs. Ming's house, to my home's left, was always tidy with cute flowers and shrubs in pots, but the Wallace brothers, to the right, had as much furniture *outside* the house as inside. Or they had until Tinja started helping herself to what she called raw materials that had clearly been cast aside. As far as I knew, they hadn't noticed her shopping in their side yard.

"Matti," Zadie blurted as Penina lowered her phone. "Where have you been? You need to sign an addendum to, uhm." She noticed Sarrlevi *and* the handclasp, though the gashes in the side of his face and tears in his clothing had to be more eyeball-demanding than our touching fingers.

My sister also noticed the handclasp, and her eyes widened as her lips pursed in disapproval.

"Matti, what's going on? Tyler has been trying to reach you to schedule your *date*." Penina noticed the blood on Sarrlevi's face and her expression vacillated, with concern trying to encroach upon the disapproval, but she'd never met him before and seemed undecided on the proper response. She settled on scowling at me.

I released Sarrlevi and shut the door. He wobbled slightly, resting a hand on the wall for support. He truly did need rest, if not the services of an emergency room, but he had that magical elven regeneration, so I hoped a night in bed would do.

"I will in a minute," I told Zadie, certain there was some update to the offer on the house. "And, ah, it's good to see you, Penina, but don't you usually call before coming over? I didn't see your car out front."

"Bob dropped me off. He's doing errands. I wouldn't park my Mercedes in this neighborhood."

"Yeah, carjackers with tools usually lurk in the bushes over there." I waved at the window, though the only thing in those bushes were birds. Mrs. Ming's eight or nine feeders in her backyard ensured our neighborhood had an overflowing population of robins, finches, and juncos.

Penina's head jerked in that direction before she realized I was joking.

"Where have you *been*, Matti?" Tinja had been staring at Sarrlevi and me since we'd walked in. "You have the aura of dragons on you."

"Because I've been with dragons. And dwarves. Though maybe their auras are less noticeable. I met my grandfather. Not the human one."

"Not *human*?" Penina mouthed.

Even though she'd known me all my life, and remembered my mother, she'd never been willing to accept that I was half-dwarf.

Or that dwarves existed. Since she'd been standing in the living room with Tinja, I had no idea how her brain was processing my green-skinned roommate. A child in a costume? Or maybe Tinja was camouflaging herself in some way.

"I'll tell you about it in a minute." I took Sarrlevi's hand again, not caring that the action prompted another lip-pursing from my sister, and led him toward the bedroom.

"You know he's all bloody, right?" Zadie asked. "He's dripping it on the floor."

"I trust you won't freak out," I called from the hallway, "unless his ear falls off."

"Gross, Matti."

Since Tinja lived in what had once been my spare bedroom/office, I had few options for guests. Only as I pushed open the door and saw my pajamas and underwear on my unmade bed did I doubt my decision to lend Sarrlevi my room.

I released his hand and lunged inside, scooping up the laundry to shove in the hamper, as I would have done that morning if I'd expected company. After tugging up the sheets and blankets in a semblance of a made bed, I plucked up or shoved aside a towel, tools, books, and device chargers on the floor, embarrassment for the mess warming my cheeks. Even though I wasn't half as much of a clutter bug as Tinja, I knew of Sarrlevi's fastidious streak and suspected he would judge me for having things all over the place. And, hell, there were bras and more panties atop a stack of laundry on the dresser. At least they were *clean*. Just not put away yet. Admittedly, I didn't always do that, not since I'd moved out of my grandparents' house and Penina hadn't been around to lecture me. What was the point of stuffing things in drawers that you would need again in a day or two?

Sarrlevi, who'd leaned against the doorjamb as I hastily tidied, didn't comment, though I was sure he noticed everything, injuries or not. Assassins were known for instantly assessing threats whenever they entered a room, weren't they? My panties might or might not qualify.

His lack of commentary attested to how tired he was—and likely how much pain he was in. He shuffled inside and gingerly eased his sword harness off his shoulders.

"Do you want help taking that stuff off?" I eyed the fresh blood that his movements prompted, his sides as gashed as his face.

"I don't know. How moved to ardor would you be by my masculine allure?"

"When you look like you just went through a meat grinder? Not very." Despite my words, the memory of him on his cot wearing nothing but an elven loincloth and bandages came to mind. The thought of getting water, washcloths, and bandages and tending to his wounds also came to mind. Less because I was a natural nurse—I wasn't—and more because it would be an excuse to touch him.

Something, I reminded myself tartly, that he hadn't invited me to do. Just because he'd told me about his past and let me hug him didn't mean he had suddenly decided half-dwarf mongrels were hot.

He grimaced as he peeled off the harness and his backpack.

"You can crash on the bed." I looked away as he removed his tunic, though I wondered why he hadn't been wearing his armor. Because he'd been in his pajamas when the dwarves arrived, I reminded myself, outside talking to *me* and making sure I was all right instead of preparing himself for a possible battle. Even if it wasn't my fault he'd made that choice, I couldn't help but feel guilty. I wondered if the gear and clothing he had with him now represented the equivalent of a bug-out bag. "I'll sleep on the couch tonight and use Tinja's blueprints for blankets."

"That is not necessary." Sarrlevi opened his backpack and withdrew some of his magical plant-fiber bandages and his folded cot. "I prefer my travel bed."

"Understandable." The cot didn't look comfortable, but it probably appealed to him more than climbing into my hastily-made bed. I tried to remember the last time I'd washed the sheets and blankets. My life had gotten busy of late. "Though I'm not sure there's room to roll out the moss rug."

"We'll see."

There hadn't been in the pantry either, but he'd made it work.

"Right. Do you need anything? Bandages? Water?" I eyed his wounds again. "A stiff drink?"

"What is a stiff drink?"

"Alcohol."

"Ah. No, that will impede my ability to regenerate my body." With his camp gear unpacked and the cot set up, he set the bandages on it, then sat to remove his boots, the muscles of his back on full display as he bent over.

I backed into the doorway, deciding to leave him to his privacy, though I was tempted to stay and watch since he hadn't ordered me to leave. Only to assess his injuries and see if I needed to find a shaman healer, not to ogle him. Or to offer to sponge off his chest and put the elven bandages on it.

Rolling my eyes at myself, I stepped into the hallway, closing the door behind me. Though I leaned my temple against the wood for a moment with my eyes closed, experiencing a jumble of feelings that included concern, regret, sorrow, and... caring for him.

Sarrlevi had lost his home and very nearly his life because he'd set up that meeting. Maybe he couldn't have foreseen the dragons getting involved—or the ex-princess *getting* the dragons involved—but he must have suspected the king was holding a grudge. The dwarven ruler was the last person Sarrlevi should have reached out to, even through a third party.

"Matti?" Penina stood in the hallway, watching me leaning my cheek against the door with who knew what expression on my face. "Who is that guy? What's going on?"

"A friend. He kind of got... waylaid."

"By the carjackers in the bushes?" She arched her eyebrows. Unlike mine, they were perfectly curved and slender, no need for plucking.

"Worse."

"So you're going to let him sleep alone in your bedroom?"

"Well, I'm not joining him in there."

"How well do you know him?"

"I met him... last month, I guess it was now."

"That can't mean you know him well. He could be a perv." Penina turned her frown on the door. "What if he's in there sniffing your panties?"

Embarrassment reared up, not because I believed Sarrlevi would do that but because I hadn't thought to run ahead and clean up my room *before* opening the door with him beside me. "He's not. Based on what I know about him, he's more likely to launder them."

That thought only mortified me more as I imagined him applying his magical cleaning kerchief to the dirty clothes in my hamper. I almost thrust the door open to make sure he wasn't and tell him such acts weren't necessary, but I caught myself. My senses told me he was where I'd left him, sitting or lying on his cot. A ton of boulders had fallen on Sarrlevi. He wasn't going to worry about my hamper.

"Tyler could afford to hire someone to do your laundry," Penina said.

"I guess that's an appealing trait in a guy." I thought about pointing out that Sarrlevi had magical laundry gizmos, but his home and everything in it had been destroyed. My guilt returned, and I slumped.

"He also doesn't get into fights."

I refrained from pointing out that *I* regularly did. "What brings you here today? Do you need something?"

"Other than for you to start leading a responsible and ladylike life?" Penina glanced toward the living room, probably toward where I'd propped my hammer against the wall.

"Yeah."

"You didn't answer the phone last night or this morning."

"Sorry." I tugged it out, but the charge had died while I'd been on the other world. "Dead battery."

I squeezed past her to plug it into the charger in the kitchen. For some reason, the toaster had been disassembled with pieces scattering the counter like breadcrumbs. What project was Tinja working on now?

"Your friends didn't know where you were either. Are you in trouble? Do you need money?"

"Of course not. Didn't Zadie mention Abbas and I accepted an offer on a house?"

"A poor offer that may or may not cover your expenses. Matti, why don't you stop working so hard for so little return and get a desk job or something?" Penina gripped my hand. "Look at your calluses. You're going to scare away men if you're in greater need of pumice stones than they are."

"I'm sure that's not true, and I'd go crazy in a cubicle. Besides, you've seen me type."

"I've seen you pound the keyboard like an orangutan, yes. But surely you know how to use office software. You must have a spreadsheet for your expenses."

"It's all right here." I withdrew my hand and tapped my temple.

"Oh, girl. No wonder you're broke."

"I'm *not* broke. We're making money on the house. We almost always do."

"*Almost.*" She drew back in horror.

When Zadie appeared, holding her laptop open for me, I sighed in relief.

"Here's the addendum. And I brought a few new listings over for you to look at too." She eyed Penina warily, no doubt having heard her advise me on a desk job. "I thought it would be best if you and Abbas picked out your next house, ideally one not located next to a werewolf-laden park."

"Right." I guided Penina to the door as she mouthed *werewolf*, and was relieved when I spotted her husband's car out front. "Your ride is here. Thanks for checking up on me, but everything is fine. I'll join you for brunch next week."

"All right." Her face brightened. "I'll invite Tyler."

"Great."

"And you'll call him, right? He said he called you, but you didn't answer." Penina's gaze turned toward the kitchen. "Where were you that you couldn't charge your phone?"

"Nowhere. It's just not holding its charge well anymore." Possibly because I kept taking it through magical portals to other realms. "I'll get it checked."

"Maybe if you're winsome and charming, Tyler will buy you a new phone."

"I don't need anyone to buy me things." I opened the door and made shooing motions. "Everything is fine. Really." I made myself smile.

Penina eyed the neighbor's house as she hustled toward the car, probably afraid the clutter from the yard would spring out and pin her mercilessly to the sidewalk.

"Where does your sister live that she thinks this is a bad neighborhood?" Zadie asked dryly.

"One of the gated communities in Shoreline."

"Ah. Big lot? View of the water?"

I nodded. "Don't forget the private gated beach."

"And a history of racial restrictions?" Zadie arched her pierced eyebrows, well aware of the pasts of those exclusive—*literally* exclusive—neighborhoods.

"Probably." After signing the addendum, I waved at the laptop. "Let's see the new houses. I trust they're not in gated communities with dubious pasts." I needed to finish my quest and close on the other house before making offers on new projects, but it didn't hurt to look.

"They are not. I've got a couple you'll like. Though the Dunston Brothers are interested in one, and you might be bidding against them. Since they egged your house while I was on the walkway, I've been checking them out. They have a reputation for bullying homeowners behind on their payments to sell to them at well-below market prices."

"Yeah, they're asses," I said, though a lot of people in the business used that tactic to get deals. As an early mentor had often told me, *You make money when you buy a house, not when you sell it.* "They don't have my skills to make something amazing on a budget."

"Your work *is* amazing. I hope you're able to save up enough to buy a nice house for yourself on Lake Washington one day." Zadie smiled, knowing that was my dream. Even if dwarves preferred underground tunnels, I loved the beauty of the water. Oh, I wasn't a good swimmer, and sailboats made me seasick, but to sit outside with a glass of wine and some cheese while the sun set over the water... That would be fantastic.

"The goal is to buy one of the old cottages there and fix it up to be nice." I'd never be able to afford something posh that had already been renovated. Besides, I wanted to put my touch on anything I lived in.

"Better act soon. There aren't many of those left."

"I know." My phone rang in the kitchen. "Hold that thought."

It was Val's number.

"Hey, Matti," she said. "Do you want to go back to that logging land with me and check out the caves Zav mentioned?"

"Did he come back?" I grimaced, not tickled by the idea of

going anywhere with a dragon after watching two of them destroy Sarrlevi's home.

"Not yet, but we've got a little more urgency now. Some general that Willard reports to is coming in person to her office tomorrow for an inspection."

"Of the empty basement?"

"Among other things. I get the feeling she's in trouble for having lost everything. Why she told her superiors about the theft right away, I don't know. She's compelled to report everything honestly, I guess, but if she hadn't said anything, it might have been months or years before anyone cared enough to do an inspection. It would have given us more time to find the missing artifacts."

The missing artifacts I'd barely devoted any brain power to contemplating.

"She didn't issue any new orders to me," Val continued, "like *find them now because my career and ass are on the line*, but I read between the lines that she would appreciate it if they were returned before the general arrives."

"And he's coming in the morning?" I glanced at the time. Days here didn't line up with the days on Sarrlevi's world, and evening was already approaching. The thought of tramping around at night in a recently burned forest where someone had tried to kill us the day before wasn't appealing, but if the lilac dragon hadn't gotten enough from my mind to clear Sarrlevi, I might need a favor from Val—and her mate—to keep the dragons from coming after him again.

"Yeah," Val said.

"How will we get there without a dragon?"

"The old-fashioned way." Val jangled something. The keys to her Jeep? "I'll come by and get you in an hour."

A crash sounded somewhere in her background. What were those vampires up to now?

"Maybe two hours," Val amended.

I hated the thought of leaving Sarrlevi, but it wasn't as if the people after my hammer were after him. The *dragons* might be, but they shouldn't know where to look for him. Besides, if they came for him, it wasn't as if I could do anything to stop them.

"All right." After I hung up, I told Zadie, "I'm not going to have time to shop for projects tonight."

"Are you going somewhere dangerous?" She glanced toward the bedroom door, maybe thinking of Sarrlevi's wounds and realizing I'd already *been* somewhere dangerous.

I sighed. "Yes."

23

BECAUSE I WAS PACING AND LOOKING OUT THE WINDOW FOR VAL'S Jeep, I immediately noticed a windowless unmarked van park across the street from my house. Magic emanated from it, and I sighed. More trouble.

Night had fallen, and the driver shut off the van's headlights immediately. I barely got a glimpse of the two shaggy heads in the cab, but my senses identified them as trolls. More mercenaries? Or other opportunists eager to earn a hundred thousand dollars?

"We've got a problem, Tinja," I murmured, glad Zadie had gone home. "A new one. Or I guess an extension of an existing one."

The magic I sensed came as much from the van as from the trolls in the cab. The auras of more trolls and likely the charms and weapons they carried. Although, so much magic emanated from the back of the van that I thought it might be more than that. Artifacts? Some of Willard's missing items?

Not likely. Even if a band of trolls could have gotten past the colonel's security, why would they be rolling around my neighborhood with their ill-gotten goods? Besides, based on the number of shelves in that basement vault, the contents would have filled *many* vans.

"I sense a lot of magic." Tinja hopped up from blueprints she'd been working on and peered out the window with me.

I'd shifted the curtains so those outside wouldn't be able to see in, but I had little doubt the trolls knew I was home. "Maybe you should hide on the roof."

Using my senses, I checked on Sarrlevi. He was still in my bedroom, probably deep in meditation to repair his wounds. I also swept out to check the area beyond my home. There could be other vans out of sight with more trolls, some maybe already sneaking up on the house.

"If they are enemies, I will thump them with my new Goblinator," Tinja said.

"What's that?"

"A cross between a cannon and a catapult. It is Earth-friendly because it doesn't require gunpowder, and the rounds are made from recycled materials. Like the coils I extracted from your appliance."

"Couldn't you have found a toaster in a junkyard for that? I *use* that now and then." Rather I *had* used it.

The trolls hadn't gotten out of the cab, but the rear doors opened. The van was large enough to hold a whole squad of thieves, if not half a platoon.

"I have observed that you usually toast your bread in the frying pan. I sense weapons, magical weapons. Those trolls may attack us."

"I'm certain they will, and I only use the frying pan when I'm making grilled cheese sandwiches, and only because someone turned my panini maker into a bath gadget."

"Goblins like a vigorous scrub for their monthly wash. It's not easy to get grease off."

I grabbed my hammer, then snatched the phone out of the

kitchen and texted Val that it would be timely if she and her stalwart tiger arrived soon.

"Get your Earth-friendly gun, and climb up on the roof, but don't shoot unless it's an emergency." I touched Tinja's shoulder. "They're probably only after my hammer."

"Maybe you and it should also climb on the roof. Don't you have a camouflaging charm now?"

"Yeah, but they've already sensed me, I'm sure, and I'm not going to hide while they lay waste to the house, which I'm positive they'll do if I disappear." Besides, I wanted to question one to find out where they were supposed to turn in the hammer. That trailer in the middle of the logging forest? Or had they been given another address? The *real* address?

Between one eye blink and the next, the trolls in the cab disappeared. *All* the trolls did. Even the van grew hazy and indistinct, like a mirage.

"Speaking of camouflaging charms," I muttered, though one that could hide squads of trolls and a van all at once was nothing I'd encountered before.

"Yes. I do not sense their magic anymore."

"I'm sure it'll be used to attack us soon. I don't want my living room torn up, so I'm going to go face them." I stepped toward the front door but paused. "Actually... let me see if I can make it to the schoolyard at the end of the block." There was a big open field there, with little that could be damaged in a battle. Unlike my house, which was distressingly damageable. "You stay on the roof. If Val comes, tell her which way I went."

"Okay."

As I jogged into the kitchen, intending to go out the back door and over the fence—no need to make it *easy* for them to reach me—Sarrlevi stepped out of the hallway. Since I hadn't sensed him, he startled me, and I half lifted my hammer to swing before catching myself.

He was bare-chested with green magical bandages plastered over the gouges in his torso, but he'd put his boots back on and carried his swords. "I sensed the arrival of trolls."

"Yeah, more hammer hunters. Someone rudely gave them my home address."

"I will assist you."

I almost told him no, that he was too injured to leap into battle, but even shirtless and wounded, he looked like—he *was*—a badass. It would be foolish not to invite him to fight at my side.

"Thanks. Follow me. I'm going to try to keep them from wrecking my house, which is a perfectly fine home in a perfectly fine neighborhood, despite what my sister says. I don't want to lose it."

All Sarrlevi said was, "Activate your camouflage charm."

"I'm trying to lead them away, not disappear."

He frowned and looked like he would object, but I stepped out the back door before he could.

The porch light was on, and I didn't flip it off, wanting to see where I was going. And if anyone was about to attack.

Though I didn't yet see anything amiss, my instincts were on edge, and I wondered if some of the thieves, cloaked with invisibility, had already made their way into the fenced backyard. Skirting my and Tinja's projects, I padded from the patio to the grass, heading for a gate. I listened and even sniffed as I tried to detect intruders with more than the senses the camouflage charms worked against.

Was that a hint of pot in the air? I had a few neighbors who smoked it, so the presence didn't necessarily mean trolls were nearby, but Abbas had mentioned that a lot of his father's people enjoyed the stuff.

A green glowing light emanated from my bedroom, and I glanced through the window on my way to the gate. I halted in my tracks.

Not unexpectedly, Sarrlevi's cot, complete with moss rug and glowing green lamp had been laid out. What I didn't expect was that the entire room had been cleared of clutter, with everything put away somewhere. Either that, or he'd incinerated everything. As I gaped at the tidily made bed, I hoped *that* wasn't the case. Even the laundry stacked on the dresser was gone. Put in the drawers? Faint magic emanated from what had been an empty wall over the headboard. Now, there were green shelves affixed to it—were those made from *vines*?—and I spotted the device chargers and some of the other stuff that had been on the floor up there.

"You cleaned my room?" I whispered in disbelief.

"And organized it, yes."

I had enemies and an imminent attack to worry about, but that didn't keep my cheeks from flushing as I imagined him tucking my underwear into drawers... I groaned. "I thought you were healing yourself."

"It was difficult to find a restful meditative state while surrounded with entropy."

"Some laundry needing to be put away is not *entropy*," I said, though I only vaguely knew the meaning of that word.

"Ssh." Sarrlevi spun, weapons raised.

I didn't see anything, but he sprang, his twin swords slashing. They clanged against something invisible.

"So much for my plan to go to the schoolyard." I raised my hammer and wondered how I could defend against invisible enemies.

It surprised me that I couldn't see Sarrlevi's opponent. With most camouflage charms, the magic was only effective beyond a certain distance.

He barked something in Elven, and a foggy mist appeared and blanketed the yard. Except in spots where it swirled, as if something was moving through it. No, *someone*. Multiple someones.

It swirled right in front of me, and I whispered, *"Hyrek,"* as I swung my hammer, instincts guiding my movements. Even when my attacker was right in front of me, I couldn't see him.

But with a *thud,* my hammer collided with something hard. It sounded like wood—a club?—rather than the metal of a sword.

Trusting someone was holding it, I kicked straight out. A masculine grunt sounded as I connected. I launched another kick higher up, but my attacker scooted back in time to avoid it.

Hammer raised, I sprang forward and swung again. The head thumped against what felt like an armored body, and something thudded into the grass.

"They have firearms," Sarrlevi warned a second before a gun cracked from above the back fence.

Afraid I was the target, I darted to the side, then sprinted for the corner of the house and the tool shed, hoping they would offer cover. Bullets slammed into the siding scant inches from my head as I lunged behind the shed.

"Damn it, this is my house, you bastards!" I yelled, wishing I had a projectile weapon so I could fire back.

Sarrlevi tossed one of his swords into the air and yanked a dagger from a sheath and threw it.

As the hilt of his sword landed back in his hand, a cry of pain sounded. The dagger had struck the shooter perched on the fence. The troll was still invisible, but I heard him fall backward, landing in the neighbor's yard with a thud and a curse. Sarrlevi sprang for another target, the mist telling him where our foes were.

Despite his injuries, his hands and feet moved with their usual incredible speed, weapons slicing and stabbing too rapidly to follow. More curses and grunts of pain sounded as he struck trolls.

Someone in the corner of the yard fired toward me, but the shed gave me cover. I wanted to fight, not hide, but it would be suicide to run into the middle of gunfire, especially when I couldn't see my opponents.

Clenching my jaw, I was forced to hunker down as more rounds slammed into the siding. One made it through the shed wall, clanging off the lawn mower inside.

A *thwump-boom* came from the rooftop. Another enemy? I groaned, but then a troll roared and something smashed into the fence. Several boards cracked or went flying.

"Got you!" came Tinja's cry from the rooftop. "All dastardly evildoers will be goblinated!"

"Try hitting their van if you can," I yelled up to her. Even though I didn't think it held Willard's stolen goods, it was possible the magic within it was what was camouflaging our foes.

"Ooooh," Tinja said, followed by an excited cackle.

Someone fired at the rooftop, knocking shingles free. I hoped Tinja was behind the chimney or other cover.

Sarrlevi, tracking people's locations by the gunshots, as well as the mist, hurled another dagger. Once more, the firing halted abruptly, our enemy crying out, then hitting the ground.

"Who is that bastard?" a male voice yelled in English, someone speaking for the first time. It sounded like a human rather than a troll. Was this a mixed band of hammer hunters?

"A fucking pointy-eared elf," someone else with a deep voice and heavy accent said. That was a troll. "Full blood. Capture him if you can."

Sarrlevi threw another dagger and hit another target.

"Screw that," the human spat.

More swirls in the mist showed someone creeping toward my tool shed, trying to circle it to get at me from behind.

"Oh, no you don't." I ran toward the stirring mist and swung, irritation that *Sarrlevi* was the one they were concerned about making me put more *oomph* than usual into my strike.

The hammer landed a solid blow, sending my invisible attacker into the fence. More boards broke, and I would later resent having to repair them, but I surged after him, my temper riled. Logically, I knew I should grab one of them to question, but I was angry that these people had invaded my home and were trying to steal my hammer. Wanting nothing more than to smash them, I took another big swing. My attacker must have scrambled away, for I swept through air.

Another *thwump-boom* came from the rooftop, followed by a clank in the street out front.

"I think their conveyance is armored," Tinja called.

"You should have used more toaster coils." I swung again, wishing I knew a command to reveal hidden enemies. Sarrlevi's mist had faded—or maybe they'd come up with a way to dismiss the magic.

A wave of unfamiliar power pulsed from the front of the house —from the van?—and a keening wail assailed me. Like some kind of boring beetle, it seemed to tunnel right through my eardrums and pierce my brain.

Gasping, I staggered and almost dropped the hammer. My instincts warned me of someone surging in from the side, and I snarled and swung in that direction. The hammer clanged against metal. A sword? Though the magical wail continued to drive pain into my skull, I pulled back, adjusted my angle, and swung again.

This time, I clipped someone's body, the hammer thudding against armor, or maybe a flak jacket. Lightning streaked from the weapon, wrapping around a human form and illuminating him, his head thrown back as he screamed. Shaking, he dropped his weapon—it was a sword, a *magical* sword—and tapped a bracelet on his wrist. The lightning halted abruptly, and I sensed magic flaring around him. A shield?

These people had a lot of magical items for run-of-the-mill thieves.

I braced myself for him to attack again, but he'd had enough and backed away, disappearing from my sight and senses.

Orange light glowed from the front yard, and smoke wafted to my nostrils. Someone hadn't lit my house on fire, had they?

Furious, I glanced at Sarrlevi and started to tell him I was going to run out front to stop it, but he was in the middle of springing into the air, first to land on the low roof of the tool shed and then over to the roof of the house. As he ran out of my view, I sensed him summoning his power. White light flashed.

I opted for running through the gate instead of across the roof and cursed as my carport came into view. My motorcycle and truck didn't yet appear damaged, but flames leaped from the structure. The bastards were *destroying* my property.

Sarrlevi, who now crouched on the roof at the front of the house, Tinja at his side with her weapon, pointed his two swords toward the street. Twin orange beams streaked from their tips and slammed into the hazy outline of the van. I still couldn't see it fully, but the beams clearly struck it. A second later, the vehicle blew up.

Pieces flew in all directions, visible now as they clattered down the street and thumped into people's yards. Several landed on the roof of my flaming carport.

Afraid that fire would spread to the house, I ran forward and yelled, "*Keyk,*" and touched the hammer to one of the support posts, willing the ice command to somehow put out the flames. Since wood was a lousy conductor of energy, I doubted it would, but I hoped in vain the magic would do something.

The hammer did grow frosty in my hand and chill the surrounding air, but the flames continued to burn heartily. It was Sarrlevi who looked down, sheathed his weapons, and stretched a hand toward the carport. That earlier weariness lingered in his eyes, and I doubted the hour or two he'd rested had done much to heal his wounds, but he once more summoned magic.

His power surprised me by angling toward my hammer like a stream of water. It enveloped it, then funneled its frost magic outward, spreading to cover the carport. The air grew even chillier and seemed to suffocate the flames. Within seconds, they extinguished, leaving the wood charred and smoking but not completely destroyed.

I slumped against the recycling bin, the top half melted from proximity to the fire, and waved a thanks to him. After the explosion, the neighborhood had fallen silent, though curtains on adjacent houses stirred as people peered out. Mrs. Ming stood on her cement stoop, a broomstick in hand, as if she'd been prepared to battle bad guys.

Tinja scrambled down a drainpipe, her weapon clunking against it. I rubbed my face, having a feeling this was about to become the weird house in the neighborhood.

Headlights shone in the street as a vehicle slowly drove up, tires crunching over pieces of the shattered van. A police car? I winced, having no idea what I would tell the authorities.

Magic still emanated from the area. I was a little surprised nobody had succeeded in shooting me, since I didn't have any fancy armor, and knew I had Sarrlevi to thank for that. The thieves might have come for my hammer, but they hadn't been able to ignore him.

As the vehicle parked, I realized it didn't belong to the police. My senses told me Val and her tiger were in it.

She parked, and they got out, the tiger immediately springing over what remained of my fence to check out the backyard. I headed to the walkway to greet Val, though she was looking up instead of at me.

"Is there a reason you're half-naked on Matti's roof, Sarrlevi?" Val asked him, her hand on the magical gun in her thigh holster.

"I invited him." I lifted a hand and stepped onto the walkway in front of Val—and between her and Sarrlevi. "Some dragons tried to kick his ass."

Sarrlevi hopped down from the roof, landing lightly behind

me, his swords still sheathed. "One was Zondia'qareshi," he said coolly, looking over me to hold Val's cool gaze.

"Because the Stormforges think you're after the dwarven king," Val said.

"He's not." I moved to stand beside Sarrlevi. "I told the dragons that. And let Zondia'qareshi read my thoughts."

Val grimaced and looked at me. "By mind scouring you?"

"Yeah."

"That hurts."

"Yes, it does. I'm hoping she got what she needed. She flew off to report to the queen, I guess, but Sarrlevi is trying to help the dwarves—the king—not hurt him."

Val met my gaze and arched her eyebrows. Asking if I truly believed that? I'd been less certain about him and what was the truth the last time we'd spoken, but I nodded firmly now.

"He doesn't deserve to be punished and rehabilitated," I told her.

"No? He did try to kill me." Val smiled faintly.

"He just saved my carport and maybe my whole house from being burned down."

"I'm not sure rescuing a carport is heroic enough to cancel out all past crimes."

I scowled at her.

"I am an honorable assassin working within the regulations and parameters established by the Assassins' Guild," Sarrlevi said stiffly. "I am *not* a criminal."

Val waved a hand. "Yeah, yeah, I know. And the punishment-and-rehabilitation gig sounds awful. Dragons are big time into it too."

"If we can convince your mate that Sarrlevi wasn't after the king, is there any chance he might be able to tell those other dragons to knock it off?" I asked her.

"The queen is Zavryd'nokquetal's mother," Sarrlevi told me,

"and Zondia'qareshi his sister. The black dragon is an older cousin. Their family holds power over the Dragon Council, which rules over all dragons and the Cosmic Realms. Thorvald's mate isn't without influence, but, if his older relatives believe I should be punished, it's unlikely he'll be able to convince them otherwise."

"Oh." I frowned at Val, though it wasn't as if it was her fault she had such in-laws, and that they'd destroyed Sarrlevi's home—and almost him. Mostly, I was distressed that such powerful and influential dragons were after him.

I've found something, Sindari spoke into our minds from the backyard.

I grimaced, reminded that I had hammer problems that I needed to put ahead of Sarrlevi's dragon problems.

24

WE FOUND SINDARI STANDING NEXT TO THE TOOL SHED WITH HIS paw on something on the ground beside the broken fence. *I sense numerous artifacts and tools on these dead trolls and humans and more out front, where their conveyance blew up, but this one I recognize. It was in the stash in the compound of the human Weber, one of many items he possessed that we gave to Colonel Willard.*

"Dead humans?" I looked warily around as Val picked up a bracelet. Though I hadn't killed the man I'd battled, I well remembered Sarrlevi's daggers thudding into people's chests, the magic of his weapons—of *him*—enough to have cut through their armor.

The thought of killing anyone disturbed me, but if we'd killed humans, even in self-defense, we—*I*—could be in a lot of trouble.

"I wouldn't have guessed a band of humans and trolls could have been responsible for that theft," Val said. "Willard's vault isn't easy to get into."

"Maybe whoever perpetrated the theft," Sarrlevi said, "sold the artifacts to these people afterward. Or gave them away to improve the odds of the hammer seekers succeeding."

These humans all wore magical rings that are continuing to render them invisible, Sindari said. *I can smell them and sense the rings when I'm very close. I believe it's elven magic. It's very effective.*

"No kidding. What happens when it wears off? And what's the proper way to deal with bodies, Val?" I watched her, hoping for a clue about how much trouble I could get in for this mess.

"Like this." Val took out her phone and dialed Willard's number.

"Are you uninjured?" Sarrlevi asked me quietly as Val moved away to talk to her boss.

Tinja had gone back inside, and clattering came from the kitchen. She was probably disassembling the rest of my small appliances to fashion more ammunition for her weapon.

"Yeah. Thanks for the help." I looked Sarrlevi up and down, amazed that someone wearing that many bandages had fought so well. "Do you need to rest longer? You're welcome to spend the night here." At least nothing on the *house* had caught fire. "I told Val I'd go with her to check out the logging area where whoever gets my hammer is supposed to take it and collect the bounty." I wished we'd captured someone who might have confirmed that they'd received the same location.

"I didn't know you'd learned that information."

"We visited the place yesterday, and magical booby traps tried to light us on fire. We didn't find anyone, but, before he left, Zavryd said he'd found some caves that were insulated from those with magical senses." I shook my head, irritated anew with the female elves. If not for their games with the dragons, Zavryd wouldn't have had to leave in the middle of his search, and we might have already found the people who had issued the reward.

"One wonders if the magical booby traps go off for everyone who enters the area." Sarrlevi eyed my hammer.

I hefted the weapon. "I had this with me, and it didn't stop anything."

"Presumably, those who set them knew you would not turn in

your own hammer. If anything, the traps may have been set to trigger quickly and violently when they detected your presence."

"I have been known to bestir people to violence."

"It's your dwarven charm."

"Are dwarves known to be charming?"

Sarrlevi smiled. "Gruff and off-putting. Some races are more charmed by that than others."

"Orcs probably like it."

"No doubt why that brute wanted to claim you."

"Too bad he wasn't my type." I didn't *mean* to glance at Sarrlevi's chest, but it happened regardless. It was his fault for running around shirtless.

He smirked, and I almost groaned, having liked it better when he'd been too injured to be smug.

"Few besides other orcs find them to be their *types*," was all he said before extending a hand toward my hammer. "If you share the location with me, I can take your weapon, pretend I'm there to turn it in for the reward, and kill whoever shows up with a satchel of money."

Half-consciously, I pulled my hammer close and hugged it. Even though I trusted Sarrlevi a lot more than I had a few days ago, I shied away from the idea of giving him the treasured weapon. The treasured weapon that my mother had made and that was all I had left of her.

"Obviously, I won't let them have it," he said, watching my reaction.

"I assumed not since you spoke of killing them. But... if I give it to you, then I don't have anything to protect myself with."

"You are with Thorvald and her tiger."

"I wasn't planning on asking them to be my bodyguards. I want to help *them*."

Val hung up and joined us again. "Willard is sending the corpse-mobile to pick these guys up. She's not happy that *humans* died here, and we may have to answer some questions, Matti."

I'd been afraid of that.

"I didn't kill anyone." At least I didn't think so. I had gotten in a couple of hard hits, but I believed Sarrlevi's daggers and swords accounted for the fallen.

"I assumed not." Val eyed Sarrlevi coolly, but all she said was, "Sindari, can you remove the rings that are hiding the bodies?"

Tigers cannot remove rings without also removing fingers. He held up a silver-furred paw, demonstrating his lack of thumbs.

"I'm not that particular on the details of how it happens, not when these guys attacked Matti, and I'd like for the corporals driving the van to be able to find the bodies." Val knelt beside Sindari and patted around to find the body, then searched for a wallet or anything that might identify him.

Sarrlevi was watching me instead of her. Waiting for me to agree with his plan?

It wasn't a *bad* idea, since Val and I hadn't had any luck getting someone to show up when we'd gone up there. An assassin might be a believable person to collect bounties, and if whoever had issued the reward was from the Cosmic Realms and not Earth, they might have heard of him. That would lend more credence to the idea. But...

"What if they know we're working together?" I asked him as Val continued her pat-down.

"Are we?" Sarrlevi smiled again, that you-shouldn't-trust-assassins smile.

"Dude, you made me shelves. Nobody makes their enemies shelves. We're on the same side."

Val arched her eyebrows, then must have slid off the ring Sindari had spoken of, for the dead man appeared, one of Sarrlevi's daggers in his chest.

"It didn't occur to me that a home improvement was the way to win your trust," Sarrlevi said dryly, unfazed by the appearance of the body. He simply knelt, removed his dagger, and produced his magical cleaning kerchief to wipe off the blood.

I was crazy to have feelings for him, and I knew it.

"Such things are the way to a girl's heart." Val stood up and brushed off her hands. Other than the ring she'd left on the ground beside the guy, it didn't look like she'd found anything. "Zav remodeled my house."

"Your *whole* house?" I asked, well aware of how much work that was. For mere mortals without magic, anyway.

"The second floor and the attic, yes. In about twenty minutes. I was suitably impressed."

I nodded, having seen Val's house. It was beautiful.

Sarrlevi's eyes narrowed. In irritation? Maybe because elven remodeling magic wasn't as powerful as dragon remodeling magic?

"These guys don't have any ID on them, and they're in the same unmarked camouflage uniforms as the dead men in the tunnel." Val nodded toward me. "It could be a coincidence, but I saw an M4 carbine among the carnage of the van too. What happened to that, by the way?" She looked from me to Sarrlevi.

"I destroyed it," he said. "An artifact inside was emitting a dreadful noise that hurt my ears."

I nodded in agreement. Had I the ability, I would have happily blown up that van myself.

"Willard's people will find the rest of the bodies and sift through the artifacts they had. Matti, can I speak with you privately for a moment?" Val pointed at the other side of the yard.

Once more, Sarrlevi's eyes narrowed. Maybe he suspected he would be the topic of the conversation.

I didn't know if Val had heard his proposition about turning in the hammer, but I would ask her opinion on it. On *him*. Did she believe me that he hadn't threatened the dwarf king? Or was she loyal to the dragons and thought them incapable of making a mistake in determining Sarrlevi's guilt or innocence? The idea of him having to endure that punishment and rehabilitation made me shudder.

"I don't think you can trust him with your hammer," Val said without preamble, speaking so quietly I barely heard her. She had to be aware of how keen elven ears were and didn't want Sarrlevi to hear.

"If he wanted it, there have been any number of times that he could have gotten it from me." Even though I'd been doubting giving it up myself, I realized my objection was more to losing it than a belief that Sarrlevi would take it and not return it.

"Have you figured out why he's here yet? Trying to find your mother?"

"He... gave me a reason." I was reluctant to share any of his story with Val or anyone else. "I believed him."

"Did something change? Because you weren't that sure about him a couple of days ago."

"I know, but he told me some stuff."

Her eyebrows rose, and I realized how lame that sounded, as if I would naively believe anything anyone told me.

"Don't take this the wrong way," Val said, "and I'm not trying to pry, but have you slept together? I know how enticing guys with magic can be and also what it's like when they put a compulsion on you."

"He didn't do that," I snapped. "And no to the other thing too. He's not into me, not like that."

I wanted to say I wasn't into him either, but Val's expression was knowing, so maybe she knew I was. Hell, who wouldn't be? Even Zadie had said he was gorgeous, and she preferred women.

"Look," I continued, "we've fought together several times now. And he lost his house and nearly his life because he was doing a favor for me. I asked him to arrange a meeting between me and my grandfather, not realizing the dwarves don't like him very much. *He* knew that, but he did it anyway."

"Didn't he tell you he was working for the dwarven king?"

"Yeah. That was a lie." Reluctantly, I added, "And maybe everything else is too, but I don't think so. Not after all this."

Val turned. Sarrlevi was walking over, his face stiff. Quiet voices or not, I had little doubt he'd caught the gist of the conversation.

His gait was stiff too, a reminder that he was injured. One wouldn't have known it to see him fight and throw magic around, but half a plateau *had* fallen on him earlier. If he tried to turn in my hammer and found it was a ruse and that he had to fight again... I grimaced. Maybe I should take Val's advice. I was already the reason Sarrlevi had lost so much. I didn't want him to lose his life too.

He stopped in front of us and held my gaze as he drew one of his twin swords, the long blade emanating magic. Val stiffened, as if she expected him to attack, but his movement was slow and deliberate, and I knew it wasn't a threat. He laid the blade horizontally across his palms and held it toward me.

"A trade for the duration of our ruse. If I disappear with your hammer, which I won't, you'll have a weapon of equal power and value." Sarrlevi cocked his head. "I would offer both of my swords, but our enemies would be suspicious if I showed up with no weapons save for the one I'm supposed to turn in to them." He must not have considered the daggers he'd retrieved from the fallen men to be weapons of substance, though they also radiated magic. "I have also not practiced often or recently with a war hammer."

I looked from him to the sword and back, considering the offer. It did seem fair, and I trusted he would want the valuable blade back.

"Where'd you get the swords?" Val asked, less trusting.

What, did she think he'd picked them up at the local 7-Eleven?

"My father," Sarrlevi said, not glancing at her but continuing to hold my gaze.

In the aftermath of the story he'd told, that sent a chill through me, but I didn't doubt that he valued the weapons—garnered through his first kill—as much as he might if he'd received them for the reason Val would assume, as a gift or inheritance.

"I've had them for almost three hundred years," Sarrlevi added.

Since he'd told me that was his age, that made me realize how young he must have been when he'd faced his father—*killed* his father. He'd called himself a coward, but it sounded more like he'd been a teenager still living at home. Hell.

Why are you willing to do this? I asked him silently, hoping he was listening to my thoughts.

You will be a target until whoever issued the reward revokes it. Or is killed.

And I matter to you?

Yes.

Because you're still hoping I'll be key in finding my mother? I arched my eyebrows. *Or because you were moved by having a woman hug you without clawing up your chest?* It was a feeble joke, especially since the plateau had fallen on him, however inadvertently, because of me.

He smiled slightly. *Yes.*

Val, standing beside me but not a part of the conversation, waited patiently until lights flashed out front.

"One of Willard's corporals is here with the corpse-mobile," she said after glancing over the fence. "Not to rush such a monumental decision," she added, waving to the sword still proffered in Sarrlevi's hands, "but I do have a mission to accomplish tonight. Perhaps you could make up your mind, so we can get going."

"All right." I hefted my hammer and offered it to Sarrlevi.

He accepted it and extended the sword to me, hilt first. "I trust you have some training with blades?"

I realized he intended me to use it if trouble found me again. "I'm pretty badass with bokken."

His eyebrows rose, and I was positive he didn't know what those were, but he nodded, as if he trusted me. And here I was debating if I could trust him. If I lost his sword, I would feel like a complete ass.

But I wouldn't. I would stick it in whoever was behind all the trouble, especially if they were tied in with my mother's death or disappearance.

"I'll need the location from you," Sarrlevi said.

Val pulled out her phone and showed him the display. "Here's the address."

He gazed blandly at her.

"I'm sure elves don't know how to use GPS," I whispered, assuming Sarrlevi wanted me to show the place to him in my thoughts, the way I had Zadie's apartment, so he could make a portal there. "And it's not like he's got a phone."

"I suppose not." Val lowered hers and looked at him. "He doesn't even have a shirt."

"Such things happen when dragons destroy your wardrobe," he said coolly, returning her gaze. "Along with your home."

"That's not Val's fault." I didn't want him to blame her, even if Zavryd's family *had* been responsible.

Returning his gaze to me, Sarrlevi stepped closer and lifted his hand toward my head, but he raised his eyebrows and paused. Waiting for permission?

"Go ahead." I was less nervous about him reading my thoughts than I had been last time. I pictured the trailer on the logging land, thought about as much as I could of the flight that had taken us there, and also formed a map in my head of the county, hoping all that together would get him to the right spot. And hoping that when he showed up, something besides magical grenades would be waiting for him.

His fingers brushed my temple and slid through my hair to rest against my scalp. Aware of Val standing and watching with her arms folded over her chest, I resisted the urge to close my eyes and lean into his hand. Though keeping them open might not have been a good idea either since I had a close-up of his naked chest, each muscle delineated as clearly as in an anatomy book.

Maybe it was good that Val was there. I successfully resisted the urge to touch his chest or do something stupid like trying to kiss him for luck.

His mental touch was gentle, nothing like the painful rakes through my mind from the dragon, and even lighter than the last time he'd done this. That urge to lean into his touch came over me again, along with a wish that he would run his fingers through my hair and elsewhere as well.

"I think I have it," he said, mentally withdrawing. Before physically pulling away, he used his magic to send a warm tingle of pleasure through me.

"Right." The word came out raspy, and I cleared my throat. "Good."

That cocky knowing smile came to his lips, and I scowled at him and stepped back. His smile only broadened. At least he didn't say anything, only inclining his head toward me and—surprisingly—Val before heading into the house to pack his gear and leave.

"I'm ready," I told Val, pointing Sarrlevi's sword toward the gate leading to the front yard and hoping to head off any further comments from her about how giving him my hammer was a bad idea.

"How similar is that in heft to your wooden swords?" Unlike Sarrlevi, *she* clearly knew what bokken were.

"Not very, but I'm prepared to kick anyone I can't manage to stab." If I'd had a safe in the house, I might have left Sarrlevi's treasured blade there and gone in with my feet and fists, weapons I *was* practiced with, but I didn't want to risk anyone breaking in and stealing it. It would be safer with Val and me, even if we were going into danger.

"Always a good plan."

"So I hope."

25

AFTER ASKING TINJA TO CONSIDER VISITING GOBLIN FRIENDS, though I didn't know if enemies would attack the house twice in the same night, I climbed into Val's Jeep with her, and we headed north. She'd dismissed Sindari, wanting to, because of the limited time he could be in our realm, save him in case we ended up fighting later.

Despite nightfall, the freeway was full of traffic, people driving home from errands. We were driving *to* our errands, errands I hoped would prove productive this time, but I worried that we wouldn't be able to reach that trailer, much less *caves* neither of us had been to, without a dragon flying us. The thought of trekking up the mountain on foot in the dark wasn't appealing.

I wondered if Sarrlevi was already there, courtesy of his portal. I supposed we couldn't have traveled together if he was going to claim to have stolen my hammer. Too bad.

"Any chance your mate will return and personally show us where the caves are?" I asked.

"There's a chance, yes, but he shared a telepathic image of the area with me before he left, so I think I can find them. The one he explored is near the top of the mountain and has a large mouth. He didn't have to tuck his wings to fly in, so we should be able to see it from a distance."

"From a distance at night?"

"Let's hope. I have a charm that lets me see in the dark." Val waved toward her thong necklace of charms. "Unfortunately, I didn't see a road or even a trail in his vision. Not a problem for a dragon... but I'm hoping to find some old logging roads up there that are still accessible." Val patted the dash of her Jeep.

"That's asking a lot in this climate. Washington might not be a jungle, but the undergrowth can spread to swallow things with impressive speed." I thought of my many battles with Himalayan blackberry brambles encroaching on the yards of houses I wanted to sell.

"I know. We don't want to arrive that quickly anyway, not if Sarrlevi is supposed to get there first. I don't pretend to understand how portals work, but Zav has told me that you can't make one from one part of the world to another. You have to go to another world first and then back to the original one. They're wormholes through space or something like that, and the travel isn't instantaneous."

"Well, if there really is someone up there, ready to give a reward for my hammer, the handoff shouldn't take long."

"I assume his plan isn't to go through with the handoff," Val said dryly. "Or so I hope."

"His fights don't usually take long either."

"He did swiftly and definitively deal with that van."

"When we left, Tinja was taking credit for that," I said, though I'd seen Sarrlevi's orange beams destroy it. "Tinja and her Goblinator."

"And that's what exactly?"

"A big gun that fires toaster coils."

Val looked over at me.

"Probably other things. She mentioned using recycled materials to make the ammunition, including my toaster coils."

"You're brave to have a goblin roommate."

"Says the person with a cadre of vampires in her basement."

"There's usually only one vampire."

"Some people would still find that an alarming number."

As we turned off I-5 and headed east, the traffic dwindled. When Val's phone rang, Willard's name popping up, she grimaced before answering it.

"We're on the way out there now," she said without a greeting. "Sorry about the delay at Matti's house, but her hammer is a hot commodity these days."

"So you said," came Willard's Southern drawl. "I'm at her house now. Corporal Spitz got some rings off the fingers of the dead. They're not from the basement vault, but a few of these other trinkets are."

"I know."

"Did you also know that there are a couple of humans in camo mixed in with the trolls? It looks like they were working together."

"Yeah," Val said. "The one I searched didn't have ID."

"None of them do. And there's no rank, insignia, or name tags on the uniforms." Willard hesitated. "There were a couple of M4 carbines too."

"We saw," Val said. "The same as the dead guys that were walled in under the house in Bellevue."

"It's a common weapon and could be a coincidence," Willard said, but she must have also been thinking about that, or she wouldn't have bothered pointing out the model.

"This implies that the recent attacks, at least this group of people trying to get my hammer, might be tied in with all that, right?" I asked.

"It's possible they learned of it, want it for their collection, and issued the reward," Willard said. "Proceed with caution."

"Shit."

Val looked over at me.

"I'm realizing there's a high likelihood that whoever is Hoovering up reactors and magical artifacts and weapons... is going to know Sarrlevi has been working with me."

"I thought you were working for *him*," Val said.

I shook my head. "All that matters is that our enemies may know we're on the same side, and he could be walking into a trap. If they don't believe he's there to sell my hammer, they'll attack him with everything they attacked us with last time. Maybe more." And he was injured and didn't have a dragon.

"I've been assuming all along there was a link," Val said. "That's why I wanted you to come back up there with me to search for clues on Willard's missing artifacts."

"They're not *my* artifacts," Willard said as I digested that. "I'm only responsible for them," she added.

"When does your general come to inspect your empty vault?" Val asked.

Willard sighed. "Early tomorrow morning."

"We'll see what we can find by then."

"Thank you."

Val hung up, turned off the highway, and stopped in front of a blue bar across a gravel road. She hopped out, touched it while holding one of her charms, and a faint *clink* sounded. She pushed the gate open and got back in.

As the Jeep headed up the dark lumpy road, I worried about what would happen to Sarrlevi when he showed up with my hammer.

26

IT TOOK THE BETTER PART OF AN HOUR TO WIND UP THE ROAD AND into the depths of the logging property. It turned from gravel to dirt and grew bumpier as we progressed, passing a mixture of old-growth forest, new growth, and clear-cut sections that hadn't been replanted. Now and then, I sensed magic among the trees. More of those grenade launchers?

Val must have sensed them, too, for she eyed the sides of the road warily and drove slowly with both hands on the wheel. "It would be nice if Zav returned soon. If not for Willard's inspector coming in the morning, I would have put this off."

"How much trouble is she likely to get in over the missing stuff?" I hadn't known the colonel long enough to have strong feelings about her, and I was still highly suspicious of the military, but Val clearly cared about her boss.

"She didn't say, but I read between the lines that it's a big deal. The government isn't happy if you lose even a stapler, much less millions and millions of dollars of one-of-a-kind, at least on Earth, artifacts."

"I didn't know they had monetary value."

"Whatever people are willing to pay. On Earth... it's a lot." Val frowned as she guided the Jeep off the road and around a log blocking it. Fortunately, there was room to do so. What would happen if we came to a spot where there wasn't? "I don't think she'd end up in a military prison, but she might get demoted and removed from her position. That would be annoying to me as well as her. I've worked for three previous commanders of that unit in the years I've been contracting with the Army. One was okay, one was a sanctimonious prick, and one couldn't give me a mission without making a pass at me, never mind that he was married."

"I imagine that's annoying."

"Very."

"I got hit on by an orc this week. That's the kind of guy I attract."

Val slanted a long look at me, and I waved away the comment. It was stupid, and I didn't even know why that incident bothered me, especially when there were far greater things to be concerned about. I admitted to myself that this reemergence of dating self-pity had started about the time Sarrlevi showed up. The desire to be hot enough that *he* would want to do more than give me a friendly pat.

I shook my head, almost wishing he had continued to be a dick. He still had his moments, like when he got smug and smirked, but now that he was risking his life for me, I was a lot more inclined to like him.

Val couldn't have read my mind—at least, I didn't think so—but she reached over and swatted me on the shoulder. "I don't doubt that orc males find women without tusks intriguing, but I hope you know that you've got plenty of attributes that guys —*human* guys—find appealing. Or is a not-human guy what you want to attract?"

"I don't want to attract anyone," I snapped, not wanting a pep talk from someone who looked like a model, even when she was dressed like Sarah Connor.

"Well, if you do and, like me, could use some help in the fashion and makeup area, you're welcome to come to one of the sword practices I have with my daughter. She's in the know with that stuff and *loves* to give advice."

"Great." Her daughter was probably as gorgeous as she was. "How old is she?"

Val didn't look older than thirty, but I also appeared young for my age. Someone had once suggested that having a dwarf parent would grant me longer than typical life, assuming I survived my tendencies to get into trouble, and those with elven blood had to be the same way.

"Fifteen."

"Oh, yes, teenage girls are just who you want giving you fashion advice."

"She's got a good eye for it. I'm not sure where she gets it since Thad—my ex-husband—considers Dungeons & Dragons T-Shirts haute couture, and you've seen *my* wardrobe."

Despite my snark, the thought of having someone to spar with who understood that my interest in martial arts was based in real-world practical dangers, rather than a desire to train for tournaments, was appealing. Maybe not the fifteen-year-old daughter, but Val knew all about orcs, trolls, ogres, and other opponents with magical blood—and magical power.

"I could come over to spar sometime," I said, "if you can promise your daughter *won't* give me advice."

"I can't do that. She gives me unsolicited advice all the time. Usually telling me to knock off the Rambo look."

I snorted. "You're way more *Terminator 2* than *Rambo*. You don't even have a bandolier."

"Only because my gun takes clips." Val winked at me before slowing down, the headlights playing over a log blocking the road.

It rose as high as the hood of the Jeep. "That one is going to be a challenge to drive around."

Its length extended into the darkness on either side of road for farther than we could see.

Val rolled down her window and stuck her head out. "I think we're still a couple of miles from that parking area. We haven't reached burned trees yet."

The reminder of us hunkering in the trailer and hoping not to burst into flames came to mind, and I winced, feeling like we hadn't been wise coming back up here. Most of those defenses might have been automated, but I had a feeling someone had been watching us and had started that fire. I couldn't imagine a booby trap so precise and effective.

"Do you hear that?" Val asked.

"What?" I rolled down the window, expecting the howls of werewolves or something to indicate magical explosives launching.

Val turned off the Jeep and kept her ears cocked. "I thought I heard a helicopter."

"Well, those are a thing in Western Washington."

"I suppose, but we're not close to any major towns now, and it's late for the forest service to be out inspecting the wilds."

I listened for a moment but didn't hear anything.

"Maybe it was my imagination." Val reached into the back and grabbed her sword scabbard. "Let's see if we can deal with that log; otherwise, we've got a long walk."

"Deal with it? With your sword?" Even if she'd had an *axe*, I couldn't imagine us getting through that massive log in a timely manner.

"*Both* of our swords." She gave Sarrlevi's weapon a pointed look.

Since he hadn't left the scabbard with me, I'd been riding with the naked blade next to my legs, being careful not to lop anything off the interior of Val's Jeep. To say it was razor sharp would have been a vast understatement.

"I'm sure Sarrlevi wouldn't be happy with me if I used his magical elven sword to cut wood."

"I didn't know making him happy was a goal for you." Val quirked her eyebrows at me.

"Given his profession, and the fact that I'd like my hammer back, making him *un*happy doesn't seem wise."

"If his sword is as powerful as mine, the log shouldn't leave a dent." Val hopped out and strode toward our obstacle. "*Eravekt!*" she commanded.

Not only her sword but Sarrlevi's glowed brightly.

"Don't tell me you *want* to be used on a log," I grumbled at it, wrapping my hand around the hilt as I opened the door.

"That's interesting," Val said, eyeing Sarrlevi's glowing sword.

Before I could ask what, a surge of energy flowed from the hilt and into my arm, along with an image of Sarrlevi battling shambling creatures with pasty skin hanging in flaps and long claw-like nails. Zombies?

I'd heard of but never seen such beings and hadn't been sure they existed. In the vision, strange green mist curled around a swampy battlefield, and two moons hung in the half-shrouded sky, muted silver light filtering through. Wherever the battle had taken place, it hadn't been on Earth. The scene and the foes brought graveyards to mind.

Sarrlevi slew the zombies, then sprang for a larger naked and gaunt figure. It crouched behind a tree with two young elven females huddled at its feet. With a series of swift sword slashes, Sarrlevi defeated the creature—a zombie lord?—and its body flopped down beside the girls. The sword beamed a sense of pride into me, pleased that it had assisted in the battle.

Less delighted by it and Sarrlevi, the elven females shrieked and stumbled away, tearing away bindings on their wrists and

ankles. Sarrlevi lifted a hand and started after them, but one
formed a portal. They sprang through it, leaving him alone in the
creepy swamp.

His hand drooped to his side. He watched until the portal
faded, and the sword shared a sense of sadness—its or his?—with
me. Sarrlevi used it to cut off the zombie lord's head, then created
a portal of his own. Off to turn the head in for a bounty? Or his
payment?

The smash of a blade cutting into wood jerked me back to the
real world, and the sword released its hold on me. Why it had
shared that, I didn't know, but the hilt was warm in my hand, as if
it was content to be there with me.

I joined Val in front of the log. Wielding her glowing sword like
an axe, she'd already taken huge chunks out of the obstacle and
waved for me to start working on it from the other side of the road.

"What was interesting?" I asked. "I didn't hear."

"That Sarrlevi's sword responded to a dwarven command. I'd
assumed he carried elven blades, but I suppose dwarves do make
the best weapons."

I thought of my mother's hammer. Even though I didn't have a
basis for comparison, I offered a firm, "Yes."

Val nodded at me and kept hacking away.

"Why didn't you bring a chainsaw?" I asked.

"I didn't think of it. I brought my camping gear, but I should
have foreseen this problem. I admit I was hoping Zav would show
back up, but that's not a plan. Sometimes, when he has to go do
dragon stuff, he's gone for days."

Dragon stuff. Like hunting down assassins, destroying their
homes, and mind scouring their friends.

Zavryd hadn't been there for that, but it had probably only
been luck that his sister had found Sarrlevi first.

"Does your sword ever give you visions?" I took an experi-
mental swing at the log. Even though I suspected Val was right

and that its magic would keep the blade from breaking or even denting, it wasn't my weapon, and the thought of having to explain to Sarrlevi that I'd broken it horrified me.

"Not really. Sometimes Storm has conveyed feelings to me. Why? Is Sarrlevi's sharing?"

Despite my tentative swing, the blade cut deep, leaving a gouge and sending shards of bark and wood flying. "Something like that but nothing related to our mission." I swung again, trying not to feel like a logger instead of a warrior. "I think it might have been one of his previous missions. It seemed proud to have slain someone vile."

"You sure it was one of *Sarrlevi's* missions? He tried to slay me, you know."

"Some people consider you vile."

"Thanks," Val said dryly. She kept cleaving into the log as we talked, the magical blade cutting off far more than a mere axe would have. "If it was his father's sword before his, maybe it was sharing one of *his* missions. He could have been some great elven warrior."

"I don't think so." I swung harder so I could catch up with Val. "I suppose he could have been a great warrior to his people and a complete ass to his family, but it's hard to imagine."

Val looked over at me. "Sarrlevi told you about his family?"

I hesitated. Maybe I shouldn't have said anything, but I had the urge to defend him. "A bit. His father sounded like a monster."

"I guess, unless you're born a psychopath, you need to have some kind of messed-up past to decide to become an assassin. Or to have been singled out by the Army and *told* you're training to become one, whether you want to or not."

"He's not a psychopath."

Val's only response was a pleased, "*Hah,*" as she made it through the log. "Magical swords are pretty handy."

As I finished cutting away the other portion, I decided my

hammer would have been better. With its ability to launch light-ning, I might have blown *up* the log. Even so, I gave Sarrlevi's sword a careful pat, wanting it to know I liked it fine.

Once the two slices had been cut away, we attempted to roll the detached section away and found that even the combined strength of a half-elf and a half-dwarf weren't sufficient. But Val had a winch on the front of her Jeep, and its 400 horsepower engine helped us tug it off the road.

Only when we were back inside did I realize she'd given me a hint about her past. "The Army forced you to become an assassin?"

"To learn to fight and deal with magical beings, yes. Before that, I was a pilot. That was what I *wanted* to be."

"Deal with them... in an assassinly way?"

"Sometimes." Her tone had grown more clipped, and I wondered if some of her orders had been deplorable. "There's a reason I got out as soon as they let me and became an indepen-dent," she added. "Willard doesn't order me to do anything morally questionable. She sends me after clear-cut criminals."

"Did the previous station commanders always do that?"

Val hesitated. "Not always."

"Then I hope we find the missing stuff so she doesn't get the boot."

"Good." She glanced at me. "If it matters to you, I don't think Sarrlevi is a psychopath. Just weird."

The urge to defend him reared up again, but I wasn't sure I could argue that someone who'd had to clean the entropy in my bedroom before he could focus on healing his wounds wasn't *weird*.

"Lots of people are," I said instead.

27

WE PASSED INTO THE AREA AFFECTED BY THE WILDFIRE—OR THE deliberately set *not*-wild fire—the blackened trunks of trees all that remained, skeletal in the wan starlight. The clear-cut came into view, a cloud of ash sifting upward around us as we drove across it toward the trailer. The structure was undamaged by the fire, but the withering remains of Val's vines were still there, entombing it.

I couldn't believe she'd called *Sarrlevi* weird and almost said so, but she spoke first.

"I don't see or sense him."

"Sarrlevi?" I asked.

"Yeah. This is still, as far as I know, where one is supposed to bring the hammer for the reward." Val gazed around at the ashes. "Though I wouldn't be surprised if they moved the meetup location after the fire. But it's where you sent Sarrlevi, isn't it? What you showed him when he was rubbing your head?"

"He wasn't rubbing my head. He was reading my mind."

"Kind of tenderly." She smirked.

"Do you torment all your allies so?"

"Yup. You can ask Sindari when I call him up."

"Maybe you should do that now." I would prefer she snark at her tiger rather than me.

"I can drive a little farther." Val waved toward a dirt road that continued behind the parking area, switchbacking up the side of a logged slope. "The caves are in that direction."

"Sarrlevi is really good at camouflaging himself."

"If he were here, I would assume he'd step out and wave at us. You, at least. I irk him."

"I suspect you irk a lot of people."

"An accurate statement." Val gave me a long look.

"What?"

"Just be prepared in case we're up here alone and have to handle anyone we encounter ourselves. I suspect— Don't take this the wrong way, but I'm sure Sarrlevi believes he can get his sword back from you anytime, whether he returns your hammer or not."

"I'm sure he does too, but just because we don't see him doesn't mean he's not here. Or *wasn't* here. Maybe he met with the issuers of the reward, but they outnumbered him and captured him. He didn't have time before this started to heal his injuries."

"Even injured, he fought a bunch of warriors at once and blew up a van with his magic," Val pointed out.

"I know. Don't tell him I said so, but he's kind of a badass."

That earned me another long look from Val.

"I'm stating a fact. I'm not infatuated with him or whatever you're thinking."

"That's good. With dragons after him, he might not be the best bet for a lasting romance."

"What if someone just wanted to have sex with him?" I meant it as a joke, especially since I'd denied being interested. But maybe I should have dropped the subject if I wanted *Val* to drop it.

"I guess that would be okay. As long as *someone* got her hammer back first."

"I don't usually include that in bedroom play."

"*Usually?*" Val smirked at me again before slowing the vehicle and frowning at the route ahead.

I sensed magic in the middle of the road. The headlights didn't show anything but dirt, but that didn't mean much when dealing with magic.

"Something in the road?" I asked.

"Yes." Val drove off the side and around the area, something that was much easier to do here in the logged area, the undergrowth almost as denuded as the trees. "I'm surprised we didn't encounter more booby traps on the way up. Zav may have triggered most of them with his crazy flying. Come to think of it, that may have been *why* he was flying crazily."

"Not to make us motion sick?"

"Maybe he wanted to trigger things since he knew he could handle the explosives and others who might come this way later couldn't. He won't admit to caring about human *vermin*, as he spent the first six months of our relationship calling the people of Earth, but he's pretty noble at the core."

I thought about teasing her for sounding a little dreamy when she spoke about him—if anyone was infatuated, it was Val—but I was pensively staring out the windows, hoping to see or sense Sarrlevi. As she'd pointed out, this was what I'd shown him, where he should have come out when he traveled through his portal. If he hadn't been met by the people offering the reward, then he would be around here somewhere, waiting for us. He'd known we were coming, so he shouldn't have left.

I refused to contemplate that he might have taken the hammer and gone. Even if I hadn't had his sword, for good or ill, I no longer believed he would betray me.

After navigating around another magical threat, we came to a dead end. There was a cleared area where trucks had staged, but the road didn't continue on. Ahead, the mountainside rose steeply, and I couldn't imagine anything driving up it, even in switchbacks. If caves dotted the slope, it was too dark to see them.

A faint *whoop-whoop* reached my ears. Val rolled down her window, cut off the engine, turned off the lights, and cocked her head to listen.

"Definitely a helicopter," she said. "Sounds like a big one."

As a former pilot, maybe she could tell the difference in helicopter size by the sound of the blades spinning. Since I couldn't, I took her word for it and let my hand fall to Sarrlevi's sword. If there were people flying around up here, maybe he *had* been captured.

Or killed. What if they'd detected the ruse and killed him for attempting it?

As I told myself he could take care of himself, I sensed magic in the distance, at the far edge of my range. It had to be something powerful, for I couldn't detect minor trinkets or artifacts that far away. Strange that it had appeared on my radar between one second and the next when we hadn't been moving.

"There's something here besides booby traps in the road." I pointed toward the mountaintop, though it had to be a couple of miles straight up from us, and what I felt seemed to be coming from behind it. Or maybe *inside* it. From within one of Zavryd's caves?

"Something powerful," Val said.

"You don't think my mother's reactor could be up here, do you?"

I didn't know *why* such a thing would be stored in a mountain, but whoever had stolen it had to keep it somewhere. Somewhere that it wouldn't be discovered by chance members of the magical community wandering past. And if Willard's stolen artifacts were magical, they needed to be hidden well out of the way too. Except for choice items doled out to hammer thieves...

"I don't know, but we can't drive any farther." Val opened the door and got out.

By the time I joined her, willing Sarrlevi's sword to stop glowing, lest it turn me into a beacon, she'd summoned Sindari.

I sense powerful magic nearby, the tiger said telepathically. *Are we heading into a glorious battle?*

"I'll be shocked if we don't end up in a fight before the night is over," Val said. "Its glory is to be determined."

All battles in which noble Del'nothian tigers partake tend to be glorious.

"Aren't you glad you won't end up in a battle doomed to be undistinguished and obscure?" Val asked me as she locked the Jeep and headed toward the slope with Sindari at her side.

Before I could decide on an answer, light appeared near the top of the mountain. It was as if someone had opened a trapdoor to the sky. Maybe they had, for an aircraft flew out from behind the mountain to hover above the area. Its dark bulky shape would have been hard to make out if not for the stars that it blotted out. It had no running lights.

"That's not normal, is it?" I asked before I realized *it* was the source of at least some of the magic we felt.

"Not in any sense of the word." Val picked up the pace and drew her gun.

With my shorter legs, I struggled to keep up, especially when we left the road and had to navigate over undergrowth and uneven ground snarled with rocks and roots. We also had to contend with trees, having reached the end of the logged area, and as we headed into them, they blocked our view of the light and the helicopter.

"Sindari," Val said, "will you go ahead and see what they're up to?"

Yes, but they're farther away than my maximum range. I encourage you to hurry if you want me to reach them before they finish whatever they're doing.

"We *are* hurrying. People with two legs aren't as swift as you."

Unfortunate.

Just climb up somewhere with a good view, Val said, switching to telepathy as the silver-furred tiger disappeared into the trees, *and let us know what you see.*

In the dark, I tripped over something and almost ended up face-first in the undergrowth. I was somewhat mollified when Val also ran into rocks and wobbled, but she caught her balance easily. Elves. We could have gone faster if we'd ordered our swords to light up, but neither of us wanted to be visible to whoever was up there.

"It would have been nice if our elven and dwarven heritage had conveyed their ability to see in the dark," Val whispered, though she'd admitted to having a charm that granted her that power.

"I agree. It would keep me from stepping on Tinja's projects when I go for water in the middle of the night. Goblins don't differentiate between tables and floors when it comes to places to store stuff."

"I've noticed."

I sensed her aura fade and realized she'd activated her camouflage charm. I did the same.

After that, we fell silent, the climb leaving us short of breath. We might have driven up high enough in elevation for the air to be thinner as well. My lungs believed that as we half-walked and half-jogged up the slope.

I sense another helicopter, Val said telepathically, saving her breath. *Maybe a third as well. Behind the mountain but heading toward the other. What are they all doing up here?*

I have no idea. They couldn't have known we were coming, right? You didn't tell anyone besides Willard, did you?

No. But you told Sarrlevi. Val didn't say it in a condemning way, but she did give me a pointed look.

I'm sure he didn't blab our secrets to people on Earth. He barely knows anyone here.

But if he came up here to turn in your hammer, as you believe, they may have learned about us and our interest in the place. Plus we were here the other day ourselves. Maybe they realized their secret base isn't that secret anymore.

That doesn't make any sense. If it was supposed to be a secret base, why give the address out to anyone who might have a shot at getting my hammer? The cave was miles from where the drop-off point had been, but still.

Maybe they were planning to move operations after they got it.

You think that's what they're doing with the helicopters? I asked. *Is it moving day?*

I don't know, but those auras are shockingly powerful. If I'd heard of helicopter technology in use on other worlds, I would assume those came from somewhere besides Earth.

Powerful in what way? I sensed the magic radiating from them, like the auras of great magical creatures, but I didn't know what it would let them do. *Weapons systems? Defenses?*

Maybe both.

I'm a mile away at the edge of our range, Sindari spoke into our minds. *And I'm watching a flying contraption hover over an opening in the mountain. It has lowered a hook and a chain. I cannot sense what's inside the mountain, and I believe the stone is blocking my senses or has been magically insulated—a camouflaging spell of some kind—but when the breeze blew from that direction, I smelled the scents of many humans.*

Humans? You're sure? Val reached out, catching me as I stumbled over a divot in the ground.

I believe so. There may be other beings I can't yet detect, but the humans smell like typical people of your world. And they are wreathed in the exhaust fumes from the air conveyances.

Exhaust as in from aviation gasoline? Val asked. *Not anything magical?*

Typical exhaust from your combustion engines. I am aware that you have different kinds of petroleum-based fuels, and I can detect the differences in scent, but I do not know the names of them.

I guess that means the magical helicopters aren't from another world.

You don't think any other races burn fossil fuels? I had no idea. Sarrlevi's house was the only place on another world I'd been.

I would ask Zav, if he were here, but I haven't heard about it, if they do, Val said. *Most worlds in the Cosmic Realms have strong magic in the land, and that's the energy source their people draw upon.*

A huge crate covered in tarps and straps is now attached to the hook, Sindari said, *and the flying conveyance is lifting it into the air.*

Damn, it does *sound like they're moving.* Though Val was huffing, the same as I, she picked up her pace. *Stolen goods. Like maybe Willard's stolen goods. Sindari, can you get close enough to stop them?*

I wasn't sure how she expected a tiger to stop an airlift, unless he could jump through the open trapdoor and attack whoever was loading the helicopter, but it sounded like it might already be too late for that.

You must get closer to me before I can get closer to them, Sindari replied. *As I said, I'm already at the edge of my range.*

We're working on it. Val began to outpace me.

Since I kept myself in good shape, and usually had the stamina of a steam engine, I found that irritating, but, with her long legs, she bounded over logs and boulders like a deer. I scrambled over them like a chubby bear.

Go ahead, I told her when she glanced back. *I'm coming.*

And I was. I might get there more slowly, but if she and her tiger could reach the top before the helicopters flew away, I didn't want to be the anchor that delayed them.

Val chopped a wave and ran faster.

A few minutes later, after she'd disappeared from my view, I came into a clearing with light spots visible on the ground. Snow, I realized. We *had* climbed substantially in elevation.

From the clearing, the helicopter was visible, the crate Sindari had mentioned dangling below it as it rose away from the mountaintop. I was still more than a mile away. If I'd had my hammer, I might have issued the storm command and tried to send a streak of lightning in that direction. It probably wouldn't have worked, as I had neither seen it shoot lightning over a mile nor had proof that it could aim its attack like sniper fire. Still, I would have tried.

I glanced at Sarrlevi's sword, the hilt clenched in my sweaty palm, and thought of his weapons shooting the van with magical beams. To my senses, that had seemed more a result of *his* power than the swords', with the blades the conduit, but I wondered if I could replicate the move on some level. Supposedly, I had inherent power of my own. And the sword clearly had power. Further, it responded to dwarven commands, at least some of them.

The crate had cleared the cave, and the helicopter headed north over the trees, picking up speed. It was about to get away with its cargo.

"Hell, let's try." I halted, needing to catch my breath anyway, and pointed the sword toward the crate, then raised it slightly to where I guessed the chain that held it was, though I couldn't see it in the dark and at that distance. "Sword, I need your help, okay?"

It thrummed in my hand, and a sense of eagerness came from it. Like Sindari, it wanted to rush into glorious battle. This wasn't exactly that, but I said, "*Hyrek!*" and envisioned it sending a beam of power toward the cable.

To my surprise, it worked. An orange beam shot out, streaking over the trees toward the helicopter's cargo. As it reached it, the beam grew fainter. Losing power?

It barely reached its target, sizzling past inches above the crate.

The orange highlighted the crate and the bottom of the helicopter, as well as someone hanging out of an open cargo door in the back.

Was that someone wearing camouflage? It was too far away for me to tell, but the man jerked back out of view.

I shifted the sword back and forth, hoping the beam had the power to cut the chain. A strange weakness came over me, and I realized the sword was drawing upon my energy for this. It was as I'd suspected when Sarrlevi had done this. He'd used not only the weapon's power but his own.

Though my legs grew weaker, as my energy was sapped, I locked my knees. I didn't want to simply startle those people; I wanted to *stop* them.

The pilot navigated the helicopter to the side but too late. The beam cut through the chain, and the crate plummeted, disappearing into the trees. Distant cracks and snaps floated down the mountainside as it struck down.

"Hah!" I feared I would collapse if I let the sword keep drawing on my power, but I had to take a shot at knocking the helicopter down. Whoever those people were, I was positive we wanted to question them, not let them get away.

But when I shifted the beam upward, it didn't do anything to the magical aircraft. It didn't even seem to strike the hull, and I imagined something like a dragon's defensive barrier around it. Given the power the helicopter emanated, I couldn't be surprised, but I swore in frustration.

Gunshots fired. The man I'd seen and two others were leaning out the open door now. A bullet cracked off a rock near me, and I swore even more. Not only did they have weapons powerful enough to reach me, but I was out in the open.

Adrenaline fueled my wobbly legs, and I ran for the nearest trees. Sarrlevi might know how to command his sword to stop bullets, but *I* didn't.

Worse, the helicopter spun around, the nose pointed toward

me. Two red lights flared from the belly, and I sensed as much as saw magical missiles fire. Toward me.

I ran faster, hoping they would detonate in trees well away from me if I could reach cover in time. But they arced to follow my path, and with uneasy certainty, I realized they were probably heat-seeking missiles. Aside from Val and Sindari, I was the only warm thing on the mountainside.

28

As the heat-seeking missiles sped toward me, the two other magical helicopters that I'd sensed earlier but forgotten about flew out from behind the mountain and into view. They were *all* heading in my direction.

Not that it would matter if the missiles took me out.

"*Eravekt,*" I commanded the sword. By now, there was little point in worrying about its light being seen from a distance.

The pair of red glows marking the magical missiles shot unerringly toward me, whipping about to avoid the trees, as if some intelligence guided them rather than onboard computer chips. Hell, maybe it did. Those things might not have been made on Earth.

Wishing I knew how to form a protective barrier around myself, I ran faster, darting wildly between trees and looking for a cliff or jumble of boulders—*anything* large and dense—to hide behind. Branches clawed at my face, and rocks made the ground uneven and impossible to traverse without wobbling.

Ferns parted, revealing a pit. Cursing, I tried to go around it, but soft earth crumbled and gave way, and I tumbled. My foot caught on a root, and my ankle twisted, pain shooting up my leg.

As I rolled into the pit, death zoomed closer. I wouldn't be able to climb out in time, and it wasn't enough cover to keep the missiles from reaching me. The pit would become my grave.

"*Keyk!*" Val shouted from up the slope as I struggled to get to my feet, not ready to give up.

Of course. The command to turn one's blade icy cold.

My ankle shot more pain up my leg and a rock slid out from under my heel, thwarting my attempt to rise. From my back in the pit, I yelled the command, hoping Sarrlevi's blade recognized it, the same as my hammer did.

As the red-glowing missiles shot toward me, the hilt grew cold, and a frosty silver glow emanated from the blade. I held it up like a shield, squinting away from the missiles and willing the weapon to shield me, to somehow protect me.

"Over here," Val barked.

As if they were wolves on the hunt for any target, the missiles veered toward her. Her sword also glowed like a frosty glacier, but she'd thrust it into the ground and stood several yards away, waving her hands. Hoping the heat of her body led the missiles away from me.

And it did. They went straight toward her, and that wasn't any better.

"Is there a command for heat?" I yelled.

Val dove off an outcropping of rock, and the missiles sped through the air where she'd been. One clipped a tree and exploded, white light flashing brilliantly across the mountainside.

Though the helicopters were the last thing on my mind then, I registered the noise of their blades. They were coming in behind their missiles, prepared to launch more if these didn't do the job.

"*Krundark!*" Val shouted as she somersaulted through the air.

She landed in a crouch, but the remaining missile kept tracking her, turning straight toward her.

As I scrambled out of the pit, trying to ignore the pain in my ankle, I uttered the command to Sarrlevi's sword. The hilt shifted from freezing my palm to warming it, and the blade's glow changed from silver to fiery orange. Its heat warmed my exposed skin, and the missile that had been streaking toward Val, who was now running down the slope and zigzagging as I had been earlier, changed course once again.

It blurred toward me. Praying I wasn't about to get Sarrlevi's sword destroyed, I jammed it into the ground and hobbled away.

Gasping with every step, with sweat bathing my face, I put as much distance between myself and the sword as I could. When I risked glancing back, I couldn't tell if the missile was going toward it or me.

Spotting a boulder, I darted sideways and pressed my back against it. Behind me, the missile crashed into the earth and exploded, the boom hammering my eardrums. As the ground shuddered, my boulder shifted, and numerous trees blew up, pieces of trunks and branches flying in a hundred directions. An entire tree sailed over my head and smashed into a pine with a great crack. Clods of dirt, rocks, and pine needles rained down all around me.

The noise of the explosion faded but brought no relief, for the *thwumps* of the helicopter blades were audible, closer than ever. Three—or were there *four* now?—aircraft were bearing down on my position.

Why had I thought picking a fight with one of them was a good idea? All because I didn't want Val to have some asshole boss? I didn't even *care* about the military or Willard's office, damn it.

I did care about losing Sarrlevi's sword. Worried it had been destroyed by that missile, I left the cover of the boulder and hurried up the slope toward a huge smoking crater.

"Thanks," Val panted, running toward me from the side. "We better camouflage ourselves again."

"I was camouflaged *before*," I said, then realized I must have *un*camouflaged myself by attacking.

"I'm guessing the charms don't hide body heat."

"A flagrant deficiency in the design."

"Yes. And the helicopters must have some magic to keep the missiles from targeting *them*. Activate your charm again anyway."

I already had, hoping that if I didn't attack again, we would disappear from the gunmen's and pilots' view.

Val reached the crater ahead of me and peered in before glancing toward the sky. One of the helicopters grew visible through the trees, and I sensed the other three flying closer. We dared not linger in the area.

I clambered into the crater, feeling the residual heat through the soles of my shoes. Sarrlevi's sword was at the bottom, but it was covered in dirt and ash and no longer glowing. I sensed magic, but I didn't know if it belonged to the blade or, like the heat, was residue left from the missile.

When I wrapped my hand around the hilt, it was cool to the touch. None of its earlier eagerness emanated from it. Nothing did.

Fear gripped me for more reasons than the enemies hunting us. What if Sarrlevi did everything he'd promised and returned my hammer, and I had only a broken weapon to give him in exchange?

Once we had the weapon, Val led the way up the slope again. Trying to make it to the crate or only to hide from the helicopters? Maybe she wanted to reach that trapdoor and hoped the cave offered protection from magical attacks.

The helicopter fired two more missiles. This time, its nose wasn't pointed right at us, suggesting our charms were hiding us from the pilot, but it didn't matter. The concern Val had voiced proved true, and the heat-seeking missiles sped unerringly toward us.

"*Keyk,*" I whispered as Val did the same.

Her blade glowed icy silver, but Sarrlevi's did nothing.

"No," I groaned.

Val frowned, saw the problem, and gripped my wrist, pulling me close. We crouched as the missiles darted around trees and arrowed toward us. As I had before, she held her sword up like a shield.

Ice itself wouldn't have done anything to repel missiles, but it seemed to mask the heat of our bodies. The magical projectiles wobbled, then veered off, circling back down the slope. They slammed into the ground where the last one had exploded, drawn by the heat of the crater.

Before I could feel any triumph at our small victory, men leaned out the door of the helicopter—out of *all* the helicopters. With rifles, they rapid-fired toward the ground. Toward us.

"We've got to find better cover," I blurted.

A statement of the obvious. Val had already released my wrist and was running up the slope.

Bullets slammed into trees and the ground all around us. Even if the men had no way to sense us, they knew roughly where we were, and I feared it was only a matter of time before they got lucky.

29

"THERE!" I WHISPERED, POINTING AND PANTING.

A rocky outcropping loomed out of the shadows, and we ran toward it. With all four helicopters flying back and forth above the trees overhead, and men firing down at us, it was a miracle that we hadn't yet been hit.

Val didn't reply—she sounded as breathless as I—but she weaved between the trees and led the way toward it. A bullet clipped off a trunk scant inches from my head. I ducked and dove toward the outcropping, finding a crevice between the rocks to squeeze into.

If the men hadn't also been firing at the ground fifty yards away, I would have been certain our camouflage had worn off. Just in case, I rubbed the charm Artie had given me one more time.

We need to figure out a way to hurt them, Val spoke telepathically from under a rock ledge a few feet away, bullets continuing to slam into the ground and trees all around us.

How much ammunition did those people have?

I hit the helicopter with a beam from Sarrlevi's sword. The sword that was now cool and dormant—or dead—in my hand. *It knocked the crate free but didn't do anything to the aircraft.*

I saw. I hope there was something valuable in there.

I did too. If not, I'd drawn their attention for no good reason. The thought of the crate containing nothing but MREs made me groan.

I have an update for you, Sindari spoke into our minds from somewhere higher on the mountain.

If it's that four magical helicopters are shooting at us from right overhead, Val replied, *we don't need that update.*

I trust not. My update is that I've sensed that your mate has returned to this world.

Is he close?

He arrived back in the city, but he flies quickly.

A bullet slammed into the outcropping, shearing off rock that tumbled down in front of me. I grimaced and wondered *how* quickly.

Thanks, Val said. *Any other news?*

I've reached the crate that your ally detached from the helicopter, and I believe these are some, but likely not all, of the artifacts from your employer's building.

That's something anyway. The rest may still be inside the cave up there.

Or they might have been moved out of the cave before we'd arrived. I didn't voice the thought.

Hold on, Val added. *Zav is talking to me. I'm explaining our situation.*

I closed my eyes and leaned my head against the rock. If we could hold out a little longer, we would have help.

The hilt of Sarrlevi's sword warmed slightly in my hand, and I squeezed it in relief, hoping that meant it hadn't been permanently damaged. A sense of confusion emanated from it.

Didn't know what had hit it, huh? I could commiserate.

One of the helicopters swooped low, the open back door visible through the trees. Two men hung out of it with rifles—no surprise there—and a third person—a woman—came into view, hefting something in her hand. It was a glowing sphere, and I could sense its magic, though the powerful aura of the helicopter almost drowned it out.

"They've got something else to try," I whispered, though I didn't know if my voice would carry over the noise of the helicopter blades, nor did I think Val would be monitoring my thoughts while she spoke to her mate.

Sindari was right, Val told me. *Zav is coming, flying at top dragon speed, but he's not close yet. We've got to buy more time.* Her telepathic tone turned grim. *And hope a dragon is a match for four super-powered magical helicopters.*

Are they that strong? I'd thought dragons were a match for anything.

They are. They might very well be made from dragon magic. I'm not sure, but I hope Zav can handle them. We'll help.

The woman in the helicopter chose that moment to lob the magical sphere toward us.

Val swore and fired. I flinched at the noise, having forgotten she had a firearm, and cracked my head on a rock. Just as well. It was time to leave.

As Val fired toward the helicopter, the magical bullets leaving streaks of light in the night air, I rolled away from the outcropping. Her bullets pinged off the hull of the craft, or maybe the shield I'd encountered earlier. Meanwhile, the glowing sphere sailed through the trees toward the outcropping.

Val fired again, this time at the sphere. It pulsed magic, and I shouted, "Get out of there!" as a premonition took me.

Not only did it blow up, but it blew up *spectacularly,* with a boom that must have been heard back in Seattle.

The shockwave hurled me into the air, ripped trees from the

ground, and lit the night like a sun. Grip tight, I kept hold of
Sarrlevi's sword as I tumbled through the air, dreading the landing. I tried to see the ground, to gauge the distance so I could roll
and absorb some of the impact, but the light from the explosion
had half-blinded me.

I slammed into a tree, and my breath whooshed out in a
painful blast that left me dazed as well as breathless. Before I
could begin to recover, I hit the ground, landing hard on my back,
a rock jabbing me between the shoulder blades. It felt like a spear-
head gouging in.

The helicopters thundered overhead. As I tried to gather my
stunned body, willing it to spring up and run, the same woman
who'd thrown the sphere leaned out of the doorway again. Her
helicopter was directly above me, not a single tree left standing to
impede her aim, and she lifted another sphere.

Though I could hear a gun firing off to my right, I had no idea
if Val was able to help. Even if she could shoot a second one of
those spheres, all her bullet had done was prompt it to explode
earlier. This close to me, the detonation might blow me to pieces.

I lifted Sarrlevi's sword, as if it might protect me. The woman
sneered and drew back her arm to throw the sphere. The *bomb*.

But someone stepped into view behind her, wrapping an arm
around her throat. Surprise widened the woman's eyes, and she
dropped the sphere.

I lurched to my feet, imagining her *accidentally* killing me as
the thing struck down, but the person grabbing her darted a hand
out to catch the sphere before it fell. He or she hurled it, not
toward me but toward one of the other helicopters. Unfortunately,
the other aircraft was too far away, and it didn't reach, instead
blowing up a hundred yards from its blades.

Even so, the helicopter wobbled in the air, the shockwave
knocking it about. The woman in the chopper above me was
pulled back and down. Shouts of anger and surprise reached my

ears over the *thwump* of the blades, and my savior stepped into view again. I glimpsed a familiar male face as he whirled with his fists up to face men charging toward him.

"Sarrlevi," I blurted.

How he'd gotten up there, I had no idea, but I would hug him later for stopping that woman.

His sword warmed in my hand and glowed, as if delighted by his proximity. As I staggered away from the helicopter, my feet, ankle, back, and everything in between hurting, more gunfire came from the ground to the right. Val was shooting at the aircraft, aiming at the windshield, as if it might be a vulnerable spot, but the bullets weren't making it through.

The craft tilted and swerved, almost hitting a tree. It lifted before striking anything, the pilot taking it higher, but I was certain the tilt had been because Sarrlevi was inside, making hell for the crew. Where had he been *before* that? Captured and tied up? If so, his escape had been timely.

"Zav!" Val cried at the same time as I sensed not one but two dragons approaching.

Zavryd and... the other one was familiar too. But not in a good way. Zondia'qareshi.

"Shit." What if she'd come not to help us but to finish off Sarrlevi?

I looked up, hoping to glimpse him again, but the helicopter was flying away from our area, and trees blocked the view of the open door. The other aircraft were also veering off. Someone onboard must have had the ability to sense dragons.

"No," I whispered, afraid for Sarrlevi.

As far as I'd seen, he hadn't had a weapon, and those people had who-knew-how-much magic. A *lot*.

Dragons ought to be able to fly faster than helicopters—though I wasn't sure if that was true of *magical* helicopters—but if our enemies had a bolt-hole in the mountains, some camouflaged hiding spot, they might disappear in such a way that even dragons couldn't find them.

Lowering her firearm, Val limped toward me—she must have also gone flying when that first sphere exploded. She pointed toward an open spot where numerous trees had been blown away in the explosion.

"Zav will pick us up there." She wiped her brow, smearing blood from a gash across her forehead.

"What about the other dragon?"

"I'm not sure, but she should be here to help. That's Zav's sister, Zondia."

"She's the dragon that mind scoured me and helped destroy Sarrlevi's home. What if she's here for *him*?"

Had Val seen Sarrlevi in the helicopter? Did she know that he'd helped us? That he might have saved my life?

"I'm sure they'll prioritize dealing with these guys first."

I wasn't. Zavryd might care about his mate and her assignment, but I doubted Zondia was here for that. She had to be here for Sarrlevi.

Val limped into the clearing and pointed her sword toward the sky to the south. The dark sleek shapes of the dragons were visible, and Zavryd's violet eyes flared with inner light. Their powerful wings flapped, carrying them rapidly toward us.

I will remain on the ground and defend this crate, Sindari announced from up the mountainside.

You just don't want to ride on a dragon, Val replied.

Correct. Also, there are many valuables here, and one of the helicopters is heading this way with a chain and hook lowered. I believe they may try to regain their cargo. It did not break in the landing.

Right. Keep them from getting it.

I will. Another air conveyance is rocking wildly. It almost crashed into the top of a tree. Did you damage it?

"Sarrlevi is in there," I blurted, then repeated the words

silently, attempting to project them telepathically, in case the tiger wasn't paying attention to me. *He's fighting them, but he was outnumbered and unarmed.*

Val glanced at me, but Zavryd had pulled in his wings to land, and she didn't speak again. When his talons touched down, she ran forward and hugged his leg before clambering onto his back.

I frowned upward as Zondia flew past without slowing. She was heading straight toward the helicopter with Sarrlevi in it.

Magic swirled under me, levitating me into the air. I blurted a surprised curse as Zavryd floated me up to join Val on his back.

She had her firearm in hand, but she also pointed at Sarrlevi's blade. "Can you make it shoot a beam again? We're going into battle."

"I can try."

Zavryd sprang back into the air, wings flapping as he carried us aloft. My stomach lurched, and I closed my eyes as we whipped through the trees.

"Whoever those guys are," Val said, "Willard is going to want at least one questioned, if not the whole lot arrested. Sneaking into a government facility and stealing all the powerful magical artifacts in the vault is a major crime."

It is a minor crime to a dragon, Zavryd informed us as he flew above the treetops. *But presuming to attack the mate of a dragon is inexcusable. I will destroy their puny flying contraptions and knock them all to the ground.*

"Do you really think their helicopters are puny?" Val sounded skeptical as she pointed toward the dark mountaintop ahead.

Surprisingly, they are not. Very powerful dwarven magic protectively enshrouds them.

"Dwarven?" I asked.

"I thought it might be dragon magic," Val said.

Dragons have no reason to build flying conveyances.

Did dwarves? My fear of heights ensured *I* wouldn't want a magical helicopter.

Zondia was winging toward two of the aircraft, including the one where I'd last seen Sarrlevi, but the other two also remained aloft and were flying fearlessly out to intercept her. Two more helicopters came into view from behind the mountain, bringing the total to six.

Twin red glows appeared on the fronts of several of them. I groaned. The helicopters had more missiles to launch.

Even with dragons, we might need more firepower than we had.

30

Several magical missiles fired at once.

"They track heat," I called. "If you can cast fire off to the side, they should be drawn toward it."

Zondia flew straight toward one of the helicopters, ignoring a pair of missiles streaking toward her. Zavryd listened to me, and bursts of magic came from him. He formed balls of fire that spun in the sky a hundred yards to either side of us. Even from that distance, I could feel their intense heat. We soon flew away from them, and the missiles that had been heading for Zavryd diverted, arrowing toward the fireballs.

Zondia was close enough, however, that the two tracking her weren't deterred. Magic swelled around her as she hardened her defenses. The missiles struck them and, with immense flares of power, blew up. Light flashed, and I squinted and turned my head.

Zavryd roared and flew straight toward the explosions to help his sister.

Val dug in her ammo pouch. "This is my last clip," she said as she locked it in her firearm. "If we're not going to get close enough for swords, I need to find a target that's affected by my bullets.

These are *magical* bullets, but so far they haven't been able to get through."

Zondia'qareshi! Zavryd called.

Despite her defenses, the missiles had knocked her out of the sky. She was still alive—I could sense her aura—but she'd landed hard and was shaking her head on her long neck. Two of the helicopters soared toward her while the rest headed toward us.

I leaned to the side so I could target past Val and Zavryd's heads and leveled Sarrlevi's sword toward one. We were closer now than when I'd knocked the crate down, so I hoped the magic might be enough to break through the helicopter's defenses.

I'm fine, brother, came Zondia's response, though she sounded dazed. *Take those maggots out of the skies.*

Surrender, verminous humans! Zavryd ordered as he flew toward our enemies. Magical compulsion laced his words, and I lowered the sword, almost overtaken by the urge to surrender. *To strike against a dragon is the greatest crime in the Cosmic Realms, and you shall die for your impudence.*

"No punishment and rehabilitation?" I lifted the sword again, then whispered, "*Hyrek,*" and Sarrlevi's sword flared with power. A beam shot toward one of the helicopters.

I'd lost track of which one Sarrlevi was in, as they all looked the same, but one aircraft was wobbling and flying erratically. Either Zondia was doing something to it—or he was.

The orange beam struck the windshield of one of the helicopters—or the barrier in front of it. Once more, the magic was deflected. I scowled, feeling useless in the battle.

Behind us, missiles exploded. They'd homed in on Zavryd's fireballs, blowing up when they reached them. Fortunately far enough back now that the shockwaves didn't disturb us.

"They *have* to have weaknesses," Val said after firing unsuccessfully at another of the aircraft.

Surrender! Zavryd tried again, though none of the pilots had so much as flinched.

"Just use raw power, Zav." Val lowered her firearm and touched his scaled back. "Something's protecting those people from your compulsion."

Fire shot up from the ground—from Zondia. This time, she learned from her brother and conjured it well away from herself.

Zavryd also created more fire, great swirling balls of it blasting into the helicopters. They momentarily swallowed the aircraft but once again didn't penetrate their defenses. Our enemies flew out of the flames and continued to attack.

"Whoever the dwarf was who enchanted those helicopters," Val said, "I want to hire him to do some armor for me."

If not by magic, I will destroy them by fang and talon! Zavryd cried and flew straight toward one of the aircraft.

Missiles exploded as they hit the ground, drawn by Zondia's fire. She sprang back into the air, her maw gaping open to show her long sharp fangs as she followed her brother's example and headed toward one of the aircraft.

As Zavryd flew toward a helicopter soaring out of one of his fireballs, one of the other choppers pitched alarmingly, the blades slicing into branches of a tree. Was that the one with Sarrlevi inside?

The aircraft ahead of us tried to veer away. It was too dark in the cab to see the eyes of the pilot, but I imagined them bulging wide as a huge black dragon flew straight at him. Faster and more agile than the helicopter, Zavryd changed course to intercept it.

"Watch out for the blades," Val warned.

Zavryd swept in from below the aircraft, a blast of power emanating from him. Something to cut through the armor of the chopper?

His body twisted as he approached, tilting Val and me upside-down, and my heart tried to leap out of my chest. His magic kept us from falling as his talons grasped onto the bottom and he hung from the craft like a giant tick.

The defenses that had repelled all manner of attacks weren't sufficient to keep the angry *dragon* from getting through. His head lunged up on his serpentine neck, and he caught the tail of the craft in his jaws, tearing a huge chunk of it free. Someone inside screamed in fear.

Maybe it was unnecessary, but I pointed Sarrlevi's sword at the nose of the craft—all I could target from my spot dangling below the battle—and summoned the magical beam again. The helicopter's defenses were down—or we were inside them—and it blasted a chunk of it off before ricocheting up and breaking through one of the spinning blades. It sheared away, chopping off the top of a tree before disappearing from view.

As Zavryd sprang free, leaving the helicopter to crash, I glimpsed the terrified face of the pilot. And gaped.

It was a terrified *bearded* face on someone short and stout who stood at the controls instead of sitting. Before, I'd sensed nothing more than the power of the craft, but as that power faded, I sensed a dwarf and... was that a *gnome* as his co-pilot? I had assumed more of the camouflage-uniform wearing humans would be behind all this.

The pilots shouted curses in their languages, unable to keep the damaged craft aloft. It smashed into the mountainside below.

Fire blasted through the night sky a few hundred yards away, and Zondia sailed after another helicopter, her talons outstretched as she roared. The pilot navigated the craft deftly, but she was as fast as her brother and swept in, using a great burst of magic to tear its defenses to pieces. She was ready to tear *it* to pieces.

A man leaned out the open door in the back and threw one of the glowing spheres at her.

"Look out!" I shouted over gunshots as Val fired at another

craft Zavryd was approaching. Whether dragons could survive a direct hit from one of those spheres, I didn't know, but one of the equally powerful missiles had almost taken out Sarrlevi's sword, and it wasn't a living, breathing thing.

Zavryd banked as missiles fired from his target. This close, they sped straight toward him. He launched flames toward them as he jerked and flew upward to evade them.

My stomach pitched into my shoes. One of the missiles exploded in the flames, but the other curved to follow us.

Fighting queasiness, I made myself summon the power of the sword again and cast a beam at the deadly projectile. The effort sapped tremendous energy from my battered body, and if I'd been standing, I might have collapsed, but the beam struck the missile.

An explosion boomed, knocking helicopter *and* dragon away from the area. My world lurched sideways, and, once again, if not for Zavryd's magic, Val and I would have pitched off his back.

As I glimpsed the ground below, my half-dwarven dirt-loving blood longed to be on it. Flying about on a dragon was madness.

I shifted my weight, tempted to jump off the next time we weren't far from the ground. Though I couldn't do much from down there, it wasn't as if I was doing a lot from Zavryd's back either.

Something flew past underneath us, startling me. It was the helicopter with Sarrlevi in it. As it arrowed toward the ground, I realized it wasn't flying but *crashing.*

I sensed his aura and that of another magical being—another elf?—as well. The door was open and a body flew out. Not his. The woman who'd been throwing those spheres, who'd tried to kill me.

A second later, the helicopter smashed into the ground. It didn't crumple or burst into flames as I expected—maybe its magic still protected it—but a piece of the hull flew off and bounced down the mountainside. A familiar blond-haired figure also flew out. Sarrlevi.

He didn't have my hammer *or* his other sword. He twisted in the air, and would have turned the landing into a graceful roll, but his momentum carried him into a tree. He hit *hard* and crumpled to the ground where he didn't move.

Two men in camouflage with guns leaped out of the crashed craft after him.

"We have to help!" I yelled, but Zavryd was flying upward again, taking off after another helicopter. "No, damn it."

He flew next to a stout pine, and, before I could think wiser of it, I flung myself off his back toward it. I had to drop Sarrlevi's sword so I could grab a branch with both hands, pine needles smacking me in the face. When I glanced down, terrified that some enemy lurking down there would beat me to it, the distance to the ground made my soul shrivel up with terror. From the dragon's back, I hadn't realized we were forty or fifty feet up.

"I hate heights," I whispered, only the awareness that Sarrlevi was in trouble spurring me to quickly maneuver hand under hand toward the trunk.

Below, shots rang out. Terrified I would arrive only to find him already dead, I clambered down the trunk. Pitch stuck to my palms, and bark scraped my belly through my rucked-up shirt. The last ten feet, I half fell and half flung myself to the ground, rolling toward the sword. My senses told me exactly where it was.

As my hand wrapped around the hilt, more gunshots fired. I still sensed Sarrlevi and knew he was alive, but I didn't know *how* alive.

Darting through the trees, my ankle, back, and everything I'd hurt that night stabbing pain through me, I rushed toward him. Someone screamed.

Poised to spring, I ran around a copse of trees with the sword raised and came upon the battle in time to see Sarrlevi pull a dagger out of his remaining opponent's chest. The man toppled, and Sarrlevi spun toward me with the blade in one hand and a gun in the other.

Once again, his face was bloody, with his clothing more torn than it had been after the rockfall. He looked like hell, but battle lust raged in his eyes, and I halted abruptly. I did *not* want to fight him.

Four fallen opponents lay at his feet, and I didn't sense anyone alive in the crashed helicopter. Fire streaked overhead, the dragons still battling the remaining aircraft, but down here it had grown still, and I felt silly with the sword raised.

Sarrlevi lowered his weapons first, though not without a glance toward the helicopter. Just because I couldn't sense anyone magical didn't mean there weren't humans left alive, humans with guns. He'd clearly gotten the one in his hand by disarming someone.

"I came to bring you back your sword," I said, lowering it.

He glanced toward the tree I'd shimmied down—damn, had he seen that ungainly descent? "I didn't think you liked heights."

"I don't. Not at all. That was a testament to my concern for—" I almost said *you*, almost admitted that I cared, but a hint of his smug smirk had crept onto his face, and his eyes glinted with humor that I was never quite sure wasn't mocking, "—my hammer. Do you still have it?"

His smirk turned into a broad smile, the kind that made him dashingly handsome when he wasn't covered in blood and bruises. Hell, even *with* the injuries, he had an allure.

I shook my head, handed him his sword, and looked away.

But he stepped forward, tossing the gun aside, and patted me on the shoulder. "I'm pleased you survived. Your hammer is in the air vessel. It and I were in the process of being captured, and—I'd hoped—being taken back to their new lair where I might have learned more. Then you and Thorvald showed up, and they realized they had to evacuate their *old* lair quickly. Unfortunately, I didn't get to learn anything."

"Sorry. Her boss wants her stuff back."

As I was thinking about trying a hug on him, Sarrlevi dropped his arm and stepped back.

"You'll want to see one of these flying aircraft up close." He started toward the crashed helicopter but paused when a dragon flew overhead, being chased by one aircraft while dodging missile fire from another. It was Zondia. I sensed Zavryd and Val, but they were more than a mile away, engaged in another battle.

Sarrlevi pointed his sword into the air. Toward the helicopter or toward *her*?

"Zavryd will kill you if you hurt his sister," I warned, stepping toward him.

An orange beam sprang from the tip of his sword. It streaked upward, not striking Zondia but the helicopter chasing her. Its defenses were still up, and the beam was deflected, but he squinted and kept firing, summoning more of his power and funneling it through the sword.

Zondia had flown out of view and the helicopter almost had when something slammed into it from the side. One of the missiles drawn by the heat of Sarrlevi's attack? It exploded, destroying the aircraft's defenses, and the beam made it through. Something blew up inside the back of the helicopter, and smoke filled the air as it sailed out of our view. Seconds later, a crash sounded, the ground trembling under our feet.

Sarrlevi lowered his sword. "As much as I would like to kill dragons at times, I would not be foolish enough to attempt to do so."

"You attacked Zavryd."

"I challenged him to a duel. Had I succeeded in killing him, which was not my intent, his people would have agreed that it was within the bounds of acceptable behavior. It's how they settled disputes in the past—and occasionally still do."

"How'd you get on the helicopter?" I walked after him, wondering what he wanted me to see, and almost halted when I spotted the elf I'd sensed earlier. But he was dead, his throat slashed.

"That one was working for them as one of their pilots." Sarrlevi pointed his sword at the body, bracelets that emanated magic on the fallen elf's wrists. "I suspect he was compelled to do so. I would not have killed him, but with so many enemies after me, I couldn't afford to pull punches."

To pull *slashes*, I thought.

Sarrlevi hunted in the brush around the downed helicopter and found his other sword. Someone must have disarmed him when they'd first captured him. When he'd *allowed* himself to be captured?

"Do you know who's running everything?" I looked at the helicopter, magic still emanating from it.

Dwarven magic, Zavryd had said, and it *did* seem familiar now that I was close to it. Very familiar. I crept toward the crash, wanting to touch the hull.

"No," Sarrlevi said. "Humans from your world, I gathered, but they spoke little. Further, they all had magical charms and were impossible to mind-read or compel. Four of them arrived in one of the helicopters shortly after I reached the vine-covered building with your hammer." He arched his eyebrows as if he knew Thorvald had been responsible for the vines. "They didn't have any money and claimed someone else had issued that reward. I got the impression they'd been startled when you and Thorvald first came up with the dragon to root around."

Sarrlevi looked toward the sky, but the sounds of battle had dwindled. I could sense both dragons, Zavryd flying toward Zondia now, and wondered if she realized Sarrlevi had helped her.

I doubted either of them had expected to find such formidable enemies here on lowly Earth.

"The four men may not have issued the reward, but they *did* want your hammer, and they believed they had weapons enough to take me down. I was still noticeably injured. It *would* have been a difficult fight, but I don't usually shy away from those."

No. Even if I hadn't seen him leap into battle numerous times that night, the blood and bruises would have attested to that truth.

"I thought about fighting them, removing their charms, and reading their minds, but they seemed like minions who might not know much. I was also intrigued by the aircraft." Sarrlevi gave me a significant look. "As you might guess, I wanted to find out if the person who'd enchanted it was still alive. I let the humans believe they had gotten the best of me, hoping they would, as I said, take me to their lair. My plan was working, until they were distracted by the new arrivals. Perhaps it may be possible to find one left alive to question, but I'm weary. I'll let Thorvald and the dragons handle that."

"Not me?" I asked, though the thought of interrogating people wasn't anything that excited me.

"You, I assume, will be more interested in checking out the aircraft." There was the significant look again. As if he expected me to twig to something.

It was only when I leaned into the helicopter to grab my hammer that I rested my hand on the frame and realization struck me like a mallet.

If Sarrlevi hadn't given me that long, knowing look, I might have doubted my ability to tell, but I could feel him behind me, watching me, and knew my instincts were right. The magic was familiar because both hammer and helicopter had been enchanted by the same person. My mother.

31

"DOES THIS MEAN SHE'S ALIVE?" I WHISPERED, HAND STILL RESTING on the crashed helicopter frame. "Or... did she enchant these long ago?"

The aircraft appeared modern to my eye, but the cockpit was mangled from an explosion, and I couldn't see much more than the hull. For all I knew, they could have been from the eighties, before I'd seen my mother shot and our apartment building burn down around her. If so, they'd been maintained well, but that was a possibility.

I looked back, but Sarrlevi was my only ally present, and he was gazing up the mountain. Because he expected more threats? I didn't sense anyone left alive around us, but there had been six helicopters at one point. I'd lost track of how many the dragons had destroyed before I leaped off Zavryd's back.

The *thwump* of the blades no longer floated on the night air, but some might have landed instead of crashed, and there might have been survivors. I *hoped* there had been survivors, because if my mother was alive... I wanted to know where she was.

Sarrlevi looked toward me.

"Will you ask Val if these helicopters were made recently? If she recognizes the model?" I waved toward my temple to indicate telepathy, though it occurred to me that, with the chaos over, I might *call* Val. If there was reception up there. I hadn't checked my phone for a while.

"Yes," Sarrlevi said, and I didn't dig for my phone.

With my hammer recovered, I could have backed away from the helicopter, but I hesitated to remove my hand, as if touching the enchanted metal might tell me something about my mother. Or that I might somehow be able to communicate with her.

"She says they are Sikorsky CH-53K King Stallions," Sarrlevi said, enunciating the mouthful of a name carefully, "which were brought online for your country's military in the last ten years. They're heavily modified."

"I guessed that when they repelled dragons and magical ammunition."

"Modified in addition to the enchantments. Customized." His eyelids drooped. "If they were made in the past decade—"

"My mother may indeed be alive," I whispered, watching his face.

As much as I wanted the stories he'd told me to be true, I couldn't forget that he'd lied to me before. It was still possible he was manipulating me, helping me so I would help him, and that he wanted to find my mother so he could complete that old mission.

"Yes," was all he said, his face a mask.

A part of me wished the dragons had mind scoured *him*. Or that I could read his thoughts. I wanted so badly to trust him. But I might not be able to fully until we found my mother and he helped her instead of thrusting one of his swords into her chest.

His gaze grew sad as he held mine, and I wondered if he knew what I was thinking. He'd said my dwarven mental defenses made it more difficult for him to read my mind, but he hadn't said it was impossible. He certainly had no trouble telling I was attracted to him.

His head swiveled toward the mountaintop again.

"Are the others coming?" I asked.

"Zavryd'nokquetal, Thorvald, and her tiger have split up and are investigating the cave and the crate that fell. Zondia'qareshi is coming."

Before he finished speaking, I sensed her. She was flying our way—quickly.

Sarrlevi had cleaned and sheathed his weapons, but he drew them again.

"If she got everything I overheard when the ex-princess spoke to you," I said, "she should know that you aren't after my grandfather."

"*If* she did and *if* she believes that what you overheard was true."

I hesitated, not sure what to say to that. It hadn't occurred to me that the dragons might believe me a dubious source, but it wasn't as if I could know if the elf females had spoken the truth. Nobody had mind scoured *them* before they'd fled.

"Maybe you should make a portal and go—" I almost said *home*, but his home had been destroyed. "Someplace they won't find you." He'd mentioned other houses. He had to have places he could go.

"And leave you here alone so she can hurt you again?"

I almost said it hadn't been that bad, but it had *not* been pleasant, and after the night's battering, my entire body already hurt. I withered up inside at the thought of enduring more pain.

As Zondia flew over the trees and found a spot to land in front of us, Sarrlevi stepped close to me, *protectively* close to me, with his swords raised as he faced her. I appreciated that, but it only made me wish even more that I could trust him without question.

"Thanks," I said, "but I don't want to hide behind you."

Besides, Zondia shouldn't have any reason to be irritated with me, to want to take *me* away.

I will take this one to the queen now, she informed us, her cool gaze locking on Sarrlevi. *She will read his mind and determine if punishment and rehabilitation are required.*

"They're not." I stepped forward, lifting my chin instead of my hammer, though if she tried to take Sarrlevi, I would crack it down on her foot. "You read my mind, didn't you? You saw the truth, that those elves were manipulating him. More than that, they *betrayed* him. They told you he was a threat to the dwarven king, right? You didn't hear it from anyone else. But he's *not* a threat to the king. He's doing all this to try to make amends, to *help* Ironhelm." I willed that to be an accurate statement, for what Sarrlevi had told me by the hammock to all be the truth. "And he helped *you* just now." I pointed toward the sky to remind Zondia of the helicopter that had been hot on her ass. "You couldn't have missed that."

Zondia's lids drooped over her slitted reptilian eyes. Did she not care that he'd helped? Feel indebted to him in any way? Maybe she'd believed she hadn't needed his help, but, even if that was true, didn't he get credit for making the effort?

I grabbed my phone out of my pocket, thinking again of calling Val, hoping she could convince Zavryd to tell his sister to knock it off, but if the queen—their mother—had requested this, maybe he couldn't do anything.

Why do you defend him? Zondia asked.

"Because he doesn't deserve *punishment.*" I didn't add *nobody does,* though I was tempted. The dragons probably weren't open to criticism of their justice system from mongrels or even full-blooded dwarves.

Even if he did not intend to target the dwarven king, he has killed many, some of royal blood. Just because he was hired and paid for those assassinations by others does not make them less loathsome.

Since I didn't disagree with that, I struggled for a convincing rebuttal.

Beside me, Sarrlevi sighed softly. Maybe deep down, he didn't disagree either. Or he believed that now that he was on the dragons' radar, there was no way to escape the fate they intended for him.

"Punish the people who hired him if you think the assassinations were unwarranted," I said. "They're more cowards than he," I added, having a vague notion that dragons might be into honor and bravery. "He doesn't deserve two years of excruciating torture for being the instrument of others' hatred and ambition. It's cold and cruel."

The punishment for those who disobey the laws of the Dragon Justice Court must be severe, so as to convince others to avoid running afoul of them. Once he is rehabilitated, his memories of the past taken and new ideals imprinted on his mind, he would be able to return to his people as a functioning and contributing member of their society. Dragons are practical, not cruel. This method of dealing with criminals is for the good of all.

I glanced at Sarrlevi, expecting him to argue against such a fate, but his face was a mask again. His weapons were still defensively up, but he seemed willing to let me do the talking. Hopefully because he believed Zondia would be more likely to listen to a neutral third party and not because he'd given up. I couldn't believe that.

Zondia prowled a few steps toward us. Sarrlevi tensed.

"Look," I blurted, stepping forward and raising my palm toward her. "Even if you're determined to do this, don't collect him now, please. I need his help to find my mother, the king's daughter and rightful heir—a far more rightful heir than the princess who hired Sarrlevi to kill my mother—her sister." I gazed steadily into those inhuman dragon eyes, though Zondia's aura was intimidating this close. *She* was intimidating. "Aren't they the royal line that your people decided was appropriate to rule Dun Kroth? You don't want to have to deal with the kind of person who would kill her sister out of ambition, do you? For all we know, maybe she's planning to get rid of King Ironhelm too."

I felt a little guilty implying that since I'd never even met Princess Barothla, but not much, not after what she'd done to my mother.

"Maybe someone should mind scour *her*," I added.

You believe Princess Rodarska lives? Zondia asked.

"I didn't before, but I do now. She enchanted *those*." I pointed to the helicopter. "Not voluntarily," I hurried to add, though I couldn't know that. "I think someone's making her work for them, building reactors and helicopters and who knows what else." A new thought occurred to me, something that might sway Zondia more than my pleas that Sarrlevi didn't deserve her people's justice. "Magic and weapons capable of troubling even mighty dragons. If we find her—and I need Sarrlevi's help to do so—we can not only return her to her rightful place in the king's court as his heir, but we can stop her from making more things to threaten your kind."

It wouldn't have surprised me if Zondia had scoffed, saying dragons feared nothing that lesser species could make, but I hoped the experience with the helicopters had concerned her at least a little. She and Zavryd might have prevailed, but I couldn't believe that battle had been easy for them. I'd been there, after all.

Our people would *approve of Princess Rodarska being returned to King Ironhelm's court and believe she would be a better heir to the throne than her sister.*

I held my breath, glad she'd stopped advancing and seemed to be considering the argument. Hopefully, she wouldn't think to ask why *Sarrlevi* needed to be the one to help me with my quest. And, hopefully, I wouldn't one day regret keeping him out of dragon clutches and next to me as I searched for my mother.

When I looked at him again, I expected to find his mask still in place as he warily watched the dragon, but he was gazing at me with warmth in his blue eyes. Because he was glad I was arguing on his behalf? Because he could tell I cared? Whatever the reason, his expression filled *me* with warmth as well. Had Zondia not been watching us, I would have stepped closer and clasped his hand, maybe inflicted another hug on him.

Very well, Zondia said, and we looked back toward her. *For now, I will not collect him for punishment and rehabilitation. Find your mother, and ensure she will make no more weapons capable of harrying dragons. She is a powerful enchanter, and she must be an ally to our kind, not a threat.*

The implication that they would have to *deal* with a threat made me uneasy, but I told myself that the dragons wouldn't have any more luck finding her than Sarrlevi had so far. And it didn't sound like Zondia wanted to head off on a hunt for her. She would leave that to us.

"We'll find her," I said.

Without another word, Zondia sprang into the air and flew off to the west. A portal formed in the sky, and she soared through it, leaving her brother as the only dragon in the world. Zavryd would also be willing to take Sarrlevi away if he deemed it necessary, but I hoped Val's mate wouldn't be gunning for him.

Sarrlevi sighed again, gazing off into the darkness between the trees. "Is it bizarre that a part of me was tempted to let her take me?"

"Yes," I answered promptly before considering why he might have said that. "You can't possibly want punishment and rehabilitation. To have your mind wiped."

Or could he? I scrutinized his face. If the story he'd told me about his father's abuse and his sister's brutal death had been true... maybe he wished he didn't remember the events. And maybe in the centuries he'd been an assassin, there were other memories he wished he didn't have.

"Maybe not the two years of punishment, but to forget everything?" Sarrlevi hitched a shoulder, still gazing into the darkness. "There's something not entirely unappealing about the idea of being born again with no memory of the past. To be permitted to return to your society, your people. But would you appreciate it without knowing what went before?" He looked at me, as if *I* might know. "Who would you be if you didn't remember who you are?"

I didn't have the answer to such a philosophical question, so all I said was, "Maybe not the kind of person who springs into battle to help an ally or brings a really cool half-dwarf lady exotic cheeses."

"That would be distressing."

"Yeah."

Sarrlevi sheathed his swords and stepped close, surprising me by drawing me into a hug. *Thank you for standing at my side*, he said telepathically and brought a hand to the back of my head and stroked my hair.

You're welcome. I let myself lean into him, *relax* into him, glad we wouldn't have to endure anymore pain that night. *I can't believe she might be alive. You seemed to know all along, or at least suspect. How?* I tilted my head back to look into his eyes.

I was aware that she was considered a very talented enchanter among her people. Further, dwarves have few enemies since they largely keep to themselves and don't bother others. I figured people would be more likely to want to use her than kill her. Sarrlevi gave me a half-smile and lifted a hand to my cheek. *Besides, dwarves are resilient and difficult to kill.*

A warm tingle zipped through my body, making me very aware of his touch.

After tonight, I don't feel resilient. As soon as the words came out, I wished I could retract them. After all he'd endured in the last twenty-four hours, he had to be in a lot more pain than I was.

Dwarves are not meant to ride dragons and climb trees. His smile widened.

I might have objected to the statement, even if I'd had similar thoughts myself, but he shifted from touching my cheek to resting his hand fully on the side of my face and head, his calloused skin warm against mine. At first, I thought he would try to read my mind, but then his magic crept into me, flowing through my whole body, warm, appealing, and invigorating.

I am not a healer, beyond some basic knowledge of dealing with combat wounds, but this should take some of your pain away until you're able to make it home and rest and regenerate.

His touch not only dulled the pain, but it made me feel so good that my every muscle relaxed, and I wanted to sink to the ground at his feet. I didn't allow myself to do that, but I did catch myself leaning into his hand, my eyelids drooping and my lips parting. No massage therapist's touch or lover's embrace had ever been so blissfully amazing. Not that he had *love* in mind, I was sure. He was just expressing gratitude, no doubt glad I'd convinced Zondia to leave. That didn't keep me from gazing through my lashes at him with molten appreciation.

Once again, he was using his power to help me, even though *he* was injured and it had to be a drain on what energy he had left.

His thumb brushed my cheek as his magic rejuvenated me, and he watched my face. My... lips? Probably because I was slumped against him like an enraptured groupie, not because he found them sexy and appealing. *He* wasn't even that sexy and appealing at the moment, not with his face bloodied. Blood even stained his short blond hair. But his magic made me forget all that, and when he sent another invigorating wave of it through me, I couldn't resist lifting a hand and touching *his* face.

The overwhelming urge to kiss him came over me. A thank-you kiss, nothing more. I knew he didn't want more.

When I leaned closer, my lips reaching for his, I expected him to spring back, or for his eyes to widen in surprise that his touch had resulted in such a response. All he did was smile that knowing smile of his, the one I usually found aggravating. Before such an emotion could arise in me, he bent his head and kissed *me*.

For a second, I was so surprised that I didn't move as his warm lips brushed mine. But my body bestirred itself to find the appropriate response, or at least the response *it* wanted to have. I wrapped both arms around his shoulders and kissed him back with ardent eagerness that didn't seem to startle him. No, he was still smiling, even as we kissed. It didn't detract from the experience, not in the least. His touch, physical and magical, put thoughts of sex in my mind. I longed to shove my hands under his torn shirt and slide them all over his muscled torso as I pulled him off into the ferns.

But before we got to more than kissing, he drew back, his magic fading from my body. "This would not be appropriate."

It took me a moment to do anything but stare at him in stunned silence, my libido humming and the ferns calling.

"Appropriate?" I rasped, my voice husky. Damn it, I was panting. Had I truly thought we would throw down on the forest floor and have sex with a crashed helicopter and bodies nearby? What the hell was wrong with me? Even acknowledging those thoughts, I couldn't help but feel stung, and my temper flared. "Not appropriate for a pretentious full-blooded elf to lower himself to be with some mongrel woman?"

Sarrlevi frowned. "That is not what I said."

"No, it *is* what you said. Back in the pantry after we met. *Elves do not mate with mongrel dwarves.*"

He opened his mouth but closed it again. Before I could decide if I wanted to say more, to remind him of other times he'd smugly looked down his nose at me and made it clear mongrels were inferior, I sensed Zavryd and Val approaching.

Sarrlevi must have too—maybe that was why he'd broken the kiss. He hadn't wanted to be caught embracing me when witnesses approached.

"Goodnight, and thank you for the assistance." Sarrlevi bowed stiffly, then drew once more on his power and created a portal. "You should be safe now."

My *safety* wasn't what had me glowering at him, hurt and bitter as he turned his back to spring through the portal and disappear.

32

After Val and Zavryd picked me up, we flew down to meet Willard, who arrived with several helicopters—perfectly mundane helicopters—and numerous soldiers. While Val reported to her, and they arranged a search of the caves, I had a half hour alone to think about where my mother might be and how I would find her.

I also had time to regret blowing up at Sarrlevi. Even if I was still hurt that he'd remembered he wasn't into me, I shouldn't have snapped and driven him away. If nothing else, he probably had ideas about where to look next. He'd *spoken* to some of these people, after all. Maybe he'd learned something from them, though it had sounded like he'd hoped to learn a lot more by being taken to their base. If we hadn't shown up, maybe that would have happened.

But did I want him to end up face to face with my mother without me there too? Invigorating magic and kiss or not, I still couldn't trust him fully.

"Did you guys find anyone left alive after the battle?" I asked Val when she came over.

"No. Most were killed by sword, bullet, or dragon talon." Val glanced at Zavryd, who'd changed into his human form and stood nearby, his arms folded over his chest. He looked like he was ready to go home. Dragons probably enjoyed battle a lot more than the debriefings afterward. "A couple more didn't have any obvious injuries on them. I think they may have taken poison to keep from being captured and questioned."

I gaped at her. "Why would anyone do that? Over some stolen artifacts?"

"There's a lot more going on than that, and you know it."

"I guess." Whoever these people were, at least some part of their scheme had been in place for thirty years, since they'd killed —no, *kidnapped*—my mother. "More than ever, I'd like to talk to my father." I looked toward where Willard was speaking with two of her soldiers as a helicopter took off, heading up to collect her stolen artifacts.

"She might be more willing to try to arrange that now," Val said.

"Do you think she can? I haven't seen anything to suggest the military isn't behind all this."

"The camo uniforms are the only things to suggest that they are, though, right? And, as we pointed out before, anyone can buy those at the military-surplus stores."

"And the rifles?"

"Firearms aren't hard to come by in this country either," Val said dryly, patting hers.

"I prefer hammers."

"I'm glad you got it back." Val nodded to my weapon. "What happened to Sarrlevi?"

"He left, presumably to take a nap on his cot. He's gotten pretty chewed up this past night and day." I didn't mention the kiss, or me losing my temper and snapping at him, though I had told her about our encounter with Zondia. Her lip had curled, and she hadn't sounded surprised that Zavryd's sister had made threats.

After her soldiers trotted off, Willard came over to join us. "It looks like all of the items from the basement, save for a few choice trinkets that they must have sold to others or selected for personal use, are accounted for. There were more crates in the cave, as well as computers and machinery, which is quite interesting."

"Interesting computers?" Val asked.

"The interesting part is that there are no power lines up here that they could have tapped into. We'll do a more thorough search in the morning, but the men haven't seen any windmills or solar panels, anything that could have collected energy for off-grid use."

"Geothermal power?" Val asked.

"Maybe, or maybe they had one of those dwarven reactors up here." Willard looked at me.

I could only shrug. Nobody had taken me up to see the cave yet, and I wasn't that eager to ask Zavryd to fly me anywhere again. Not unless it turned out that there were some clues about my mother up there.

"We'll take everything back to headquarters," Willard said, "and see if we can dig up anything, but I have a feeling they'll have wiped the drives before leaving. They had time to pack up. Another hour, and you would have missed them completely."

"I'm confused," I said, "about the whole side thing with my hammer. Why did they decide after all this time that they need it? And why give the world of bounty hunters and reward seekers their address up here? Maybe they figured nobody who went to the trailer would have a dragon to fly around and look for nearby caves, but isn't it strange that they didn't pick a more remote meet-up location? Just in case?"

"Unless *they* weren't the ones who put out that reward," Val said. "Maybe someone was trying to lead you up here."

I touched my chest. "Me? I'm not important to anyone. Except maybe Sarrlevi, who wants my help finding my mother."

Willard and Val exchanged looks, and I knew neither of them

trusted him. I'd defended him enough that night, and since I still had my doubts, I didn't say anything.

"He might not be the only one who wants you to find her," Willard suggested.

"The only other people I know of who might care and are on Earth are the two dwarves, Artie and Hennehok. Hennehok apparently believed my mother was alive, but I haven't been able to find and speak with him yet." I spread my arms.

"I'll have my intel people do some more digging to see if they can figure out who put out that reward," Willard said. "I remember being surprised how easily we found the address. At the time, I assumed whoever issued the reward wanted the hammer badly enough to throw out the details and turn-in point far and wide, but now I wonder if we were *meant* to discover this place. And if someone assumed that orcs and trolls wouldn't be able to get that weapon away from you."

"If so, someone is giving me a lot of credit."

Willard shrugged. "We'll see. Regardless, I appreciate you two finding the missing items. I wish you'd found that reactor too, especially if it was up there until recently, but at least I shouldn't have to worry about losing my job." She smiled grimly. "I'll arrange payment for your services, Thorvald. You too, Puletasi. Combat bonus."

"You don't have to pay me for helping you, Willard," Val said. "Though Matti may want pay. Her carport got torched and her fence torn down."

I grimaced. "Don't remind me."

Val thumped me on the arm. "At least the house was still standing when we left."

"Yeah."

"Though you did leave that goblin with the large toaster-coil weapon roaming around on the premises."

"Because she's my roommate."

Zavryd walked over. "Is it not time to return to our domicile, my mate?" he asked Val, his eyelids drooping. "You know what going into battle with you puts me in the mood for."

Willard snorted. "Your dragon is horny again, Thorvald."

"He's talking about smoked ribs and meat loaves," Val said dryly.

"As appetizers to the main course, yes." His eyelids drooped further as he continued gazing at Val.

I looked away, wondering if anyone would ever look at me like that. He might enjoy meat loaf, but I had no doubt he had more than that in mind. Why it was *appropriate* for a dragon and a half-elf to hook up, I didn't know, since an elf and a half-dwarf couldn't. Though I supposed that was just an excuse for Sarrlevi and that he preferred his own kind.

"Go home and get some rest—or whatever," Willard said, waving at me as well as the two of them. "Puletasi, I'll let you know if there's anything interesting on the computers or we find out who put out the reward."

"Thank you, Colonel." I glanced at Val, though she'd clasped Zavryd's hand, and they weren't paying attention to us. "Do you think it would be possible for you to get me in to see my father? I want to see if he knows anything more about what happened thirty years ago—and who might have my mother now."

Willard hesitated, and I wondered if she cared about where my mother was. At the least, she cared about that reactor. Her superiors would be delighted if she could find one or more for humankind, especially if people had already figured out how to make it produce electricity that our technology could use.

"I may not be able to arrange that," she finally said, "but I'll see if I can pull some strings."

"Thank you."

"And get you a combat bonus. Lumber for fences and carports isn't cheap."

"No, it's not," I said, "but the greater danger is that if I don't show up with some soon, my roommate will get creative and start recycling materials gathered from the neighbors—and my kitchen —to use in the rebuilding."

"That is a great danger. Trust me, I know." Willard didn't mention Gondo by name, but I was sure she had him in mind.

EPILOGUE

I REPLACED THE BURNED CARPORT SUPPORTS WITH THICKER POSTS than before, having a notion of carving them when we finished the rest of the repairs. Maybe with bears or elephants or other particularly sturdy animals. I'd already purchased a special stain that was supposed to be fire resistant. Steel would have been even better, but I loved the character of wood and couldn't bring myself to use metal. Unless I found my mother and could convince her to stay with me long enough to teach me to enchant metals.

An enchanted carport wouldn't be weird, would it? If I was going to be targeted again, the whole property ought to be enchanted. If Tinja's goblin booby traps had done anything to deter the invisible trolls, I hadn't noticed it.

"From up here, that looks very good." Tinja gave me a thumbs-up from the roof.

She was supposedly replacing a few singed shingles, but her mussy hair and rumpled shirt suggested she'd been taking a nap in the afternoon sun. More than once, she'd hinted that she would be willing to draw up blueprints for a rooftop deck if I would install it, as if the two tasks required equal time and effort.

Fortunately, Abbas had come over, and his help went much further. Bangs from behind the house announced his work on repairing the fence. It sounded like he was almost done. I vowed to ask if he needed help with anything around *his* house, or maybe I would volunteer to carve something for him.

My phone rang. My sister. I thought about ignoring it, as I had let two calls from Tyler go to voice mail, but she might drive over again if she thought I'd gone missing.

"Hey, Penina," I answered.

"Tyler says you haven't returned his calls," she said without preamble.

"It's been an eventful couple of days." I almost mentioned the damage to the property, but I didn't want her to worry.

"Are the events over?"

I hesitated. Were they?

I hadn't heard from Val or Willard and didn't know if they'd found anything interesting in the computers and crates they'd recovered, nor had Willard called with a new assignment for me. Sarrlevi also hadn't come back. I hoped because he was recovering from his wounds, not because I'd snapped at him.

As far as I knew, he still wanted to find my mother and believed I was his best bet for that, so he ought to be back before long. It wasn't as if I wanted him here, breathing down my neck as I did the repairs and urging me to assist him on the hunt, but a small part of me missed his company. Maybe not *that* small a part.

"Matti?" my sister prompted.

"Sorry. Yes. I may have a couple of days that aren't as busy."

"Good. Call Tyler, okay? You said you would."

"I will." Why not? I'd agreed to it earlier, so I felt obligated, and maybe it wouldn't be that bad.

Besides, it wasn't as if I could have a romantic future with someone who thought I was an inappropriate mongrel.

"Good. And don't let any weird beat-up guys in your bedroom. That's the kind of thing that puts off a possible boyfriend."

A twinge of longing went through me as I thought of my still-clean bedroom, including the braided vine shelves that Sarrlevi had magically anchored to the wall. Why had he *done* that? Surely, not only because he couldn't rest in a messy room.

"Talk about sending mixed signals," I muttered.

"*Exactly.* You don't want Tyler coming by to pick you up and finding another guy there."

"I'm sure." Another call came in. Willard. "I need to go."

"Call Tyler," Penina said by way of a *goodbye* before hanging up.

I rolled my eyes as I answered Willard. "Hello, uhm, Colonel." Was I supposed to call her that or *ma'am*? I had no idea.

"I like you better than Thorvald already," Willard said. "You have better phone etiquette."

"Are you supposed to talk about your independent contractors behind their backs?"

"It's not behind her back. She's sitting in front of me with her leg and her dirty boot slung over the armrest of my chair."

"Hey, Matti," Val called. "You get your combat bonus yet?"

"Yes." I'd been bemused when a corporal in a black sedan with government plates had driven up and handed me an envelope with cash in it. Apparently, independent contractors didn't get checks or direct deposits. Maybe Val—and now I—didn't officially exist, as far as the military was concerned. Fine by me. "I split it with my business partner and intern, who, as she informs me, is woefully underpaid for her extreme value."

I eyed the roof, snores floating down. Tinja must have been up late doing homework—or disassembling my appliances.

"You don't have to split your earnings from your government work with your home-renovation partners," Val said dryly.

"No? Don't you use your pay to buy meat for your dragon?"

"Yes, but we're married. What's mine is his, and what's his— well, dragons aren't into money and don't have a lot, but he compensates me in other ways."

"She doesn't want to hear about your bedroom exploits," Willard said.

"That's not the *only* way," Val said. "He flies me around and helps me beat up bad guys too."

"It's good that you found each other."

"Obviously."

"Anyway, Puletasi," Willard said, "this isn't what I called about. We're still going over the computers, and I've got a team up in that cave dusting for prints."

"Do caves hold fingerprints well?" I asked skeptically.

"Not usually, but there were a few flat surfaces. It looks like it was kind of a lab as well as a storage and office facility. What I *have* learned so far, by bribing numerous informants, is that a dwarf was the one to put the reward out for your hammer and feed interested parties the address of the logging operation."

"What dwarf?"

"Nobody knows. They said he was hooded and magically shrouded."

"The only male dwarf on Earth that I know about is Hennehok, the engineer," I said. But if he'd been a friend of my mother's, why would he have wanted me to lose the hammer?

"I wondered if it might be him, and I've had someone check his cabin a couple of times, but he hasn't returned."

Had I given her the dwarf's address? I didn't think so. Had *Sarrlevi*? I would be stung if he was on Earth, talking to Willard, and hadn't stopped by to see me. Maybe Willard had simply found out about the dwarves on her own.

"Artie's Axes has a *temporarily closed* sign out front too," Willard added, "and she hasn't been home for a while."

I stared pensively at the cracked cement of the driveway. Was Sarrlevi the reason the dwarves had disappeared? Had they gone back to their own world?

"What about my father?" I asked.

"I'm still working on it."

"Really?" I couldn't tell if she meant it or was brushing me off.

"Really," Willard said firmly, not sounding annoyed by my doubt. "He's not only locked up, but I can't get anyone to acknowledge that he exists. One wonders if it's because of what he knows as much as because of what he's done."

"He didn't do anything except defend my mother and try to save our lives when soldiers stormed our apartment."

"I'll keep working on it, but I can only press so much. If a superior officer tells me to quit asking questions, I have to obey."

"It might be better for someone with stealth magic and the ability to create portals to visit him," Val said in the background.

"I'm going to pretend I didn't hear you say that," Willard said.

"Do I have to pretend?" I asked, though I didn't know how Sarrlevi or anyone else could open a portal into the middle of a restricted area on a military post they'd never visited before. Since I'd never been permitted to visit, it wasn't as if I could guide him.

"Just don't get caught if you try anything," Val said, "or Willard will have to pretend she doesn't know you."

Willard's grunt might or might not have conveyed agreement. She definitely wasn't going to sign off on infiltrating a military prison.

But maybe, if there *was* a way to sneak in with magic, I would have to try. With the dwarves gone, who else did I know who might have useful information to lead me to my mother's captors? Only my father.

"Thanks for the update, Colonel," I said and hung up.

Unless Val's mate was willing to fly me down to Fort Lewis, I wouldn't be able to do anything until Sarrlevi came back. *If* he came back. Until he did, I would be stuck waiting around, mulling over what the people who had my mother might have been doing to her—or making *her* do—for the past thirty years. I couldn't imagine being enslaved for that long and not being allowed to visit my family. Did she want to? It was hard to believe she wouldn't, that she was voluntarily working for our government or whoever was behind all this.

"I need to take my mind off all this," I muttered, looking at my phone. After taking a deep breath, I dialed Tyler's number.

"Hello, Matti," he answered right away. "Thanks for calling back."

"Sure. Sorry it took a couple of days. I've been busy, but I was wondering if you'd like to get coffee sometime."

"I absolutely would."

"Good. Perfect." We set a time and place, and I said goodbye, feeling I'd fulfilled my obligation to my sister. And maybe it would be a nice date. The distraction I needed with a guy who wouldn't send me mixed messages.

No sooner had I had the thought than a goblin pedaled up on a kid's bike, a few boxes tied to the back. *Special deliveries*, a sign dangling from the handlebars read.

He pulled into the driveway and honked a horn three times, even though I was right there.

"Are you here for Tinja?" I glanced at the roof, wondering if she had a date.

The snores had stopped, and she peered down.

The male goblin tipped a hat made of stacked bicycle chains supporting what looked like the spinning plate from inside a microwave toward her.

"I have a delivery for Mataalii Puletasi." He opened one of the boxes in the back.

I watched warily, though I didn't sense anything magical, except for the goblin himself.

Tinja must have been curious about the delivery—or maybe the goblin—for she shimmied down the drainpipe to join me. "Who knows your full name?" she asked.

"Not many people." I almost wondered if Tyler had sent something, but he would have used FedEx, not GoblinEx.

Whistling, the goblin produced a gift basket and offered it to me. Was that... cheese? *Pink* cheese such as came from another world?

"Tips are encouraged." He winked at Tinja. "In lieu of money, I'll accept kisses."

I pulled out a five-dollar bill, not wanting my roommate to feel obligated to put her lips on a stranger. Besides, Tinja's eyes were for the basket of cheeses, not the delivery goblin.

"Thank you, ma'am." He tipped his hat again and pedaled off.

"Is that *dokdok* cheese?" Tinja clasped her hands in front of her chest. "Who sent it? A suitor?"

"It had to be Sarrlevi."

Tinja's forehead creased, and she gave me a concerned look. "He's *not* a suitor, is he?"

"Definitely not. He's..." I pulled out a large jar, its contents hidden by a fabric covering. A tag dangling from a ribbon around the lid read *A cornucopia of pickled exotic root vegetables from across the Cosmic Realms.* Emotion knotted in my throat, and I shook my head, at a loss for words.

"A deadly assassin with a reputation for ruthlessly slaying anyone who crosses his path?" Tinja suggested.

"I think he mostly ruthlessly slays those he's hired to slay."

"A distinction which does not make him a suitable partner."

"I know." But I hugged the pickled vegetable jar to my chest and wished...

Hell, I didn't know what I wished. I'd just made a date with another man, one who thought I was cute and not a *mongrel*.

Sarrlevi and his mixed messages could sod off. But I planned to enjoy the heck out of the gift basket.

THE END

AFTERWORD

Thank you for following along with my *Legacy of Magic* series. If you enjoyed Book 2, *Betrayed*, please consider leaving a review.

If you would like to continue on with the adventure, you can now order Book 3, *Trolled*. (I've been waiting a long time to be able to use that as a title for a fantasy novel!)

For updates and bonus extras, you can sign up to my fantasy newsletter:

https://lindsayburoker.com/book-news/

Made in United States
Orlando, FL
30 December 2022